THE CHAMPAGNE GIRLS

The sparkling sequel to The Wine Widow...

Young, beautiful, buttressed by the wine fortune of the House of Tramont, the future for Netta and Gabrielle must surely be rosy. They are the Champagne Girls, two cousins who enjoy the finest things in life in La Belle Epoque. Yet for Netta, propriety demands that she give up her one passion – music – to make a socially acceptable marriage, and for Gaby wealth cannot protect her from a broken heart. Meanwhile the family face the threat to the vineyards posed by the phylloxera beetle – and the consequences of their involvement in the scandalous Dreyfus affair.

THE CHAMPAGNE GIRLS

The Champagne Girls

by

Tessa Barclay

Magna Large Print Books
Long Preston, North Yorkshire,
BD23 4ND, England.

British Library Cataloguing in Publication Data.

Barclay, Tessa
    The champagne girls.

    A catalogue record of this book is
    available from the British Library

    ISBN   0-7505-2007-8

First published in Great Britain in 1986 by W. H. Allen & Co.

Copyright © 1986 by Tessa Barclay

Cover illustration © Len Thurston by arrangement with
P.W.A. International Ltd.

The moral right of the author has been asserted

Published in Large Print 2003 by arrangement with
Tessa Barclay, care of Darley Anderson

Books Ltd.

Chapter One

When the wedding gown was delivered by a little pony-drawn dressmaker's van bearing the magical name of Maison Worth in gold lettering and attended by two anxious assistants, everyone in the Tramont household stopped whatever they were doing. The kitchen-maids stole up to the back landing so as to watch it pass, in a deep rectangular box tied with gold ribbons. The butler stood to attention as it was taken upstairs.

Madame de Tramont's maid Estelle allowed Mademoiselle Netta to watch the unveiling. Layers of tissue paper were removed. The bed, specially spread with a fine cotton cloth which would later enfold the gown, received it as it was gently lifted out by its shoulders.

'Oh, good heavens,' groaned Netta. 'It's *lavender!*'

'And why should you complain, young lady, if it is?' Estelle demanded. She was allowed to scold the granddaughter of the house: she was a servant of many years' standing.

'But lavender is such an *old* colour!'

'Old? Not at all! It's charming and very

suitable,' twittered the chief vendeuse, alarmed in case something went wrong at the last moment with this prestigious order.

'Suitable for a wedding? It's a widow's colour!'

'But your Grandmama is a widow, my love–'

'She's a bride, isn't she? Isn't that what all the fuss is about? She's getting married...' At last, she ended to herself. And perhaps it was too late, really. Fifty-six... Could an old lady of fifty-six really want to get married? From her viewpoint of nineteen years, fifty-six seemed the end of the road to Mademoiselle Nicolette Hopetown-Tramont. And Lord Grassington, although of course a darling, seemed so ... so ordinary. If Grandma must marry, why couldn't she choose some handsome, intelligent Frenchman instead of this grey-haired foreigner?

But everyone knew those two old fogies had been in love for years. And now poor Lady Grassington had died of the bronchitis brought on by those terrible damp acres she insisted in living upon, and so at last Grandpapa Grigri and Grandmama could get married.

The gown had been spread on the bed. Layer after layer of frilled silk and lace made the skirt, lavender and cream in alternating rows. There were bows of moiré to define the front panel at the hem. The narrow-boned waist and one had to admit, Grandmama still had a girl's waist – was edged with velvet where it fitted into the skirt. The front bodice consisted of ruched silk muslin edged with folded ribbons, among which space had been left for the corsage of violets Grandmama would wear to the ceremony.

Netta was interested to note that the skirt had no bustle. Well done Grandmama, she thought – always abreast of the fashion. The bustle had come in with a great wave of ebullience but had gone out again last year, much to Netta's relief. Energetic and active, she'd found it a great nuisance, although the mode at the moment insisted on skirts so tightly wrapped with frills and narrow flounces that it was like having your knees tied together. One must of course obey that dictates of fashion, but Netta couldn't help longing for the day when designers would decree loose, easy-fitting skirts.

The chief vendeuse waved at her assistant. The assistant brought forward a flat box, which she proceeded to open.

'Oh, not another lace cap!' protested Netta.

'Now, Miss, enough of this silly criticism! You know your Grandma always wears a cap – it's part of her stock in trade.'

'You'd think that at her own wedding she'd forget the business of promoting Champagne Tramont and the Widow's Vintage– Oh!'

She broke off, entranced. From the box had emerged a little flat oval disc of some stiff fabric covered in moiré and edged with tulle and Parma violets. 'Oh, but that's pretty – that's really pretty!'

'And chic, too, don't you agree, Mademoiselle?' said the chief vendeuse, looking with approval at this eager girl whose voice chimed liked the song of a happy angel, and who might yet become a great leader in Paris society and style.

Netta was worth looking at. She was perhaps too slender for current fashion as yet, but the boning and corseting thought necessary for every lady had given her line and the right curves of hip and bosom. Even in her tailored morning dress of dark grey velvet, she sparkled – grey-green eyes alight, russet hair gleaming with health, cheeks aglow from a brisk early-morning walk.

'Try it on,' suggested Estelle, holding the hat out to Netta.

She drew back. 'Oh no. No one else but Grandmama must wear it. It's special, isn't it? In place of a wedding veil...'

Wedding veils were popular this season in Paris. Specially made by the great fashion houses, or pieced together from heirlooms of Mechlin and Chantilly, they flowed down from elegantly dressed coiffures sparkling with diamante and white blossom. But, from what she'd heard from both Mama and Grandmama, neither of them had ever worn one.

Grandmama, according to the legend, had been too poor to afford a proper wedding gown. She'd been married to Grandpapa ages and ages ago in a grey cotton dress – how odd it sounded! And yet romantic, because she and Grandpapa had had a dreadful time persuading the Tramonts to let the marriage take place.

Mama's wedding had been even more romantic. She'd run away – actually run away to Gretna Green, the place where the blacksmith married you over the anvil according to Scottish law. Well … not quite, perhaps. Every time this tale was told, Mama would laugh and say she was married in a respectable church in Perth with a priest and two witnesses, but she had to agree she'd had no wedding gown and no veil. 'Flowers I had,' she would add, with a glance at her husband Gavin. The 'flowers' were pressed still in her prayerbook – a sprig of heather he had brought her from the moors around the town.

How strange it all seemed if you thought about it. Mama at odds with Grandmama, running off to get married without permission, almost banished to Portugal with Papa until the aftermath of the terrible war of 1870 brought them back to the wine estate at Calmady.

Everyone kept on saying what hard times those had been. German troops riding the country, a huge sum of money to be collected by the French as an indemnity before they could have their lands to themselves again, vineyards devastated by gunfire and the manoeuvring of cavalry...

Well, twenty years later there was no sign of it, Netta said to herself as she smoothed the folds of the rich wedding gown so that it could be wrapped and hung up for this afternoon's ceremony. Nor had there been throughout her life, so far as she could remember. Quite the reverse. Money seemed to flow into the Tramont family just as the famous wine flowed into the casks at vintage time.

Netta had grown accustomed to being talked of as an heiress. She and the other young ladies of the great wine families were watched and commented upon as they threaded their way through the season in Paris and London. The Champagne Girls, the inheritors of the fortunes earned by the great wine of celebration – life for them could only be full of splendour and enjoyment.

'It'll be your turn soon, I shouldn't wonder,' Estelle remarked as they stood back to look at the swathed gown on its stand. 'Only you'll have white, of course.'

Netta said nothing. She didn't like to think

about it. Of course she'd have to marry one day, and probably soon, as Estelle suggested – after all she was nineteen and it would be a strange thing if she wasn't a bride by twenty. It was expected, and she would be glad to fulfil her family's expectations of a brilliant match.

And yet... And yet... Freedom was delightful! Since her debut two years ago she'd had such a good time, flirting and playing with handsome young men, always avoiding any serious relationship. As she danced like a butterfly in the sunshine of the Belle Epoque, everything was fun, everything was modern and exciting. Engineers erected a great column of metal in the heart of Paris and called it the Eiffel Tower. In London the great American circus Barnum & Bailey put whooping Red Indians and performing elephants on show at Olympia. A Republican government might rule in France, but it did nothing to limit the gaiety and extravagance of the populace, and particularly of the rich.

Netta considered it one of the most rewarding times to be alive – comparable only with the Renaissance in Italy or the days of Classical Greece. Not that she'd have liked to be a Greek, no, no – not for her the almost oriental seclusion of the Athenian ladies.

Mama might shake her head and sigh that she was flighty. Papa might frown a little and remark that she had exceeded her allowance by an even greater margin this month. None of it really mattered – she knew they loved and admired her, not only because she was a pretty, intelligent girl but because she had something precious – a talent.

Already young intellectuals had written poems about her voice. It was tremendously flattering... Yet it was unsettling too. What was the use of having a 'golden gift', as her teacher called it, if she was destined only to use it in stuffy drawing rooms after dinner? Because that of course was all that could come of it, especially once she was married. Husbands, she suspected, didn't like their wives to be seriously interested in music.

'Have you let Grandmama know the gown's here?' she asked as they came out of the great bedroom in a group.

'Oh, my goodness, Madame de Tramont prefers to treat the whole thing as run-of-the-mill,' said Estelle with a shake of her grey head. 'I really believe, mademoiselle, that she's less excited than any of the rest of us!'

The two vendeuses made complimentary remarks on Madame's self-control, wished everyone luck on the occasion of the marriage, and were shown out of the handsome back door with tips equally handsome in their reticules. Netta, after glancing into the drawing room and the morning room and finding them both empty, went to survey the gown she herself would wear that afternoon.

Monsieur Worth had almost begged to be allowed to produce what he called 'a unity' for the ceremony – the bride in a gown which would supply a theme for all the other ladies. But Grandmama had quashed that idea on the first visit. 'Monsieur, don't be absurd! An old woman like me, made the centrepiece of a pretty tableau for the photographers? Certainly not!'

Mama had therefore been left to supervise the dresses of the other female members of the Tramont household. Netta would be in pale blue *mousseline de soie* with cream flowers and a cream and blue bonnet, while her nine-year-old cousin Gabrielle – whom Mama insisted on calling 'the bridesmaid' – was to wear a concoction of voile and taffeta in the same shades.

This had deeply offended young Gaby, who already had a decided view of herself as a person. 'But I'll look like a *doll!*' she protested. 'Please, Aunt Alys, don't make me wear this dress!'

'My darling, just this once... To please me ... I want everything to be perfect for Grandmama's wedding.'

'Other people's grandmothers don't have weddings!' cried Gaby. 'I don't see why we should have one who does!'

'Now, Gaby, your great-aunt is entitled to

15

a lovely happy day on the day she marries Grandpapa Gri-gri – you wouldn't want to spoil everything?'

'N … no… No… All right, then. But don't make me wear this thing on my head.' 'This thing' was the wreath of forget-me-nots Monsieur Worth had concocted. His 'theme', which he secretly hoped to carry out, was to have each of the ladies adorned with different small flowers on their headgear.

'Gaby, sweetheart, if you're going to wear the dress you might as well wear the headdress,' coaxed Netta. 'Look at me – I'm putting up with all these cream freesias–'

'But you *like* dressing up! Mama, you know I hate it! Please don't make me wear it.'

Gaby's mother, Madame Fournier-Tramont smiled and shook her dark head. 'As your Aunt Alys says, my angel, just this once… We all have to dress up for the wedding and, only think how lucky you are! If it were Netta's wedding you'd probably have to carry her train and handle a posy as well. Just to wear a garland – that's not asking much for Grandmama.'

'We-ell … I s'pose not… All right then.' And, despite her protests, the little girl looked surprisingly beautiful while the 'bridesmaid's' dress was being tried on. Her vivid dark eyes and raven-black hair rescued the outfit from sugariness.

She inherited her looks from her mother, Laura. Daughter of a New York banker, Laura had come into the Tramont family by her marriage to Robert Fournier-Tramont.

Robert had gone to America some twelve years ago. Why he had gone was something of a mystery – it wasn't an easy journey for him, lame as he was, and certainly he could ill be spared from the business for the length of time necessary for the long sea passage. Of course, the members of the great wine families travelled: but generally it was to places where their wares were already in demand or where a market could be opened up.

What Robert could possibly intend to do in California was an enigma, nor had it ever been explained.

He had in fact gone to meet his father. Only Robert and Madame de Tramont knew the secret – that Robert was not the son of Paulette, Madame de Tramont's sister, but of Nicole de Tramont herself and Jean-Baptiste Labaud, former chief of cellar on the Tramont estate.

It had taken Robert years to extract his father's name and whereabouts from Nicole. She had persisted in saying it could do no good for him to know, that the mere fact of his existence was unknown to his father, that it would only bring unhappiness to the man and his innocent wife.

'Aunt Nicole, of course I won't go blundering in and cause an upset,' Robert pleaded, time and again. 'All I want to do is write to him – tell him I exist. Is that too much to ask?'

'Robert, my dear… You know I would tell you if I thought it were right. But he's a long way away, you could never meet – what's the point?'

He took her hand. They were good friends, closer than many mothers and sons, although the relationship between them was thought of by the world as that of aunt and nephew.

'It's hard to explain, Aunt Nicci. Partly it's to do with Mama's husband – with Auguste…'

Auguste Fournier had deserted his wife and children a little over twenty yeas ago, leaving Paulette, Nicole's sister, with no one to provide for her.

As always, Nicole had stepped into the breach. She'd pulled together the little builders' business that had been Auguste's supposed livelihood, she'd arranged for an income for the deserted wife. Later, when Nicole discovered she herself was pregnant, Paulette had volunteered out of gratitude to take the expected child and bring it up as her own. This she had done, so that until he was a young man Robert had always thought of Paulette Fournier as Mama.

18

There had never been a 'Papa'. Madame Fournier was accepted as a widow, although within the privacy of the home it was acknowledged that 'Papa' was probably alive somewhere, eking out a living as a seaman.

It came as a bombshell to Robert when at last he had to be told that he was Nicole's son. A time of great unhappiness had ensued. Robert escaped from it into the French Army, which almost at once was engulfed in the attempt to stop the German invasion of 1870. The wounds he received still marred his physique, although he managed very well with one stick considering that the doctors had said he would never walk again.

Nicole had never perhaps understood Robert's need to know his father. 'Papa' had been a bad lot, but then 'Papa' had not been his real Papa. When he found that out, it was only to be told that the man responsible for his existence had been another 'deserter', a man who had packed up and left France. 'It had to be so, my dear. Everything was complicated enough as it was. It was better not to tell him.'

'But I want to know, Aunt Nicole. I want to know if he's someone I can respect. You tell me he was a good man – I want to know that for myself.'

'No, dear. It's better not.'

And for years she held by that decision.

What changed her mind? She learned, by the interchange of news that took place in the world of wine-making, that Jean-Baptiste's wife had died. His children by that marriage must be grown and out in the world by now. It was safe to tell Robert the name of the man who had sired him.

'My dear, before I give it to you, I want your promise that you'll act with caution and tact.'

'Something has changed?'

'Yes, Robert. Madame Labaud died last year. It says in the *Journal de Vinicole Mondiale* that Jean-Baptiste had done no research for about six months due to anxieties over his wife's health.'

'That's his name? Labaud?'

She nodded. The soft lace lappets of the widow's cap she always wore swung gently with the movement. Her face was pensive, sad. 'Jean-Baptiste Labaud. A fine man – tall and strong and honest.'

'Labaud? But I've seen articles by him in the *Journal* – good God, Aunt Nicci, he lives in California!'

'That's right.'

'California!'

'You see, my mother-in-law – Old Madame – she'd made everything impossible by interfering and meddling...'

Her voice died away. She was back in the past, reliving the agony of that day when

20

Jean-Baptiste told her he was leaving France.

How she had loved him! Even now she thought of him with affection and respect. But of course he would have changed, after all these years. He would be a true American, though somehow she could never quite bring herself to believe that. Just as she could never bring herself to believe that even Jean-Baptiste would produce wine worth drinking from grapes produced on the other side of the world...

Everything was different now. She herself wasn't the same woman as that passionate young widow of twenty years ago. She'd rebuilt the House of Tramont, literally and figuratively, after the Franco-Prussian War. She'd survived the death of a daughter and the anxieties of Robert's illness. He had recovered well: better still, he had been reconciled to her after bereavement brought them together. Now he had taken her name legally, as had Gavin her son-in-law. The two men helped her to manage the business.

The House of Tramont flourished under their care. It was only fair that Robert should have the reward he'd wished for so long – that of knowing his real father.

True to his promise, he wrote a careful letter to Jean-Baptiste Labaud, saying that Madame de Tramont had given him permission to approach him and would vouch for the truth of what he now related. If Monsieur Labaud would do him the honour to reply, they could correspond with one another, enough to get to know each other a little.

'Perhaps he'll take no notice,' Robert murmured to Nicole when he confided the letter to the post.

'He'll reply,' Nicole said with assurance.

She was right. As soon as could be – although that wasn't too soon, since the mail service between France and western America was not of the best – a letter came. Two letters, in fact – one to Nicole reproaching her for keeping her secret so long.

'My dearest girl, I understand your reasons and respect them, but I can't help being stricken to the heart to learn after all these years that you and I produced a son. Write to me, Nicci, tell me what he's like! From his letter he seems a sincere and earnest young man better educated than his Papa, of course, and I daresay brought up to be a gentleman. He tells me he helps in the business. What does he do? It would be nice to think he inherited some of my ability with the wine. My own children are quite uninterested, although Alain is a decent enough assistant-manager.'

Correspondence between the two families flew back and forth. It ended with an invitation from Jean-Baptiste to Robert – to come to California so that they could meet. 'I can't come to France, my boy. If I left here, the wine-making would go to pieces in two days. These Americans! They understand nothing about vintage. Besides, it wouldn't be a good thing for me to turn up again in Calmady, nor would I fit in too well with the grand life you lead in Paris. Come, dear boy – you might like the New World.'

It was a big decision. Robert's health was good, but getting on and off trains and boats presented difficulties, and as for stage-coaches! However, Jean-Baptiste assured him that the train would take him to the West Coast, and although from there he would indeed have to go by Wells Fargo the road was good and the distance to Bracanda Norte could be covered in about a day and a half.

With many misgivings Nicole de Tramont let her son make the trip. She wondered if his body with its mended bones would stand up to it, and whether his eagerness to meet his father would end in pleasure or disappointment.

It was to be a six months' trip. As Jean-Baptiste said, it was hardly worth making the effort if he allowed less time, because the sea passage to New York was long and the train journey across the continent

23

almost equally so.

In one respect Robert was lucky. He had no difficulty with the language. His mother had always insisted that her daughters and her supposed nephew should learn English and German, and of course once Alys settled at home with her English husband the language became almost as common in the Tramont household as French.

But he found the Americans strange. New York itself was extraordinary, with buildings apparently trying to poke a hole in the sky – and in fact that was their name, 'skyscrapers'. The food was unspeakable, good wine was unobtainable, even in good restaurants because even if it was in stock, it was badly handled.

During the long transit of the continent he sent back letters from stations where the train stopped to take on passengers or mail. Respect began to creep into the phrases: 'So vast a country... Little towns huddled at the railheads... What struggles the settlers must have endured... Yet there is activity. There must also be prosperity, though I have no chance to see it...'

When he reached San Francisco he wrote to say he was staying overnight, to rest and prepare for his venture into the old-fashioned stage-coach system. Always his letters were suitable to be read aloud to other members of the family at Calmady, taking it for granted he was on a journey of investigation into the Californian wine industry.

But his first letter from Bracanda Norte contained also a single sheet, folded over and marked 'Confidential'.

'I have met my father. I must tell you how much I like him. We have had several long talks. Though he would wish to acknowledge me, we have concluded that it would be needlessly cruel to his other children to reveal our kinship. My role here is as a visitor from the region where he was born, a member of the family with whom he was once employed.

'My father has some shares in the wine company, Bracanda Norte Winery. There would be no problem in making a post for me here and this has already been hinted at but I shan't take it up – it would look strange to my half-brother Alain, for they have no work for a manager of buildings since in this country they as yet care too little about the warehousing of the wine.

'Besides, if I stayed here, I think it would become clear that there is a relationship – we are not unalike in features. Gossip would spring up. You know in the little world of wine-makers news is handed on sooner or later – through shipping agents it would undoubtedly get back to France, and harm your reputation, dear Mama.

'That is the first time I have ever

addressed you by that name, Mama, and I think it must be the last. It would be dangerous to let it become a habit. I conclude this note by saying merely that I regret not having had the chance to grow up in a family with such a father and mother. I believe it will be best if you destroy this note—Your son, Robert.'

Nicole wept over the letter, and kept it for several days, taking it out in the privacy of her bedroom to read and re-read it. But in the end she obeyed her son's command and held it in the flame of a match. It scarcely mattered that the truth of their relationship had to be kept secret. All the world knew that on the death of her sister Paulette she had adopted both her nephew Robert and her son-in-law Gavin as joint heirs of the Tramont name. Everything she owned would be divided between them. If she sometimes showed more affection for Robert than for Gavin, that was only natural – she'd known him since he was a child, whereas Gavin, though in every way a fine son-in-law, had only come into her life a few years ago.

All the other letters that Robert wrote from the United States were for public consumption. He returned in the autumn on the *Gallia*.

But he didn't rush straight to Calmady, which was strange, as the wine harvest was just over and the grapes were being pressed. It was an anxious time, one he usually shared with Nicole and Gavin.

Instead he made use of their newly-installed telephone to call from Paris. 'I have some matters that will keep me here a day or two, Aunt Nicole. How is the pressing going?'

'Not well. The juice from nearby seems very "heavy". I'm going tomorrow to take a look at what they're producing on the côtes. How are you, my dear boy – have you recovered from the effects of your trip?'

The question really meant, Have you got over the shock of meeting your father for the first time? She waited anxiously for his reply.

'What? Oh … yes… All that is behind me now. Aunt Nicole, you don't mind if I stay on in Paris?'

'Of course not, Robert. But you won't stay away too long, will you? It's six months and more, you know.'

'Yes, I know … I'll be at Calmady by the end of the week.'

It was very strange.

'It's a woman,' Gavin declared when Nicole wondered why he should linger in Paris.

'Robert? Never!'

'Dearest Belle-mère, even Robert can fall in love, you know!'

Nicole didn't reply that Robert had been in love once, tragically. That was all in the past. Delphine was dead, seldom spoken of because the memory was too painful for those who knew the story.

She had almost taken for granted that Robert would go through the rest of his life faithful to that memory. She had never wanted it so, but Robert was so grave and quiet in his ways that somehow it had seemed suitable he should remain a solitary figure.

Yet Gavin was proved right. When Robert at last came home to the country house at Calmady, he had a request to make after the first excitements of reunion. 'Aunt Nicole, when we go up to Paris for the winter, may I ask you to call on a friend of mine?'

'Certainly. I believe I heard that Antoine Delahaie and his wife had taken an apartment in–'

'It's not Antoine. It's someone I met on the *Gallia*.'

'Ah, a new acquaintance. Of course, Robert – I'll leave a card. What's his name?'

'It's a lady.'

'Aha!' cried Gavin, with a glance of triumph at his mother-in-law. 'Didn't I say so?'

'S-sh, Gavin... There's no need for an uproar–'

'But it's so unlike Robert to make friends

with a lady! What's she like, Robert? Young? Pretty? What's her name?'

Robert took the boisterous inquiries with his usual tranquillity. 'She's Laura Simeon, from New York–'

'An American?' exclaimed Alys in amazement.

'Good gracious, Alys, Americans are people like the rest of us. Go on, my boy,' urged Nicole, now thoroughly curious. 'From New York – yes? On a visit?'

'With her mother. They're staying at the Crillon. I gathered that they intended the usual round – the art galleries, the museums, the opera... They have friends and distant relations here but ... it would be nice if we could help them enjoy the city.'

'Yes, of course, we must come to their aid,' Gavin agreed, 'and if in doing so we increase our acquaintance with this pretty American, that's only the just rewards for a good action.'

'I haven't said she's pretty.'

'But she is, isn't she?'

'Yes.'

'And young? And witty?'

'Not witty. Laura's rather serious, I think.'

Teased by Gavin and urged by Alys, Robert revealed that the young lady was the daughter of a New York banker, a third generation American of French extraction. They had met on the boat at the captain's table, but their friendship seemed to date from the moment when he rescued her hat from sailing overboard by trapping it with his cane.

He didn't speak of the hours they'd spent together, in long conversations that ranged from their past travels to their present plans, their intentions for the future, and their secret hopes and beliefs. A sea voyage is like a forcing house – relationships flourish in the enforced idleness and the continual meetings. By the time the *Gallia* docked it felt as if they'd known each other forever.

Nicole took to Laura at once. The others were less enthusiastic. They thought her too quiet, too introspective. 'But don't you see, that makes her exactly right for Robert!' Nicole declared. 'He's quiet too, and so reserved that I never expected him to get involved with any young woman – certainly not with any of those in our set.'

'Mama,' Alys said, colouring, 'I don't wish to seem snobbish, but the family seem to have come from nowhere.'

'They came from Bordeaux–'

'That's not what I meant, Mama, and you know it. As far as I can gather from what Madame Simeon says, her father-in-law landed in New York without a sou.'

'Yes? And so?'

'We-ell...'

'Alys, I had very few sous when I was a

30

girl. Being poor is no disgrace, especially when the first Monsieur Simeon in New York seems to have done so extremely well–'

'But Mama... The name...'

'What? Simeon? What of it?'

'Don't you think it's Jewish?'

'Certainly.' Nicole frowned. 'You aren't going to say anything against the girl on that score, Alys? We may be Catholic by tradition but we're not devout, don't let's pretend we are.'

'I didn't mean that, Mama. I meant... Well ... it can be a social disadvantage.'

Nicole sprang up and walked about the room, her black taffeta skirts rustling against the dark Brussels carpet. 'My dear child, I should think the House of Tramont can survive any snobbishness it meets on that point. I won't hear any more of this, Alys, do you understand me? Robert loves the girl – you can see that in the very way he turns to greet her. And she loves him. He deserves his happiness after all that's happened to him. So that's the end of it.'

'Very well, Mama,' said Alys, surprised at the warmth of her mother's manner. It was odd, sometimes – Mama could be as strong in her affection towards Robert as towards her own children and grandchildren.

The families had the usual conferences, although in the case of the Simeons it had to be done through the mother only. The father signalled his good will from New York and promised to come for the wedding. Nicole expected some slight problem over the religious ceremony but to her relief there was none – it seemed that if the Simeons were of Jewish origin they had let that go in the three generations since they reached the New World. Laura, serious and attentive, took instruction in the Catholic faith and was received.

The following year their first child, David, was born.

As she bent over the cradle Nicole felt the tears welling. Who would have thought that her darling son would ever find this happiness? The joy of a son of his own, the blessing of a wife who adored him... She felt a surge of love not only for the child but for the mother who had brought Robert this gift. And when two years later little Gaby was born, the Fournier-Tramonts were, in their quiet way, the happiest family in the world.

That happiness had never been marred. Even the troubles of the wine-making world couldn't disturb it. Laura played no part in that, and if sometimes Robert was worried he kept it from her. On the whole life had taken a tranquil turn for the Tramonts, and their excitements were generally of a joyous kind.

Not that young Gaby considered the

wedding of her grandmother a joyous occasion. She was made to eat a light lunch and lie down for an hour before getting dressed for her part in the ceremony.

'I'm too old to take a nap!'

'No one too old for that,' said Nanny in her thick Portuguese-French. Flori had been brought as children's nurse by Alys and Gavin from the vineyards outside Lisbon where Gavin had been employed. Still, almost twenty years later, she'd never mastered the French language. She found it an advantage when dealing with recalcitrant children – when they were stubborn she simply refused to understand.

'Well, Grandmama's too old to get married!' insisted Gaby.

'Never too old for that, either.'

'Well, I think weddings are stupid, anyway! I'm *never* going to get married!'

'*Verdadeiro!* No one will take you!' But Flori knew it was untrue. The child was destined to be a beauty. She had the dreaming dark good looks of her mother, enlivened by a flash and spirit that couldn't have come, in Flori's opinion, from either mother or father. Sometimes it seemed to the nurse that there was a strong likeness to Madame de Tramont in Gaby – but that could hardly be, since Nicole wasn't the child's grandparent. That brave, eager liveliness must come from some earlier forbear, it seemed.

Alys Hopetown-Tramont tapped at her mother's door at two-thirty in the afternoon. She found her, as she expected, wide awake and sitting at her escritoire looking over some documents. 'Mama, I knew you wouldn't be resting!'

'My dear, time enough for "resting" when I no longer have the energy for work. Well, what is it?'

'Nothing important. I just wanted to chat with you. This is such an important day!'

Nicole nodded. She put her pen down, turning in her chair to face her daughter. 'Does it upset you in any way? That I should be marrying again, so late in life?'

'Mama!' Alys flew to her, to drop a kiss on the widow's cap of black and white lace. 'Fifty-six isn't so very "late"! And I told you at the outset, when it was first mentioned – I'm only too happy that you and Gri-gri can have a life together at last.'

Nicole smiled. 'It will be strange. I've been The Widow Tramont so long…'

'The Marchioness of Grassington – it's an elegant title.'

'And that too is strange, Alys – and ironic. You won't remember, but Old Madame was so keen to have the title back – the de Tramont title. She worked half of her life, trying to make your father the Marquis de Tramont. It does seem odd that *I,* the peasant girl, should be the one to bring

34

nobility into our household!'

Lord Grassington had explained to Nicole that of course the title could not be inherited by any of her family – his son William would be the next Earl. Likewise his estates and his money, which were considerable, would be handed on to the heir. 'I can only offer you myself, really, dearest,' he'd said in an apologetic tone when he had set it all out for her.

'Gerrard, you're angling for a compliment! You know you yourself are all I ever wanted.'

'Yes, I know, but it's nice to hear you say it after all this time, Nicci.'

They had been lovers for almost twenty years – discreet, devoted. Gerrard's wife must not be hurt, his political career must not be damaged by scandal. They had waited the obligatory year after Emma's death.

It was a greater change for Nicole than for Gerrard. She had agreed to spend at least half the year in England so that he could attend parliamentary sessions and look after his estates.

It meant handing over control of the House of Tramont to Gavin and Robert. She did it gladly, reserving to herself those things she did best – correspondence with shipping agents, visits to foreign markets. Six months in England and perhaps two more spent in travel she wouldn't be seen nearly so much at Calmady.

'But I'll always be there for the vintage, my boys,' she had assured them. 'It's not that I don't trust you... It's just that I could never be happy anywhere else in the world in September!'

The plan was that the honeymoon should be spent first in a tour of those parts of Germany now considered romantic thanks to the works of Herr Wagner. Business could later be done with some rich importers in Berlin. In August Gerrard wished to be at home to open the grouse season on his moor. In September, they would come to Calmady to watch the first vintage produced under the aegis of the two young men.

Alys could hardly envisage it. Ever since she came home in 1873, Mama had been the guiding spirit of their lives. What would it be like without her in their handsome house in the Avenue d'Iena? What would it be like without her in the great mansion in Calmady? What, most of all, would it be like without her in the cellars, in the pressing-house, in the gleaming new laboratory where the tests were carried out on the new wine?

Estelle knocked, to bring in a tea-tray laid out in the English style. They drank a cup, and then the maid reappeared. 'Time to get dressed, Madame,' she said, tears gleaming on her lashes.

'Yes, I suppose so.'

'I'll stay and help, Mama.'

'No, dear, you go and put on your own finery. You know you and the others must go first to the Mairie.'

Alys nodded, kissed and hugged her, went out.

Nicole de Tramont turned to her maid. Today, for the first time in a quarter of a century, she was to wear colours. Today she would put off forever the widow's weeds that had become her trademark.

It was a great change – for herself, for the House of Tramont...

Chapter Two

Although the wedding was quiet and dignified, next day seemed flat by comparison. Netta Hopetown-Tramont went for a brisk walk in the Bois, lingering at La Potinière to hear the latest gossip. The talk was all about Madame de Greffulhe's party of that evening.

'You'll be going, of course, Netta?'

'I haven't had an invitation, Cosette.'

'As if that matters! You and she are so alike

in your interests – she'll want you to be there. I hear Monsieur Rimsky-Korsakov is to be among the guests. Tomorrow he is to conduct some suite or other with the Orchestre Pallarde–'

'Yes, "Prince Igor" – from an opera by his friend Borodin, about a captured Russian prince.'

'Good gracious, then perhaps it will be worth listening to! At least it won't be in four movements and send one to sleep.'

'Cosette, you're impossible! Why do you go to concerts if you haven't any interest in music?'

'Dearest, you know very well,' Cosette Sisimonde said with an expressive pout. 'It's because Mama makes me. Now you, on the other hand, are very strange. You actually go to concerts and operas without your mama. But it's very naughty of you, because you never trouble to follow up any of the advances the young men make.' She linked her arm in Netta's to draw her away from the rest of the group. 'Mama was saying only the other day that if you had put yourself out, you could have had Monsieur de Brigonte – he positively pursued you in the Opera Bar.'

'Not at all,' Netta said, laughing. 'It was simply that he went to fetch me an ice, and when he returned, I'd moved somewhere else.'

'My goodness, if Monsieur de Brigonte was looking for me, I'd take care to be where he could find me.'

'Cosette, you know as well as I do that the only thing to recommend Monsieur de Brigonte is his inheritance. Otherwise he's of no interest – he has protruding teeth, inflicts his opinions on you, and never listens to what you say in reply.'

'Oh, if that's all–!'

'Don't make light of it. I'd rather die an old maid than marry the likes of Esme de Brigonte.'

'Don't say such things! Or if you do, touch wood! Really, Netta... Sometimes you alarm me. You'll end up with an arranged match if you keep frightening off the possibles.'

'As far as I'm concerned, de Brigonte is impossible. Besides, though he goes to the opera and looks solemn, he isn't the least interested in music.'

'As if that matters, Netta!'

'It matters to me,' Netta said with emphasis, stabbing the ferrule of her parasol into the turf. 'I simply couldn't live with a man who can't even recognise the main tunes from *Carmen*.'

'My dear!' sighed Cosette. They walked a pace or two, arm in arm. They had been schoolfellows, still kept up a friendship although their outlooks were so entirely different. 'Tell me... Do you think I should accept Henri Margotier?'

'Cosette, you don't really want my opinion on that. I think he's a waster.'

'Ye-es... But Papa is willing to pay off all his debts and settle something on him. There's a lot to be said for him. His family have money–'

'But they've washed their hands of him because of his gambling. No, no, Cosette, if you've decided to take an arranged suitor, get Papa and Mama to find you someone more considerate than Margotier.'

'How difficult you are to please! Margotier's a ne'er-do-well, de Brigonte is dull. There aren't so many left, you know, Netta. I should have taken one of the half dozen on offer in my first season, instead of being so choosy. But I still thought then I might fall in love.'

'And so you might, still.'

'Heaven forbid! The more I see of love-matches, the more I think it's best to leave it all to the parents.' Netta was shaking her head, and Cosette went on: 'It's all right for you! You can put it off as long as you like, with your family's money behind you! But mind you, I still don't think you'll ever find a husband who'll put up with your ideas to have a career in singing.'

'We'll see,' said Netta, 'we'll see.'

That evening she went with her mother

and her brother Philippe to Madame de Rime's at-home. Philippe, in his usual gentle way, went at his mother's instructions to make himself agreeable to a group of young ladies. At eighteen Philippe was still too young to be taken seriously as a possible husband by any of those present. Netta was shepherded towards a set of chairs where the chaperones took their ease and kept their daughters by them until a suitable young man came to claim their attention.

Netta never minded such manoeuvring. So long as she was left alone to talk or be silent with the young man, she was quite happy. She could generally escape when she wanted to, to gossip with the girls, or perhaps look at the books in the library or play with the other children.

On this occasion, she discovered she was being held prisoner. It was clear that her mother was expecting someone in particular. 'Mama, it will really be best if you tell me whom it is I'm waiting for. Then I can go and amuse myself, and come back when I see him arrive.'

'You'll stay here, child,' Alys said with a playful tap from her fan. 'I know you! You'll find the music room and never be seen again all evening.'

'No, I promise. I'll stay in the salon. Who is it this evening, Mama? Georges Filimor again? Or someone new?'

'My darling, I can't imagine how we ever brought you up to be so unladylike! It is quite unseemly for you to talk in this way of the young men you may encounter.'

Mademoiselle Quebrouille, chaperoning her niece, leaned across to nod agreement. 'Young girls these days... Where do they find these forward notions? I put it down to the unsettled political climate, you know.'

'Political?' Alys was surprised. 'I hope my daughter is not influenced by politics, mademoiselle!'

'You misunderstand. I mean these continual changes – from Emperor to Republican President – from one code of manners to another... Under a Republic, you know, morals are always more relaxed than under a prince.'

The two ladies became involved in an argument about the government which had come into office after the flight of Boulanger last April. Netta seized the opportunity to move gently away towards the windows. They stood open to the terrace, with steps down to a small formal garden. Outside, the April night was balmy. In a house some distance away, a small orchestra was playing a Strauss waltz.

Netta knew the words. She began to sing them under her breath. 'Springtime, Springtime, beautiful time, Beautiful season of Springtime...'

'How charming,' remarked a male voice. 'A nightingale in the garden – and so early!'

She turned. Leaning against the balustrade in the shadows was a young man in the required evening dress. The red light from the end of his cigar showed up a thin dark chin and full lips over the gleam of his dress shirt.

'M'sieu, you startled me!'

'I apologise. But it was so surprising to hear someone singing to herself at this dirge of a party.'

'You aren't enjoying it?'

'I never came across a duller set of people – that is, until I met you.'

'Come, come. You haven't "met" me. And all you know about me is that I hum Strauss to myself – that's not very interesting.'

'It's interesting compared with anything else I expected to come across here this evening.'

'I wonder that you came at all, since it isn't the sort of gathering you enjoy.'

'Orders are orders,' he said lightly. 'My father threatened to cut off my allowance if I didn't attend.'

'How cruel! But you'll endure the torment, because you need your allowance.'

'Who doesn't? Besides, I'm not likely to come to any harm. Some blue-stocking girl is to be introduced and then I can make my escape.' He drew on his cigar in enjoyment.

'Now you – you clearly share my views on the company.'

'You think so?'

'You shouldn't have crept out to be alone with the bushes in their tubs.'

'You're quite mistaken. I didn't come out because I find the company uninteresting.'

'Why, then?'

'I have reasons of my own.'

'A lady of mystery? And that reminds me we haven't introduced ourselves. I'm Frederic de la Sebiq. And you are?'

'Nicolette Hopetown-Tramont.'

'Ah! Now that's very interesting!'

'It is? I can't imagine why?'

'You will find out, Mademoiselle,' he said. There was amusement in his tone.

'Well, I had better go indoors again. Mama will be looking for me, I dare say.'

'No, stay. Let's get better acquainted.'

'Not at this point, m'sieu. I'm sure Mama wouldn't approve of my being alone with a man who hasn't been properly introduced.'

'She won't object,' he said with great assurance.

'She won't? What makes you think not?'

'Mama's always approve of me. I'm welcomed by every Mama in Paris.'

You have a high opinion of yourself, thought Netta inwardly. Aloud she said, 'All that may be true, but for my own ease of mind I should prefer to go indoors. Good evening, sir.'

'No, wait!' He caught her by the arm. 'Wait, I want to know more about you.'

'Let me go, Monsieur de la Sebiq–'

'No, a moment longer. Let me take you so that the light shines on your face. I want to see what you look like.'

Angrily she dragged her arm free. 'Sir, if you want to inspect my looks, you can do it in the salon where it's less like inspecting one of your horses. Excuse me.'

She walked quickly back through the windows into the salon. Her mother had by now noted her absence but wasn't perturbed, though she was surprised to see Netta marching in, not from the music room but from the terrace, with her colour considerably heightened.

'There you are, my dear! Is anything wrong?'

'Nothing at all, Mama. I just stepped outside to look at the stars.'

Alys sighed. What could you do with a nineteen-year-old daughter who went out to look at the stars alone, instead of waiting to be invited by a suitable young man?

'Sit down, Netta. Compose yourself. You look a little flustered.'

'No I'm not!'

'Don't contradict. Use your fan. If this young man appears, we don't want you looking like a pink shrimp.'

45

Netta quelled the annoyed repartee that rose to her lips and fanned herself with too much briskness. Really, life was insupportable! First of all she had to submit to coming to Madame de Rime's when she would have preferred to go to Madame de Greffulhe's music party. Then she was impertinently inspected by a young man who hadn't even the right to speak to her since he hadn't been introduced. And now Mama was telling her to make herself look pale but interesting for a gentleman who was so very late in appearing.

They were holding a conversation with young Monsieur Perron and his bride when out of the corner of her eye Netta spied their hostess forging her way towards them. Her heart sank. The young man she had in tow was certainly the one who had offended her on the terrace.

Though she hadn't been able to see him clearly, there was no mistaking that slightly arrogant tilt of the head, and the cigar… Surely he wasn't going to have the impertinence to be presented smoking a cigar?

'My dears, I want to introduce Frederic de la Sebiq, who has expressed a sincere desire to know your family. Frederic my dear, pray make the acquaintance of Madame Hopetown-Tramont and her daughter.'

'Enchanted,' murmured Frederic de la

Sebiq, bowing over Alys's hand. Netta took good care to be busy folding her fan, and satisfied herself with a cool nod.

'Dear Frederic has just come back from service in Indo-China,' explained Madame de Rime. 'Such heroic exploits! I'm sure if you tease him about it, he'll tell you some details.'

She moved off, to order a footman to bring them refreshment. Monsieur de la Sebiq looked questioningly at the empty chair beside them. Alys made a little gesture of invitation. He sat down.

'So, you have been fighting in the French Union of Indo-China,' said Alys with a smile of approval. 'That of course accounts for your tanned skin, m'sieu. The life must have been very exhausting, apart from the dangers of war.'

He took up the subject she had begun, shrugging a little. 'The dangers were not too great. A cavalry regiment had really little part to play. But the climate is certainly tiring. I am glad to be home where one can walk about without growing weary in ten steps.'

Alys glanced at Netta. It was now her turn to take part in the conversation, to follow up the young man's remarks. She could for instance say: 'Which is your regiment, m'sieu?' or 'Did you take part in the capture of Tonkin?' or – if she preferred to get away

from war, which would be very ladylike –
she could ask: 'Now that you are home,
what shall you do, m'sieu?'

Netta, however, took none of these
openings. She had turned her eyes towards
the approaching footman, and when he
offered a tray she took a glass of wine. 'I find
I'm hungry too,' she said, to no one in
particular. She got up, moved off easily and
without haste towards the table with
canapés and other tasty morsels.

Behind her she could feel her mother's
angry eyes boring into her. Well, let her be
angry! She had cut him dead, and it was all
he deserved. 'Some blue-stocking,' indeed!
And even if he were a war hero, that didn't
give him the right to be so patronising.

When she had been served with a little
plate of goodies, she took up a position
beside the Perrons. Lucie Perron, who was
recently enough married to remember her
single state, whispered to her: 'Ought you
not to go back to your mama? She's keeping
Monsieur de la Sebiq with her on purpose.'

'I don't wish to know him,' Netta said with
a little huff of annoyance.

'Netta, my dear! You can't snub a man
your mother has particularly sought out for
you.'

'Oh, can't I! Just you wait and see.'

She remained on the other side of the
room for the next twenty minutes. Monsieur

de la Sebiq, his conversational powers exhausted, bowed and moved away from Alys. Alys rose and sought out her wayward daughter. 'Well, you've ruined this evening quite adequately so we'll take our leave. Come along.'

Netta knew she was in disgrace. But she didn't care, even when her mother remained grimly silent in the carriage all the way home to the Avenue d'Iena.

In the drawing room Papa was still up, reading and quite clearly waiting for them. 'Well, my dears? Did you have a nice time?'

'Not at all,' said Alys. 'Your daughter behaved like a barbarian.'

'What?'

'She cut Monsieur de la Sebiq absolutely dead. I don't understand her.'

'Netta, you didn't?'

'I treated him as he deserved, Papa. He offended me.'

'He what? Nonsense! He was introduced in proper form and–'

'While still holding his cigar in his left hand, I noticed!'

Gavin gave a half laugh which he covered with a cough. 'Oh, Netta, now my dear… The man has been overseas among fellow-officers for two years! You must forgive him a few rough corners.'

'It's not only that. He was out on the terrace while I was there–'

'Netta! You didn't tell me that–'

'I'm telling you now. I took a great dislike to him. Without troubling to find out who I was he spoke disparagingly of the girl he'd been invited to meet, and then he tried to … to…'

'What?' cried Alys in great alarm.

'He tried to drag me into the light to look me over.'

'Oh,' said her father, with a sigh of relief. 'Oh, well … that perhaps was not quite–'

'From what he said, it was clear his father had ordered him to be there. Was this to be a match asked for by the older Monsieur de la Sebiq?'

'We-ell…'

'Oh, Papa, don't shilly-shally. It sounds as if they're pressed for money. Was I to repair the family fortunes?'

'My dear child, how does it come about that you talk of such things? I'm sure I never brought you up to be so forward! Really, Papa, you must speak to her. She's becoming quite … quite odd. Two seasons out and not even engaged – and acquiring such peculiar manners…'

'Now don't be cross with her, Mama. She's got plenty of time to get a husband'

'You think so? She'll be twenty next year! Everyone she came out with will be married by then!'

'There will always be plenty of suitors for

Netta's hand, my love.'

'But will she ever make up her mind to take one?'

'I certainly shan't take anyone who talks about me as if I were a hateful duty he has to endure!'

'Netta, go to bed! It's to be hoped you'll wake up in the morning with more sense than you have now!'

'Goodnight, my dear,' murmured Gavin, submitting his cheek to be kissed. 'You've been a bad girl, but we forgive you.'

When the door had closed on her, Alys broke out: 'I wish you would be more severe with her, Gavin! She's being very difficult!'

'At least she doesn't want to become a nun,' he retorted.

Alys shuddered. The family had had a great fright some four years ago when Philip, at fourteen, had come home on school holiday declaring that he wanted to train to be a priest.

The family had been in uproar for almost a month. The boy was adamant that when he returned to the seminary he would put his name forward for the priesthood. His parents had told him they would refuse permission, and certainly take him away from the rather devout institution he attended.

Neither Alys nor Gavin had anything against the church. But they had always taken it for granted that Philip would follow his father into the House of Tramont. There was, of course, Robert's little boy David, but at seven years old he was having bronchitic troubles which seemed to foretell a possibly limited role.

It was his sister Netta who talked Philip out of it in the end. He had always confided in her and respected her, for though only a year his senior she seemed so sure of herself in every way. 'Phip, of course if you really have a vocation, you must follow it. But remember this. As a priest you'll have to deal with the problems of very ordinary people, won't you?'

'I suppose so, if I'm given a parish...'

'But – now be honest – how many ordinary people have you ever met?'

'What?' the boy said, looking up in surprise with his dark grey eyes.

'You've been brought up on the estate, it's true, but you don't really mix with the wine-workers, now do you? And you've been to the seminary since you were eleven, and all the boys there come from families that are ... well, you'd say fairly aristocratic, wouldn't you?'

'I suppose so. But we go out to visit the poor'

'Oh yes! Ten minutes with some poor old man in an almshouse, give him half an ounce of baccy, and off you go in the school

52

cart! My dear little brother, we do that at the lycée too, only we visit poor old ladies and give them hand-knitted mittens. But if I look into myself truthfully, I have to admit that I don't know anything about those old ladies. And...' she hesitated. 'I've never said this to anyone else but I don't really enjoy visiting them!'

'Oh, Netta...'

'Be honest, Phip – do you like those old men? Do you know them at all.'

'We-ll ... of course we have to stick to the timetable and–'

'No excuses! Have you ever sat down with one of them and listened to his troubles? Have you ever volunteered to do more than is required by the school?'

'No, but–'

'All I'm saying, Phip, is that you may have a vocation but it doesn't seem to have much to do with a wish to serve ordinary people. And if that's what you were asked to do after you were ordained, how could you make a start?'

'But other men learn through their parish duties–'

'But other men perhaps come from more ordinary walks of life. They're the sons of farmers, merchants, teachers ... I don't say you shouldn't train for the church, Phip dear – all I say is that you should delay the decision until you've finished your ordinary education and seen at least a bit of the world.'

He didn't agree at once. But two days later he told his anxious parents that he'd thought it over and though he felt he would one day enter the priesthood, he'd decided not to take that path as yet.

Luckily, according to their view, the notion had faded. At a new school he had become more interested in the classics for their own value, and was planning to go on to university to read Greek. Since he was handsome in his own quiet, inoffensive way, they had hopes that when he finished his studies he would marry well, but whether he would ever play much part in the wine firm seemed doubtful. He was so much a dreamer... But young David, luckily, had survived all his chest complaints to become a sturdy schoolboy so that the Tramonts, looking to the future, felt that in him they had a boy to carry on the family name.

As to Netta, the Hopetown-Tramonts had had no fears. They had known she would make a glittering entrance into society and were sure she would find a husband without any efforts on their part.

'If only she would fall in love,' mourned Alys as they sat discussing the latest disappointment.

'She may well do so. After all, Alys, she *is* only nineteen.'

54

'At that age I was married and a mother!'

'Yes, of course – but let me remind you, you were even more wayward than Netta!'

'Ah, Gavin!' She leaned against him to let him put his arm about her in consolation. She still preferred him to any man she had met in twenty years of marriage.

'If she's taken a dislike to this young man, it's no great loss. An ex-cavalryman, after all...'

'But Helene de Rime vouches for him. She says he's charming.'

'He doesn't seem to charm Netta, which is the important point.'

'Where is the man who will, my love?' sighed Alys. 'I can't think what she expects.'

'More than a formal arrangement, I suppose... Perhaps you could have another chat with her, dear.'

'I've chatted with her until I am at a loss for words. I had great hopes of Monsieur de la Sebiq – Helene spoke so well of him, and the family of such good standing... And having just come back from a war ... I thought it would lend him some extra fascination.'

Gavin laughed, dropped a kiss on her head, and said as he released her: 'Netta is not easily fascinated, dearest. It may be my Scottish blood breaking out. But try another talk with her. It's the beginning of the season – try at least to get her to look more seriously at the young men. Last year it was all "hither and thither" with one fellow after another but nothing came of any of it.'

'Yes, dear,' his wife said with a sigh. She had small hopes of making any headway.

But, as instructed, she called her into her little study after Netta came home from her usual morning walk. The study was a less formidable place than it sounded; it was where Alys carried out correspondence about various charities in which she played a leading part. She also studied sale-room catalogues there. She was beginning a quite interesting collection of Old Masters.

'Now, Netta, your father asked me to speak to you seriously about your future. Don't frown and fidget, dear. Sit down and listen to me.'

'Mama, we've been over all this already–'

'But that was before you almost literally turned your back on a very nice young man–'

'He wasn't "very nice". I thought him quite odious.'

'Oh, good gracious, how can you talk such nonsense. You couldn't have exchanged more than ten sentences with him – you weren't out on the terrace long enough for more!'

'Those ten sentences were enough!' Netta gave an angry jerk of the head, which caused a tendril of bronze-coloured hair to escape from the carefully pinned side-curls. She put up an impatient hand to capture it and tuck it back.

'Well, let's leave Monsieur de la Sebiq aside for the moment – though mind you, I'm by no means so ready to let the acquaintance go as you are. I'm thinking of inviting him to a five-o'clock.'

'If you do, I shall go out!'

'Netta, don't be absurd!'

'Is it absurd to want to have some … some sensitivity from the men I meet? Some respect?'

'My dear, don't tell me Monsieur de la Sebiq was really disrespectful–'

'Oh, I suppose not. It was all very playful and complimentary in its silly way…'

'Then what are you complaining of?'

'I don't want to be "played with"! I'm sick of being treated like a pretty doll! At first it was fun, I enjoyed seeing the men fluttering around me – but when you come to listen to them, they all sound the same. "How charming you are, how pretty you look, what a pleasure to be with you" – it's all quite meaningless.'

'It means they like you.'

'No it doesn't! It means they're looking for a decent-looking girl with money who will do their social standing a lot of good when they get married.'

Alys stared at her daughter. Stated

nakedly, this was indeed what the social season was all about.

'You see?' challenged Netta, making fists out of her hands and shaking them in the air. 'You can't deny it!'

'Well, I … I want to see you well married, my love…'

'It's so unfair!' Netta cried, strange tears springing to her eyes.

'Unfair?'

'You married for love, so did Grandmama! Why am I expected to marry for family aggrandisement?'

There was a long silence. At last Alys said, 'Come here, dear.' She patted the cushions of the chaise longue on which she was sitting. Unwillingly Netta came to her. Her mother took her hand and went on: 'Your father and I want you to fall in love, we really do. But you show not the least signs of it – you have a million friendships and no sweethearts. Most girls of your age have been in and out of love half a dozen times, Netta. The problem is usually how to keep a daughter from making the wrong alliance, not how to get her to make one at all…'

'Is there something different about me?' Netta asked, almost in a piteous tone. 'Am I incapable of falling in love – is that it?'

'Oh, child!' Alys put the palm of her hand to her daughter's cheek, looked into the grey-green eyes. 'You're a sweet, good, affectionate girl! Of course you can fall in love like all the rest of us. Only…'

'What?'

'I wonder if your head isn't full of other things?'

Netta lowered her lashes. She didn't want to meet her mother's anxious gaze. She knew that after the first excitement of her 'white ball' and her launch into society she'd become less and less amused by the activities of her social set. She hadn't exactly dropped out, but she'd certainly made far fewer engagements for the season ahead than for last year, and only half of what she'd had for the first one.

'One thing I notice, Netta. Last night you almost dropped out of our engagement with Madame de Rime – you said you'd rather go to some music party at the Greffulhes. You always make time to go to your singing lessons. You're always ready to cancel another arrangement to go to a concert. You always insist on being on time at the opera–'

'Mama–'

'Let me finish. I've no objections to your making music your chief interest. There's a lot that can be done for charity through musical gatherings and subscription concerts–'

'Mama, one doesn't take an interest in music to help the charities–'

'There's where we differ. There's where

my anxiety rises. Netta, you mustn't let yourself become *odd* about music. It's good to be a patron of the arts, but–'

'I can't bear to hear you talk like this!' cried her daughter, jumping up. 'A patron! Who dares to talk of being a patron to Gabriel Fauré? To Vincent d'Indy? Music is far more important than–'

'Netta, Netta! Don't make such an outcry! Goodness, I'm not attacking these people, whoever they are–'

'They're two of the most important composers in France, that's all!'

'Well, well, I have nothing against them, nothing at all. Netta!'

Her daughter ceased her angry pacing about the room and turned to face her.

'This behaviour is exactly what I mean when I say I'm worried about you. I want you to have accomplishments, and if you have chosen singing, well and good. I love to hear you sing. You give great pleasure to your friends–'

'But Mama, you don't understand! Singing in a drawing room, usually to the accompaniment of a friend who isn't sure of the fingering...' Netta sighed. 'What must it be like to sing with an orchestra? To hear one's voice rising above the violins and woodwind?'

'Netta!' Now Alys had risen too, and took her daughter by the shoulders. She gave her a little shake. 'I never heard such nonsense! Sing with an orchestra? You're not speaking of … public performance?'

'Why not? Monsieur Leroux tells me I have a voice. Why shouldn't I use it?'

'Not in that way.' Alys stood back. 'Listen to me, Netta. I had no idea that things had got to this state. Now I understand why you've been so difficult about everything. Your head's full of nonsense about being a professional singer–'

'It's not nonsense! I could–'

'No you could not! Monsieur Leroux may tell you you sing like an angel, but that's mere flattery – of course he flatters you, he's made good money from his fees. But that's all over now. No more music lessons.'

'Mama!'

'No, Netta. I see now that I should have put my foot down months ago. No more lessons. I forbid you to go to Monsieur Leroux's studio any more. I will write him a note telling him his services are no longer required.'

'Mama, you can't treat him like that! He's not a servant! He was one of the greatest baritones of the French Opera!'

'He's clearly a silly old fool if he's been filling your head with dreams of that kind,' Alys said, with more anger than she'd ever shown in a conversation with her daughter. 'Now understand me, Netta. You will not go to Monsieur Leroux's studio again.'

Netta said nothing.

'Netta? Did you hear me?'

'Yes, Mama.'

She had heard. But she intended to disobey.

Chapter Three

That afternoon Alys had an engagement to go with Philip to the University, to meet some of the scholars who would be his instructors in the autumn. The family's engagement diary showed that Netta was to go with a party of young ladies to see a fashion show by a new young designer.

'Enjoy yourself, my dear,' Alys said to her in token of forgiveness, 'but don't buy anything.'

Cosette Brissiac and her cousin picked Netta up in their carriage. At the show, Netta watched two or three costumes on display then whispered to her friend, 'I'm going to slip out now, Cosette. Don't say anything.'

'Slip out?' gasped Cosette. 'Where are you going?'

'Don't look frightened. I'm only going to my singing teacher.'

'Oh.' Cosette was not quite convinced. 'And how are you going to get back?'

'I'll take a cab.'

'A cab!'

'Oh, Cosette, people do it all the time!'

At the door of Monsieur Leroux's studio, the maid received her with a smile. But when the old singer came into the studio he looked puzzled. 'I didn't expect you, mademoiselle.'

'No, it's not one of my days for a lesson–'

'I didn't mean that.' He picked up a small sheet of stiff paper from the top of the piano and waved it at her. 'This came by hand after lunch. Your mother has discontinued your instruction.'

'Oh!' Netta was taken aback. She hadn't thought her mother would move so fast. 'Oh, Monsieur Leroux, I'm sorry ... I wanted to tell you about it myself...'

'What is the reason? It's not explained in the note. I thought perhaps you had got engaged and therefore–'

'No, no, it's nothing like that. We had a ... a disagreement this morning. Mama feels I'm taking my singing too seriously.'

Leroux wished she would sit down. He had got up from his afternoon nap to receive her and still felt bemused, and his embonpoint seemed to weigh heavily. But Netta was pacing up and down, so he was forced to remain standing. Such were the rules of etiquette with a young lady of good family. Had she been one of his ordinary pupils, he could have ordered her about.

'Monsieur Leroux, you've told me I have a really good voice. Mama says it's just flattery. Is it only that?'

He was offended. 'Mademoiselle, there is no need for me to flatter. I have other pupils among your acquaintance – do I tell them that they sing well?'

'I… No, I don't think you do. Is it true, then? Do I really have a voice worth training?'

'I no longer have any interest in flattering you since your Mama is no longer paying me fees. You have an exceptional voice. But if you don't believe me, I can give you an introduction to a teacher whose opinion would be totally above suspicion.'

'Who?'

'Alfonsini.'

'Alfonsini!' This was one of the great names in opera. He had dominated the stage for twenty years and then retired when gout became too great a problem. As a teacher, the old singer had a reputation for being severe, difficult, but utterly honest.

'I see you are impressed. As a matter of fact, it has crossed my mind once or twice that it would be good to send you to Erneste, to see what he thinks. But there seemed little point if you were only taking lessons as a hobby.'

'Would you give me the letter of introduction?'

'Now, you mean?'

'Yes, please, m'sieu. I very much want to know whether it's worth fighting to go on with my lessons.'

'Very well, Mademoiselle Tramont. Pray be seated. It will take a moment.'

He went out of the room. When he came back with an envelope, he was smiling. 'Even if you don't come back to me for lessons, it's good to know you feel so strongly... How will you get to Monsieur Alfonsini?'

'I have a cab waiting downstairs.'

He raised white eyebrows. 'My word! This is a sudden surge of independence? Does your mama know what you are doing?'

'Not yet,' Netta replied with a little shiver of apprehension. What Mama was going to say didn't bear thinking of.

The address of Monsieur Alfonsini was in a respectable street not far from the Opera House. Once more she told the cab driver to wait. 'Will you be long, mademoiselle?'

'I don't know … perhaps… Why?'

'I'll just give Jo-Jo his nosebag if we're going to be hanging about.'

'Oh.' This was new to her. She had never dealt with horses that had to be out all day on the streets. 'I think that may be a good idea. I'm likely to be about half an hour.'

Monsieur Alfonsini had a pupil. She could hear the girl singing as she was shown into the downstairs waiting room. The servant took the note she offered and hurried upstairs.

She heard the girl stop singing. She resumed again almost immediately. The servant reappeared. 'Monsieur Alfonsini says he will have to keep you waiting about five minutes. He also says, since you are asking for an opinion, pray be so good as to look over this song.'

It was a very simple piece by Franz Schubert, which she already knew. However, she sat with it in her hands for the requested five minutes. She saw with surprise that her hands were trembling. It was suddenly a great ordeal, to be heard by Ernesto Alfonsini.

And why was she doing it? She still didn't know.

Her mind had been in a whirl ever since her mother gave her command that morning. She had wanted to see Monsieur Leroux, to tell him she was sorry at the abrupt way he was being dismissed, and to beg him perhaps to plead for her. But all that had changed now. She was going to speak to Alfonsini.

It was the difference between talking to a friendly old uncle, and approaching a king.

Alfonsini had trained some of the greatest singers now appearing on the international stage. The fact that Leroux even thought it worth while to send her to him for an opinion showed that it was important.

The servant reappeared to show her upstairs. The upper room was long and comfortably furnished, but most of the room was taken up with a grand piano, a small group of chairs on which rested various musical instruments, and a comfortable couch on which the maestro himself rested.

He made no effort to get up as she was shown in. Nor did he speak. He watched her come in and come close.

'Good afternoon, Monsieur Alfonsini,' she said in a trembling voice, seeing that he expected her to speak first. 'I'm Nicolette Hopetown-Tramont.'

'So this note informs me. Forgive me that I don't rise to greet you. My foot is troubling me.' He waved a hand. 'This is Lipeti, my pianist.' A thin old man at the keyboard nodded at her. 'Did you look over the song?'

'Yes, M'sieu. I already know it.'

'Good. Lipeti, play. Mademoiselle, when you are ready...?' His hand waved her towards the piano. His couch was placed so that he could watch and listen while leaning back on his cushions.

The pianist played the introduction. Netta drew a deep breath, then launched herself into 'Hark, Hark, the Lark'.

She had sung two verses when the accompaniment died away. She glanced up from her score. Alfonsini was waving once more at the pianist.

'That's enough of that one. Lipeti, give her *"Dove Sono"*.'

Lipeti ferreted in a pile of music on the piano top. He handed her the copy. Netta was scared. This was new to her, and was moreover from an opera by Mozart – nothing like the pretty, easy pieces she'd spent most of her time on.

But she'd seen *The Marriage of Figaro* many times and knew the aria. More than once she'd thought she would like to sing the piece, the wistful lament for days when love was new and faithful.

She launched into the music, reading without difficulty and catching at the phrasing from memories of other singers. This time she was heard through to the end. Whether that was good or bad, she'd no idea. More importantly, Monsieur Alfonsini struggled to sit upright, picked up a stick from the floor, and got to his feet.

'Well now ... Lipeti, where's the *Rigoletto?*'

'I have it here, Maestro.'

Alfonsini limped over, took the score from the pianist's hand, and turned the pages rapidly. His thick moustachios seemed to quiver over the pages like antennae. 'Here,' he said. 'Try that.'

It was *'Caro Nome'*, one of the greatest soprano arias in the repertory of opera. Netta looked at him in horror. 'You want me to sing this?'

'Don't you think you can?'

'Well … I can … I suppose … but…'

'Stop stuttering. Lipeti?'

With a look of amused mischief, the little old man launched into the long introduction, which ought to be played by a full orchestra. Netta pulled herself together. Either she was going to sing, or she wasn't. Standing here feeling frightened was pointless.

'Caro nome del mio cor', Festi prima palpitar…' The first line was easy enough. It was when you came to the sudden leaps and the broken notes that you had to watch out. She knew she didn't do it well, but it was an astonishment to her that she did it at all. Monsieur Leroux would never have dreamed of letting her loose on anything from *Rigoletto.*

'Well…' said the maestro when she quavered to a halt. 'You'd never seen it before?'

'No, sir.'

'Not bad, then.' He had a strong Tuscan accent, very attractive. 'Perhaps you are not a Verdi singer. But then perhaps it's too much to ask for passion at first sight at four o'clock in the afternoon. Have you sung choral music?'

'In a choir, you mean – yes, at school, and
with the church on one or two occasions –
we did the Mass in B minor last Easter at
Calmady'

'Ah, Bach! That is a thought. Lipeti, have
we got "Sheep May Safely Graze"?'

'No, Maestro – you gave it to
Mademoiselle Tiraine to study.'

'I know it, sir.'

'Oh, do you think you do? Lipeti let's see
if the young lady "knows" it.'

He stood only a few yards away, watching
with ironic amusement as Netta began to
sing after the introduction. Already she was
regretting having blurted out that she'd
learnt it. It was a very, very difficult thing to
sing, asking for purity of tone and perfect
breath control.

But, she said to herself, if he wants to find
out my weaknesses, I may as well let him see
them. Or, if possible, prove him wrong.

Something came to her aid as she began
on the repeat of the long, simple melody.
She'd sung the first phrases well, but now
she'd instinctively taken hold of the music –
she was no longer letting the accompanist
force her along at the rhythm he wanted to
impose. She lengthened the tempo, let her
breath swell out the notes.

When silence fell, and she looked at
Alfonsini, he was standing with both hands

clasped on his ebony cane and his head bowed. He stayed so for a few seconds. Then he glanced up and snapped his fingers. The pianist leaped up, to set a chair behind him. Alfonsini subsided thankfully into it.

'Well,' he remarked. 'You can sing.'

'I … I can.'

'Have you had any other teacher than Leroux?'

'No, sir.'

'Thought not. These damned French teachers they concentrate too much on elegance. You were at a loss in the Verdi, but you liked the Mozart. You may be a Mozart singer.'

'Sir, I–'

'But when you sang the Bach, you stopped being frightened. There's something there. How old are you?'

'Nineteen, sir.'

'Um… The voice is green, of course. But you've plenty of time to ripen it. What are you planning to do?'

'Planning? I … I…'

'Do you always stutter like this?'

'No, sir,' she replied, pulling herself together. 'No, in general I can make myself understood without trouble. It's just that – to tell the truth, I've no plans, I only wanted to know whether I really could sing.'

'What you need is a woman teacher, of course.'

'Really? Why do you say that?'

'Because you're young and shy and well brought up. You wouldn't like this, for instance.' He advanced upon her, limping heavily, but with one arm outstretched and the fingers of his hand splayed at about her midriff.

She drew back hastily.

'There, you see? You wouldn't like me to touch your diaphragm. Yet it is necessary to feel the rib-cage, to see whether it is extending properly. And necessary to mould the spine, to make sure you stand properly. Look at you now, feet together and hands politely linked. If you stood like that while you sang a big aria you'd never have the muscle power. No, you need someone like Signora Mangioni in Milan–'

'Oh, that's quite out of the question, Monsieur Alfonsini. My parents–'

'You can't go to Milan?'

'No, sir.'

'Um ... Mademoiselle Licelle might take you, but she's got a lot of pupils and they don't really get enough time. You need someone to concentrate on you a little, get rid of your well-brought-up manners–'

'Would you give me a letter of intro-duction to Madame Licelle?'

He hesitated, then shook his head. 'If you're going to train in Paris ... I'd rather take you myself. If you could come to terms with the fact that your body is just an instrument, and that I have to poke you about sometimes–'

'You'd take me, sir?'

'I've just said so, haven't I?'

She gulped. She'd expected nothing like this. It was such an honour that she hardly knew what to say. 'Monsieur Alfonsini, do you really think I could sing in opera?'

'Of course.'

'I could have a career?'

'We-ell… You have the beginnings of a voice. As to a career, that's a different thing. A singer needs good health, a certain ruthlessness – and luck. All the same, you have several advantages. You're pretty, you have personality, and from the look of your clothes you have money. All those things are very helpful. And I of course am not without influence – if I took you as a pupil it would have its effect.'

Netta's mind was racing as she tried to take it all in. 'How long would it take, m'sieu? Before I could make my debut?'

He pondered, tweaking his moustache. 'Two years? Three? Three, I think, because you have a few French "trimmings" to shed before you can really address the big roles in Italian opera – although you might get by on vocal agility at first.'

Three years… 'Sir,' she said, clasping her hands in great earnestness, 'please tell me.

Would you really take me as a pupil and teach me for three years?'

The old Italian glanced in exasperation at his pianist. 'Tell her, Lipeti – do I generally talk like this to people I don't want to teach?'

'No, signore, you generally tell me to show them the door within five minutes.'

Alfonsini raised his shoulders in a huge, expressive shrug, as if to say, 'You see?'

'I have to speak to my parents. It may be very difficult to persuade them. They are not in favour of my taking my music seriously–'

'What?' It was an explosion of annoyance. 'Who are they, these philistines?'

'My father is Monsieur Hopetown-Tramont, of the House of Tramont, the champagne-maker–'

'Ah!' the old man stared. 'You're one of the Champagne Girls?'

'Yes, sir.'

'A champagne heiress who wants to make a career in opera?' He was shaking his head. 'No, no. I think I have misled you. I could see you had money, of course, but I thought ... I thought you came from some lesser background. No, mademoiselle, I'm sorry. I think we had better forget all I've just said. You have a very fine voice – one that I should have enjoyed bringing to perfection. But I don't think the project is likely to begin.'

'I'll speak to my father—'

'Will you? And what will he say?'

'I'll convince him!'

The old teacher took her by the elbow and led her to the door. 'Do as you like, mademoiselle. I don't expect to see you again, however. And all I can say is, it's a waste... Good afternoon.'

When she reached home, Mama was nearly at the end of a five-o'clock with some friends, and Papa was upstairs changing for dinner. If the butler noted that she paid off a hackney cab, it wasn't his business to remark upon it. She sent a message by her father's valet that when he had dressed she would like to speak to him privately for a few minutes before he went into the drawing room for his pre-dinner drink.

The reply was that he would see her in the library. He was glancing through a newly delivered copy of the London *Times* when she came in.

'Well, kitten, if it's about your singing lessons, you're out of luck. Mama has already told me the story and I go along with her decision.'

'It can't be dismissed quite as easily as that, Papa.'

'Oh?' He frowned at her. Although still only in his mid-forties, he had gone grey early, and the adoption of a beard and moustache after the mode of the English

Prince of Wales made him seem older. He didn't look like a man to argue with, even though he was an indulgent father as a rule.

'I went to see Monsieur Leroux–'

'Netta! Although you promised Mama you would not?'

'I promised no such thing. She asked if I heard what she said, and I said I heard. But I felt I owed it to Monsieur Leroux to explain. And I wanted to ask him–'

'I'm surprised to hear excuses for wriggling out of your promise. I think you know that what you did was wrong.'

'Not at all, Papa! What I did was right, the more so as Monsieur Leroux sent me to see Monsieur Alfonsini.'

'Who?'

'Ernesto Alfonsini – he's the best teacher in Paris. He–'

'If he were the best teacher in the world, you would still have no reason for going to see him. You are to take no more music lessons.'

'You can't say such a thing, Papa! You have no right!'

Gavin sprang up from his chair, letting *The Times* fall about in disarray. He towered over his daughter. All at once he was very formidable.

'Nicolette, that is quite enough. You forget yourself.'

'No, Papa.' Although she was frightened,

she refused to back down. 'Monsieur Alfonsini told me I had a fine voice. He told me he would accept me as a pupil for the next three years. Papa, he wouldn't have done that if he didn't believe I had the chance to make good in opera–'

'*Nicolette!*' The shock in his tone was so great that she drew back in alarm. He seemed to catch a breath then said: 'Have you a fever? Is there something wrong with you? For I can't account for your words in any other way.'

'But Papa, you must listen! Monsieur Alfonsini said it might take three years, and of course I would need determination and luck, but he said I might be able to tackle the great roles.'

'You are not suggesting, girl, that you should appear on the operatic stage?'

'I … I… Yes, of course, Papa. That's what Alfonsini said.'

'You've taken leave of your senses. Opera? *Opera?*'

'But Papa, you like opera! You've gone every season. And I've heard you express admiration for Mademoiselle Tettrazini.'

'Of course I admire Tettrazini. I also admire the little ballet girl in short skirts who leads the corps in the Faust dances. But I would no more think of allowing you to dance in scanty clothes than let you sing in opera. What are you thinking of?'

'But Papa. Mademoiselle Tettrazini–'

'Stop talking about Tettrazini. She's a pretty lass and has a fine voice, but she could never be invited to the house. You know that as well as I do. Theatrical people are not of our world. We may admire them but we can never *know* them.'

'But all that is changing, Papa. People invite–'

'People invite performers to play or sing at an evening drawing room – certainly. But they are paid off and let go through a side door. And even then, these are the more respectable kind. Opera singers – you know as well as I do that they have the morals of...' He broke off. Even in the midst of his indignation he recalled that you couldn't use an expression like that to a young lady of nineteen.

'Oh, I know their amours are talked of, but that's just gossip.'

'Perhaps so. But do you imagine I could let you be spoken of in that way, Netta? And it isn't just gossip. It's well known that Mademoiselle Emante could never have received leading roles last season if she hadn't gone to bed with the directeur–'

'Papa!'

'Do you imagine I could let you enter a world like that? Leaving aside the fact that it's totally unsuitable, that you are quite unfit for it by birth and upbringing, where would it lead? Whom could you know? Who would receive you?'

'But you can't ask me not to do anything with my talent – because I *have* talent, Papa, the maestro said so!'

'I wish he had had more sense than to fill your head with this rubbish.'

'It's not rubbish! And I know it isn't – I felt it, myself, this afternoon, when I was singing for him. I felt the … the *power* of my voice–'

'Now that is quite enough.' Gavin Hopetown-Tramont took a turn about the library, stooped to gather up the scattered pages of *The Times,* and straightened, having gained control of himself.

'Netta dear,' he said in a gentle tone, 'I can see you're sincere in all this. But you're too young to appreciate how impossible it all is. For your own good, I must expressly forbid you to think of it again. You are not to go on with your singing lessons. That is my decision. I agree with your mother – it's been a mistake. Luckily it's not too late to retrieve it and within a day or two I think you'll see things in their proper perspective.'

'You have no right to prevent me from going on with my music.'

'We not only have the right, we have the duty. We daren't let you ruin your life over some foolish notion. People of our class don't become opera singers, Netta. It's as simple as that.'

'But … what am I to *do* if I don't train?'

'You'll get married, set up a household, have children – what else?'

'Papa … that's not enough…'

He put a hand on her shoulder. 'That is a wicked thing to say.' His manner was calm and sad. 'You know I'm not a religious man but I think there is such a thing as sin, and you are verging on it, daughter. Your duty as a woman is to marry and be a comfort to your husband and his children. Anything else is mere absurdity.'

There was so much weight in his words that she was silenced, though she wasn't convinced.

'Now go to your room and change for dinner. I shan't tell Mama what's passed between us, it would only upset her. In a day or two, when you've got the better of this nonsense, you may feel like confessing it to her yourself – I leave that to you. But in the meantime you are to put it away, behave properly, and give her no cause for uneasiness. She has had enough fatigue with the wedding of Grandmama and the arranging of Philip's university career. I don't want her worried any further. Is that clear?'

'Yes, Papa.'

He called her back from the door. 'One moment. You said "Yes, Papa" – is that another sophistry? Are you saying merely that you agree not to worry your mama, whereas I am to believe you are agreeing to behave?'

Tears welled up. She turned and fled. It was truly dreadful to have angered Papa to the extent that he would use that tone to her.

All the same, she couldn't think he was in the right. All that nonsense about the wicked life of the opera stars – how could it possibly be true? From what Alfonsini said, you had to be strong and determined to keep your career going – how could you possibly waste strength on philandering?

She saw, of course, that her father was inexorably against the idea of letting her study any further. There was no question of getting lessons with Monsieur Alfonsini.

But the maestro had mentioned a woman teacher in Milan. What name had he given? She searched her memory but failed to recall it. Twenty-four hours later, when she was thinking about something totally different, it popped out of some pigeonhole in her mind. Signora Mangioni…

She decided to make one more attempt to get the approval of her parents. She sought out her mother one evening, before they went to change for an evening preview of a water-colour exhibition.

'Mama, there's something I have to tell you.'

'Really? Come in, dear, sit down – I shan't

be a moment, I'm just doing this note to Cristale about the garden party on Saturday.'

'Mama, it's about my singing.'

Her mother threw down the pen so that it scattered little ink blots on the paper. 'Netta, I hope we're not going to have another upset!'

'I don't *want* to upset you. I want you to understand. I really do have a voice worth training.'

Alys looked at her with something like sympathy. 'My dearest girl, I know that. I know you have a beautiful voice. That's not the point. Your situation in life prevents you from doing anything with it. You must accept that fact.'

'But why? It's madness—'

'Netta, if you had been born lame, you would have had to live with it.'

'You're not saying that having a good voice is a *handicap?*'

'It is, if it's going to prevent you from being content. You cannot, simply cannot, do anything with your talent – not in any serious way. You may sing at social gatherings and with the church choir, as you have done up to now. You have had enough training for that. More would be unseemly.'

'I can't believe you mean this!'

'I do mean it. I'm thinking of your own good.'

'What was that poem I learnt in the English class? "That one talent which 'tis death to hide, Lodged with me useless…"'

'Don't overdramatise, dear. Whoever it was who said that, his situation doesn't concern you. You are a young woman with your whole life ahead of you. I don't want you spoiling it with absurd ambitions that cannot be fulfilled.'

'You refuse to let me study any more?'

'Just so. Now, dear, I shall have to re-write this letter. Please leave me in peace – and let's hear no more of this nonsense.'

As she let her maid dress her for the evening, Netta was making plans. And later that night, when all the household was asleep, she rose silently.

She dressed without calling her maid. She packed a few things in a valise and stole downstairs. In her mother's study she sat down before the escritoire. With trembling fingers she took out notepaper, dipped the pen in the ink, and wrote:

'Dearest Mama and Papa, I have gone to study with a great teacher of singing. In a few days I will write again to give you my address but in the meantime please don't worry about me, I have plenty of this month's allowance with me and I have taken my pearls to sell if need be.

'This is for the best. I could never be happy now, knowing that I have the ability to make a career in music and yet not making the effort. My love to you both and to Phip. Your daughter, Nicolette.'

Chapter Four

Things went badly in Milan from the start.

Netta imagined she knew the city, from a visit two years ago. But that had been with a governess in charge and under the tutelage of the Contessa di Peghirino, an authoritarian Roman matron who saw to everything.

Now she found that her Italian was quite inadequate. So were her funds – she couldn't afford the kind of hotel she was accustomed to, where servants ran about if you lifted a finger. She understood her mistake after a couple of days, consulted with a wondering receptionist at the Hotel del Angelo, and removed to a little pension in a side street.

But worse yet was the meeting with Signora Mangioni. The signora was unable to receive her for almost a week. It took that long for Netta to understand she must offer a bribe to the servant.

When she was at last allowed into the elegant drawing room, Signora Mangioni greeted her without ceremony. 'I can spare only five minutes. What is it you want?'

'I want to study with you, madame.'

'*Prego?* Your Italian is poor. What did you say?'

'I've come to ask you to take me as a pupil.'

'Ah! I understand. When did you wish to commence your lessons?'

'Well... Immediately, madame.'

'Signorina, you are being absurd! I have no vacancy for a student at present.' She picked up a diary from her desk, flicked through it. 'No, nothing this year... Perhaps in January?'

'But madame! I've come from Paris on purpose to take lessons—'

'Indeed! Who sent you? Who is your teacher?'

'I was told of you by Monsieur Alfonsini—'

'Ah, Ernesto...' The signora looked momentarily impressed, then frowned. 'He should know better than to send me students on the expectation I can take them at once. Where is his letter?'

'I ... er ... I have no letter, madame.'

'What?'

'I didn't get a letter from Monsieur Alfonsini. I ... I didn't think of it.'

'Indeed?' The great teacher rang the bell at her side. 'You are not a pupil of Alfonsini's. You are trying to carry out some trick.'

'No, madame, I assure you. Monsieur

Alfonsini, heard me sing, he said he himself would take me as a pupil but–'

'I really have no more time to waste on you, signorina. If you really are a protégée of Ernesto's, you will come to me with a proper letter of introduction. But even if you do, I cannot take you until next year.'

'But, madame – please–' The sturdy maidservant was already at Netta's elbow, waiting to usher her out. 'Madame, I've come on purpose to take voice lessons – what am I to do?'

'If I were you I'd apply to the conservatoire. They may take you. Good morning, signorina.'

Outside in the broad avenue, Netta found her head whirling almost as if she were about to faint. It was the disappointment. To be dismissed so curtly! It had never happened to her in her life before.

For the first time it began to dawn on Nicolette Hopetown-Tramont that the world was no bed of roses. Up till now, her wishes had always been attended to. She hadn't always got her own way but when she was refused, it was with kindness and usually a reasoned explanation.

To be turned out of someone's drawing room as if she were some sort of trickster was a new experience. To be told she wasn't important enough to receive even the chance of lessons until next year a terrible blow. And the thought of going to the conservatoire was unnerving. There would be a large number of students with whom she would have to compete for the interest of the instructors.

But she never even reached that point. When she applied at the information office, she was told that there was an examination system. And the next exams were not until the autumn.

She had written home when she settled in the Pensione della Croce. The letter had been full of hope: 'I expect to see Signora Mangioni soon and begin lessons immediately. Please don't worry about me. I'll write again in a week or so.'

Now she must go back to the boarding-house and write that Signora Mangioni had refused her. She must ask for money. She still had her pearls but she didn't want to sell them unless it became absolutely necessary. She hoped that her parents would continue her allowance; they weren't cruel or hard-headed, they'd wish her to have funds to live decently while she studied.

This was naïve – not in her judgement of their kindness, but of their anxiety. As soon as they learned her address, Gavin Hopetown-Tramont boarded a train and headed straight for Milan. He called at her pension, found her there looking through a newspaper trying to translate advertisements for singing teachers, and ordered her to pack and come home at once.

'Papa, you shouldn't have come. I've no intention of coming home. I'm here to study music.'

'I told you already, Netta. That's quite out of the question, even though I understand this Signora Mangioni is one of the greatest–'

'She refused me, Papa. But I'll find someone else.'

'What?'

'There are dozens of teachers in Milan.' She pointed to the newspaper.

'Netta, don't be nonsensical! You can't go to a teacher you pick out of a newspaper!'

'Why not? Milan is a great centre of–'

'Damn it all, girl! You could end up with your throat cut! This is a big city, with all the dangers that go with it! And you – look at you! A wide-eyed innocent! You are coming home this minute, Netta, if I have to tie you up and carry you.'

She was shocked by what he said, by his vehemence. But she couldn't believe what he said. So far, well-dressed and with enough money to get by, she'd had no problems.

She shook her head. 'No, Papa, I understand that you're worried, but there's no need. Truly there isn't. Everything will be all right. I've written to Monsieur Alfonsini to ask him to write me an open letter of introduction, and with that I know I'll find a good teacher in the end. Meanwhile I shall go to someone respectable–'

'How will you know? How will you know it isn't some vulture who–'

'Papa, how absurd you are!'

They argued all that day. He took her out to dinner in hopes that a good meal in proper surroundings would make her see the deficiencies of the little pension, but she chattered on with bright determination about her plans. When he tried to insist she move back into the Hotel del Angelo, she refused. She understood his tactics.

Next morning he returned to the attack. He found her a little shaken. Last night, as she was going upstairs after he parted from her in the hall, a man had tried to follow her into her room. It was the very first time in her life any such thing had happened to her, and she had been very frightened.

Luckily the landlady had been coming downstairs with an armful of linen. She had said briskly, 'Come along now, Signor Matteotto, this isn't the kind of young lady you're looking for!' and hustled him away. Later she explained to Netta that Signor Matteotto had taken too much wine, and she mustn't be put out about it.

'Does he lodge here?' Netta demanded,

still quivering with fright and indignation.

'To be sure.'

'How can you allow a man like that to stay in your house?'

'A man like what? Good gracious, signorina, there's nothing wrong with Signor Matteotto! In general he has the sense to look for his pleasure elsewhere.'

It was so unlike anything she'd ever encountered that Netta couldn't sleep, although she bolted her door and put a chair under the knob.

Her defence against her father's argument remained firm, nevertheless. She would wait for Monsieur Alfonsini's letter, she would find a teacher, she would study singing. Privately she added that she would be very careful in any encounters with men.

She would have carried on the fight for as long as seemed necessary – she was sure of that.

On the Thursday, Papa took her for a drive in the country and a visit to a villa full of art treasures, which was intended to reawaken her to the kind of life she was used to. But she found she felt unwell as she walked through the great shadowy halls of the villa.

She said nothing to Papa. It was only a headache, or something she'd eaten – the food at the pension was heavier and more oily than she was accustomed to.

But when she tried to get up next morning

she was attacked by a fit of shivers that made her fall back on the bed. The room spun round. She crawled back under the covers. Next moment she was too hot. She threw the covers off.

Some time later – she had no idea how long – Papa's face swam into view. He was saying something, but she couldn't make out what. She told him, 'It's all right, it's just a cold,' but no words came out. His face swam away again, in a purple and grey mist.

When she came to herself again, she was lying in a pretty bed in a strange room. A nun in a white habit and stiffly-starched apron was sitting by her side. When Netta croaked a sound of interrogation, the nun said in good French: 'It's all right, mademoiselle. Your father will be here later. You're in a private nursing home.'

'Nursing … home…?'

'You have had malaria. How do you feel?' A cool hand touched her brow. Her wrist was taken in firm fingers.

'I … feel funny… Very weak…'

'Yes, you have had quite a bad attack. Now drink this, and lie quiet.'

Netta accepted the bitter liquid. Shuddering, she lay back on her pillows. After a time she slept.

When she was convalescent she learned that malaria was still quite common on the plain of Lombardy. She had been unlucky enough to be infected soon after her arrival in the city but the symptoms hadn't become severe until after about two weeks.

'It's a blessing that I was here,' her father remarked, holding her hand between both of his and stroking it. 'Just think, Netta, if you'd been alone in a strange city!'

In her weakened state, the mere thought brought tears to her eyes. 'Oh, what should I have done?' she murmured.

'Mama has been so worried, Netta! Now you see, you must come home.'

'Yes, Papa.'

In the middle of the month of May, when she was still quite weak but up and about, she was carefully transported by slow stages to Paris. Her mother came to meet her halfway, at Lyon. Alys was so relieved to get her daughter back that there were no recriminations, no scoldings. They fell into each other's arms.

The season was still in full swing in Paris. Netta had a couple of days rest, and then was expected to take at least some part in what remained of it. Cosette came to see her while she remained indisposed.

She could hardly wait for the maid to leave the room before embarking on a list of questions.

'My *dear!* Whom did you go with? Is it anyone I know? How did your parents find you? Was there a great row?'

Netta stared at her, pale lips parted in utter incomprehension.

'Oh, you were a sly one! Not the least hint of it until that day at the fashion show! And yet, you know, I supposed I should have guessed. I hear you were downright rude to Frederic de la Sebiq, and that could only have been because your heart was already given–'

'What on earth are you talking about, Cosette?'

'Of course, everyone thought I would know all about it and wouldn't believe it when I said I was in the dark.'

'You couldn't be more in the dark than I am. What is this all about?'

'Netta, of course, you have to pretend nothing awful has happened, but you needn't pretend with *me!* I'm your friend.'

Netta, looking at the avid face and eager, rather unkind smile, doubted it. 'What am I supposed to have done, Cosette?'

'Supposed to have done? I suppose the details differ slightly in *your* version–'

'Do I take it you think I eloped with some unsuitable man?'

The coldness of her tone made Cosette blink. She hesitated. 'There's no need to be angry, Netta. I'm sorry you were dragged home from Venice – Venice, how romantic!'

'I was brought home because I fell ill. There was no "dragging". I went to Milan, not Venice, to study music with a former star of La Scala. That's the whole history of the thing.'

'Oh, come, now, Netta! Oh, really! With a friend like me you don't have to keep up such a tale.'

'Cosette, it's the truth. I ran away from home to take singing lessons from a great teacher in Milan.'

Cosette shrugged her pretty shoulders and looked offended. 'All right. I see you don't intend to tell me who you went with. But at least tell me this – is it all over? Or are you going to see him again?'

'There was no man, Cosette. I assure you. I went on my own to Milan.'

'A likely tale! If you think I'll believe that!'

'Cosette, if you can prove that I have been involved with any man in the way you mean, I'll ... I'll give you that Chinese ivory fan you always admire so much.'

'What?'

'Or any other thing of mine that you like. If you can produce one single iota of evidence–'

'Oh, goodness, I don't go in for games of that kind! And in any case you kept it so terribly secret I daresay it would be impossible'

'I didn't keep it secret. If you like to ask my singing teacher, Monsieur Leroux, you'll find that I went to his studio that day

I left you at the dress show.'

'Is that where you used to meet him? At your singing teacher's?'

Netta got up. 'Cosette, I see it's useless to talk to you. We're having a conversation that makes no sense. It would be best if you left now.'

'You're asking me to leave?' Cosette cried, too astonished to take it in.

'Yes, please. I still don't feel absolutely a hundred per cent, and it's exhausting trying to talk to you if you insist on going on like this.'

'But ... Netta...'

'I haven't done anything wrong – not in the way you're suggesting. I didn't have a lover. I wasn't with a man. I only wanted to study with a great teacher.'

'Are you really asking me to believe you went to Italy to study music?'

'Yes.'

'But what on earth *for?*'

'To be an opera singer.'

'An opera singer?'

'Yes. I was told by someone I respected that I had the ability. I wanted to study seriously.'

'To go on the *stage?*'

'Yes.'

It was so bizarre as to be utterly convincing. Cosette was silenced. After a moment she said, 'Everyone thinks you went with a man.'

Netta shivered. 'Yes,' she agreed, 'I can see that they do.'

'In fact…'

'What?'

'When they heard you were ill, a lot of people said… But I always told them that was going too far…'

'They said what, Cosette?'

'Well … *you* know… It seemed to follow…'

'What?'

'Well … a baby…'

'What?' cried Netta, shocked to the heart. She felt herself go cold and faint at the thought.

'Netta! Netta! Oh, I'm sorry! Oh, Netta dear, don't…' Cosetta sprang to the bell and pulled it violently. By the time the maid appeared, Netta was recovering. All the same, Cosette begged that a glass of brandy should be brought, and that Madame Hopetown-Tramont should be told her daughter was unwell.

As soon as Alys appeared, Cosette took her leave. She had a feeling she was decidedly unwelcome just then.

When she had sipped the brandy and recovered a little, Netta confided to her mother what she'd just learned from her schoolfriend.

'Oh, of course,' Alys said grimly. 'What else did you expect?'

'Mama, I can't go back into society knowing people are saying things like that!'

'You can and you will! If you once begin to cower away, the story will gain credence. You'll go to Helen de Rime's At Home tomorrow evening, and everyone will see that the stories are untrue.'

'They won't! They'll titter and gossip.'

'Only those who prefer lies to truth. You *look* like someone who's had malaria, Netta – you still have that faint yellowish tinge to your skin. And as for the supposed lover when they find they just can't put a name to him, they'll get tired.'

'Mama, please don't make me go through all that.'

'I'm sorry, my precious,' Alys said with complete sincerity, 'but if you're to retrieve your reputation, it must be so.'

Netta bathed and dressed the following evening with great reluctance. Her mother sent her maid to apply a tiny scrap of rouge and powder to counteract the skin tints left by the malaria. She had lost a little weight, which didn't help matters where fashion was concerned but which would bear evidence to the matrons in the evening that she certainly hadn't had a baby.

The rich pink silk rustled as she made her way in the wake of her mother into the salon of Madame de Rime. They were rather late: Alys had planned it thus, so that as many people as possible would see for themselves that all the gossip was untrue.

So it was a grand entrance. Helen de Rime hurried over to greet them, flustered and somewhat put out that her old friend should make her stage this scene for her. She prattled a welcome, looked about hopefully for someone who would join them and ease the situation.

But most of those present were staying where they were, eyeing Netta with interest masked by cool politeness. One or two of the young ladies were visibly giggling behind their fans.

Netta wished she could sink through the floor. If her colour had needed rouge before she set out, it was too high now. She stood with her chin up, resolutely staring at a corner of the ceiling. Soon she must move to join one of those unfriendly groups – or be trapped forever in this moment, like a fly in amber.

'Good evening,' said a voice from behind them. 'How pleasant it is to meet you again after all this time, Mademoiselle Tramont.'

It was Frederic de la Sebiq.

Chapter Five

Where one leads, others will follow. After Frederic's intervention, Netta's first evening engagement went better than she'd feared.

It was decided by the arbiters of society to accept the story that her month's absence had been due to a severe bout of malaria, though how she'd come to contract that ailment was never fully explained.

One of the tales that was told concerned Mademoiselle Hopetown-Tramont's wish to study music. This came from Cosette Brissiac, who wasn't fully believed because she was known to prattle. But it was as good an explanation as any. Besides, one couldn't really 'cut' the Hopetown-Tramonts. They had *so* much money, and their family went back on one side to a good monarchical supporter so that one might antagonise, for instance, the Comte de Paris – who of course stuck to his own little coterie of the Faubourg St Germain, but all the same, it was better not to annoy the possible future King of France.

Beside, Mademoiselle Hopetown-Tramont was this year's Lady-President of the Charity of the Little White Flowers, and if one offended her she might very well cut one off the list of subscribers – and then how would one get tickets for the Grand Charity Ball in June?

Soon the gossip columnists, instead of speculating over Netta's whereabouts, were cooing again about her good looks and her exquisite taste. 'We note,' they remarked, 'that yet another heart has been added to the sleeve of that delightful young lady. Monsieur Frederic de la Sebiq is now seen in her company as well as Monsieur Parlau and Monsieur André de Harlangier. The haut monde waits with bated breath to see if she will choose from among these devoted admirers.'

Netta still wasn't ready to 'choose'. Her experiences had shaken her so that she was now very unsure of herself. She had never been ill before, except for the usual childish ailments. The feeling of not being in control of her own body, of losing touch with reality, was frightening. She still had nightmares that grew out of the illness, and were fed by the bewilderment of her first days in Milan and the brief encounter with the man at the boarding-house.

A certain languidness possessed her. She didn't even feel like arguing that she should take up her music lessons again with Monsieur Leroux. She was content for the moment to drift.

Her parents didn't urge anything upon her. They were in the first place only too thankful to have her back safely within the fold. And in the second place, they had more important matters to think about.

An event had occurred which they'd been dreading for years. Phylloxera had reached the Champagne region.

This deadly disease of the vines, brought over to the continent of Europe from America, had slowly been making headway through the vineyards from the south. It had first appeared in Provence in 1863, but little anxiety had been felt then – it was a new disease, it would be counteracted by some new spray or powder.

Not so. In the next quarter of a century it had erratically made its way through the vine-rows. In 1869 it had been at work in Bordeaux but also in Portugal. The Rhône valley felt its power in the year of the Franco-Prussian War. Then unexpectedly it appeared in strength in the New World and in Australia where a beginning had been made on producing wine.

By 1887 it was in Africa, both Algeria where the French were promoting the wine industry, and in South Africa where the European vines had been healthy and strong for twenty years. The following year the Italian vineyards were decimated.

Almost the only winefields that had not

been touched were those of Champagne. 'Ah,' said some of the wiseacres, 'it's because our climate's too cold for the insect that carries the disease.'

Once again, not so. Phylloxera had been seen this year near the River Marne, on a small stretch of vines owned by a small grower.

Netta's father and her Uncle Robert were too concerned about the outbreak to care whether or not she was having a successful season. And even her mother and Aunt Laura took part in the anxiety.

The onward march of the insect seemed inevitable. Nothing seemed to stop it or cure the disease it inflicted. The vines yellowed and died, no grapes were produced.

And if no grapes were produced, no wine could be made. The fortunes of the Champagne Girls would disappear in the useless fight to save the industry.

The family went as usual to Calmady in September. The grape harvest was in full swing. All was well – a good pressing, rich and well-flavoured. The relief was almost palpable.

Grandmama had come with Grandpapa Gri-gri as she'd promised. They stayed on for the shooting, to which guests came from time to time throughout October and November.

'Which of these young men are you

considering, dear?' Grandmama asked Netta, pointing at the group at the edge of the wood.

'None of them, Grandmama.'

'Indeed? Isn't it time you made your mind up, Netta? You can hardly appear unmarried for a *fourth* season.'

There was asperity in the tone. Netta was surprised. She glanced about with some anxiety, not wishing to have anyone hear the implied reproof, but they were standing far back from the *battues,* with the servants waiting to serve the luncheon.

'Grandmama, you know André de Harlangier as well as I do. Would you like to be married to a man who brays like a donkey when he laughs?'

She saw her grandmother hitch up her thick coat collar to hide a smile. 'Well, aside from the noise he makes, he's a very worthy young man.'

'Is he? Perhaps he is.'

'Are you looking more favourably on ... who is that one in the brown knicker-bockers?'

'That's Louis Nanillet. He's already proposed and been refused.'

'What was wrong with him? Did he smile too widely?'

'Oh, Grandmama! He hasn't got two wits to rub together.'

'He's quite good-looking...'

'So is a poodle dog. But one wouldn't want to marry it.'

'Netta, you must really be more reasonable. Your parents are quite worried, and I begin to sympathise with them. You *must* make a choice soon.'

'I don't see why!' Netta burst out, swinging away from her grandmother to swish impatiently at an inoffensive clump of bracken. 'It's only convention that insists a girl has to marry in her first two or three seasons.'

'It's quite a good convention, my dear, because it means, quite frankly, that she doesn't get too long in the tooth.'

'Grandmama!'

'Oh hoity-toity! You're still a very pretty girl – but watch out, my love. There are younger, prettier girls coming along all the time. One day you'll find the men aren't flocking to your door any more. And then it'll be an arranged match, with perhaps even the awful André de Harlangier – and how shall you like that?'

'Oh, Mama and Papa would never make me marry someone I really disliked.'

'Don't play fast and loose with their good nature, then, my lass! Come now, Netta, you're a sensible girl. You must *see* you can't go on for ever without taking your proper place in the family. By now you should be married and expecting your first baby.'

Netta blushed. 'Need you put it in such bald terms?'

'Why do you close your eyes to it? Your parents want you settled and with children of your own – it's part of the scheme of things. There must be someone you'd be happy with. How about this young captain of cavalry – the one who rallied round so handsomely after your foolish little jaunt to Italy?'

'You mean Frederic... I must admit, I think better of him than I did when we met at the outset.' She thought with gratitude of Frederic's support on that first occasion after her illness, and his amused acceptance of a platonic friendship ever since. 'The only trouble is, Grandmama – we really have absolutely nothing in common.'

'That can't be true. You meet at various events in Paris – he escorted you to at least one ball...'

'All he seems to know anything about is backing horses and playing cards. He wouldn't ever have bothered to make my acquaintance if his father hadn't forced him to. And from what I can gather elsewhere, I was selected by old Monsieur de la Sebiq because I looked a good healthy specimen. Cosette says the de la Sebiq blood has got so thin you can't distinguish it from water except in a good light.'

'I hope you don't pay attention to

anything Cosette says,' reproved her grand-mother. 'The de la Sebiq family goes back to the Knights Templar–'

'And their house in Provence is about the same age. I hear it's a crumbling ruin.'

'Well, good gracious, no one is asking you to go and live there! I'm sure your papa would make a useful settlement on the marriage, and I hear that the boy could be found a place in the business.'

'You've obviously had a long talk with Papa about this!'

'Little minx! You're pleased at the thought of having us all on tenterhooks about you!'

'No, truly, Grandmama, I'm not. I … I really wish I could be the kind of daughter Mama seems to want. I even wish I could fall in love with Frederic. But somehow I … I just don't. And he isn't in love with me, and don't pretend that he is. He doesn't want to be a married man. He told me so himself.'

Grandmama made a sound of vexation. Really, how were they to get anything settled if the young people talked themselves out of marriage so easily?

'I'll be entirely honest with you, Netta. Pierre de la Sebiq is quite in earnest about having his son marry into the Tramont family. He wants to see the family carried on – they'll die out if Frederic doesn't marry and have children. He's even quite resigned to the idea that his son will become part of the House of Tramont and take part in the wine industry.'

'Frederic doesn't know anything about the wine industry!'

'He drinks wine, doesn't he? He knows good wine from bad? Besides, nobody would expect him to assume responsibility for anything important, like the blending. All we want in your husband is that he helps to keep the House of Tramont going.'

'It sounds so ... so cold, Grandmama. Too much like a business transaction.'

Lady Grassington threw out her hands. 'Then fall in love, Netta! Lose your heart to someone! We're at the stage now where we almost don't mind who it is, so long as he's respectable and a bachelor! Find yourself a handsome, decent young man and we'll all give our blessing – but don't wait too much longer because we're all getting anxious...'

Thinking over the conversation afterwards, Netta had to admit that her grandmother had stated the case accurately. It was she herself who was to blame. She was beginning to believe she was incapable of falling in love. And now that her health was fully restored, she found herself yearning again to go back to her music. That seemed to be the really important thing in her life. Which must mean she was a very odd character indeed.

Spring approached, and with it the awful thought of yet another season in Paris, with everyone staring at her and making calculations about her age. She was saved from it by the kindness of Lord Grassington, who proposed she should come with him and Grandmama on a trip, half-business and half-pleasure, to Austria and Hungary.

She hadn't any doubt they hoped she might fall in love with one of the exquisite young dandies of the court of Francis-Joseph. But nothing of the kind occurred, and by the end of August they were in England for the grouse season. From there she went home for the wine harvest.

There was an air of anxiety at Calmady. The weather had been poor. The grapes were not of the best. But thank God, no phylloxera among the champagne vines.

A large house-party had assembled for the celebrations which followed the tasting of the first pressing. Frederic was among them, and at the ball he partnered her for one of the early dances. When supper was announced, he brought her some food and a glass of wine in the grape arbour on the back of the house.

They ate for a while in companionable silence. Then he said, with a sudden shake of the head: 'Where's this going to end, Netta?'

She had her glass halfway to her lips. She

withdrew it, staring at him. 'What do you mean?'

'Are we to go on forever, meeting at parties, smiling across to each other from opera boxes? Because if so, I think I ought to warn you I'll have to bow out. My father's getting restive. He says he wants me married before he dies.'

'Oh, good heavens, Frederic – he's not about to die, is he?'

'Well, he's not getting any younger. He married late, you know.'

His tone was light enough, but she could tell he was in earnest. 'I'm sorry,' she said. 'Parents can be troublesome, I know from my own experience. I've had hints from everyone about settling down and so forth.'

'Do you ever intend to do it?'

She set her wine-glass on the little gilt table at her side, and studied the feathers of her fan. 'I don't know that I've ever quite resigned myself to it. I had ambitions of my own, you know...'

'Ambitions?' He was puzzled. 'Of what kind?'

'I wanted to be a singer.'

'A singer!'

'It's why I went to Italy – you know, last year, when everyone was saying I'd eloped. I wanted to study music.'

'Netta!' he said, utterly astounded.

'You mean, you thought I'd gone off with

109

some man?'

'I... Well, it wasn't my business what you'd done. I heard people gossiping, and when you turned up again I thought you looked scared and desperate so I... At any rate, I thought you'd shown a bit of spirit, which is more than can be said of most of 'em.'

'Oh, Frederic!' She laughed, and patted the fine worsted of his sleeve. 'Well, the truth is, I wanted to be a singer. Still do. In Budapest, when my grandmother and Gri-gri were hobnobbing with their friends, I was at the State Opera listening to Herr Mahler conducting Verdi. They hoped I was getting romantically involved with the handsome young hussars.'

Frederic ate some devilled game, then sat looking thoughtful. 'You never have been "romantically involved"?'

'Not to the extent where I thought it was important.'

He cleared his throat. 'Don't think this ungentlemanly of me but... Am I right in thinking you'll be twenty-one next birthday?'

She shrugged and nodded. 'The sere and yellow.'

'Well, it's time to come to terms with the facts. You've more or less got to take someone, Netta.'

'I suppose so. But what I want is a man who'll let me pursue my music studies, who'll understand that I have some talent and want to use it, even test it by appearing in public... And where in the world is there such a man?'

There was a pause. Then Frederic held out his hand. 'Here, perhaps?' he suggested.

'You?'

'Why not?'

'But ... you're not the least bit interested in music!'

'I admit it. But you don't ask for a husband who'll share your enthusiasm – you only want one who'll tolerate it. And I've a very tolerant nature.'

'You'd let me study opera?'

'Oh ... now ... Netta, be reasonable.' He withdrew the hand he'd been holding out. 'Opera? No, that's going too far. I'm quite willing to sit in the audience and applaud as you sing *The Messiah* or something respectable of that kind. I don't think you can ask me to applaud if you sing *Carmen* – that's asking too much.'

'You'd really let me study?'

'If it's what you want.'

It was an extraordinary offer. She hesitated. 'And what do you get out of it, Frederic? For I know you too well to think you'd do this out of sheer magnanimity.'

'Who, me?' He laughed and made a little grimace. 'I get a decent income, I hope, and a cessation of criticism from my father. And

I get a pretty wife who won't be too irritated if I follow my own pursuits.'

'Your own pursuits... That means horses and cards...'

'I'm afraid so, my dear.'

'And women?'

'It's not tactful to ask such a question.'

'I shouldn't be jealous, Frederic. I just want things to be clear. If you had affairs, you'd be discreet?'

'Of course,' he said, shocked. 'I wouldn't dream of hurting your feelings, Netta. I really do like you quite a lot. I feel we could make a go of this, in our own peculiar way.'

She smiled. 'We certainly shall be a peculiar pair! Will you mind if people stare at our way of life?'

'Not a bit. We'll have our compensations.'

Once more he held out his hand. Now she took it. He said, teasingly, 'It's usual to kiss on becoming engaged.'

'Ah, well... If we must.'

He drew her towards him and kissed her directly on the lips – a kiss of warmth and affection, but without passion. She returned it in the same spirit. After all, it was only to seal a bargain.

The families were greatly relieved when the young people came to them with the tidings. It was something they'd hoped for all along, so they congratulated themselves on their forbearance while they launched into the legal negotiations of the marriage settlement.

The lands and estate of the de la Sebiqs were found to be mortgaged to the very chimneypots. Gavin wasn't very pleased. Nothing would actually be coming to the Tramonts except the decrepit house in the Midi and the young man himself.

He, however, showed himself quite willing to give up the Army and take a junior post in the management of the House of Tramont. He made no objections to any of the legal restraints connected with Netta's dowry. He agreed to have his wife keep the name of Tramont in her married title, and to have any children of the match known as de la Sebiq-Tramont. His father muttered a little at this, but was persuaded in the end.

As soon as Easter was over, the wedding took place – a very splendid affair with much white tulle in the wedding-train and many chaplets of stephanotis on the bridesmaids' heads.

'Thank God,' Alys said privately to Gavin, 'she can enter society this year as a married woman – it would have been *too* embarrassing to have her do the season again as a single girl.'

But it could hardly be said that Netta entered society. True, she came to Paris, and took up the quarters in the east wing of the house in the Avenue d'Iena which had been allotted to the young couple. But she had occupations of her own. She didn't accept the invitations to become involved in the committee work of charities.

And when her mother inquired what on earth she was doing with herself, she received the astonishing answer: 'I'm studying with Monsieur Alfonsini.'

'Studying! Netta, what are you thinking of!'

'You know I always wanted to, Mama,' the young Madame de la Sebiq said sedately.

'You must be mad! What will Frederic say when he hears of it?'

'Mama!' cried Netta, quite shocked. 'You don't imagine I would do it without my husband's permission?'

'Frederic knows of it?'

'Of course.'

'But, Netta … how can he allow … I thought it was all agreed that you would forget this nonsense!'

'It isn't nonsense, Mama. I do wish you'd realise that!'

'Well,' Alys said, recovering from her astonishment, 'I suppose Frederic feels there's no harm in lessons…'

'Frederic agrees that I may sing in public–'

'Netta!'

'In due time, Mama. Not yet, of course – Monsieur Alfonsini says I'm not ready. But one day I hope to prove to you all that I have something to offer the world.'

'Frederic will never agree to any such thing.'

'But I tell you, he does agree. It was part of our bargain.'

'And what bargain was that, pray?' her mother demanded in a sharp tone.

'When we decided to get married,' Netta said, with a little shrug. 'We made a compact – he would go his way, and I would go mine.'

Her mother heard this with growing dismay. 'Child,' she said, biting her lip, 'what sort of a marriage is this? A mere business arrangement?'

'Oh, come, don't look put out! You were beginning to think you'd have to talk me into an arranged match. The only difference is, Frederic and I made our own arrangement.'

'That's not what I meant. I meant … is it a *proper* marriage? A marriage in the true sense?'

'Oh, that!' Netta said, laughing. 'All that is perfectly in order, Mama.' The tone of satisfaction was justified: Netta had been surprised and pleased to find that the part of the marriage she'd dreaded – the actual going to bed with Frederic – had brought pleasures beyond her expectations.

Alys didn't know what to make of it. She told her husband her problem, ending with,

'You must speak to Frederic, dear! You must tell him to put an end to this nonsense!'

'Alys, you know better than to ask me to interfere between husband and wife.'

'Dearest, you must. Otherwise we shall find ourselves looking ridiculous before the whole of Paris one day.'

'I thought you promised me that when Netta was married, we'd have no more worries?'

She sighed deeply. 'It seems I was wrong!'

Gavin didn't want to get involved. However, after a little family diner one evening, when the two men were sitting over port and cigars and the women were in the drawing room, he said, 'My boy, my wife was a bit perturbed the other day over something she heard from Netta.'

'Really? I'm sorry to hear it. Nothing serious, though?'

'Your mother-in-law tells me our daughter is taking singing lessons – with your encouragement, it seems.'

'Oh…' Frederic drew on his cigar. 'I don't exactly encourage it. I just tolerate it.'

'But Frederic! You know the idea is that she's going to sing in public one day.'

'No, no,' his son-in-law said, smiling. 'It will never happen.'

'How can you be so sure?'

'To take lessons in a studio with a great teacher is one thing. But to get up on a stage in front of a thousand people is another. You must have heard of stage-fright?'

'I don't know if you're right. She's very determined–'

'In any case, it's going to take a year or two, so M. Alfonsini says. By that time, Father-in-law, I hope she'll be too busy with her babies to bother about such nonsense.'

Gavin drew his brows together, then smiled. 'Of course! That's a relief! Why didn't her mother think of that!'

He was glad to put the problem from him because, to tell the truth, something much more important was claiming his attention. Reports were coming in from Calmady that the vines were looking sickly.

He went to the estate to meet his mother-in-law and Lord Grassington, who had asked to be kept informed. So many things could go wrong during the growing of the vines that there was no reason as yet to suspect anything more than normal damage from a succession of weather hazards.

The new vines had been layered-in as usual in February, chosen from the healthiest and most prolific plants. There had been a rather severe frost in late spring – in fact, around the time of Netta's wedding, which had caused the vineyard-workers to shake their heads and speak of evil omens for the young couple.

But then better weather arrived, the vines

117

put forth their leaves, the usual spraying began, and all seemed normal – a little touch of the disease called oidium, but nothing out of the ordinary.

Now, however, it was July and the grapes hadn't formed. The leaves were yellowing. Spraying seemed to do no good – there was no insect on the leaves, no mildew to be seen, nothing a spray could reach.

'Now, Nicci,' Lord Grassington said to his wife, 'you mustn't worry. It may be nothing. You know how strange the weather's been this year – the plants may just have been chilled too much to produce–'

'Gerrard dear, stop talking nonsense. You know and I know that there's something more than weather blight affecting the vines – or Gavin wouldn't have sent word.'

They were breakfasting together in their room before going down to face the day. It was a frightening morning. Already, out on the slopes, a worker was digging up sample vines at intervals of twenty yards, to examine the roots. By the time they went downstairs and out to the sheds, the little cart had come in and the vines were laid out for them to look at.

The weather was thundery. The clouds were an army of rolling grey monsters overhead. Gavin watched his mother-in-law approach and thought for the first time that she really wasn't young any more – nearly sixty, too old to be facing this anxiety.

'Well, Gavin?' she said as she entered the long, airy shed.

'They're on the table, Belle-mère.'

'Give me the glass.'

He handed her the big magnifying glass. She bent over the table, without touching the vines. She examined the roots of first one, then another, then a third.

'Gerrard?' She handed the glass to him. He in his turn inspected the plants.

As he straightened she said, 'There's no doubt, is there?'

'I'm afraid not.'

'What does Mellisot say, Gavin? How widespread is it?'

Gavin shook his head. 'He hasn't taken samples from every acre but all the vines are yellow in just the same way. The inference is that the roots are all attacked.'

She was silent a moment. He could see she was trembling. 'No grapes from Calmady this year?'

'I'm afraid not, Belle-mère.'

'It can't be so... No matter what might happen – frost, hailstorms, mildew attacks – there have always been *some* grapes to harvest.'

'Not this year, madame. I'm sorry.'

She put out a hand blindly. Her husband took it. 'Take heart, my dear,' he urged. 'Though Calmady's vines have been attacked, it doesn't follow the whole region is the same. You can blend champagne from other vineyard's wines – you've done it before, when Calmady's crop was poor.'

'But we've never had *none* of our own, Gerrard…'

'I know, I know. But so long as there is enough juice in the Champagne region to make wine, we can make champagne – a small vintage, I know, only a few hundred bottles perhaps, but we'll keep it going, we'll blend with last year's wines.'

'I have this terrible feeling, Gerrard–'

'Don't frighten yourself with terrors that perhaps don't exist. Come along, Nicci, let's go and look at the other vineyards. And we'd better be quick, because if they have good grapes and they know we want them, the price will go up by the hour.'

She laughed, a little unsteadily, but allowed herself to be led out to the light carriage that was awaiting them. But they both knew that the neighbouring vineyards had diseased vines. They had been visible when they drove from the railway station the previous day. And the reports filtering through had been of alarm, of growing dismay…

Their pretty team of ponies trotted down the road – a well-made road now, financed by La Veuve Tramont years ago to facilitate the moving of her wine. Everything in the neighbourhood spoke of Nicolette de Tramont's good business sense, her interest in the well-being not only of herself but of the whole winefield. She had made donations for village playing-fields, for fountains and memorials to those who died in the war of 1870. She had paid for the rebuilding of the church. The small vine-yardists who produced the rows of grapes normally sold their fruit to the House of Tramont while it was still on the vine. La Veuve Tramont herself used to come and bargain with them. Later, as the firm grew larger and more prestigious, she sent others to do the bargaining. But her wine was famous, they were happy to contribute to its fame.

Now she came to again to speak to them. Not in the black widow's weeds that had become her hallmark, but in a morning costume of brown and ivory, the heavy silk tailored to her still-trim figure.

The owners of the little vineyards hurried to greet her, cap in hand. Everywhere the story was the same. The vines were dying. What could they do? They looked at her beseechingly. She had led them for so long – showed them how to improve their cultivation, how to be more efficient in their business methods. Now she would tell them how to save their vines.

'I'm sorry, Jules,' she said, 'I'm sorry, Marie. I don't know what to do.'

She and Gerrard had set out early. Now it was well past lunch-time. The weather was heavy, hot and sultry.

'Come, my darling,' Gerrard said, taking one of her hands in both of his. Through the fine kid he could feel the slender bones, feel the trembling. 'It's time to go back to Calmady. You're tired now, you need something to eat.'

'I'm not hungry, Gerrard.'

'But nevertheless... We'll go home. You've had enough.'

She said no more against it. He helped her in, took up the reins and shook them. The ponies obediently started forward. He glanced at the clouds. There would be a downpour soon – he hoped they could get home before he had to stop and put up the carriage hood.

Nicolette was very silent.

'Are you all right, Nicci?'

'Perfectly all right, Gerrard. Just – as you said – tired.'

'We'll think of something, dear. Don't worry about it.'

She made no reply. He said to himself, Be quiet, you fool.

For what could be done? Where the disease had already struck, no vines would grow. Phylloxera came, and destroyed the plants. Once in the area, it remained. The insect overwintered ready to attack the roots of the newly-planted cuttings. The plant, deprived of nourishment, died.

There would be no grapes in the Champagne region this year. There would be none next year – and for how long? No one could tell. If the vines all died and the insect went elsewhere, it was possible to re-plant with cuttings from unaffected areas – but in the end the phylloxera aphid came back and the plants succumbed again.

Vineyards elsewhere had produced grapes sporadically after the first attack, but the uncertainty, the scanty crop, the immense waste of time and effort had taken their toll. Many great vineyards had already ceased to exist.

They must face the fact that The House of Tramont was about to go under. Perhaps not at once, but in a year or two – in four at most – if there was no Veuve Tramont champagne there would be no House of Tramont.

They made their way home through the narrow white-chalk roads to Calmady. As the light carriage came in, the first drops of the thunderstorm began to splash on the flagstones of the courtyard.

'Ah,' said Nicolette brightly, holding out her hand to catch them, 'here comes the rain.'

'Quickly, Nicci – we don't want to get soaked!'

'No, I'm coming.'

Gerrard jumped down, throwing the reins to a stable lad. He went round to hand down his wife. She stepped out, and then gave a little cry.

'Gerrard!'

'What, dear? Oh, careful – you'll fall!'

He thought she'd missed her footing on the folding steps of the carriage. But she continued to topple forward. He caught her in his arms. Her head fell back. He lifted her, sudden fear making his grip convulsive.

'Gavin!' he shouted. 'Alys!'

The servants came scurrying. The butler helped carry her ladyship into the drawing room. They laid her on a sofa. Alys came running in from the dining room where she had been awaiting them.

'What's happened–' She broke off. 'Oh, Mama!'

She threw herself on her knees by the sofa, took Nicolette's limp hand in hers. She leaned over her, examining her face. 'Mama, Mama! What's wrong?'

But there was no word, no sound from the pale lips. The Widow of Tramont would not grieve any more over her lost vines.

Chapter Six

The cortège was long. So many people joined it that the village of Calmady was engulfed in a sea of black.

The family had wished for a simple ceremony. But first there had been a delay while the medical certificate was issued – after all, Madame had died very unexpectedly and had been a British citizen, the wife of a British peer, when she died.

Then the government had requested a further wait. The Minister of Trade himself wished to attend the funeral. The death of such an esteemed member of French society, a leader of the French business world – it must be acknowledged by a public tribute.

All the workers of the region came, although they were needed in the fields now that August was nearly upon them. Or they would have been, had the vines been healthy...

All the negociants and owners from Rheims and Épernay were there, all the heads of great wine families who might have still been holidaying on the Riviera – all were there, following the coffin.

Among them was a tall, white-haired old man, who spoke the French of the Champagne region but with a strange overtone from some other land.

'May I present Monsieur Jean-Baptiste Labaud?' Robert Fournier-Tramont said, leading him to Gavin and Alys. 'He used to work on the estate, many years ago.'

'Oh, the gentleman you visited in America... How very kind of you to come, Monsieur Labaud.'

The old man shook hands, bowed. His face was set, his mouth grim. Nothing would have kept him away from Nicci's funeral, not even her high-flown title from the English milord. He lowered his eyes but glared at Lord Grassington under his brows. Couldn't he have looked after her better?

'Who is he?' Gerrard inquired, watching him as he turned, stiff-backed, from the closed gates of the family vault of the Tramonts.

'He's my – my friend from California.'

'He didn't come all the way from California?'

'No, he was in New York on business when he heard.'

Somehow the two men were never introduced. Jean-Baptiste stayed out of Gerrard's way, and Gerrard was too busy receiving condolences from people of importance.

Jean-Baptiste had accepted hospitality in

Robert Fournier-Tramont's house in Rheims. He moved about the old city, renewing acquaintance with those who were left of his days at Calmady. He toured the vineyards in a pony and trap.

'It's bad, my boy,' he said to Robert. 'I've never seen sicker looking vines than those out on those slopes.'

'You don't need to tell me,' Robert said, striking angrily with his stick at a stone in his path.

They were strolling in the formal garden of his town house. Tubs full of geraniums made a brilliant show in the mild sunshine of an August day on the Marne. Small shade trees glimmered with white dust from the chalky soil, dry after a week without rain.

Jean-Baptiste was silent for a moment. He himself had been lucky – the grapes in his valley of California hadn't been ravaged by phylloxera.

Yet.

That was the word that had always to be spoken silently in congratulations over healthy plants. There was absolutely no way of knowing when the insect would arrive. Some freak of wind direction, some chance importation on cuttings – who could tell how it came? All that could be said was that once it came, it brought havoc to the vines.

'We're working on it,' said Jean-Baptiste. 'We're trying to find an antidote.'

'Damned if I can see how an antidote can be applied to the roots,' Robert retorted. 'If you start scraping away the soil to apply a chemical, you're likely to damage them just at the moment when they need to be strongest.'

'I know, I know... But American viticulture is spending a lot of money on the investigation, Robert. And you know one thing Americans have plenty of is money. And what they call "know-how".'

'If they "know-how" to kill these particular plant-lice, I hope they share the knowledge quickly. Otherwise we're dead men.'

His father wheeled to take his shoulder in a vice-like grip. 'Never speak like that, Robert! Never even think of defeat! We'll find a way to stop this damned insect.'

Robert gave him a grim smile. 'Fighting talk. I hope the phylloxera bug hears you!'

They strolled on a pace or two. Anyone with a little insight might have seen that they were related, for though one was tall and strong and white-haired and the other thinner and somewhat lame, there was a resemblance in the set of the head, the carriage of the shoulders.

'Who's in control of the firm now?' Jean-Baptiste asked, with some anxiety. 'Not that simpleton of an English lord?'

'He's not so simple,' replied Robert. 'But

no – it was all settled in legal contracts before they got married. Gavin and I have joint control, in trust for our children.'

'Huh!' growled Jean-Baptiste. 'Those two youngsters of Alys's aren't going to do much. The boy's got his head in the clouds – d'you know, he asked me if I had ever read any Greek. Greek! And the girl – my God, she's a charmer, but she doesn't seem to know a thing about the grapes.'

'Not much. She has a good palate, though – she's always made useful comments about the blending. Not that that matters much,' he concluded in a sombre tone, 'since it doesn't look as if we'll have anything to blend this year and probably next.'

'What about your two? Are they showing any interest?'

'David says he wants to be a lawyer.'

'Well, at – how old – thirteen? That's not a bad ambition. My lad wanted to be a train driver. What about the girl?' For in the matter of growing wine, the women were as important as the men.

'Oh, it's a bit early for her to know... She's only eleven, after all. But,' added Robert thoughtfully, 'if she ever took up the wine, she'd be good. She's got ... I don't know ... something. Character, enthusiasm'

'And looks, by heaven! *What* a little beauty. I must say, Robert, you've given me grandchildren to be proud of!'

'I just wish I could tell them–'

'No, no, my boy. No, better not. Sleeping dogs, sleeping dogs...' They stood for a few moments looking at the goldfish in the ornamental pond. Jean-Baptiste threw in a leaf, watched the pretty fish rise to the surface without fear, to investigate. 'Stupid creatures ... comes of leading a sheltered life.'

'Well, they won't be sheltered much longer,' Robert said. 'We'll have to cut down on expenses in a big way after this year's disaster. I may even have to sell this house.'

'Shall you mind that, boy?'

'Well, the children were born here ... Gavin asks us to move in at the manorhouse.'

'I think you should.'

'You do?' Robert said, surprised. 'We might get in each other's way if we were so close.'

'I'd like you to be there, Robert. I'd like to think you were protecting what your mother built up.'

'Oh, there's no need to "protect"–'

'Yes, there is. I'm not saying anything against Gavin – he's a good man, he's made little Alys very happy. But he's not a Champenois. The wine to him is something you make and sell. To us it's something more.' He paused, studied his son. 'I'm right, aren't I? You care about the wine?'

Robert hesitated, then nodded. Until that moment, he'd never thought of it in those terms. But being asked to speak out, he understood in that moment how dear the place was to him, the estate with its vines, the great wine that flowed from its grapes, the precious knowledge that enabled them to make a drink no one else in the world could make.

'The time could come when Gavin might think of selling up.'

'Selling up?'

'Oh, if you can't grow grapes, you might be in dire straits for money.'

'But who'd buy a vineyard where you can't grow grapes?'

'Financiers take risks like that all the time. They might see a use for the land – I suppose you could grow other things, and the caves, Robert – the caves where we keep the wine ... I've no doubt there could be some new use for the caves. Don't let it happen. Hang on to what Nicci built. One day there will be wine again – hold on until that day comes.'

'So long as it isn't delayed too long, Jean-Baptiste. Your American scientists had better be quick.'

'It doesn't depend on them. It depends on *you*. You're your mother's only son. Defend the heritage. So long as Champagne Tramont lives, Nicole Tramont will never die.'

When his father had gone, Robert felt strangely alone. There was no reason for it – he had a wife and children whom he adored. Yet Jean-Baptiste was someone special. And what he had said was important.

'We've got to fight back,' he said to Gavin and Alys as they sat in the estate office after a long session with the lawyers. 'Monsieur Labaud was telling me that in America they've invested big sums in trying to find a way of counteracting the phylloxera bug. Here, where it's a damn sight more important, we're doing almost nothing!'

Alys looked momentarily startled at his vehemence, but nodded.

'We've sat quaking with terror of the thing long enough,' she said. 'It's time to start fighting back.'

Gavin put a hand on her black-clad arm. 'My love, what can we do? You know none of the usual chemicals have any effect on this creature.'

'Then we must find other chemicals.'

'Alys, research is going on – at the Pasteur Institute, for instance.'

'But as Robert says, Gavin – not urgently enough. We must get a group of botanists and viticulturists to concentrate entirely on the problem–'

'You are saying we ought to hire them?'

His wife stared at Gavin. The idea hadn't occurred to her until he said it, but now that it was said, it seemed obvious. 'Yes, that's it! We must finance research into the phylloxera beetle!'

'My dear, think what you're saying! The cost–'

'The cost if we don't is that our vineyards are going to die! You remember, Gavin, before we left Portugal to come home – Señor Medadia's winefields - nothing but rows of yellowing leaves. Phylloxera had forced him into selling–'

'We are never going to do that,' Robert interrupted, so as to have his position clear. He could hear the words of his father as they shook hands in farewell: 'Sell warehouses and stores and jetties if you have to. New buildings can be built. But never sell land, Robert – you can't rebuild the land.'

'Are you in favour of this idea of financing our own research?'

'Yes, I am.'

'Have you thought about the expense?'

'Not so far – Alys has taken me by surprise. But no matter what it costs, we ought to do it. Perhaps we could get other vineyardists to come in with us.'

'That's possible. A joint effort...'

'But we should make a start, on our own if need be. Every week that passes without research is a week wasted.'

For the next few days the senior members of the Tramont family discussed the project.

Alys argued in favour with more passion than she could understand. She hadn't realised, until now, how important the House of Tramont was to her.

Gavin, although not entirely against it, was worried about the drain on their capital. This year they were going to make no wine. Next year, they might make some but that was a gamble, depending on whether or not their cuttings were attacked.

'We'll be living from hand to mouth, you understand,' he said. 'If we're to keep Champagne Tramont going, we'll have to draw on stocks, and of course put the price up – and say what you like, even our most devoted customers are going to baulk at giving up a month's income for one bottle. So we can't finance the research project out of income. It'll have to come out of capital – and that's *dangerous*, Robert!'

'I know it's dangerous. We must economise in every other way, that's all.' He paused and gave his quiet, wry smile. 'I accept your invitation to move in here with your family. We ought to get a good price for the Rheims house – and that, of course, can go in the kitty.'

'Ought we to sell the Paris house?' Alys asked, with a tremble of the voice that she couldn't prevent. The house in the Avenue d'Iena was dear to her. She had helped her mother choose it and furnish it. From there she had launched herself into society as an influential married lady, had sent Netta out into the season and seen her glitter like a jewel against the setting of Parisian elegance.

Gavin hesitated, glancing at Robert. Robert said, pulling at his chin in thought: 'Not as yet, perhaps. That would be a signal to the world that the House of Tramont is in trouble – and we don't want to give that impression if we can help it. But there are buildings we could sell ... for instance, our transport facilities will be under-used this year at least and perhaps for the next year or two. We could either sell or rent some of the storehouses.'

'We could close down part of the Paris house,' Alys said, stiffening her sinews. 'After all, we really only use it for three or four months of the year as a family. The rest of the time, only Netta and Frederic are there. We could close down all of it except the east wing.'

'That doesn't sound too comfortable,' protested Gavin, thinking of the beautiful Netta living in a dust-sheeted house.

'Too bad,' Alys said with determination. 'And another thing – Frederic's got to pull his weight! He's a dear boy, and I don't want to be hard on him, but he can't expect to draw a handsome salary for playing at selling wine.'

'Especially as there's almost none to sell...'

'What are you going to do – cut him down to bread and water?'

In the end Frederic was given the task of acting as liaison between the research chemists at the university and other Parisian institutes, and the laboratory which was set up at Calmady. At first he was unwilling – it involved him in a lot of travelling back and forth, putting a decided spoke in the wheel of enjoyment: no long late-night card games, visits to the races curtailed.

But as he began to take hold of the role, he found he enjoyed it. Moreover, he was good at it. His natural easy charm and the friendships he'd already made enabled him to cajole money out of unexpected patrons. He brought groups of interested parties together and somehow made them work in harmony.

'Perhaps you should have gone into the diplomatic corps as a boy, and not the Army,' his father-in-law said with some admiration.

'It's a funny business. I was always in trouble at St Cyr for arguing with the instructors! Yet now I seem to be able to smooth people down...'

'Thank God for it. I hear you've arranged a debate here next week?'

'Here' was the Paris house. The debate was to be between three groups of researchers, each pursuing a different line, and each eager to tell the others that they were on a wrong track.

'Yes – if you hear the police have been called, don't worry! Feelings run high on the subject of who is wasting money and who isn't – because of course they know how vital it is to find a barrier to this awful little insect.'

'What does Netta make of all this?' Gavin said, still regretting that his lovely girl had had to give up her house to such workaday matters.

'Oh, Netta... She hardly takes any notice. If there's a row going on in the sitting room, she can always go off upstairs and practise some scales.'

Gavin clapped him on the shoulder. 'You're a decent sort, Frederic! I've heard scarcely a word of complaint from you about the way things have turned out – though it can hardly be what you expected.'

'Well, no,' Frederic agreed, tapping ash off his cigar and watching it fall neatly into the ashtray. 'I never saw myself as a ... scientific go-between. But it's interesting, you know. I have private bets with myself, who's going to chuck his papers in whose face, things like that. Almost as good as horses!'

As the months passed, the family poured money into the research. But nothing useful emerged. Trials were made in various parts of the world with new compounds, new systems of spraying and of sterilising the soil – to no avail.

'I try to do what you commanded,' Robert wrote to his father, 'but the House of Tramont may be about to die after all, my friend. Since you left, after that disastrous harvest that you saw, we have had yet another, with no grapes worth pressing in the Champagne region. We have sold some very important assets, but so far no land - although Gavin is seriously suggesting we uproot the vines and turn to some other product.'

'Courage!' Jean-Baptiste replied. 'Research may eventually rescue the wine industry. Here on this side of the Atlantic, scientists have discovered wild vines that are immune to the bite of *Phylloxera vastatris!*'

Phylloxera vastatris... Well-named! The insect, by laying waste the roots, caused the leaves to become dry and lifeless.

Wine production had almost come to a standstill. Not only in the north of France, in the region of the fine sparkling wines, but everywhere – Bordeaux, the Rhône, the sherry regions, the Chianti mountain-range of Tuscany, the hill slopes where Hock was produced – all of them were stricken, halting, productive only now and then as the hated creature came and went at will among the vines.

Yet, against this sombre background, family life went on. Philip Hopetown-Tramont graduated from the university with honours. Tall, slender, he blinked at the world from behind his gold-rimmed spectacles. What was he to do with his talents? He could read Greek, was an expert on the literature of the first century BC and especially the drama...

But what use was he?

'Don't worry about it,' his mother soothed. 'When things are better and we have some funds to spare, you can go to Athens perhaps, and help the research on the Greek theatre.'

'Mama, why did you let me waste all that time! And the fees – you should have brought me home and made me earn my keep!'

The truth was, Alys and Gavin had talked it over and decided the boy was best-placed in the libraries of the Sorbonne, happy and busy. He had no head for business. He wasn't like Frederic who, after an initial distaste, had proved a great asset. Philip was the kind of young man who would buy a gold watch costing five francs at a fair and be surprised when the gold wore off. He was the kind who believed everybody's hard luck story.

But what, actually, was he going to do? They didn't have the money to send him abroad to do private archaeology, which had been the original intention. Frederic came to the rescue. Among his many friends and acquaintances there was the owner of an erudite journal; Philip was given a post as assistant editor at a minute salary, his job being to read and approve the contributions concerning the classics. He would have rooms in the Paris house, looked after by the small staff that ran the establishment for Netta and Frederic.

'I know very well it's a do-nothing job,' Philip sighed to his sister. 'I ought to be ashamed of being so useless!'

'Darling Phip, if you feel like that, what about me!' Netta cried. 'Now that I've had to stop and look around, I find the world's been going to pieces – and I never even noticed!'

Netta was in a very emotional state. She had had to cancel her debut as a singer, having discovered she was pregnant with her first child.

At first she had been delighted. It was time she gave Frederic a son, she felt. But the baby signalled its presence by making her desperately sick, not only in the mornings but off and on throughout the day. Her teacher, Alfonsini, had at once forbidden her to go on with her lessons.

'You know how strenuous it is to use the voice properly,' he scolded. 'And now you strain the stomach muscles with this continual sickness. No, no – you must stop, you could do serious damage either to the child or yourself. No more lessons, no more singing, until after the baby is born.'

'Maestro, please!' She didn't want to give up now. Her first appearance on the concert platform was only a few weeks away.

'No, it is final. You remain silent, my nightingale, until at least three months after your baby is born.'

She had to bow to his authority. But what with that, and the changes wrought in her by the baby's presence, she was liable to dissolve in floods of tears at any moment.

'Netta, you at least were doing something that would please the world,' Philip said, innocently unaware that his family would have been seriously displaced if Netta had actually sung in public. 'Whereas I... What use am I, really?'

'Oh, you're useful just by being you, Phip!'

It was true. People came to him and told him their personal problems. He never knew how to solve them, but he listened with deep attention, always caring and kind in his responses, always anxious and concerned on behalf of the confidant.

But he was unaware of this virtue. He saw himself as someone who loved a quiet life, who shirked the major issues. And now that he'd become aware of the financial straits of the House of Tramont, he reproached himself as something of a parasite. 'I'm nothing like as useful as David is going to be,' he mourned to his sister. 'You can tell already – he's got a business brain, that lad!'

His uncle Robert's son was now fifteen, taking his studies at the lycée in his stride. Comically, he had done more. By involving himself in the production of a little booklet on how to do well in exams, he had actually made money – not quite enough to pay his school fees, but enough to allow him to return his allowance with lordly indifference.

'But, my boy,' his father protested, 'what happens when all the boys in your school have bought a copy of this masterpiece?'

David raised dark eyebrows. 'They already have. I'm now selling it in other schools, through an advertisement in the *Youths' Magazine*.'

Robert stifled a laugh. 'What do your masters think of all this?'

'We-ell, at first they were bothered, because they somehow thought it was a book telling boys how to cheat. But you know, Papa,' David said with a puzzled shake of the head, 'that would be pointless. What's the use of cheating at exams? You end up not having any proper qualifications and of course you'd get nowhere in life.'

His father didn't explain that that wasn't necessarily true. He had a feeling that

Netta's husband Frederic had passed most of his academic tests by cheating - and yet Frederic was doing relatively well in life, thank you. It was true he'd married for money, and the family was now in the process of losing it at a rapid rate, yet Frederic enjoyed himself.

'Shall you let Gaby have copies of the book to sell among the girls at her school?' he inquired.

David looked shocked. 'Certainly not, Papa! That would be a very unkind thing to do.'

'Really? Explain that to me.'

'Well, it would mean an awful lot of young ladies would leave school with certificates saying they were clever – and you know men don't like clever women, so how would they find husbands?'

This time Robert couldn't prevent the laughter that bubbled up. 'David, you're a tonic! When things look black in the business, I know I can always find some antidote in your view on life!'

David pulled down the fronts of his short school jacket and bowed. 'Always at your service, sir,' he said. Then, looking a little less pleased with himself and the world in general, he added, 'Are things so very bad, Papa?'

'Couldn't be worse. No one seems able to help the wine industry to save its vines.'

'How about these resistant vines in America? Your old friend at Bracanda Norte was to keep you informed.'

'And has done so. But you understand, David – we cannot make good wine from these nondescript American grapes. So now the viticulturists are experimenting with grafts. We shall have to graft the Pinot grape on to the root of the wild vine – and then wait and see if the graft takes, and if the grapes we get are true Pinot...'

'How long will the tests take?'

'It's to be hoped they'll come to a conclusion one way or the other before our money runs out. But don't you bother your head about that,' Robert interrupted himself quickly. 'Life has always had its ups and downs in the winefields.'

David recounted the conversation to his sister Gaby as they walked to church next morning for the Easter service. 'Papa says not to worry about it, but you can see it's on his mind all the time. Now I understand why I didn't get the Rover Safety Bicycle he promised me for my birthday.'

Gaby, exquisitely turned out in a pale pink cotton walking suit and the first straw hat of spring, couldn't take that altogether seriously. 'You didn't get the bicycle because Mama thought you'd kill yourself on it,' she remarked, opening and closing her parasol a little to discourage a hovering fly.

'No, it's not that, I'm sure it isn't. I think there's a real problem over money.' He bent to glance under the parasol, to say the next thing very seriously. 'There may not be enough to give you a coming-out, Gaby.'

Gaby's face lit up. 'Oh, good!'

'What?'

'Oh, I'm sick of hearing about coming out!' she cried. 'Everybody keeps on about it – the hairdresser, the girls at school, even the teachers...! I don't think so badly of the older girls because it's going to happen for them in a year or so. But the rest of us! Honestly, David, it's sickening! All they think of is their White Ball, and who'll be offering for them in their first season, and whether the styles are going to be in their favour that year. At the moment they're all in a state because the wasp waist seems to be going out. That's to say, those that have got slim waists are bothered. The rest of us don't care.'

'There's nothing wrong with your waist, Gaby,' said David with brotherly frankness. 'In fact, I think most fellows would say you were quite attractive.'

Most fellows would have said a lot more than that. Gaby was not very tall – at thirteen she perhaps had a lot of growing to do. But her features were perfection itself, or so it seemed to those who preferred brunettes. She had an oval face, like the subject in an Italian portrait of the seventeenth century. Her brown eyes were enormous, fringed with thick dark lashes. Her lips were of a rather dark red, against which her white teeth would flash when she laughed.

And Gaby laughed often. Unlike her mother, whom she physically resembled, Gaby soared and darted along the surface of life like a swallow. She wasn't shy or nervous – she grasped opportunities for enjoyment or excitement when they came, and used them to the full. She was a true Champagne Girl, even though the fortunes of the Champagne Girls didn't give reason for as much gaiety as formerly.

Gaby was a great supporter of her Aunt Netta's ambitions to be a singer. Of the whole family of Tramonts, she was perhaps the only one who took Netta seriously. In fact, there was a warmer relationship between these two than between Gaby and her mother, for Laura Fournier-Tramont was always a little restrictive to her spirited daughter.

'I look forward so much to the day when Gaby will be out in the world,' Laura would say to Robert. 'She needs something to expend all that energy on.'

'My dear, that's at least four years away.'

'Yes, and meanwhile we must just hope she behaves herself better at school and pays attention to her lessons. Luckily, now that Netta is expecting a baby, she's a better example to the child.'

Robert smiled and sighed. 'It will be good, won't it, when Netta's baby arrives. I only wish...'

'What, my love?'

'That Aunt Nicci could have lived to see it. A great-grandchild in the Tramont family... How she would have loved that.'

The coming of Netta's baby was the main point of interest for them that year, something pleasant to turn to when the business news continued bad. Yet on the day the child, Pierre, was born, another event occurred which was to have an enormous effect on the family.

Captain Alfred Dreyfus, a total stranger to them, was arrested on a charge of treason. They had never met him, never heard of him. But he was to shatter their lives.

Chapter Seven

There had been a meeting of scientists at the house in the Avenue d'Iena, to exchange news and ideas so as to have something to think about over the Christmas holiday. The men were struggling into their heavy surtouts, in preparation to face the biting Paris wind, when the front door burst open.

Philip Hopetown-Tramont surged in, brandishing a copy of *L'Union.*

'They've done it! They've found him guilty!'

He had come in with so much energy that he jostled some of the visitors. They sorted themselves out, staring at him.

'Who?' Frederic asked. 'What are you talking about?'

'Dreyfus! You see how they are – they've released it only to conservative rags like this! And three lines, that's all.'

'May I?' asked Professor Saurcy. He took the crumpled paper from Philip's hand, smoothed it out, and read aloud while others came to look over his shoulder.

'Captain Alfred Dreyfus, tried in camera on charges of treason to the state, was found guilty yesterday by a unanimous verdict of senior officers trying the case.'

'Oh, that's bad,' muttered Saurcy, 'that's very bad...'

'What's the punishment for treason? Is it still the guillotine?'

'My dear fellow, surely we're not so inhuman as to behead people–'

'But what's he done?' ventured Leneuf, at a loss. 'Have we ever heard what he's supposed to have done?'

'No, and you never will!' cried Philip, his

mild blue eyes flashing behind his rimmed glasses. 'The whole thing's been carried out under cover – you can tell it's a put-up job!'

'Now, now, Phip,' Frederic soothed. 'Calm down, calm down. Gentlemen, I believe some of you have hackney carriages waiting.'

'Oh yes, yes of course…' With murmurs of 'Bad business' and 'I'm afraid I don't really know what it's all about' the gentlemen took their leave. While they did so, Philip's father emerged from the sitting room where the informal meeting had been held. He had in his hands the notes he'd gathered up from the various chairs.

'What's all the uproar about?' he inquired. 'Oh – hello, Phip, you're home early?'

'Come in and calm down,' Frederic said, ushering them all into the warm sitting room. 'We don't want to alarm Netta – she's upstairs with the baby, it's his bedtime, you know.'

Gavin smiled to himself at this aspect of Frederic as a family man. Surprising what a three-month-old son could do to a man…

But his own fully-grown-up son was in the sitting room, divesting himself of his outdoor coat as if he were having a fight to the death with it. 'I can't believe it! Where's the justice if a thing like this can happen?'

'What's the matter?'

'Alfred Dreyfus,' Frederic said by way of

explanation. He went to the side-table, where he poured a glass of the wine left over from the refreshments offered to the scientific group. 'Here, drink this. You look as if you need it – though why you should be in such a state over Alfred Dreyfus, I'm damned if I know!'

Philip accepted the wine, gulped down a mouthful. 'You don't understand, Frederic! Half the journalists in Paris are up in arms about this!'

The other men exchanged an amused glance. Philip was hardly a journalist. Yet since taking up the post with the *Scholarly Chronicle,* he had mixed with a different set of people. The reporters on the magazine, those sent to take shorthand notes at intellectual meetings, came from all walks of life and were used to staying in contact with men on newspapers and gossip magazines.

Intense interest had been aroused by the charges brought against Captain Dreyfus. The newspaper world naturally expected to be given some details. But nothing of the sort. A great clamp had come down, like an iron hand. Nothing was released, nothing was even allowed to be hinted at in the press.

Journalists became annoyed and resentful. They had a *right* to know what was going on. They expected to learn more at the trial.

But then came the announcement that the

court martial was to be held in secret. Well ... perhaps that followed, since Dreyfus had been charged with passing on documents to the German High Command. Presumably national security was involved. But there were always ways of getting to know what went on in a courtroom.

Not in this case. The trial lasted two days, ending yesterday, December 22nd. The usual privates and sergeants and military clerks, normally very bribable, had refused every inducement. The word among the Paris pressmen was that they seemed scared to death.

Why the intense secrecy? Why so much anxiety over the trial of a nonentity serving as a fetch-and-carry officer on the general staff?

There seemed to be two answers to the questions. Either Captain Dreyfus had done something extremely damaging to the safety of the French nation, or he could say something to the detriment of some important officer or minister if the evidence were published.

Depending on which half of the Paris press you represented, you could choose your view. The conservatives decided that Dreyfus was a traitor of the very worst kind. The radicals were sure the government were involved in some monstrous cover-up. Presumably the verdict would give at least some explanation of what had been going on and, the radicals insisted, if Dreyfus were not acquitted it would be a crime against French justice.

Philip, always apt to take up lost causes and befriend lame dogs, had been muttering for some time that something bad was being done to Alfred Dreyfus. The whole thing was demonstrably unfair. The censorship over press speculation only showed that the government were afraid to come out in the open with their charges because they knew they were absurd.

'Some of the fellows are going in a deputation to the Ministry of Justice tomorrow,' Philip said. 'We *must* get the facts about this conspiracy!'

'What conspiracy is that? The one Dreyfus has been involved in?'

'The one he's a victim of, Father! There's no doubt–'

'There's plenty of doubt,' Gavin intervened, frowning at his son and smoothing his beard with an impatient tug. 'One imagines the government wouldn't have brought a charge if there were no grounds–'

'Then why don't they make them public?'

'But if it's to do with military secrets?'

'Good God, Father, if he really passed on the stuff to the Germans, what's the point of keeping the evidence secret?'

Frederic gave a laugh. 'He's got a point,

Father-in-law! And you can be sure of this, my friends – the German High Command is laughing and rubbing its hands to see the French Army making itself ridiculous.'

'You agree it's ridiculous, then, Frederic? There, Papa! Now Frederic knows the army–'

'All the same, it's going too far to accuse them of conspiring against this captain. Why should they? Why should they do anything so disgraceful? We have to suppose, my boy, that the men at the top are decent and honourable.'

'Oh, now…' Frederic said, on a note that held some cynicism.

'You see, Papa?'

'What does that mean, "Oh, now"? Are you saying the general staff are scoundrels, Frederic?'

'They're men, like the rest of us,' was the reply. Frederic was selecting a cigar from a box whose contents were low. His conscience told him he ought to economise, but it had been a long afternoon, it was cold and dark outside, and he wanted to relax over a good smoke.

'But you don't think they have any reason to victimise Captain Dreyfus, surely?'

He shook his head. 'I know nothing about it. All I say is, you shouldn't regard the court martial judges as beyond reproach. Senior officers can have a very blinkered view, you know. And Dreyfus is ... well ... there were problems.'

'You knew him?'

'Not at all. He was an artilleryman, I believe, before he was called to the general staff. No, he never crossed my path. But some officers are popular and some are not, and the gossip among my military pals is that Dreyfus was not well-loved.'

'You're not saying they would find him guilty on insufficient evidence, just because they didn't like him?'

Frederic took his time about lighting his cigar before replying. 'Hm... It probably didn't help him. If material has been going missing from the files and they had to find out who had taken it, for example ... Dreyfus is the kind of man who might spring to mind as a criminal.'

'How do you mean, Frederic, would "spring to mind?" Has he a bad character? Is he in debt, or something of that kind?'

'He means, Papa, that Dreyfus would spring to mind because he is a Jew.'

'What?'

'Captain Dreyfus comes from a rich Jewish family. His father is a manufacturer of–'

'Come, come, my boy! What has that to do with anything?'

Frederic snorted.

'Freddi, stop being cagey and come out

154

with it! Is there truth in what Phip is saying? Would the officers of the general staff suspect Dreyfus simply because he's Jewish?'

'Of course.'

'Frederic!'

'If you're going to disbelieve what I say, why d'you ask me? I tell you, Father-in-law, there are men on the general staff who hate the idea of having Jewish officers in the army. If anything goes wrong, well, inevitably, it's *their* fault. They're not natural soldiers, you see – not like us true-blue French with our martial inheritance and our background of chivalry.'

'Well ... I must say I... This is all very distressing... But all the same, he's had a fair trial. I mean, you can't say there was no evidence against him – they couldn't possibly have brought a case if there had been no evidence.'

'There may have been evidence, Father,' Philip intervened angrily, 'but we're not to be allowed to know it. Those damned autocrats!'

Gavin shook his head at his son in bewilderment. 'I can see it's a bit ... odd. But I don't see why you have to get so bothered about it, Phip.'

'It's because of Aunt Laura.'

The other two men gaped at him.

'Aunt Laura?' Gavin echoed. 'What's it got to do with Aunt Laura?'

'Aunt Laura is Jewish.'

'Oh, don't be absurd!' said Frederic. 'Aunt Laura is a Catholic – she goes to church with the rest of us most Sundays.'

'Her people are Jewish,' Philip insisted. 'Great-Uncle Simeon in New York – the very name, it's Jewish.'

'Oh, if you're going to go by names,' laughed Frederic, 'I know a fellow called Korngold but if anything, he's a Calvinist–'

'It's not a joking matter!' Philip cried. 'From the moment Dreyfus was arrested and charged there have been all kinds of sneers and innuendos about–'

'Good God, boy, nobody thinks about that kind of thing.'

'I wager Aunt Laura thinks of it,' Philip insisted.

'Nothing of the kind. Your aunt never gives it a thought, I'm sure.'

He was wrong.

In the New Year, when the ground around the village of Calmady was grey with frost over hard clay, Laura Fournier-Tramont received a letter. She read it several times, her dark brows drawn together in perplexity and something like pain. When her husband came in from his morning ride around the estate she had hot coffee brought, and then handed him the letter to read.

'I want your opinion, dear,' she said.

Robert read it. He sat silent after he had

156

put it down.

'I have half decided to accept the invitation,' his wife said.

Still he said nothing.

'You don't think I should?'

'Laura, you don't enjoy committee work. Even when you sat on charity committees, you got nervous and upset.'

She chuckled. 'That was one of the compensations for losing so much of our money – nobody invites me on to charities any more, I'm not valuable enough.'

'There you are, then.'

'But this is different, Robert. This isn't a charity, it's a demand for justice.'

Robert hesitated. 'My dear,' he said, 'how do we know that justice has not been done?'

'Because everything has been done in secret! And Captain Dreyfus has continually insisted he is innocent.'

'But surely – every criminal insists on his innocence if he can.'

'Monsieur Dreyfus is not a criminal, Robert.'

'How can you know? You have no acquaintance–'

'Phip went to the Ecole Militaire to witness the ceremony where he was stripped of his regimentals. He told me the man seemed to be bewildered at what was being done to him. He cried out to the detachments from the Paris garrison, "Soldiers! An innocent man is being degraded! Long live France!"'

'Phip should not have told you anything about it,' Robert said angrily. 'Why should he inflict his political views–'

'I asked him, Robert. I spoke to him by telephone, asking if he would be in the party of journalists invited to witness–'

'You asked him? It was your idea? But, Laura! I had no notion you took any interest in the case!'

She sighed. Choosing her words with delicacy, she said, 'It was forced on my attention.'

'But why? Why?'

'There have been little remarks... Oh, of course, dear, you wouldn't notice. And people forget when they speak in front of me that I have Jewish blood...'

'Laura!' He leaned across to take her hands. 'Laura, people say silly things – it's simply a manner of speaking, an old habit that dies hard.'

'Yes, of course, I know that. But ... when they spoke of Dreyfus as naturally guilty because he wasn't a true Frenchman–'

'Oh, that's nonsense! He's from Alsace – I was brought up there. No one is more French than a man from Alsace since the Germans annexed it in 1870!'

'Robert...' She shook her head. 'You're being naïve. They didn't mean only that he's from Alsace. They meant that he's Jewish.'

Her husband didn't know how to gainsay it. He had heard the men in clubs discussing the story. They took it for granted Dreyfus was guilty. The newspapers were almost unanimous in supporting the verdict: *Patrie, Eclair, Libre Parole, Matin* – everyone except perhaps *L'Autorité,* and the world knew that the editor of that journal was a Bonapartist, likely to disagree with anything a Republican government did.

And in most of the reports, the point was always made that Dreyfus was a Jew. If he had come from the south of France, no one would have kept on pointing out that he was a Provençal or a Dauphinois. There was a difference, and Robert couldn't deny the fact.

He went back to the original plan. 'I don't think you are suited to political activity, dear. I can't understand why the committee wrote to you at all – yours isn't a name that springs to mind in connection with a campaign of this kind.'

'They already had my name,' Laura said, colour coming into her thin cheeks. 'I wrote to Madame Dreyfus expressing sympathy after the "degradation".'

'You did! I had no idea of that, Laura!'

She said nothing. It began to dawn on Robert that his wife had been unhappy for some weeks now, and he hadn't even been aware of it. He drew her closer by the hands he was holding and kissed her on the cheek. 'Of course, sweetheart. If you feel so strongly about it, you must join this Committee for Open Justice. But I must warn you, it's a hopeless cause.'

It certainly seemed so. A few good-hearted people worked hard, writing letters to anyone who might have influence on the possibility of bringing into the open the evidence against Alfred Dreyfus. They had no success over all the months of 1895, and yet their work was noticed, both by those friendly to them and those who thought they were either wrong-headed or working to annoy the government.

On a day in the beginning of the following year, David Fournier-Tramont was delivered to his home in Calmady by an anxious teacher.

'David!' cried Laura, called to the sitting room by a flustered maid.

He had an arm in a sling and a piece of sticking plaster on one temple. There was a yellowing bruise along his jawline. He drew back with a grunt of pain as she tried to put her arms about him in alarm.

'Don't Mama – I've got a broken collar-bone.'

'But how? What happened? Monsieur?' She turned to the black-clad teacher.

'There was a fight, madame. Your son is better off than the other boys, I assure you.'

'A fight?' Laura was amazed. David never indulged in fisticuffs. He had his friends and his enemies, of course, but he never settled differences with blows.

'The school doctor set the collar-bone and, as you see, has treated the contusions and cuts. He says he'll come to no harm. But we thought it best, madame, that he should come home to recuperate.'

'Of course, of course! My poor silly boy, what have you been up to?'

'Nothing, Mama.'

'Come now, to get into a fight is not nothing. What was it all about?'

'Nothing important, Mama.'

She turned to the teacher. 'Can you explain this, sir?'

She thought the teacher looked embarrassed. 'There's nothing to explain – some boyish upset, that's all. But the other boys … I mean, particularly the ringleader…'

'Ringleader?' Laura cried in alarm. 'You mean my son was set upon by a gang?'

'I regret I don't know what happened, madame. All we can say is that there was a battle on the playing field yesterday afternoon and that David rendered one of his assailants unconscious. Unfortunately, that boy is the son of a rather influential man… Madame, I think it would be best if you kept David at home for the rest of the term.'

161

'Until after Easter? Certainly, if you wish it.'

'We can perhaps then discuss whether he can come back for the summer term—'

'*Whether*...? Sir, he must come back – he has to sit his exams.'

'Of course, of course, there should be no problem by then. Everything will have calmed down.'

Laura saw that he didn't want to be drawn further. She remembered her duties as a hostess, ordered refreshments, sent a man to see that the carriage horses were rested and given oats. When she had seen him off about an hour later, she went to David's room.

The lad was sitting at a table by the window, a book in front of him. As she came in, he hastily turned a page with his good hand. But he hadn't been reading.

'David, what does all this mean?'

'It's nothing, Mama. Just a stupid fight.'

'But you never get into fights.'

'This was different.'

'How was it different? And why did a whole group of boys set upon you? What had you done?'

'I'd done nothing!' he flared. 'It was *them!*'

'They had done something wrong?'

Her son had recovered himself. 'You wouldn't understand,' he muttered.

'Of course I'd understand. Tell me.'

But he stubbornly refused.

It was extraordinary. He'd always been close to her, closer than her daughter Gaby. But she couldn't get anything out of him.

When Robert came home from a business trip to Rheims, he had to be given the news. He looked taken aback, and she saw that he was tired and in pain – sometimes his back troubled him greatly after a day spent travelling.

'I'm sorry to wish this on you, Robert. But he won't tell me what he's been up to.'

'I'll speak to him,' he said. 'Leave it with me, Laura.'

He limped up to his son's room. David was changing for dinner. He turned with his stiff collar in one hand, collar-stud in the other. 'Oh… So you've come to read the riot act, have you, Papa?'

'I've come to ask what the devil's going on! What have you got yourself into, you young fool?'

'I haven't "got myself into" anything–'

'Well, I'd say you're in some disgrace – brought home and told to stay there!'

'It's damned unfair!' cried David, throwing the collar on his dressing table in anger. 'It should have been Boiledieu who was sent home!'

'Who's Boiledieu?'

'He's the one who's the main troublemaker. As a rule I just ignore him, but yesterday he went too far!'

Robert eased himself into a chair. 'Your mother says you won't tell her what it was all about.'

'Papa, I can't tell *her!* She's the last person...'

'What?' His father jerked upright in his chair. 'What are you saying, David?'

'It was what they were saying about *her.* They were calling out things...'

'About your mother?' Robert was totally at sea. 'What could they possibly be...' Then the faintest of ideas began to form. 'David?'

'They were saying she was a treacherous Jew, who supported the traitor Dreyfus.'

There was a long silence.

'Her name's among those on the heading of those letters they sent out, isn't it, Father? Somehow Boiledieu's father had got hold of one and told him about it, and ever since then Boiledieu's never stopped going on and on about it. I didn't care at first – it was just a load of rubbish about busybodying and things like that. But this last week...' He looked at his father. 'In the past few days they've been going on and on about Grandfather Simeon and his "dirty money" and American interference and how Mama's a foreigner who ought to keep her nose out of France's affairs and ... and ... well, I hit him.'

Good for you, thought Robert. Aloud he

said, 'It seems he hit you, too.'

'Him and four of his friends. He's got a lot of friends. He's a popular chap, as a matter of fact – I quite liked him until he got going about Mama and how she wasn't to be trusted because she was Jewish. I said to him, "In that case you've got to say I'm not to be trusted either" and he said nobody could trust a Jew and that we were all foreigners who ought to get out of France.'

Robert sighed. 'What nonsense.'

'Papa, it'll be better if I don't go back at all. Boiledieu isn't going to apologise and if he doesn't, I'll hit him again.'

'Now, look here, David–'

'I know what I'm talking about. It's not that I mind taking him on – it's that Professor Spirron says it's disrupting school discipline.'

'He doesn't blame you for it, surely.'

'No, no – if he'd thought I was in the wrong he'd have expelled me. I tell you, I mucked up Marcel Boiledieu good and proper, and I didn't do too badly on Thigreau either!' There was a faint pride in his own exploits. But his basic good sense was dictating his words. 'Even the masters are beginning to take sides. Of course, most of them don't want any bother and those that are interested in Dreyfus think he got what was coming to him. But one or two are beginning to say perhaps there was

165

something fishy in the case, and the poor old Prof wants me out of the way so he can have some peace.' He paused, colouring up and looking absurdly like his mother in that moment. 'The only solution would be if Mama gives up her campaign work – and we ought not to ask that.'

'But your exams, David–'

'I can sit those somewhere else. I'm officially entered, all the paperwork's been done.'

'But what about tuition?'

'Oh, I can keep up to standard with my books. If I feel a bit uncertain you can hire a tutor for me. But I'm not really worried, Father, I'll do all right without the lycée.'

They discussed it for a time. Then Robert said: 'It may be that you're right. But don't talk to your mother about it. I'll tell her some tale, it'll be all right.'

'Just as you say, Papa. Now help me with this rotten collar – I can't manage with one arm in a sling.'

Robert went to his room afterwards to change. Laura was already in a dinner gown, and waved her maid out as Robert came in.

'Don't worry about it any more, dear,' he said. 'It was a boyish fight about name-calling.'

'But David doesn't fight–'

'This was different, my love. You forget his

age. At seventeen, if someone makes a slighting remark about a certain young lady, you get very angry.'

'Oh, goodness!' She gave a muffled shriek of laughter. 'It was about a girl?'

'I'm afraid so. So don't ask him anything about it. He's very tender on the subject.'

'Of course not, my dear.' She helped him out of his jacket – he had dispensed with a valet as an economy, although Laura kept her maid. 'So David is interested in a young lady,' she said. 'What an extraordinary thought...'

'Not at all. He's just at the age... If you see a few letters winging back and forth, don't remark on it. But as a matter of fact, she may not be as keen as David.'

'Who is she? Anyone we could know?'

'Oh, no, darling. The daughter of a tobacconist in Épernay. It's just one of those little flirtations. It'll die a natural death.'

He was ashamed of the fluency with which he invented the lie. Between them there was an almost total honesty which had seemed as natural as the air they breathed.

He couldn't help feeling a secret resentment against the Dreyfus Affair, for causing him to lie to his wife.

Philip Hopetown-Tramont was much more active than his Aunt Laura and was working with a much less respectable group. Some radical journalists, some political commentators, a few intellectuals from the university, and one or two self-educated trade unionists – these made up his colleagues.

'I don't know what you think you're doing!' his father, Gavin growled. 'Moiret is an anarchist – I suppose you know that?'

'Nothing of the kind, Father. That's one of those libels the conservatives invent to discredit'

'If they catch him with a bomb actually in his hand, will you believe it then? I tell you, Philip, your getting yourself in with a bad lot!'

With surprising stubbornness, Philip resisted Gavin's attempts to make him toe the respectable line. He was less easy in shrugging off his sister's anxieties.

'You're putting yourself in a very odd position, Phip. Papa says these people are nihilists or anarchists or something. Of course I see you'd want to support a cause you think is just – that's just like you. And you want to help Aunt Laura. Though why a respectable married woman should get involved…'

'You'd be surprised at the kind of woman who gets involved, Netta.'

'Should I?' She studied him with interest. 'Have you one in particular in mind?'

'Not at all. Though there is a young lady who is a supporter of Dreyfus–'

'Well now! Has she a name, this young lady?'

'She's called Elvire Hermilot.'

'Elvire!' said Netta, raising her eyebrows at the literary allusion.

'Her friends call her Elvi.'

'Oh? And is that what you call her, little brother?'

'I have that honour,' he said, stiff with embarrassment. He took off his glasses and began to polish them, a trick he had when he needed to avoid a direct glance.

'Well, well… How long has this been going on?'

'Nothing is "going on". I was able to be of service to her when her position was made untenable by the unwelcome attentions of her employer. I was able to find her a post with a law firm in the same building as the *Scholarly Chronicle*–'

'Her employer! What are you saying? She's a working girl?'

'There's no need to make an outcry, Netta! Grandmama Tramont was a working girl at first.'

'Grandmama? Your thoughts fly to the family, I see. Are you thinking of bringing this working girl into ours?'

'There's no question of that at present. I am Mademoiselle Hermilot's friend.'

'And what does she work at, Mademoiselle Hermilot?'

'She's a steno-dactylographer – very useful to our group because she can go to meetings and take quick shorthand notes.'

'Phip, Phip...' She was half laughing, half anxious. How like Phip to fall in love with an earnest little anarchist-nihilist short-hand-typist.

There had been murmurings in the family that it was time Philip settled. At going on twenty-five, he'd shown no sign of interest in marriage.

Perhaps in normal times the Tramonts would have been busying themselves finding a suitable match. But things weren't quite what they used to be for the Tramonts. They had slipped down a rung or two of the social ladder. It had first become noticeable after La Veuve Tramont's funeral – there had been fewer personal visits of condolence than one might have expected. Instead, cards had been left, letters of polite grief had been sent.

A great event such as a birth or a death was a useful way of changing one's relationship with a family. A signal was sent out by the warmth or tepidity of reaction. The Tramonts had noted that some of the haute bourgeoisie with whom they'd been close were now perceptibly more distant. Very well... It was understandable. Times were hard, the Tramonts couldn't cut such a figure in society as formerly.

170

Then the almost complete closing of the Paris house had followed. No more great balls and parties to which people longed to be asked. No more invitations to sit on the committees of important charities, those bases from which social power was wielded. No more five-o'clocks at which discreet decisions were made about which young man was suitable for which young lady.

This change wasn't as distressing as it might have been. The menfolk were too busy trying to save the champagne trade and, rather to Gavin's surprise, Alys was playing an active part. Laura, less commercially minded than her sister-in-law, gave her spare time to the Dreyfus Affair. Frederic was proving useful not only in handling the scientific administration but in dabbling profitably on the Bourse, bringing in a little extra income when it was most needed.

To Netta, the change had been a real blessing. Contrary to all expectations, she'd gone back to her singing after the birth of Pierre, and now she found there was less opposition than there used to be.

Partly it was because society in general had become more tolerant of 'bohemianism'. It was true, one wouldn't be too happy if a son actually wanted to marry a girl from the corps de ballet, yet it was permissible to meet the great dancers and actors without too much embarrassment.

Then there was the changed status of the Tramonts. Formerly Netta's misdoings would have seemed a terrible blot on their escutcheon. Now her actions seemed less wrong, and hardly important compared with the fact that the House of Tramont itself was in danger.

So Netta had resumed her lessons, had sung in one or two charity concerts. So far the music critics hadn't been asked to take her seriously.

But in October she was to make her real debut, with a recital in the Salle Berlanger at Nancy. Her head was full of thoughts and plans for the great event. She was having a special gown made, of ginger paper-silk and velvet, in the new 'princess' line which would accentuate her slender elegance with its unbroken sweep from shoulder to heel. She was to have a new hairstyle. Frederic had given her a set of tortoise-shell combs set with brilliants to enhance the smoothness of her bronze-coloured hair.

She was very nervous, and yet she was confident. She knew she had a voice, and she had learned how to use it. True, this recital wasn't of the best music – mere drawing room songs, most of them. But, as the maestro said: 'To sing a "nothing" song well is the test of a good voice. And it endears to the public, no? They love to hear what they themselves sing in the bath, but sung well!'

The recital was booked for a Sunday afternoon, that favourite hour of relaxation for the whole family. What could be more enjoyable to the textile-makers and iron-masters of Nancy than a leisurely family lunch in a good restaurant, a little stroll by the banks of the Meurthe to settle the stomach, and then a little concert of pretty songs by a pretty woman? Especially, the wives said to each other, since she was a Tramont of the House of Tramont, and would be sure to wear something really delicious.

Netta was so immersed in the preparations that she didn't notice an event which was very important for her brother Phip and her Aunt Laura.

The London newspaper the *Daily Chronicle* published a report that Alfred Dreyfus had escaped from prison. When repeated in France, the news brought a sudden surge of interest in the traitor on Devil's Island, and a good deal of nodding and 'I told you so' because of course, if he was in the pay of the Germans, the Germans would have helped him escape.

The report was entirely false. How it arose was never clear. But a cable from Lebon, the Minister for the Colonies, to Cayenne brought a complete denial: Alfred Dreyfus was safe in solitary confinement in his cell.

The governor of the penal colony had seen him himself that very morning.

Whoever started the story had done Dreyfus no service. The governor was instructed to build a double palisade round the prisoner's cell, and to shackle him to his bed every night. At first, since the warders weren't allowed to speak to the prisoner, he had no idea what was going on – his appeals for an explanation of this additional cruelty were ignored. But Bravard, the governor, was so ashamed that he complained of his orders to his immediate superior, the Governor of French Guiana. He in his turn tried to make it clear in cables to Paris that the former Captain Dreyfus had not escaped, could not possibly escape, and never would escape.

Of course, cables back and forth between Paris and the penal colony couldn't be kept entirely secret. Some of the facts leaked out. The newspapers leapt on the story. The anti-semitic press started a scare that the 'international Jewish conspirators' were going to buy off the warders on Devil's Island with their vast sums of money. *Le Figaro* replied with a reasoned case on the impossibility of escape and described, with great vividness and some sympathy, the conditions under which Dreyfus was held. It was at this point that the nightly fetters were discontinued but the double wall remained, cutting off Dreyfus from even the sight of the trees and the sea, his one comfort in a situation of loneliness and hardship.

In *L'Autorité*, the editor announced that he was far from certain that the trial had been fair. He said a few unkind things about military judges, commenting on their clannishness and lack of enlightenment. Other papers took up the challenge, one of them reporting with apparent certainty that Dreyfus had made admissions of guilt on two occasions.

A National Deputy, Castelin, announced that he would speak on the case at the reopening of Parliament.

There was talk in the newspapers of a *bordereau*, a list, which had been the chief evidence at the trial. It was being murmured that the *bordereau* was not in Dreyfus's handwriting after all.

By now it had become known in military circles that an officer called Esterhazy was probably involved with Dreyfus in the passing of information to the German Embassy and might, in fact, be the real culprit. But it was essential to keep such knowledge from the general public. It couldn't be permitted that anyone should think the Army had made a mistake.

The staff at GHQ let it be known that they wanted support, public support, from right-minded junior officers and former officers.

Frederic de la Sebiq had it murmured to him at his club: 'I say, old fellow, oughtn't you to tell your in-laws to stop meddling with things they don't understand?'

'My dear chap, it's not my place to tell my in-laws anything – I'm very much a junior member of the family.'

He didn't mention the conversation to anyone. He regarded it as just another example of the top brass getting in a state over nothing.

Netta, totally unaware of it all, got to the concert hall on the great day in plenty of time. She'd had a light lunch and a glass of white wine, as Alfonsini commanded. Her accompanist had tested the pianoforte so that he was sure it was in tune – a thing one couldn't always be certain of, even in a provincial capital.

Alfonsini himself had made the trip to Nancy. It was a great compliment. He seldom travelled beyond the gates of Paris, unless it was to hear a world-famous protégé in a new role.

He greeted Netta as she came from the greenroom to the wings of the concert platform. He made a little gesture with his thumb. 'A good audience! Almost every seat taken!'

'I hope they've come to hear the music, not just to look at Nicolette de la Sebiq-Tramont!'

'It doesn't matter why they've come! It's how they feel when they go away that's important.'

'Yes, maestro.'

'Now, remember – if you feel tension, clasp and unclasp the hands three times behind the back.'

'Yes, maestro.'

'Deep breaths. Don't rush into the Delibes – it's a good song to bring up the interval, but you want to leave a good impression while they drink their iced lemonade and discuss you.'

'Yes, maestro.'

'Richard, are you ready?'

'Yes, sir,' said the accompanist.

'Remember, Richard – don't let her rush into "The Fair Maids of Cadiz"–'

'I won't, maestro.'

'Very well, *avanti!* Good luck, my child, God bless you.' He gave her a little push to go in the wake of the pianist, then made the sign of the cross on his breast as she walked on stage. His little nightingale, his crystal-clear songbird...

Netta had been warned not to try to descry her family in their place near the front. Frederic was there, and her brother Phip with, she thought, his young lady. Her mother was there, but not her father nor her uncle Robert; they had been unable to leave Calmady, since it was the time of the grape

177

harvest – another miniscule crop.

She saw a sea of faces, mainly a blur. It did perhaps drag at her attention that on one side of the auditorium there seemed to be few hats – ladies in an audience were noticeable for their hats. It must mean the block of seats was taken up by men. How very flattering...!

Richard had given only the most cursory response to the spatter of applause that greeted them. He arranged his music on the music stand. He opened the first book at the dog-eared page: 'On Wings of Song' by Felix Mendelssohn, the perfect concert-opener.

He caught Netta's eyes. She didn't nod, but the message was passed. She was ready.

The introduction rippled out. Netta took a breath.

Then from the hall came a shout. 'Dreyfusard! Dreyfusard! Down with her, down with her, Dreyfusard!'

Richard raised his eyes from the music. Netta had faltered as she was about to sing the first note. A hot fierce colour had risen in her cheeks.

'Sing!' hissed Richard.

'Down with her, down with her, Dreyfusard! Silence her, silence her, traitor's friend!'

It was a chant. The thing sounded as if it had been rehearsed. And it came from the block of seats that Netta had already noticed.

'Sing!' urged Richard, and began the introduction again.

But the chanting was so loud she could scarcely hear him. And her throat had seized up, as if a steel gate had come down inside it. A red blur came and went in front of her eyes. She stood, scared and at a loss, centre-stage in front of the piano.

'Gentlemen, gentlemen,' called the manager of the hall, coming partly on to the platform. 'This is uncalled for–'

'Shut up, shut up! Off, off! Off the platform! Down with the enemies of the Republic!'

'Gentlemen, Madame de la Sebiq-Tramont is here as a singer–'

'Singer? Can't sing a note! Boo! Boo! Off, get off!'

'Stop it! You stupid, ill-mannered louts.'

'Who's a lout! You're a villain!'

'Sit down! You're treading on my foot!'

'Oh, shut up, you old fool! You – who're you to call me a lout?'

'Down with the Tramonts! Friends of the traitor! Down with Tramonts!'

'Gentlemen, gentlemen!'

But the manager's bleat of complaint was lost in the uproar.

Netta glanced blindly about. From the wings Alfonsini was beckoning, mouthing something she couldn't hear. He was saying, 'Come off, it's no use.'

Something whizzed past her ear – a piece of orange peel. She winced, although it hadn't touched her. Another missile – an egg, it splattered against the piano. Richard sprang up and fled, scattering sheets of music.

Frederic de la Sebiq forced his way down the side aisle and up the little flight of steps to the stage. His dark face was darker yet with anger. He took Netta in his arms, his back a shield against further attack from the crowd.

'Come, darling,' he said in her ear. 'Come away.'

He led her to the wings. Alfonsini was weeping, beating his fists against the proscenium edge.

'Vandals!' he moaned. 'Savages! Pay them no heed, *bambina mia* – they are not important.'

But they were. They had booed Netta de la Sebiq-Tramont off the stage.

Chapter Eight

In the months that followed the police were to become accustomed to brawls arising out of the Dreyfus Affair. On this occasion they were taken by surprise, so there was a long delay before the fighting groups were separated, the upturned chairs and smashed mirrors cleared up, and a safe conduct arranged for the members of the Tramont family trapped in the Salle Berlanger.

Frederic and Netta had a room booked for the night at the Hotel Meurthe-et-Moselle. But the commotion followed them there. Netta, already in a nervous state, was driven almost into hysteria by the shouting and bawling under their windows. They were smuggled out by a back entrance and put aboard the Paris train. Alys Hopetown-Tramont was escorted in her carriage back to Calmady by a stalwart constable in plain clothes.

It was only when they were safely at the Avenue d'Iena that Netta realised her brother was nowhere about.

'He's seeing Mademoiselle Hermilot home, no doubt,' Frederic suggested. 'Shall I look in his room?'

'No, if I never see him again it will be too soon!' cried Netta. 'This is all his fault – he and his stupid devotion to the Dreyfus cause!'

'Now, darling, calm down. You know you don't mean that.'

'I do, I do! I've *told* him and *told* him not to meddle in politics! After all, what have the Dreyfus family to do with us?'

'Nothing, of course, and I'm with you on

that score. I wish Phip would show some sense... But there you are, he never seems to see what's under his nose, which is that protesting about a criminal's sentence is likely to get him in trouble.'

'If he got in trouble himself, I shouldn't mind!' Netta flashed, with much more unkindness than she really felt. 'But why must he drag *me* into it? The most important day of my life—'

'Oh, come now, Netta.'

'It was, Frederic, it *was!* I've been working for it so long...'

Frederic, though not in the least sentimental, couldn't help being a little hurt that his wife should place her debut as a singer above her wedding day and the birth of their child. But he could see she was upset and not quite responsible for what she was saying. He decided to have a very serious word with his brother-in-law when he came home.

Philip didn't come home at all that night. Frederic thought nothing of it or, if he did, took it for granted he was staying with the little dark-haired *belle amie* in her apartment somewhere near Montparnasse. Netta was persuaded to take a soothing drink recommended by Monsieur Alfonsini to help her to sleep, and the big old house in Avenue d'Iena settled down to rest.

On the Monday, one or two friends from

182

the world of music came to comfort Netta. Frederic, having business appointments, left soon after breakfast. When she asked, as an afterthought, 'Have you seen, Phip?' he shrugged, shook his head, and raised his eyebrows expressively.

It even brought a momentary smile of sisterly indulgence to Netta's lips.

Philip was shown into Frederic's office at the House of Tramont's business premises about mid-afternoon. This in itself was unusual – Philip seldom came there because he took no part in the business.

'We-ell,' Frederic said with heavy irony, 'so here you are at last! I trust you had a comfortable night?'

'Frederic,' said Philip, 'I've come to ask for your advice.'

'About what? How to conduct your love affair? Now, now, my boy – I'm a respectable married man these days, – or at least that's the impression I like to give.'

'This is rather serious, Frederic. I'd be glad if we could discuss it without jokes.'

'Oh? Really?' He was taken aback at the heaviness of the tone. As a rule his brother-in-law spoke with hesitancy when he was pressing any claim for attention on his own behalf.

A dreadful thought seized Frederic. Could it be – oh, wearisome prospect! – that the little Hermilot was expecting a baby? If so

... well, the money would be found somewhere to pay her off, but these days any additional expenditure was very unwelcome.

'Sit down, sit down, Phip,' he invited, gesturing at the heavy mahogany chair which stood across from his desk. 'Shall I pour you a drink?'

Philip sat down, rather suddenly, as if his legs had all at once given way. He said, 'I don't want a drink – I mean, not wine or brandy but I'd be glad of something to eat and a cup of coffee. I don't believe I've eaten since lunchtime yesterday.'

'Phip!' Now Frederic was really perturbed. This was more than a hitch in a love affair. When a man forgets to eat, it's serious.

He rang his bell, his secretary appeared. 'Michel, ask the concierge to fetch coffee and croissants from a café – and be quick about it.'

'Yes, sir.' The young man looked with curiosity at Monsieur's brother-in-law, who had an odd appearance – pale, strained, a little dishevelled. One would almost have said he was suffering from a hangover except that Monsieur Hopetown-Tramont wasn't the sort.

'Now, come on, out with it,' Frederic urged when the door closed behind Michel. 'What's wrong?'

'Oh, nothing's wrong – not really, it will all

sort itself out. But you see ... I'm not very accustomed to this kind of thing so I need some advice.'

'On what?'

'I know you'll put me right, Frederic. It's the kind of thing you're good at, having been a soldier and all that.'

'What's my military career got to do with it?'

'Well, you're accustomed to handling them.'

'What, for God's sake?' Frederic was totally baffled.

Philip took off his glasses and began to polish them on a none too clean handkerchief.

'Could you show me how to handle a pistol?'

For a long moment Frederic gaped at him, his black brows arched in disbelief. Then a rush of terrible thoughts: these stupid friends of Phip's – anarchists – violence as a political tool – assassinations...

'Phip, what tomfool scheme have you got yourself involved in now? Because I warn you, I'm not helping you to stage an attack on some right-wing deputy.'

Philip breathed on his lenses to moisten them, polishing assiduously. 'It's nothing like that. I need to know because I don't want to look a fool. I've got to fight a duel in the morning.'

185

Frederic gave a gasp, but it became a laugh. 'Oh, Phip... You really gave me a fright about the pistol! I thought you were going to...' The words began to die away. His brother-in-law seldom made jokes, and when he did, they were always little innocuous sallies, nothing like this mad idea. 'Phip, you're not in earnest.'

'Oh yes.'

'A duel?'

'Yes. In the Bois tomorrow.'

'But ... but ... nobody fights duels these days.' As he said it he knew it was untrue. The code of duelling died hard. It might be against the law, classed as a criminal act like common assault, but men still met each other in the grey light of dawn on matters of honour.

It was particularly well preserved among the officers of the Army and the Navy. One of Frederic's former classmates of St Cyr had had to retire from active service after losing an eye in a duel.

'What happened?'

'I went after the ringleaders of that attack on Netta's debut,' Philip explained. 'Most of them were officers in mufti from the Sixth Corps stationed at Nancy, but the men who took the initiative boarded a train for Paris about nine o'clock last night. I followed them – I lost them at the railway station but by that time I'd heard them calling each other by name. I started making inquiries for them as soon as it was light today—'

'But why? Phip, what on earth did you think you'd achieve?'

'I wanted to reason with them, so they'd apologise,' Philip said, frowning and shaking his head in bewilderment. 'I wanted to tell them... But they wouldn't listen.'

'Tell them what?'

'We know that Captain Esterhazy was the real culprit in the Dreyfus Affair, Frederic. There's enough evidence to bring a case against him and pressure's building up to do just that.'

'You thought you'd achieve something by explaining all that to them? And for God's sake, where was all this?'

It had taken place at a small café near the Statistical Section office, a place used as a club by the young staff officers. Philip had tried but failed to gain admittance to the office of the tall, noisy young man who had taken the lead in shouting abuse at his sister. But at lunchtime the group appeared, ready to continue the celebrations of yesterday for their victory over the forces of political disaffection.

Philip approached them, asked to be allowed a moment of their time.

'I want to explain to you, Lieutenant Daubert, that you're in error—'

'You know my name?' Daubert said,

looking up in surprise from the menu.

'Yes, monsieur, I do. I took the trouble to find it out. I felt that once you'd had it explained to you how wrong you were–'

'Wrong?' exclaimed the lieutenant of Zouaves. He got to his feet, jarring the table so that the wine spilled out of the glasses already filled for his companions. They protested cheerily. As yet no one foresaw that things were going to turn serious.

'Excuse me, I know it's a strong term to use, but you behaved very badly yesterday because you were misinformed – or at least, didn't have the information. I want you to understand what a mistake you made, and then I want you to apologise to my sister.'

'Your sister? Who on God's earth is your sister?'

'Madame de la Sebiq-Tramont.'

'What? *What?* I say, fellows! Just imagine what the cat's brought in! This is one of those damned Tramonts!'

'Jules, Jules, not so loud, my boy,' urged one of his friends. 'You're spoiling our appetites. What's it all about?'

'I'll tell you what it's about! This worm of a Tramont dares to come here – *here,* on our own turf! – and tell me I've been in the wrong to let his family know what we think of them and their crooked friend Dreyfus.'

'That's just the point,' Philip persisted, thrusting down the impulse of anger that kept upsetting his good intentions. 'Captain Dreyfus isn't a crook. We know almost for certain that Major Esterhazy was responsible for the bordereau–'

'Esterhazy? You don't by any means refer to Major Marie-Charles Walsin-Esterhazy?'

'That's the man,' cried Philip with eagerness. 'You know of him.'

'I say, you chaps! This toad is slandering old Marie-Charles!'

'Shame!' cried the others, laughing and digging each other in the ribs. 'Saying bad things about old Major Mocha-Mug himself! Can't have that, can't have that!'

Major Esterhazy was a figure well-known to them. Tall, thin, yellow from old sunburn, he showed signs in his face of the years he had spent abroad in the Foreign Legion. They weren't especially fond of him, but he was a soldier, for God's sake, a former Zouave – you couldn't let a mere civilian cast aspersions on him.'

But they were still good-humoured about it.

'This officer, Esterhazy,' Philip went on, 'he will almost certainly be court-martialled on a charge of treason.'

'Rubbish! Twaddle! Throw him out, Daubert!'

Nothing loth, Lieutenant Daubert caught Philip by the lapels of his jacket, spun him round, and began to march him away from the table. A waiter, already alarmed at the noise, came scuttling to prevent violence. 'Messieurs, messieurs...'

Philip cannoned into him, unable to stop himself because of Daubert's thrust from behind. The waiter fell, Philip on top of him. Daumier stood back, laughing.

'Oh, you tripped! Poor old chap! Diddums hurt umself?' He helped Phip up, dusting him off but in doing so flipping his cravat askew, slapping his shoulder with the back of his hand.

'Monsieur, don't do that!' Philip said, giving him a shove that made him stagger backwards.

'Hey!' cried the audience, delighted. 'He's got some spirit after all! Thought he was going to let you throw him out without a fight, Jules.'

'He's not going to fight. He's a Tramont, isn't he? You couldn't expect anything like decent behaviour from the likes of them. What kind of a bunch can they be, anyhow? Letting one of their womenfolk get up on a public platform to make a fool of herself before strangers?'

'Leave my sister out of it,' Philip said hotly. 'You did enough damage yesterday–'

'No we didn't, not nearly enough. Come on, lads, let's rush him out and throw him in the gutter, to join his sister!'

'Don't dare touch me!' said Philip. All at

once his tone had changed. His voice was low and hard. The others paused, staring at him.

'I say...' began a younger officer at Daubert's elbow. 'Don't let this get out of hand, Jules...'

'Don't worry, it's nothing,' Daubert said in loud contempt. 'Look at him – a snivelling civilian! He and his sister are a well-matched pair – she's a slut and he's a fool.'

'And you, sir, are a cad and a mannerless oaf,' Philip replied.

'Jules, Jules... He doesn't understand...'

'He understands well enough to insult me! Sir, you will retract that remark.'

'No, sir, I will not. I'll go further – you are a coward, because you attacked a woman before her friends then slander her behind her back. You're a rotten coward!'

A deathly hush had fallen. The group of men were staring at the two protagonists. Even the officer who had tried to restrain Daubert was silent.

Daubert reached up to his epaulette strap, drew his gloves from under it, and slapped Philip across the cheek, hard. 'You'll give me satisfaction for that!'

'Certainly.'

Afterwards it was dreamlike. The younger officer, Lenotre, took Philip aside. 'Apologise,' he begged. 'Apologise at once and everything will be forgotten.'

'What I have to apologise for? It was he who insulted my sister and my family.'

No amount of anxious advice would serve. The situation couldn't be altered. Lenotre said: 'It's your privilege to name the weapon, then.'

'Weapon?'

'I'd take pistols, if I were you. Jules is quite a good sabreman, and I daresay you've never...?'

'No, never.' He didn't add that he'd never handled a pistol, let alone a sabre.

'Very well. We'll regard this as my having called on you as per protocol. It's best not to drag this sort of thing out – the police are hot on preventing duels if they can.'

It was only then that Philip thoroughly understood what had happened. He was expected to fight a duel at five next morning in the Bois de Boulogne.

'So you see I need to have some advice about how to cock the thing and aim it,' he explained to his brother-in-law as he eagerly drank the coffee Michel had brought...

'You're not going through with this nonsense?' Frederic shouted, beside himself with horror at the mere idea.

'What else can I do? He insists on satisfaction or an apology – and I can't apologise.'

'Of course you can! Dammit, Phip, a man like that, who'd start a public uproar to spoil things for a harmless woman – I mean, he's nothing but shit! Why do you have to bother about him? Write him an apology!'

Philip was shaking his head. 'It's just what he expects me to do. He thinks I'm a spineless idiot.'

'But, Phip – you could be killed – or badly injured…'

'Then show me how to use a pistol so I can at least shoot back!'

In the end Frederic had to agree to demonstrate how a pistol worked. 'I've got one, not a duelling pistol though, at home in my bureau. You go home and wait for me there. By the way, who's going to be your second?'

'Well, I thought … you, Frederic?'

Dear God, groaned Frederic inwardly.

As soon as he'd got rid of his brother-in-law he told his secretary that he was going out for the rest of the day. He took a hackney to the office of the Statistical Section, gave a note and a good bribe to the corporal on duty, and was admitted in due course to be taken to the room where Lieutenant Daubert worked.

As soon as he saw the man, Frederic knew his mission was useless. He knew the type – big-chested, bombastic, loud-voiced great on talking about 'honour' and 'duty' but with no sensitivity and few morals.

But he had to try.

'Lieutenant, as my note explained, I come representing Philip Hopetown-Tramont–'

'Then you should speak to my second, Lieutenant Lenotre.'

'No, monsieur, it's you I need to talk to. My brother-in-law isn't a fit antagonist, Lieutenant. He scarcely knows one end of a gun from another. When there's shooting on the estate, he almost never takes part. He'll be at a total loss in this affair.'

'He should have thought of that before he started calling me names.'

'Come, monsieur, I think we both know that it was you who started it. You were to blame by distressing my wife–'

'Oh? So *you're* the husband!' Daubert laughed in contempt. 'It's you who should have come after me, monsieur. Why send a boy to do a man's work?'

'I didn't send him. And frankly, I considered you so much beneath my contempt that I never even thought of demanding satisfaction.'

'Sir!'

'Come, come, don't pick a quarrel with me too.' Frederic still had his officer's air of authority and was the senior of Daubert by about eight years. He commanded respect. 'I'm here to try to stop the first one. Monsieur Hopetown-Tramont came to me asking how to handle a pistol – just think of that, lieutenant. He's going to face you

194

tomorrow morning but he hasn't a clue how to do it.'

Daubert flushed and shrugged. 'That's his concern.'

'You mean you're quite ready to shoot a helpless target? You think that's a way to satisfy your honour?'

'The meeting has to take place. If you're asking me to back out … well, I can't.'

'Yes you can. Your fellow-officers will understand. They wouldn't want you to score a bull's-eye on a defenceless man.'

'He'll have a pistol, too!'

'But doesn't even know how to cock it. And his eyesight is so bad he couldn't hit a barn door.'

Daubert couldn't allow himself to feel ashamed. He jutted his jaw. 'Get him to apologise and I'll accept. That's the best I can do.'

'He won't apologise. Would you, in his place?'

'Well, no…'

'Come on, man! You know it's all wrong! 'Call it off.'

'No, I can't do that.' It was true, he couldn't. It wasn't in him to admit he'd been totally in the wrong from the very first in suggesting the barracking of the recital by Madame de la Sebiq-Tramont. All the same, he understood that his antagonist in the duel was very much his inferior in every

195

respect, and it was like shooting a sitting duck to take him on.

'I'll tell you what I'll do,' he said. 'I'll shoot to the side.'

Frederic bit his lip. 'Are you a marksman?'

'Pretty good, pretty good.'

'You can guarantee not to hit him?'

'Thousand devils! Of course I can! Can you guarantee that this nincompoop won't hit me by sheer luck when he takes wavering aim?'

Frederic had to be satisfied with that. It would be better still to prevent the meeting, and that might still be accomplished. When he got home he took his wife aside.

'Netta, the damnedest thing has happened. Phip's got himself involved in a duel.'

She was incredulous, and then, when he had explained, she was terror-stricken. But he reassured her. 'It's all right, if it actually does take place, I've Daubert's word that he'll shoot wide. So Phip's in no real danger. But honestly, it would be better if you could talk him out of it. He's fond of you, Netta – see what you can do.'

She flew to her brother's room to fall on his neck and berate him for his foolishness. For once in his life Philip was angry with her. He disentangled her arms from around him, pushing her away.

'This is nothing to do with you, Netta. I'm astonished that Frederic told you.'

'He told me so I could put a stop to it.'

'How? By persuading me it's unimport-ant? You know better than that–'

'If it's about the stupidity at the concert yesterday, forget it, Phip! It doesn't matter.'

'But it does matter.'

'No, no, I don't really care if they wrecked my debut. It's not important.'

'I was there, Netta. I saw your face–'

'Well, I was surprised and upset... Yes, I admit that. But really, now I think it over...'

'It's not only that, Netta. It's things that man said. You didn't hear him. He despises us!'

'Who? Us Tramonts?' For she recalled the chant, 'Down with Tramonts!'

'Yes, the Tramonts, and anybody who sympathises with Dreyfus.'

'Oh, God, forget Dreyfus, Phip! What's he really got to do with us?'

'I understand now,' Philip said in a low tone, 'for the first time, I really understand, that Dreyfus was a victim. Until today I wanted an open trial, no secrecy, the evidence produced – that's what I wanted. But now that I've met Daubert and his friends I see that we have to demand more. We have to demand that the people who preyed on him are brought to justice. They're bad men, Netta – really bad.'

'But to bring them to justice, you don't have to fight a duel, Phip.'

'If I back down, it'll make them worse. They despise us, think we're useless and spineless. I have to fight Daubert just to show him we're not like that!'

'No, no, don't talk nonsense! If this man has done something wrong—'

'Oh, not him. Probably he's not personally involved. But people like him hate people like me, and there comes a time when you have to make a stand.'

'Please, Phip darling, don't talk yourself into heroics! You know it's not your kind of thing—'

'Yes,' he said, with unexpected bitterness, 'that's it, isn't it? Poor old Phip, full of his high-flown notions, never really facing the real world. Well, this is real, Netta, and I'm facing it.'

'But you can't shoot? You know nothing about duelling!'

'I'll learn all I need to know tomorrow morning, Netta.'

'But you'll be facing a man who—'

'I know who I'll be facing. And I only have to do it once, after all. When it's over he'll know we're not contemptible. That's all I want.'

She couldn't move him. She left his apartment to hurry down to Frederic. 'He's determined...'

'Yes, I was afraid of that.'

'There must be *someone* who could make

him see sense … Mama, perhaps?'

'For God's sake, no, Netta! If he really means to go to the Bois at dawn, the last thing he wants is emotional scenes with his mother – and besides, she couldn't get here in time to stop him.'

'I know!' Netta cried. 'Mademoiselle Hermilot!'

'Who? Oh, the *petite amie*... Well, that might be worth a try. Can you get hold of her?'

'I'll find her!'

She remembered that Mademoiselle Hermilot had a post with the law firm in Philip's building. Although it was now seven in the evening, she flew to the telephone. When the operator at last found the number and put her through, there was no reply. She asked if there was a telephone in the concierge's office. Yes, there was. She was connected.

'Who's there?' came a very loud voice. The concierge was one of those women who distrusted telephones – frightening things that rang when you were busy.

Netta explained that she needed to get in touch with Mademoiselle Hermilot from the notary's office.

'Oh, they've gone, madame. All gone home half an hour since.'

'Do you know Mademoiselle Hermilot's address?'

'No-o... Wait, I believe she once asked to have a package sent on if it was delivered here. Pamphlets and that, it was...' A long delay. Netta could imagine the woman searching among scraps of paper. 'Yes, here it is. Forty-seven Rue de Gons, that's in Montparnasse.'

'Is there a telephone number?'

'No, madame.'

Nor could the operator help. 'There's no telephone in the name of Hermilot nor for that address, madame.'

Netta seized a wrap before running to the door. 'I'm going to find her, Frederic. I've got the address.'

The building was a neat little three-storey block at the top of a steep hill. The concierge came out of her lamplit office, mouth full of bread and cheese, to say that Mademoiselle Hermilot wasn't at home.

'Do you know when she'll be back?'

'Generally she's home by now if she's coming. Gone to one of her meetings, I shouldn't wonder.'

'Where? Have you any idea?'

'Well, I haven't seen much of her over the weekend, see. She went to some affair at Nancy yesterday, came in a bit flustered-like, didn't stop for a chat as she often does. Went out early this morning as usual, never said if she'd be home her regular time. Lessee... Was it tonight she was to be at the

Trade Union office in Rue Lussier? Or was that tomorrow?'

'Rue Lussier? What number?'

'Dunno. You can't miss it, though. It's got a red flag in the window.'

Netta got back into the cab, calling to the driver to go to the Rue Lussier as fast as he could. It was true, you couldn't miss the shop that was the headquarters of the Paviours and Road-menders Union – but there were only two men there, painstakingly going over the books.

'No, lady, the meeting Mademoiselle Hermilot was coming to is tomorrow. Sorry.'

'Have you any idea where she might be this evening?'

'Did she mention anything, George? Lemme think … I believe she said she couldn't come tonight to help with the books 'cos she would be at Avenue Allenton.'

From place to place, address to address, Netta pursued Mademoiselle Hermilot. At ten o'clock she went back to Rue de Gons, hoping that she might have come home. But no.

'May I come in and wait? Surely she can't be long now!'

'Just as you like, madame.'

She waited till one o'clock. Mademoiselle Hermilot didn't appear. The concierge's husband came out, frowning, to say they would like to lock up now, if you please.'

'But Mademoiselle Hermilot hasn't come home yet!'

'Nor won't, neither. This must be one of the nights she stays with a friend – Mademoiselle Dalbie, perhaps, or that little widow over near Père Lachaise.'

Exhausted, Netta gave up. The man found a cab for her, she drove back to the Avenue d'Iena. Her husband and her brother were nowhere to be found.

She never thought of going to bed. She fell asleep sitting up in an armchair, waiting.

It was bad luck for Philip Hopetown-Tramont that he had chosen his brother-in-law as confidant. Frederic, although he had never been the kind of officer typified by Jules Daubert, was bound by the same code of honour. It never occurred to him to do the one thing that would have prevented the duel. He didn't call the police.

Instead he took his brother-in-law out to a shooting range on the outskirts of the city, and there in the covered gallery he attempted to teach Philip how to handle a gun. It was a hopeless task: Philip had no aptitude for it. In any case, Frederic's old army revolver was nothing like the elegant duelling pistol that would be produced from its case by Daubert's seconds.

At about the time that Netta was returning home, the two men went to a hotel nearby,

202

where they had some food and a few hours' sleep. Then, a little after four in the morning, they set out for the Bois.

As they reached it, a light rain was falling. The trees were draped in a grey cloak. Frederic was cheered by the sight. If Philip couldn't see well normally, his opponent wouldn't be able to see well because of the weather.

The cab rolled along the well-made road. Frederic was looking out for signs of the meeting-place. Lieutenant Lenotre stepped out from the shelter of the trees, holding up a hand to stop the driver.

A small group of officers was waiting on the edge of a clearing somewhat into the woods. Daubert, an older officer who would act as umpire, a man wearing the regimentals of the Medical Corps, two others in mufti. There was also an army groom to hold the coats and hats.

'It's my duty to ask if the matter can be resolved by an apology,' Lenotre inquired, looking past Frederic to Philip.

'He's the one that should apologise,' Philip replied, jerking his head angrily at Daubert.

'You are determined to settle the matter by use of arms?'

'Yes.'

'Very well. Colonel Sissincourt?'

The older man came forward, summoning

Daubert. He gave them instructions on how they must conduct themselves: twenty paces which he would count off, turn when he called the command, and fire at his signal. Honour would be satisfied by the discharge of both weapons, blood drawn or no blood drawn. Agreed?

Agreed.

Frederic caught Jules Daubert's eye. He gave the very faintest of shrugs, meaning, 'He still can't shoot – remember your promise!'

Daubert nodded.

The two men selected weapons, Daubert giving Philip preference as a gesture to his inexperience. They stood back to back. The colonel asked if they were ready. 'Very well. I begin counting *now*. One, two, three...'

The distance between them seemed very short when the counting ended.

'Turn. Fire!'

They turned. They fired, Philip stretching out his arm and trying to sight along it as Frederic had explained. But the rain was on his glasses and he couldn't see a thing. His shot went sailing off into the rain.

Daubert, true to his promise, fired one foot to the right of his opponent.

It was just the greatest bad luck that the bullet struck a tree-trunk ten yards away, ricocheted off, and winged straight into the heart of Philip Hopetown-Tramont.

Chapter Nine

Emile Zola was being given a conducted tour of the vine rows close to the manor-house. It was an exceptionally fine July day, so the fields were busy even though it was a Sunday. The sixth spraying had been done, and the third hoeing, so soon it would be the time for the second leaf trim. There is always work to be done in a vineyard in July even if the weather is poor, but if the sun shines the sense of urgency becomes almost frantic.

'Well, I am of course no expert,' Monsieur Zola said, pausing with hands behind his back to study the plants, 'but they look exceedingly healthy to me, mademoiselle.'

Gaby Fournier-Tramont, his escort at the front of the group of visitors, gave a little smile and a sigh. 'At last! The grafts seem to be successful at last. We have had a very anxious time, you know, Monsieur Zola.'

The great novelist gave her a glance that was admiring though somewhat patronising: 'It's unusual for a young lady to be so knowledgeable about matters of business, Mademoiselle Gaby...'

'I'm not knowledgeable. It's just that here

at Calmady we live and breathe the vines. And of course the success or failure of the new method has meant the difference between life and death to wine production.'

'And now these plants from America ... is that correct ... will make your fields immune to the insect?'

'Not exactly. Our native vines will always succumb to the phylloxera aphid, it seems. But by importing American roots and grafting upon them, a certain amount of protection can be given. It appears the insect either doesn't attack the old wild vines or, when it does, makes little headway. From these roots our own grafted vines can take nourishment, as you see.' She made a little gesture with a gloved hand at the healthy green on the vine leaves. 'This is the second year of grafted vines in full production. We've put all our vines in one basket!' She laughed, anxious to keep the great man entertained.

To tell the truth, she didn't find him good company. He was so self-centred, so self-important. But he had done something vital for the cause of Alfred Dreyfus so it was necessary to be grateful to him, to show concern for him, to offer him hospitality and admiration.

Behind her the rest of the Tramonts and their friends were following in desultory groups. Her brother David was squiring

Mademoiselle de Caillavet, at whose salon an equally great writer, Anatole France, had often spoken strongly in favour of Dreyfus. One of the lawyers involved in Zola's defence had given his arm to Gaby's mother and was bending his knee to listen to some quiet comment from her.

The senior menfolk of the House of Tramont were at the back of the group, standing about, evidently talking about the possibilities of this year's grapes, or deep in conversation that excluded thoughts of their surroundings.

And indeed there was plenty to talk about. So much had happened in the last year!

Cousin Philip's death had changed everything. The efforts of the Tramont family to get justice for the killing had been thwarted, almost sneered at. The examining magistrate who heard the evidence against Jules Daubert ruled that there was no case and was privately heard to say that he couldn't be expected to help a bunch of Dreyfusards to drag down an honourable officer. Daubert himself was quietly given a transfer to service in Tunis, to get him out of harm's way.

Although until then Gaby's father and her Uncle Gavin hadn't been too keen on Phip's support of Dreyfus, the tragedy of his loss and the contempt with which they were treated had brought them to understand his feelings. Uncle Gavin had accepted an invitation to join a committee, had given what money he could. Papa had spoken in public demanding a re-opening of the case. Not one member of the family thought of protesting when Netta, with advice from the grieving Elvi Hermilot, began to work with various little groups in Paris, carrying on where her dead brother left off.

Due to the efforts of the 'Dreyfusards', Major Esterhazy had been given a court-martial. To the amazement and despair of all those who knew the facts, the court cleared him.

Emile Zola perhaps wanted a 'cause' to which he could pin his colours. He had just finished a great trilogy of novels – *Lourdes, Rome, Paris* – and was suffering from a feeling of listlessness, of lack of direction. And of course as a radical and a socialist he was interested in anything that would unsettle a conservative government.

The various workers in the cause of Dreyfus supplied him with information. Netta herself had hurried to and from his house in Paris with folders of letters and pamphlets. During the thirty-six hours after Esterhazy was acquitted, Zola composed a long open letter to Felix Faure, President of France. It listed a catalogue of misdeeds and injustices, each prefaced with the words, 'I Accuse'. He named names, cited facts. He had ended with: 'As for the people I accuse, I do not know them … I bear them neither ill will or hatred … let them dare to bring me to the Assize Court and may the examination be made in the light of day. I wait!'

On January 12th 1898 he took the letter to the offices of *L'Aurore*. It's editor Georges Clemenceau, later to be known as The Tiger, had the idea of running it under the banner of 'I Accuse!' The paper went on sale first thing in the morning. By the evening, two hundred thousand copies had been sold.

Consternation followed in the Chamber of Deputies. The government decided to play everything down. But a petition was started, signed by almost everyone of significance in France's cultural scene – among the names were Monet, Anatole France, Marcel Proust.

Now members of the Chamber of Deputies began to lose their tempers with each other. Insults were exchanged, the Palace Guard had to be called to stop the fighting that broke out.

Duelling almost came back into fashion. Journalists and politicians on either side of the cause called each other out. Clemenceau fought Drumont, Picquart fought Henry. Clerics bewailed the disintegration of law and order.

Zola's invitation to bring him to court was

accepted. He was arrested and held until charged with libel in February. His defence was that he could substantiate every accusation. Therefore dozens of witnesses were called – and though the case was ostensibly against Emile Zola, the prosecution found itself having to listen to story after story which reflected on the justice of Dreyfus's imprisonment.

The newspapers published scores of columns of almost verbatim reporting. Major Esterhazy began to look less and less honourable. The famous bordereau, the chief evidence against Dreyfus, was almost certainly written by Esterhazy – although it might have been produced at the instructions of someone higher up. If anyone had been selling information to the Germans, it looked as if it wasn't Dreyfus.

Nevertheless the court ruled against Zola. He hadn't proved that his accusations against named officers and ministers were true. He appealed on technical grounds, glorying in the notoriety the trial had brought him and, to do him justice, pleased that he had brought in some much needed light and air on the Dreyfus Affair. He was released pending further proceedings.

Now, in mid-July, he was about to be re-tried at a court in Versailles. Hence this gathering at Calmady on the preceding weekend, for it was clear to everyone that the courts intended to find him guilty again. This time, there would be no grounds for appeal. The sentence, which was likely to be severe, would be final. The purpose of the little weekend conference was to persuade Emile Zola to leave France.

But for the moment he preferred not to think of that. He had had a pleasant visit with the Tramonts, was being escorted on his afternoon walk by an exceedingly beautiful young lady, and all was well with his world.

'So, Mademoiselle Gaby,' he said, tugging at his little Vandyke beard, 'you didn't have a "white ball" for your coming out.'

'No, it would have been inappropriate, don't you agree – considering that we were still in deep mourning for Philip. And to tell the truth, I was pleased. I've never liked this idea of a big fuss.'

'I can only say it's a great shame, mademoiselle. You would have been a huge success.'

She smiled and gave a little bow in acknowledgement of the compliment. 'I shall have my small success, perhaps, next week. I'm having a little provincial coming-out party here at Calmady.' She took off a glove, to run a hand along a vine branch, gently and with affection. 'This is where we belong, after all. Paris has almost become a place where we go merely to do battle.'

'Ah, you can say what you like, but Paris is the centre of the world,' he replied with the conviction of a Parisian born and bred. 'And the battles we do there are the cynosure of all eyes. No one can really be a success in France unless he captures Paris – either figuratively or metaphorically.'

'There's truth in that, of course, m'sieu. Cousin Netta is good at that part of the fight. I try to be a help to her, but–'

'You are too young and beautiful to spend your time on politics, mademoiselle.' He took her hand and kissed it.

She was amused at the clumsy compliment but hid the fact. It was important to keep Monsieur Zola in a good mood. They *must* persuade him to leave the country if the court condemned him. For what use was he to them if he was in prison? They needed him free and able to write, even if it had to be from abroad.

After an early dinner that evening Gaby's father escorted Zola and the other guests to the station. When he came back the family were awaiting him in the drawing room.

'Well, Robert?' Gavin demanded as his partner limped in and sat rather heavily in a corner of the sofa.

Robert nodded. 'Yes, he's agreed. He had enough of prison when they shut him up after "I Accuse". We're making travel arrangements for him to go to England.'

'Papa, maybe the judges will acquit him,' David put in.

Everyone turned to stare at the young man. 'If you really believe that,' his Aunt Alys said grimly, 'you had better give up studying law at once – you're too naïve to survive.'

The family party broke up for the night. They were anxious yet determined. Things were moving at last. Although they were still not winning, the government was greatly on the defensive. In time, in time... In time there would be justice.

Although the sentence against Zola of a year's imprisonment was what they had expected, they were downcast next day when the news came through. But then friends in Paris telephoned to say that Zola was safely off across the Channel. He would go on with his campaigning in the friendly security of England. Alys had already written to dear old Grandpapa Gri-gri asking him to give hospitality to the writer and make sure he found a comfortable billet for his sojourn abroad.

Now it was time to turn to family matters. Gaby's coming-out ball was to be the following Thursday. It was an awkward time to be giving it, with work so pressing in the winefields. But it was the earliest date that Laura Fournier-Tramont had felt able to arrange.

Her nephew Philip had been killed at the beginning of October. His parents and sister had been in deepest black ever since. At least six months had to be allowed to go by before the question of Gaby's coming-out could be discussed, and then of course it was too late for Paris, even if they could have afforded the season.

Now, nine months into the year's mourning, it would be allowable to have a ball, nothing elaborate, and that was all to the good because there would be less expense. Alys Hopetown-Tramont had agreed to attend briefly and to wear colours – perhaps grey or heliotrope. This hint to their friends and neighbours brought a good number of acceptances. All the same, there was an awkwardness. People didn't like being too mixed up with a family who embraced the cause of Dreyfus so openly and fervently. And who actually invited that awful M. Zola *to the house!*

'Well, my dear, I'm sure we've done all we can,' Laura observed as they sat in her little boudoir ticking names on lists. 'The menus will arrive tomorrow I wish the printer had been more prompt but there are always these little hitches...'

'Oh, Mama, people can see what's on the buffet table! We don't need menus!'

'Gaby, dear, people like to take them home as keepsakes. And this is a rather special

214

occasion so they'll want them all the more.'

'You mean they'll want them as mementoes of actually sitting on the same chair as that firebrand Zola, or eating off the same dish as the singer Netta de la Sebiq-Tramont.'

Laura smiled. Gaby's outspoken style always amused her. There had been a time when she'd worried about it – because her friends used to shake their heads and say it would drive away prospective husbands. But everything was different these days. Her outlook on life had changed completely. Little things didn't trouble her any more.

Not that a husband for Gaby was exactly a little thing. But Laura had come to the conclusion that her daughter wouldn't settle easily into matrimony and that it would be better to let her stretch her wings a little first. After all, Gaby's cousin Netta had taken her time about making a match, and look how well that had turned out.

The ball on Thursday was a slight bow of recognition to convention, Laura felt. The rest was up to Gaby – if she didn't wish to launch herself into the marriage market, well and good. The death of her nephew Philip had made the elder Tramonts realise how precious were their children – to be loved and valued rather than forced into some mould that the rest of society respected.

Events at the Tramont ball turned out

quite differently from all expectations, however.

There were eighty guests, about half of whom were expected to dance. The mothers of the young ladies had been at work for some days ensuring that their daughters' *carnets* were suitably full of partners. Young men weren't so plentiful as might have been the case in a Paris ballroom and so Laura had accepted two or three strangers – all of course vouched for by families well-known to her.

There was a six-piece orchestra, locally recruited, to play the required waltzes, gallops and two-steps. They were rendering a country-dance, allowable since this was a provincial ball, when noises from outside began to drown them out. There was the sound of wagon-wheels, men's voices raised in shouts.

The dancers faltered, the music began to die. Now the guests could make out the words of the shout.

'Down with Tramonts! Down with the dirty Dreyfusards!'

'Oh, my God!' gasped Laura, putting out a hand blindly for her husband.

He grasped it. 'Don't be afraid, Laura. It's just some bunch of hooligans.'

'But how did they get in?'

Only too easily, of course. None of the estate staff would have expected interlopers.

A wagon trundling along the road to the mansion – who could have expected it to bring trouble-makers?

Grooms and gardeners came running. They found a flat-bed wagon pulled up on the terrace outside the house. To get there it had ploughed through the shrubbery. Two heavy horses had been set free from their harness and, cut across the rear with whips, had gone galloping off in fright through the flower-beds.

A band of men were standing on the wagon, holding banners and bawling. The grooms grabbed at them, to haul them down. One man was kicked in the head and went down, blood streaming from a bad scalp wound.

The male guests had reacted after their fashion. Some had run to the windows to order the hooligans off, others had retreated to the far side of the room.

Robert put his wife into a high-backed chair. 'Stay there, dear.' He moved towards the windows. Some of the older men fell in beside him. Among them he noticed Marc Auduron, junior partner in the law firm who handled his affairs in Rheims, and Grossard, the head of the bottle-making firm.

The scuffle on the terrace had turning into a big fight. Worse yet, when they got out there the guests found there were reinforcements coming through the shrubbery – at least another dozen men, silhouetted against the summer sky.

The gamekeeper of the estate happened to be near the house, on his rounds – he'd really come to peep in through the windows and see Mademoiselle in her pretty white ballgown. Lasalle understood the problem at once. He brought up his shotgun, slapped it closed. 'Hey!' he shouted. 'Clear out or I fire!'

'Yah! Traitors! Rotten bastards–'

Lasalle fired one barrel into the air. 'The second barrel goes through you lot! Now clear off!'

The men retreated, leaving the injured groom on the flagstones. Lasalle ran after them, with others of the estate staff.

Gaby Fournier-Tramont sped to the dais on which the orchestra was sitting, instruments loose in their grasp.

'Play!' she commanded. 'Play, boys!'

The 'boys', most of them old enough to be her father, tucked violins under chins, put trumpets to lips. The leader banged with his foot – one, two. The band broke out into the tune they'd been playing when they were interrupted: 'High the summer garland raise, Round our village take your ways...'

Gaby wheeled to the room. She threw out her hands. 'Let's dance, my friends!'

A broken cheer rang out. Men offered their hands to ladies. The ladies, a little pale, tottered back into the double line of the country dance. The men, looking determined, made hands-across and partners-swing. Gaby's partner took her by the elbow and led her down the middle of the rows.

His name was Lucas Vourville, unknown to her until that evening, friend of a friend in Epernay but from a family owning engineering works in Lille. He was tall, very fair, and about twenty-two years old. He was also greatly smitten by the extraordinary good looks of the girl who now re-met him in the turns of the country dance – her flashing dark eyes, her minute waist in its finely-boned gown of white tulle and pale pink rosebuds...

If he hadn't admired her before, he certainly would now, after her bravery. How wonderful, to lead them back into the dance without caring for the intruders!

There came a smashing of glass as they danced to the end of the row. The terrace window came in, sending smithereens towards them that sparkled like ice crystals. Lucas clasped her in his arms bodily and swung her round so that his broad-cloth-covered back caught the shower.

The trespassers had been driven back out of the garden. But in the dark, and taken by surprise, the servants couldn't get rid of them. There was easily-found ammunition among the bricks for the rebuilding of the loading-shed. Now they came hurtling through the windows, lobbed from beyond the terrace.

'Are you all right?' Lucas asked Gaby, taking the excuse to hold her close.

'I'm fine,' she said, making no attempt to release herself. She was trembling, and quite frightened, but she was also elated in some strange way.

All her life Gaby had been surrounded by handsome men. Her father's sombre good looks, Uncle Gavin's open English features, Cousin Frederic's almost Latin charm, even her brother David's dreamy goodness... But Lucas Vourville was different. She thought he looked like some young sun-god from a Greek temple.

She had been educated at a strict girls' school. There, her schoolmates went through the usual romantic dreams and crushes on such males as were available – but in actual fact there had been few opportunities to be in close contact with a man.

Now she found herself held close against the fast-beating heart of a tall, handsome stranger. And she felt her own heart melting away within her breast.

'Well, sweetheart,' Robert said next day to his wife, 'despite all the interruptions, it seems to have been a successful ball.'

'I don't know how you can say that!'

mourned Laura. 'Madame Auduron's gown was ruined by flying glass. And as far as I can see, the police are quite unable to say who was responsible.'

'I didn't mean that, Laura. Of course we suffered some damage, and I suppose we ought to offer to pay for Madame Auduron's gown. What I meant was, did you see our daughter as she said goodbye to Lucas Vourville?'

'Oh, that... Well, of course... They were brought unexpectedly close together by the incident of the stone-throwing.'

'You mean you think it was just the mood of the moment?'

'Whatever it was, Robert, we mustn't let it run away with us. Who is Monsieur Vourville, actually?'

'Well, his invitation was obtained and vouched for by the Rollins, wasn't it? The Rollins are very respectable people, dear.'

'We shall see what comes of it. If he's visiting with them and goes elsewhere soon, we may not see him again.'

'Oh... Do you really think that?'

Laura nodded her dark head. But then she added with a faint smile, 'It might be as well to make a few inquiries about him, all the same.'

Messages as to the family's welfare poured in as soon as a reasonable mid-morning hour arrived. The telephone never stopped ringing with regards and good wishes. Although not all the neighbours approved of the Tramonts' involvement with the Dreyfus affair, they had a wholesome landowners' respect for property – the thought that strangers could surge in and wreck a social occasion was abominable.

Lucas Vourville came himself with Adrien Rollin in the afternoon. Anxious inquiries were made as to the health of the ladies after such an upset to the nerves. Somehow it happened that Lucas Vourville spirited Gaby off to a shaded corner of a vine arbour, there to be unearthed when it was time and more than time for the afternoon call to end.

'I really had better make some investigations into him,' Robert said when he heard about it.

The information obtained was quite acceptable. The Vourvilles had been iron-masters, had now gone over to heavy engineering. They weren't extraordinarily rich, but then neither were the Tramonts in these hard times. There was a married sister, the alliance very suitable, a haut-bourgeois family in Belgium.

'Well, if he comes asking for Gaby's hand, I shan't close the door on him,' Robert said.

But that was just the problem. The young couple seemed to be so wrapped up in each other that they were content to be swept along without looking about them. Robert, after a few weeks and at Gavin's instigation, took the young man gently to task.

'I must ask you, monsieur, whether you have any intentions other than a long friendship with my daughter?'

Lucas was taken aback. 'What? Oh – I ... I...'

'I have no objection to the friendship, of course. Only it must not be so exclusive. Since you came to our ball in July, she has scarcely spoken to anyone else.'

'Oh, I'm sorry, monsieur... Yes, I suppose that's true... Well, then... Yes, of course ... I ... I...'

'Have you any reluctance to think of marriage?'

'Not at all,' said Lucas. In fact, his family had been hinting that a good match would be gratefully received.

'In that case, may I ask you to go home and speak to your father, and then if you wish to continue the relationship with my daughter, you might return with some proposals?'

'Certainly, sir, of course. I'll go to Lille in the morning.'

Gaby moped and grizzled all through his interminable absence – a whole four days. When he returned, he went straight to Robert with a formal proposal for Gaby's hand.

'So now we don't have to keep trying to snatch moments alone together. We're officially allowed!' he said with a chuckle to Gaby.

She rested her head against his shoulder. 'I shouldn't get too optimistic. Mama's very kind-hearted, but she'll keep an eye on us, you know.'

Laura intended to do just that, but things were happening again in the matter of Captain Dreyfus. Colonel Henry, long known to be implicated in the affair, had been forced to admit forging two letters used in evidence. Rather than face a court-martial, he committed suicide. And immediately after that the man whom the Dreyfus supporters considered to be the arch-enemy had fled to Belgium.

Naturally the Dreyfus family had filed an appeal to the Minister of Justice for a re-opening of the case. Laura was deeply involved in helping. And normally her little daughter would have been acting as helper, writing letters on her behalf on the newly bought typewriter. Well, let the child enjoy what was rightfully hers – the joys of falling in love. Laura would manage without her.

So, unsupervised, Gaby wandered about the grounds with Lucas. Kisses and caresses became more and more passionate. Gaby's soul seemed to be unleashed when he touched her. And Lucas was a sexually knowledgeable young man, accustomed to having girls surrender to his charms. His career at university had been a succession of easy conquests among the midinettes and shopgirls.

Soon he was begging Gaby for more. 'Why not, dearest heart? We'll be married soon, as soon as our families have sorted out the settlements. Why should we wait for someone else to tell us when we can belong to each other?'

'No, darling... It would be wrong... Mama would be so upset...'

'But she need never know! It's so easy, Gaby. We can meet in Paris.'

And it was indeed easy. Gaby had only to say that she was going to Paris to give some help to her Cousin Netta, who had a concert coming up soon. Laura, unsuspicious, gave her permission. Gaby took the train to Paris, her heart hammering at the thought of what she was about to do but full of yearning to give herself utterly to the man she loved.

Lucas had told her he had a friend with a little apartment in the Rue de Rome. She took a cab, was set down at the door. The concierge knew better than to take any notice of this little beauty who, with cheeks flushed in love and apprehension, ran up the stairs.

Lucas opened the door when she tapped on it with gloved knuckles. She fell into his

225

arms. From that moment everything was a perfect and lovely dream, as he carried her into the bedroom. His hands tenderly undid the tiny buttons of her boots, his lips kissed her instep, his voice murmured in her ear as he slipped the embroidered lawn underwear from her shoulders.

Afterwards they lay in bed in each other's arms. 'One day I'll tease you about all this,' she told him lovingly. 'When you're an old married man and you look at a pretty girl, I'll say I know you're capable of enticing her into wickedness...'

'How can it be wicked to be so in love?'

'Oh, of course it's not wicked – nothing you could ever do would be wicked or wrong, my darling!'

But their time together was over for now. She had to dress and hurry to the Avenue d'Iena, where she was sure her Cousin Netta must see in her face that she had just spent two hours with her lover.

They were able to meet twice more in the little apartment. Then Lucas was summoned home to Lille for some business reason. Gaby pined, but each night as she fell asleep with his photograph in her arms she was sure he'd be back next day.

A week went by, oddly enough, without even a letter. Then her mother requested Gaby to come to her in her boudoir.

'My darling,' she said, after gesturing her

to the chaise longue beside her, 'are you very, very set on marrying Lucas Vourville?'

Gaby, who had been about to lie back and dream of him while her mother talked about something else, sat up. 'What a strange question!'

'But what's the answer?'

'Of course I'm "set" on marrying him. I love him!'

'Yes, dearest. But ... you see ... there's a problem...'

'What problem? What problem can there possibly be? We love each other, our families want the marriage–'

'Well, that's just the point, Gaby. We do want the marriage, but the Vourvilles are asking for financial terms that we can't possibly meet.'

'What?'

'You must understand, Gaby – although the Tramonts are by no means poor, our money is tied up in our land, our warehouses, our stocks of wine such as they are. Our Monsieur Auduron – of the law firm, you know he specialises in company finance and he says we can't possibly produce the sum Monsieur Vourville's lawyers are asking for as part of the bargain.'

Gaby gave a great laugh of relief. 'Oh, if that's all! It's all nonsense. Lucas doesn't care about the money. He'll tell them not to be silly.'

Laura looked away. 'Darling, Lucas was sent for to come home so that they could give him this news. As far as I can gather, he isn't going to come back unless we can agree on the money matter.'

'Nonsense!'

'Don't say that to me, Gaby. Don't rush along like a torrent, heading straight for a waterfall... Has he written to you since he went away?'

'Well, no...' A chill touched Gaby's heart at the question. It was odd. She had written every day to Lucas, but she had had no replies. 'He's busy, I suppose – arguing with his silly parents and his silly lawyer!'

Laura took both her daughter's hands. 'I'm afraid the match is going to fall through, my darling. You must brace yourself–'

'No!' She sprang up, wrenching herself away from her mother's gentle grasp. 'You don't understand! Of course we're going to be married! We must, we must!'

Laura was shaking her head. She got up, to catch at Gaby before she ran out. 'Gaby, I'm afraid you must face the disappointment – Lucas either wants to back out or has let himself be persuaded–'

'No, no! He never would! You don't understand!'

In floods of tears, she ran to her room. She threw herself on the bed, sobbing and beating the silk counterpane. For a long time she wept, angry yet afraid.

But her courage reasserted itself. She sat up, wiped her eyes with the palms of her hands, and went to her bureau. There she wrote a hasty note.

'Dearest, I've had the silliest discussion with Mama about our engagement. She says your family want to break it off. I know it's all nonsense but you and I had better meet so as to decide how to put things right. I'll be at the Rue de Rome on Wednesday at four o'clock. Yours who belongs to you, Gaby.'

She was at the apartment ten minutes ahead of time. The concierge, with a little *moue* of surprise, let her in. 'M'sieu didn't let me know he was coming today...'

'He'll be here soon.'

But he was not. She waited and waited. The sky began to darken with the coming of the late September evening. The concierge came into the room, noisily letting herself in with her key.

'I must ask you to leave, mademoiselle. This is a private apartment and you have no right here.'

'No, please!'

'I must ask you to leave, mademoiselle. The rooms are needed.'

Gaby stared at her in the dusk, then went red with shame. Of course. Some other

229

loving couple were due to come here this evening. This wasn't the apartment of a friend – it was a house of assignation.

She sprang to her feet, almost knocking the woman over as she ran out.

How could she ever have been such a fool...?

Outside she hurried along the street, blinded by something not yet tears. She found herself outside the Tramonts' Paris house. Yes, of course ... Cousin Netta...

She went in and in a voice almost unrecognisable told the maid she must see Madame de la Sebiq-Tramont. After a moment she was shown up to Netta's bedroom, where her cousin was changing for an evening engagement.

'Gaby! My God, little cousin! What's the matter?'

'Netta! Oh, Netta!' She threw herself into her cousin's arms. The floodgates opened. She let hysteria claim her. 'Netta, he doesn't want me! He's let me down!'

'What? Who? Gaby, Gaby, quiet now – Gaby, sit down!' With one hand Netta was ringing for the maid. When she came in she called over the sobbing girl's head, 'Smelling salts and brandy! And Jeanette, telephone the Malvasons and say the master and I shan't be able to make it to their dinner party.'

About ten minutes later Frederic put his

head round the door. 'What's going on?' he said. He was in white tie and tails, ready for the evening. 'Jeanette tells me you've cancelled.'

'I'll explain later. Telephone Calmady, will you, darling, and say that Gaby is with me, quite safe and sound. I can't quite understand whether they know she's come to Paris or not.'

'But what's it all about?'

'Not now, Frederic.' She was chafing Gaby's cold hands, kneeling at the side of the boudoir armchair in which she'd placed her.

Presently she had some strong hot coffee brought in. Gaby sat up and with trembling hands held the big cup to her lips.

'Now, my dearest girl, tell me so I can understand. What has happened?'

'Lucas has cried off.'

'Oh, no…'

'Mama told me on Monday but I didn't believe her. I thought it was some silly mix-up over the money.'

'Ah, Frederic mentioned that Auduron was shaking his head over that.' Frederic, who of course took part in the discussions about the financial side of the match, had confided that the Vourvilles were asking for a very large investment in their engineering works. It seemed they wanted to expand into some new technique and regarded the dowry of their son's bride as a sensible way to finance it.

'I wrote to him ... I told him I was sure it was a mistake ... I expected to meet him today...'

'To meet him? In Paris? Where, Gaby?' Netta asked, shocked.

'Never mind, it doesn't matter. We had a place. But he never came. I waited hours. Hours and hours. But he never came, he never even sent a message.'

'But you should not have been meeting Lucas in such circumstances in any case!'

'Oh, Netta, how could he do this? We have to get married! We belong to each other! He can't just turn his back on me after what we've been to each other!'

'Gaby,' Netta said, drawing her young cousin's head against her shoulder. 'Tell me... You and he are lovers?'

She was almost ashamed of even asking the question. It couldn't possibly be. Young innocent, trusting Gaby – *surely* no man who had been asked to the Tramonts; house would ever do such a thing.

But she felt Gaby's head nod.

'Oh, darling...'

'I love him so much! It seemed right that we should give ourselves to each other... We were to be married, it was good and right...'

Netta sat with her arm about her little cousin. Only two things were clear to her now. One was that Lucas Vourville had treated Gaby very badly, and the other was that Aunt Laura must never know what had happened.

Things were bad enough without making them worse.

Chapter Ten

Netta had no trouble persuading Gaby's parents to let her stay a day or two more. As for her unchaperoned escapade to Paris, it was put down to a little crisis of nerves over the uncertainty of her engagement.

Two days later Robert and Laura Fournier-Tramont came to the house in the Avenue d'Iena. They brought with them the formal letter of regret from Lucas to Gaby, enclosed unsealed papers from the Vourville lawyers ceremoniously withdrawing from negotiations.

Gaby read it, dry-eyed. As she handed it back to her father she said, 'Must it be kept?'

'No, the legal papers are enough.'

'I should like you to burn it.'

'Certainly.' He stepped to the fireplace, threw the paper on the flames, then with a poker knocked the flinders to pieces. His dark face was grim.

'Don't blame yourself, Papa,' Gaby said. 'He just didn't love me enough.'

'Adrien Rollin feels he is to blame,' her mother said in a shaky voice. 'Since he shares our views on the Dreyfus Affair, he didn't make too much of an issue of it to the young Monsieur Vourville. But his people dislike that. And then Adrien thinks he put too much emphasis on our money and local prestige. And you know ... our house does look as if we still have plenty of money.'

Especially for the ball, thought Netta. She herself had been unable to attend, but she had seen the preparations. She could imagine the sparkle of the chandeliers, the profusion of flowers, the excellence of the food.

She suspected that her aunt had used her personal allowance, from her father Arnold Simeon in New York, to finance it. Since she became interested in the Dreyfus Affair the money had gone into paying for necessary expenses on that score but, for her daughter's coming-out, Laura would have deflected it to this one great event.

'You aren't to blame, my love,' Robert said, anxious as always to shield his wife from distress. 'I was too informal over the opening of negotiations. You remember, I sent Lucas back to Lille to speak to his people. He probably went under all sorts of delusions. I should have got Marc Auduron to draw up a paper to take with him.'

'It's no one's fault. Please stop trying to account for it. Let's stop even thinking about it!' Gaby ran out of the room.

Laura brushed away tears from her eyelashes with her knuckles. 'What's to happen now? No matter how discreet we've tried to be, this must harm her future prospects.'

'Let her stay on in Paris a while,' Netta suggested. 'The season is over, there are few to gossip and giggle about it – fewer than at Calmady, where I do recall they looked terribly in love whenever you saw them.'

'If I ever meet that young man again, I'll kill him,' Robert said through gritted teeth.

'Now, dear,' Laura said, putting out a hand to calm him. He took it. They sat side by side, looking sad and weary.

By and by they left. Robert had business at the Paris office, Laura had to see colleagues at the campaign HQ.

When Frederic came home he'd heard the latest news from his uncle-in-law. 'It's a rotten business,' he remarked as he sat in their room, watching Netta do her hair in a new fashionable style of side coils.

She shrugged.

'And yet, you know, they may come together after all, in time.'

'Never!' Netta cried, with so much

vehemence that her hand jerked and she tangled a comb in her hair.

Frederic came to stare at her reflection. 'How can you be so sure?'

'It's something I can't explain – a man wouldn't understand.'

'Oh, feminine intuition and all that,' he said, taking hold of a strand of tangled hair and giving it a tweak. 'Well, stranger things have happened, my angel. I could tell you of a case where a very cantankerous young lady put all sorts of difficulties in the way of a match with a very excellent young man, but in the end they got married. Though whether that was a good idea,' he concluded, 'I really can't say, for she leads him a dog's life.'

'That was different,' Netta said, repairing the damage to the hairstyle. 'There was far less emotion involved between us two.'

'Ye-es.' Frederic didn't sound entirely convinced.

'And you were far less avaricious than this young man, and us Tramonts had more money at the time.'

Frederic pulled her head back, using the strand of hair as a tether, and kissed her on the lips. She struggled free, gasping.

'I can't breathe, all upside down like that!'

'All right then, let's try again.' He drew her to her feet and kissed her with an urgency she recognised.

'No, now, Freddi – dinner will soon be ready...'

'Who cares? Not even Gaby – she doesn't care if she eats or not. And I'm not hungry. For food,' he ended, as he guided her to the big double-bed.

'Oh, Freddi, you're so...'

'What?'

'Loveable,' she said, as she wound her arms about him.

Downstairs in the drawing room, dressed for dinner and waiting to be summoned to the dining room, Gaby Fournier-Tramont scarcely noticed the long delay. She was deep in her thoughts.

Her reflection in the mirror as she changed had told her she looked as pretty as ever. Prettier, perhaps, since her dark eyes seemed larger and had a haunting, plaintive look that was somehow attractive.

She could still catch any man she wanted, she told herself. The trouble was, she didn't want anyone but Lucas. Well, so much the better. She'd take her time about finding a husband. And she wouldn't let her emotions get the upper hand again.

She knew now that there was a side of her nature that craved to be satisfied. But she also knew – didn't she? – that you didn't have to be married for that. When it came to choosing a husband or a lover, she'd take care always to be in control.

Netta found her difficult to entertain for the next week or two. She was quiet, introspective, unwilling to undertake activity. But Netta had many activities she must attend to.

In the first place there was her own career. She had her lessons as usual, and there were two concerts looming up.

Then there was renewed energy in the Campaign for a Re-trial. After the suicide of Henry and the flight of Esterhazy, the friends of Captain Dreyfus were renewing their efforts. It was clear that the evidence in the first trial had been corrupt. Surely the government would grant a new one?

In February of the following year the old President died. At his funeral an idiot called Deroulede, a member of the Chamber of Deputies, tried to stage a coup d'etat. His plan was to introduce a quasi-dictatorship.

Even the conservative members were shocked at that. A groundswell arose. In the upper ranks of the government of France, it was clear, there were many self-seeking, wrong-headed men.

At the end of February the Senate passed a law sending the Dreyfus Case to the Appeal Courts. In June the Court ruled that there should be a re-trial. A week later the news came that Alfred Dreyfus had left Devil's Island, the most hideous of prisons, to face the courts and establish his innocence at last.

The surge of events caught up even Gaby Fournier-Tramont. Her mother's joy at their success was so pure that it would have been selfish, almost obscene, to tarnish it with her own petty unhappiness. She began to take part in the organisation of support meetings, to help draft letters to the press and then to copy them out on the machine that few as yet had mastered, the typewriter.

Yet the verdict of the Appeal Court judges had brought penalties with it. A feverish anti-semitism seized some of the population. It was even believed by some that the Appeal Court judges – all forty-six of them – had been bribed with Jewish money.

The Tramonts suffered public execration as did all Dreyfus's supporters. Theirs was a greater suffering because Gaby's mother was of Jewish blood. Gaby felt the sting of the charge, but made herself ignore it. It was true – Jewish blood ran in her veins. But she was a Frenchwoman first, foremost, and always.

The re-trial was held in Rennes, that old prefecture of Brittany, with its beautiful old parliament building used as the law courts. It had survived a fire, lasting seven days, which had destroyed most of the city in the early eighteenth century. 'If it survives the intensity of the Dreyfus Trial, it will be a monument indeed,' said Emile Zola.

Everyone in the pro-Dreyfus camp was confident. So many of the original witnesses against him had been discredited – it was impossible that, in a new trial, he could fail to be given back his freedom.

Little Elvi Hermilot, who had worked so hard in the cause both before and after the death of Philip Hopetown-Tramont, came to the Avenue d'Iena on the great day to await the verdict. 'He will be acquitted, I know he will,' she said in a tremendous voice, 'and Philip won't have died in vain.'

The women of the Tramont household smiled at her. She was a strange little creature, very earnest, desperately anxious for justice and for the betterment of mankind. She gave lessons in the slums of Paris in her spare time, trying to teach the wild neglected children to read and write so they could get decent jobs.

'Philip should have been here,' Alys said. 'He should have shared the triumph that he worked for. But oh, what I really want is for it all to be over!' She glanced about apologetically. 'Forgive me, Laura – I don't want you to think I begrudge the work and time we've all put in. But I'm so *tired* of being at odds with my neighbours, with seeing our name in some of the papers classed with criminals and traitors...'

To Netta's surprise Alys began to cry. She went to her, putting a protective arm about the shaking shoulders in their half-mourning of grey silk. 'Don't cry, Mama. It *will* be over soon.'

It was known that the counsel for the defence would finish his summing up of the case about noon. The Tramonts expected the verdict to be announced soon after lunch, and then either Robert or Gavin would telephone the news to them. But the prosecuting counsel had asked for the right to reply and although this was unusual, it was allowed. The seven officers acting as judges had retired after his final speech.

The ladies amused themselves by playing with Netta's little boy Pierre. At five he was lively and active, very like his father in appearance, dark, curly-haired, recently barbered out of his baby locks.

Five o'clock came. Netta ordered afternoon tea, as was the fashion, but few touched the pretty English-style sandwiches or the tiny iced cakes, although they all drank thirstily. When it was cleared away, Gaby and her mother strolled out into the little formal garden for a breath of the fresh September air while Netta went upstairs to see her son put to bed.

When they heard the telephone ringing faintly in the hall, they all hurried towards it.

Netta took the receiver from the house-maid. 'Yes, speaking – yes, Papa. Yes. *What?*'

It was an explosion of amazement. The others gathered round her, trying to hear the tinny voice in the earpiece.

'When? But that's… No, I'll tell her at once. Au revoir.'

She turned, took her Aunt Laura's hand. 'They found him guilty.'

'Guilty!'

'By a verdict of five judges to two.'

A stunned silence grasped them all. Then the sturdy little Mademoiselle Hermilot began to sob. 'No, no! It can't be! After all the work, all the evidence of fraud and conspiracy we unearthed! And Philip … Philip…!'

Gaby went to her. 'Don't,' she whispered. 'It's bad enough for his mother and sister – don't.'

The other girl made a big effort to check her sobs. The women stood helplessly staring at one another.

'Should we telephone to Madame Dreyfus?' Alys said, keeping her voice steady with an effort.

'No, if they have any decency they have let her be with her husband.'

They had heard from the men who attended the trial how pitiful Alfred Dreyfus looked – thin, ill, a scarecrow in his uniform, unable to swallow French food now and living almost entirely on milk. Their own dismay and despair was as nothing compared with what the man and his family must be undergoing.

Elvi Hermilot took her leave, with a friendly hug from Gaby and a promise, not entirely meant on Gaby's side, to meet again. When Frederic came back from the office Laura, Alys and Gaby accepted his escort to the station for the evening train to Calmady. They were too exhausted by the long anxiety of the trial to have the energy for a renewed campaign yet – and besides, who knew if that was what Madame Dreyfus would want?

Netta had a concert to give next day, a Sunday. It was in honour of St Cloud, whose memorial day was a few days earlier. The concert was to be held in a hall of Versailles, near where he died. Alfonsini always insisted that the evening before a concert she must eat sparingly, read some relaxing tale or listen to some undemanding music on the Gramophone, and go to bed early.

This ideal advice she tried to follow, but it was useless to go to bed. She had looked at a portrait photograph of her brother, taken on the birthday before his death, and over her there rushed a flood of memories – Phip polishing his glasses as he murmured about Mademoiselle Hermilot, Phip chasing a boy who had been tying a tin can on a stray dog's tail...

'And he's gone, and what was the use?' she cried to Frederic. 'He faced up to just the kind of man who served on that panel of judges – Army men, blinkered, unable to admit they could possibly be wrong.'

'Darling, do come to bed. You'll be fit for nothing in the morning. You won't be able to sing a note.'

'Aunt Laura has worn herself out over it. Did you see how frail she looked today?'

'I wonder your Uncle Robert lets her go on. Perhaps he'll put a stop to it now.'

'Put a stop to it?' She had been pacing up and down the bedroom, but now turned to stare at her husband, who was propped up on his pillows paring his nails.

'Well, what's the use now? They'll never allow a new trial.'

'But they must!'

'Darling, the army have done all they intend to do. They've reduced his sentence to ten years.'

'He'll never survive that long! They *can't* send him back to Devil's Island!'

Frederic knew only too well that they could, and perhaps would. He still had friends among army officers for there were those in the army who sided with the Dreyfusards although it did their career no good – and they told him that the senior ranks were furiously determined to condemn Dreyfus once and for all. They *could not*

244

admit he was innocent. Too many officers would be condemned for perjury if they did. The honour of the French Army would be gone for ever.

'It's gone already,' Frederic would murmur in response to such remarks. 'If you saw the foreign press regularly, as I do in the course of business, you'd know that every nation looks at the French Army and recoils in horror.'

But that, he knew, would only make the generals close ranks. Foreigners...! What did they understand of the honour of France?

Netta slept badly, rose with a slight headache, but was encouraged to hear when she tried a few scales that her voice hadn't suffered. Unfortunately such peace of mind as she was striving for was done away with when her father telephoned from Calmady to say that Aunt Laura had had to have the doctor. 'It's a chill, nothing serious, I think. But if anyone from the campaign office rings you asking for her, say she ought not to be disturbed for a day or two.'

'She was broken-hearted yesterday, I could see it.'

'Your mother wasn't any too happy either. She's tried to put Phip's death behind her, but yesterday it all came rushing back...'

'I know, Papa. I'm sorry.'

He sighed. 'You're a good girl, Netta.

You've done a lot for the campaign.'

'Not as much as I should have…'

'Nonsense. Well in the circumstances, you'll understand if we don't come to your concert, won't you?'

'Of course, Papa.'

'Sing well, dear.'

Frederic comforted her when she told him the news. 'Don't worry, Aunt Laura only needs rest. And as for Mama-in-law, she's got so much commonsense… She'll get over yesterday.'

He accompanied her to the hall. Alfonsini wasn't there. He was growing too old to jaunt about to halls outside Paris, he said. But his accompanist and assistant, Lipeta, was there. He smiled and made a sign for good luck as she went into the green-room.

It was a concert with a small orchestra, and a trio of singers who would sometimes sing in harmony and sometimes solo. They had rehearsed earlier in the week. The order of songs had been finalised. Moucherouz, the conductor, had decided to put Netta first with a rendering of the *Exsultate Jubilate* by Mozart so as to open in a fine, rousing fashion for the local saint.

The waiter for the green-room brought a pitcher of water for the singers. The baritone who was to sing second was humming a few half-notes to himself. Netta went outside into the corridor to take a few deep breaths to calm her nerves. There, on the stone floor of the corridor, lay a newspaper that had fallen out of the waiter's pocket.

Idly she picked it up, smoothed it out. A cruel caricature leapt up, almost as if to slap her in the face.

It showed Alfred Dreyfus, labelled 'Traitor' so there could be no mistake, being wrapped in chains like a bundle of rags and being carried to the ship for transportation back to Devil's Island. The caption read, 'Rubbish goes back where it belongs.'

She shuddered and threw it down. The orchestra ended their muted tuning up on stage. The conductor came into the passage, pulled down the front of his morning coat, patted his cravat, and gave his hand to Netta. 'Ready, madame?'

She was led on, to a brisk outbreak of applause and some hissing. A small anti-Dreyfus claque had come to the hall – it was only to be expected, she was resigned to it these days.

She took her place to the left of the conductor's dais. Moucherouz frowned at a clatter of sound as a clarinettist dropped his spare reed. He nodded at the musicians for complete silence, then glanced at Netta.

She didn't look back at him. She was staring out at the audience, clearly visible in the September sunshine streaming in at the

247

tall windows of the hall.

They too had looked at that cruel cartoon. They too might be horrified as she was, or in favour of its message.

She took a step forward. 'Ladies and gentlemen—'

'Hah?' grunted Moucherouz, twisting towards her more fully.

'Ladies and gentlemen, yesterday a great wrong was done – renewed, I should rather say. Captain Alfred Dreyfus was once more condemned for a crime he didn't commit.'

'What are you doing?' hissed the conductor.

'We came here today in a celebration of the life of a saint very dear to the French, a man who turned his back on the chance to rule because he preferred goodness and charity.'

'St Cloud, St Cloud!' cried a party of youngsters from the local school which bore his name.

'St Cloud escaped with his life despite the cruelty of those who ruled France at that time. Friends, another good man has not escaped – he has been condemned to five more years of wrongful punishment—'

'Not wrongful! Deserved every day of it!'

'What are you *doing?*' cried Moucherouz in subdued fury. 'Either sing or get off my platform!'

'Frenchmen, Frenchwomen – we can't go

248

on punishing this man! We're here to honour a saint of our church – if our church means anything, it stands for truth and justice!'

'Justice, justice!' echoed voices in the audience, the pro-Dreyfus element.

'Remember what St Paul said,' Netta went on, her trained singer's voice ringing through the hall. '"Be not deceived; God is not mocked: for whatsoever a man soweth, that shall he also reap." What can we reap but the whirlwind when we refuse to admit our guilt and release this innocent man?'

There was a strange little silence. Those who agreed with her hesitated to applaud, those who disagreed were held back by unwilling respect for the scripture she'd quoted.

Netta glanced up at Moucherouz. 'I'm ready,' she said.

The baritone marched on to the stage. 'I object to this,' he said in loud tones to the conductor. 'I didn't come here to take part in a propaganda meeting on behalf of that traitor!'

'Monsieur Allier, please go back to the wings. The concert is about to begin.'

'Not until I make it clear that I am not a party to this disgraceful conduct of Madame de la Sebiq-Tramont! Ladies and gentlemen,' he went on, sweeping his portly body round to address the hall, 'I am against

249

what Madame has said. I ask her to withdraw it.'

'Withdraw, withdraw!' chanted the claque at the side of the hall.

'I can't withdraw what I said,' Netta replied, speaking low to Allier. 'I meant every word.'

'Then I refuse to take part in this concert!'

'Come, come, m'sieu,' urged the conductor, 'passions run high over Dreyfus but we're here to make music!'

'Not I! Not until I get an apology for the disgraceful behaviour of Madame!'

'I shan't apologise,' said Netta.

'Very well. Monsieur Moucherouz, either she withdraws from the performance or I do. I refuse to appear on the same stage with her.'

'Don't be an ass, Allier! We can't rearrange the items at this late stage.'

'Sir, I have my reputation to consider! I am a chief baritone at the Opera Français – I cannot let my name be linked with a plea for leniency to that traitor!'

The manager came on. 'What's happening?' he asked, huddling against them so that his voice wouldn't carry to the front row. 'Are you going to start the concert or not?'

'No, we are not!' declared the baritone, and marched off.

The manager and the conductor gaped at

each other. 'Oh, madame, what have you done?' wailed the manager, wringing his hands.

He turned to the audience. 'There will be a slight delay in opening the concert. Please be so good as to remain in your seats.'

'No, no, no,' chanted the rowdies. '"No delay, start today. That's the rule we must obey".'

'M'sieu, madame, please follow me.' He led them off the platform. The orchestra, shuffling uneasily and glancing out at the restless audience, remained in place.

In the green-room Moucherouz wheeled on Netta. 'How dare you do such a thing? If you think I came here to conduct an orchestra for a madwomen, you are mistaken!'

'Madame, you could have started a riot–'

'I'm sorry, gentleman. I know you think it was wrong. But I had no idea I was going to say a word until I stood there.'

'Allier's gone,' reported the doorkeeper.

'Gone? Where?'

'Out of the hall. He's left.'

'Oh-h!' wailed the other singer, a contralto who had remained in the green-room throughout. 'We can't do the programme without Allier!'

'It's absurd! It's outrageous! D'you know what you've done, madame? You've put an end to this concert!'

'I'll have to refund the money,' the manager wailed.

'I'm sorry, monsieur–'

'It's no good saying you're sorry! You'll suffer for this, let me tell you, madame!' stormed Moucherouz. 'I won't be made a fool of in public and so I warn you!'

The audience could be heard growing noisily restive. The manager went to announce that the performance was cancelled. Frederic appeared with Netta's cloak. 'My love, what a mad thing to do!'

'I'm sorry, Frederic,' she said, and began to cry.

'Now; now... Come along ... I've got a cab outside, if we go quickly we can avoid any trouble.'

At home she went completely to pieces, shuddering, crying, cold to the marrow and then suffused with pulsing heat. Frederic sent for the doctor. 'A malarial attack, that's all.'

'Malaria!'

'I h-had it in M ... Milan,' Netta said through chattering teeth.

Twenty-four hours later she was returned to something like normality. She sat up in bed sipping broth, looking at the newspapers which recounted her extraordinary outburst.

'Although we cannot recommend such actions to other performers, we salute the courage of Madame de la Sebiq-Tramont for saying in public what many decent citizens must feel in their hearts. Who now can follow the tortuous course of the evidence against Captain Dreyfus? It fills many volumes, and much of it has been clearly shown to be false. Madame de la Sebiq-Tramont spoke for many of us when she said, as we hear, that the church should stand for truth and justice. Much has been made of the fact that the French Army is defending the honour of the Catholic church as well as its own. What we ask now is – does our church really demand further suffering? Or, as is rumoured, will the President listen to the pleas of those like Madame de la Sebiq-Tramont and extend a pardon to Alfred Dreyfus?'

'Perhaps it did some good,' she murmured.

'Darling, you were lucky to get out of that hall without having your head knocked off!'

'I never thought of that. I wasn't the least frightened.'

'Well, I damn well was! Never do a thing like that again, Netta!'

She gave a wavering smile. 'It's hardly likely, is it?'

Next day she was allowed up. Monsieur Alfonsini came to see her, leaning heavily on his cane. With him he brought the concert manager who handled Netta's bookings.

'My dear,' he said, after kissing her gently, 'you have done a very rash thing. Laurent is very upset.'

'I'm sorry,' said Netta. She had already said she was sorry a score of times – to her father who had telephoned in great alarm, to Elvi Hermilot who called in person to scold her, to Moucherouz and the contralto Lili Spezza.

'It's not enough to be sorry. You must repair the damage. And how it's to be done I don't know,' Laurent said, brushing at his moustache and beard with angry fingers. 'I have had two cancellations already – the Orchestre du Midi refuses to have you sing with them.'

'Good God, the entire Orchestre du Midi can't be anti-Dreyfus?' Frederic put in, half-laughing.

'Who knows? They don't want to associate with her. They don't want someone so unreliable and odd as their soloist. And the same goes for the management of the Salle de Fecamp. You've scared off a lot of possible engagements, madame. And there are plenty of hungry singers they can book instead.'

Netta knew she was in disgrace. 'What ought I to do?' she inquired in a timid voice.

Alfonsini sat down beside her, taking her hand in both of his old, dry palms. 'You ought to go abroad.'

'Abroad!'

'To sing. Laurent can get you engagements in Belgium and Germany, probably also England—'

'No!' cried Frederic.

Alfonsini shifted so as to look round at him, his old bones creaking in protest. 'She cannot sing again in France for at least a year.'

'She can't go abroad!'

Alfonsini looked at Netta. 'Madame Netta?'

She shook her head. 'No, I can't go abroad. I have a little boy. I have a husband and family. I'm needed here.'

Alfonsini shrugged expressively. 'Then you must remain silent. You cannot perform in this country until the memory of your escapade has faded. Managements and fellow-artists may forgive you in time, but I think it will take at least a year.'

They discussed it for an hour but when the two men left they had remained firm. Laurent had said he would refuse to look for any engagements for her for the foreseeable future – he dared not attract the resentment of other artists. She could of course find another manager but he doubted if anyone would take her. Alfonsini said sadly: 'Your job was to sing, not to be a politician. Leave politics to those who can't sing.'

When they had gone, Netta and Frederic

had a light meal together. Then she went up to look at her little son, peacefully asleep in his nursery. She couldn't leave him to travel the world as a singer. It was impossible.

By and by Frederic came to find her. He coaxed her to come away into the warmth and light of their bedroom. 'My dear, I know you're unhappy, but that will pass—'

'Oh, you don't understand!' she burst out. 'You've never understood! You thought I was just playing at being a singer, but it's important to me!'

'Netta, I may have thought at first—'

'I could be a great singer! I could really!'

'You are a great singer, my love,' he said, taking her in his arms and holding her close so that her little gestures of anger were stifled. 'When I hear you sing, you make me believe there really are angels in heaven.'

She was still. Then, raising her head to look into his eyes, she said, 'But I always thought you regarded it as ... as a sort of hobby...'

'It pleased you. That was enough for me. I've always wanted you to be happy, Netta – that before almost everything.'

'But ... but...' She was staring at him. A strange thought was growing, filling her mind. 'You ... love me?'

'Oh, my darling wife – what a question to ask!'

'No, no – don't laugh, Frederic. Apart

from the fact that we get on well with each other and have made a go of things – Freddi... Do you love me?'

He nodded, a mixture of laughter and wistfulness in his dark eyes. 'It happened. I woke up one morning and found I was in love with my own wife.'

'Oh, dear God!'

'Does it shock you so much?'

'Yes – no – I just never–' She put her head against his shoulder. 'Have I been a great fool, Freddi?'

'Never mind about that. Do you love *me?*'

She snuggled against his shoulder.

'Do you know,' she said in a voice he could hardly hear. 'I believe I do.'

Chapter Eleven

Nine days later Laura Fournier-Tramont died of pneumonia. Minutes after she breathed her last the newsboys were out on the streets of Paris and the big cities shouting, 'Dreyfus Pardoned! The President Acts!'

'If only she could have known,' Gaby said later, looking back on that day with its strange mixture of sadness and triumph. 'It would have meant so much to her.' But at least, she thought, Aunt Alys had got her wish. It was over at last.

It was by no means over. The reverberations of the Dreyfus Affair were to echo over the heads of the French for seven more years until at last, in a complete reversal of former opinions, Alfred Dreyfus was decorated with the Legion of Honour. But the Tramonts didn't feel compelled to take part in the campaign to clear his name totally – they had done what they wanted to do, they had helped to give the prisoner his freedom so that he could undertake that fight himself.

In any case, the Tramonts had problems of their own.

Arnold Simeon and his wife had come to be with their daughter in her last illness but arrived too late to see her alive. Gaby and Pierre could scarcely remember them. Last time they'd seen them, they'd been small children and Grandpapa Simeon had seemed tall, dark, severe. Now he looked an old, tired man, and Grandmama Simeon had hair that was almost pure white under the black veil for the funeral.

Before he left to take ship for New York, Arnold had a conference with the men of the House of Tramont. 'How's business?' he asked, with a wry glance.

'Not good. That damned phylloxera is still chewing at our vines. We here at Calmady

258

have planted where we can with grafted plants, but it's an expensive process, Monsieur Simeon.'

The old man didn't want a lecture on viticulture. He knew nothing about that. What he wanted was something different. The death of his only daughter had stricken him. He wanted to draw his relatives closer.

'Our vines in America are immune to this bug – am I right?'

'Yes.'

'Whyn't you sell up and move to America, then?'

'To do what?' Frederic asked, astounded.

'To make wine, of course. Plenty of wine made in California and round the Great Lakes.'

Robert thought fleetingly of his father, Jean-Baptiste Labaud, at Bracante Norte. For him the idea had attractions. And yet ... Jean was in his seventies now – what was the point of removing to California to be with him when he might not live many years longer?

Gavin was already shaking his head.

'You can't make champagne in North America,' he said.

'Why not? It's just a sparkling wine–'

'No, no. No other sparkling wine is champagne. Only the wine made *here*–' Gavin threw out a hand to indicate the mist-wreathed landscape outside the mansion's window – 'only *our* wine is champagne.'

'You mean to say that you're going to go through all this expense, grafting French twigs on American roots, just so you can grow the damned things in this rotten climate?'

The three wine-makers looked at each other. Then Robert said calmly, 'Yes, Father-in-law. If that's the only way we can save the champagne grape, it has to be done. And it can only be done here.'

'You're mad,' grunted Monsieur Simeon.

Frederic grinned. 'I think you may be right,' he said in his strongly accented English, 'but that's how it has to be.'

Before them, he knew, lay a great struggle. The small wine-growers of the Champagne region were stubborn, conservative, suspicious of change. The bigger firms, the negociants, might want to replant with grafted vines, but the families that owned the little vineyards couldn't believe their own vines, the true vines of Champagne, wouldn't withstand the pest. Besides, they begrudged the money for grafted plants prepared in expensive hothouses and nurseries.

It was all a plot, they were sure – a plot on the part of the negociants to force them into subjection. They began to band together to withstand what they thought of as the underhandedness of the big firms. Already this year, at harvest time, there had been hard words between growers and buyers over the price offered for grapes. The crop had been poor, vineyards had expected big sums for what was available, but the great houses had not been as generous as they'd expected.

Sometimes, after Arnold Simeon had left, Robert dearly wished they had accepted his offer to find finance for a new beginning in America. At least there they might have had some peace from the bickering that went on in Champagne.

Money became very tight. A family conference was called, with even young Pierre and Gaby taking part. 'We have to find capital to finance the re-stocking of the rows,' Robert said. 'We have to offer money on favourable terms to the small growers so that they'll buy the grafted vines. Otherwise we won't get anything to press, and we'll have smaller and smaller vintages.'

'What did Maqueras Fils put in that so-called vintage they sold this year?' Frederic asked. 'I had a London shipper call in on me in Paris, and he was furious over what he'd got from them. He practically put a gun to my head to make me swear Veuve Tramont's wine was made from Champagne grapes.'

'It's said Maqueras bought grapes from the Yonne. I don't know how true it is,' Gavin said. 'But you have to remember that

Maqueras have a funny idea of "vintage" – that stuff they're marketing has only been in cellar two years.'

'Terrible, terrible,' sighed Robert.

He was often depressed these days. The death of Laura had hit him hard. Gaby had come home to stay at Calmady to 'look after him', although he never paid the slightest heed to her pleas that he work less hard and rest his lame foot.

'One of the big problems is getting the grapes. We've got to convince the vineyard-owners other than the big firms to grow grafted vines. They ought to see that if makers can't get Champagne grapes because of the phylloxera, they'll go elsewhere.'

'Only if they're prepared to tell lies about the wine,' Gavin put in.

'We-ell...'

A silence ensued.

'So where's this money to come from?' Gavin went on, brushing up his moustache with his knuckles. 'The bank isn't going to lend us funds to lend to other people.'

'We must sell the Paris house.'

'No!' cried Netta, springing instantly to the defence of the place she now thought of as home.

But her husband was already nodding. 'That makes sense. Property on the Avenue d'Iena is fetching very high prices.'

'But – but–'

'You could come and live here, Netta,' Gavin said. 'After all, it is the family home.'

'Yes, dear,' agreed his wife. She leaned forward to touch her daughter fondly on the cheek. 'It would be nice to have you close at hand, Netta.'

'But the men need somewhere to stay when they have business in Paris.'

'Oh yes – quite true. But we could take a little pied-à-terre, my love. No need for a damned great house – excuse me,' Frederic added with a glance of apology at his mother-in-law for the swearword.

'You're quite right, Frederic, it is a damned great house. And it's also full of damned expensive furniture - you know Mama filled it with antiques when she bought it, all in keeping with the architecture and all that. So there's money in the furniture too. The Americans are great at buying French furniture. The silly British too,' Alys added with a grimace at her British husband.

Netta gave up trying to argue against it. She could see the menfolk had made up their minds, and anyhow, it hardly mattered any more. She had given up the idea of pursuing a singing career seriously. She was now nearly twenty-nine years old, and if she had been going to set the world of music alight, she should have done it by now.

Too many other things had intervened.

Life itself seemed to have diverted her from time to time from the direct path she should have followed if she had been destined to be a star of the concert platform.

The sale of the Paris house caused some comment in the gossip columns. The House of Tramont must be going through hard times indeed, hinted the journalists.

The year had turned and the new century had begun when the last private belongings of the Tramonts were loaded aboard a pantechnicon to be taken to Calmady. Netta turned her head away as it drove off.

'Courage, my love,' Frederic said teasingly, 'the natives out in the wilds won't eat you.'

'But I've grown so accustomed to Paris, Freddi...'

'It will be better for Pierre. He can run wild a bit. Paris is for adults, not for children.'

It was true that at Calmady little Pierre seemed much more at home. His mischievous temperament was less troublesome, he could rush about, play with the dogs, get under the horses' feet, beg for rides on the carts, and have a lot of fun. Gaby spent much of her time with him, while Netta helped her mother run the house and estate.

'We mustn't allow Gaby to stay around the house so much,' Alys said to her daughter. 'It's lovely of course to have her take Pierre out for walks and so forth, but it's no life for a young girl.'

'Do you think she's ever really recovered from that business with the awful Vourville?'

'Who knows? But time's going by, you know, dear. Perhaps we ought to do something about finding somewhere else for her.'

'Oh, do you think so, Mama? Gaby's so independent...'

'But she'll soon be twenty-one! Who would ever have thought a Champagne Girl would still be unmarried at that age!'

Netta sighed. She'd found that nickname a burden. It pre-supposed a certain kind of girl, a certain kind of life – and these days there was hardly the kind of money to support the legend.

'We ought to find her a nice young man,' Alys went on, 'someone who understands the circumstances of the wine industry and doesn't expect too much of a dowry at present. Someone from our own circles.'

But Gaby had already found someone – not at all suitable and certainly not from her own circles.

She met him on an outing with Pierre and his nurse, Flori, who had come to France from Portugal with Alys, had decided to become a fat little old lady when she turned forty, recognising that she would never now get married but that the Tramonts would

265

always look after her even if there were no children to nurse. She'd cared for Netta and Philip, Gaby and David, and now there was little Pierre.

He was too much for her and always had been, since the day he took his first step. But Mademoiselle Gaby seemed willing to do all the running about, so they would ramble about the grounds and the countryside, Gaby actually looking after the little boy and Flori acting as chaperone.

Pierre liked to beg a lift from one of the carters going out from the wine cellars. He'd be given a ride to the crossroads, where he would be set down to await the arrival of Gaby and Flori at their more sedate pace.

One afternoon they found him sitting on the shoulders of a great chestnut draught-horse, one of a pair drinking at the horse trough. 'Look at me, look, look, I'm riding the horse!'

'Ooh-h – be careful, Master Pierre!' shrieked Flori, trying to waddle a little faster.

'He's all right,' said the carter easily. 'Aren't you, lad?'

'I'm fine, I'm a big grown-up driver with a pair of big horses!'

The man took off his cap as the two women arrived. 'I was sure you wouldn't mind,' he said. 'I'm Louis Peresqueau. Of course I know who you are, ladies.'

'Come down this minute!' Flori cried.

'No, no,' said the carter. 'Leave him alone – he's all right.' He glanced at Gaby. 'Can I give the two of you a lift back to the gates, Mademoiselle Tramont?' In the neighbourhood, the name was usually shortened to the one the villagers thought important – the name of the wine house.

'Yes, do, do, Aunt Gaby! And I'll drive the horse from up here!'

'That would be very nice, Monsieur Peresqueau.'

He put his hands to her waist then without apparent effort swung her up to the driving seat. He looked up at her. She had coloured, because his hands had lingered a moment before he took the trouble to lift her. She should object now, if she wanted to. But the moment passed, and he turned to Flori.

For her he set two boxes, one on top of the other, helped her clamber up, set one of the boxes on the flat bed of the dray as a seat, and settled her. Flori grasped the back of the driving seat grimly. She was sure she was going to be shaken to death.

Peresqueau took hold of the headstall of the nearer horse. 'Up, my beauties!' Obediently the two great beasts turned away from the trough, the unwieldy vehicle turned a great circle in the crossroads, and they were heading at a slow pace towards Calmady.

'Faster! Faster!' shouted Pierre.

'No, no, lad, we can't go any faster or we'll bruise the ladies' tender portions.'

Gaby heard Flori give a gasp of horror, and she herself felt a start of surprise. But then she reflected that the man was a simple creature, unused to dealing with ladies of her class.

'Do you work for Monsieur Trusoit?' she inquired to cover the embarrassment.

'Me work for a master? I should say not. Didn't you see my name along the side? This is *my* wagon.'

'Oh, you work on your own account. How splendid.'

He tilted his head to look up at her. He had light greenish eyes, like one of the great cats. 'Oh, yes, I'm sure you're impressed,' he said drily.

He had put his cap in the front pocket of his coarse blue smock. His hair was a vigorous rich brown, springing up in a curling shock. He had a beard that covered his jaw up to the earline in little crisp ringlets. One tanned forearm and hand were visible where he grasped the headstall to lead the horse.

'You – you do cartage for the House of Tramont?'

'Occasionally. When they need extra haulage. Could do with more work from you – you might put in a word for me with your papa.'

'Monsieur!' cried Flori in protest.

'It's all right, Flori – it's a joke.' She said to Louis Peresqueau, 'You don't lack a good head for business!'

'Oh, a poor man like me has to use what chances he gets. Don't often hobnob with one of the ladies of the house.'

Pierre was bouncing about on the mare's shoulders, urging her to move faster despite the restraining hand of her master. The big, good-natured beast plodded on uncomplainingly, nodding in unison with her partner as they covered the half mile to the estate.

On the journey Gaby learned that Louis lived in a cabin a little to the west of the village of Calmady, that he was a widower, that he planned to buy another team and wagon in about two years' time if all went well.

When they stopped at the entrance to the estate, he swung Pierre down in one great swoop that caused the boy to scream with terrified delight. He lifted Flori down just as easily but with more sobriety. Then it was Gaby's turn.

He looked up at her. She met his glance. He held up his arms. She leaned forward into them.

While Flori fussed with Pierre and prevented him from embracing one of the great feathered hooves in love and gratitude, Louis Peresqueau unnoticed picked up Mademoiselle Tramont, held her close against him as he brought her to the ground, and rubbed his bearded chin against her cheeks before letting her go.

Scarlet and speechless, she stared at him.

'You must come and visit me one day,' he murmured as he put a hand on the wagon to swing himself aboard. 'Artists have painted my cottage – they call it "picturesque".'

'I hardly think so, monsieur. But thank you for the lift.'

'It was a pleasure – one I've been looking forward to for a long time.'

'What?'

'Oh, I'd noticed your nephew liked to get a ride with the carters. It was just a matter of arranging to be there one day to pick him up.'

'How dare you!'

'Of course it wasn't the lad I was interested in. Now there's a compliment for you!'

'Mademoiselle Gaby!' called Flori, trying to hold Pierre back from dashing up the drive to tell Mama about his ride on the big horse.

'If you come to see me, leave *her* behind,' Louis said with a jerk of the head towards the nursemaid. 'Fat old thing...'

'I'm certainly not going to—'

'Oh yes you are,' he said. He sprang up into the driving seat, picked up the long whip from its stanchion. He used it to give a little salute against his brown hair. 'You'll come sooner or later.'

'Never!'

But she was wrong. It took nearly a month before she gave in, during which time she kept running across him here and there – in the village, at church, in the lanes, at a christening party for one of the little vineyardists.

What she heard about him was disturbing. 'He's a bad lot,' Flori asserted. 'Half gipsy, you know – nobody trusts him.'

'He's a wonder with horses,' said the chief groom at Tramont. 'Anything wrong with a beast, and they send for Peresqueau. Mind you, he always makes sure he gets paid – never does anything for nothing.'

'Oh, what a one he is for the girls,' said the village seamstress with a giggle. 'I can't keep my apprentices away from him.'

'Poor young man, poor young man,' said the curé, sighing. 'Widowed so early... A tragic accident, but at least there were no children left orphaned.'

When she went to Louis's cottage, it was he who led her there. They had met as if by accident at the big vintage party on the estate. He danced with her, one of the lilting waltzes from a successful operetta. The

271

touch of his hard hand on her back, the scent of plain soap and male sweat, the sound of his whispered words... Something seemed to rise up within her to meet the physical enticement.

Lucas Vourville had taught her to enjoy sexual passion. Now she discovered that she had needs that could only be assuaged by surrendering to the challenge of Louis Peresqueau. When he said goodnight, he murmured that he would wait for her at the wooded edge to the estate. She slipped out when at last the house quietened down after the party.

It was turning towards dawn. A grey light was in the sky already. She ran though the dewy grass, her party dress drenched with the moisture, her little high-heeled shoes soundless on the wet soil.

She didn't see him at the meeting point. He was just suddenly there, engulfing her in his embrace. She let herself fall against him. He kissed her, her mouth, her cheeks, her neck, her bare shoulder where it rose from the party dress.

'Come on,' he said roughly.

He hurried her through the woods, down the rough embankment, into a lane that deteriorated into a mere track. In a curve of the chalky hillside, a light could be glimpsed.

'My place,' he said. He led her through a

gate. She could hear the sound of horses stamping and moving in a big shed behind the little house. He pushed open the house door. The interior was dimly lit by a lamp on a table, beyond which she could distinguish another door.

He said nothing as he led her to it. She could see the whiteness of the sheets, the ghostly outline of the bed canopy. His arms were around her. They fell on the bed together, wrapped in each other, held together already as if by bands of iron.

'I've always wanted you,' he grunted. 'From the minute I first saw you, my little beauty. Come on now... Come on... You're mine, aren't you?'

'Yes,' she gasped. 'Yes. Oh yes.'

And within moments it was true. He had taken her and made her his own, a prisoner to the sheer animal fulfilment he brought with his lovemaking.

He wasn't a bit like Lucas, who had been clever, gentle yet exciting, considerate yet demanding. Louis was careless, sometimes almost cruel. He had no pretty turn of phrase, no pretence of chivalry. Yet each time she told herself she wouldn't see him again, she found herself hurrying to be with him. It was a kind of enslavement.

Before Christmas had come round, she'd discovered the truth of the head groom's saying, that Louis Peresqueau never did anything for nothing. He began to demand her help in furthering his career.

'Your family does a lot of business in this area,' he mused. 'I don't see why they couldn't put some work my way.'

'But they do already – didn't you tell me you did haulage for us?'

'Oh, but only when the big companies are hard pressed. What I mean is, they could give me a contract. See, Gaby, if they'd give me a contract I could get credit from a bank and buy that other dray.'

'Well, it seems to me it would be more sense for you to get a contract as a self-employed haulier with one of the haulage firms.'

'No, no – I tried that – they give you jobs that take you miles away, miles and miles, and it exhausts the team, and you have to pay outrageous prices for feed in areas where they don't know you.'

She listened with sympathy, offering little suggestions when she thought they might be useful. Always she came up against the same obstacle – Louis didn't want to take orders, he wanted to be entirely his own master.

'But even if you got a contract from some big winemaking firm in the Champagne area, Louis, you'd have to take orders from somebody. The chief of cellar, or the transport manager.'

'That'd be different. That'd be between

equals. Look, Gaby, why don't you see what you can do about having work put my way?'

She tried time and again to explain that there was nothing she could do. Such matters were settled by her father or her uncle.

At last he came out with it. 'I'd think if you really cared a damn about me you'd *want* to help me get a good contract! All you have to do is speak to your father!'

'Oh, yes!' she riposted. 'Can't you just imagine the conversation? "Listen, Papa, there's this man I'm sleeping with, and he wants you to"–'

He seized her by the wrists. 'Don't make fun of me!'

'Louis!' She pulled away, but he held on fiercely. 'Louis, you're hurting me!'

'Huh! That's not all I'll do! Who do you think you are, making fun of me?'

'I wasn't, Louis, really I wasn't. I was just trying to show–'

'Oh, you always think you know best! Such a great lady, with such a marvellous education!'

She sat up in the bed, rubbing her wrists. After a long silence he said: 'All I'm asking is for you to introduce my name into a conversation, that's all.'

'But ... Louis ... the menfolk hardly ever talk about things like that to me.'

'Every winemaking family always talks

about winemaking–'

'Yes, of course, but not about transporting casks or hauling timber.'

He let it go for the time being but returned to it again and again. His temper, always chancy, would rise. She began to be physically afraid of him.

One evening she was dressing for dinner in her room at the mansion of Tramont. Her little nephew came running in, looking for a place to conceal himself in a game of hide-and-seek. Hard on his heels came his mother, pretending not to see him kneeling behind his Aunt Gaby at her dressing table.

'I wonder where he can be?' Netta asked the air, twirling around in the pretty room. 'I–'

She broke off. Her eye had lighted on her cousin's arms, upraised with her hairbrush so that the loose sleeves of her robe fell away. There were dark bruises on the slender forearms.

She stood staring at Gaby. Pierre, unable to keep quiet in his excitement, leapt out. 'You didn't see me, you didn't see me!'

'No, you were invisible! Run along now, dear, Flori will be looking for you in a minute for your bath.'

'Oh, Mama!'

'Go along, love.'

Pouting, the little boy raised his face to be kissed goodnight by his aunt then left the room. Netta closed the door behind him. Then she came to her cousin and took her hands in both of hers. She drew them out towards her. Then she let go and pushed back the sleeves of the robe.

'How did you get those marks?'

'I walked into a door in the dark a day or so ago...'

Netta turned the hands over. The marks went right round the wrists.

After a pause she said, almost in a whisper: 'It's a man, isn't it?'

'What are you talking about–?'

'I see now. You stopped being unhappy some time just after the vintage. But recently you've begun to seem ... drawn, anxious...'

'I don't know what you're talking about.'

'Who is it, Gaby?'

'No one. You're imagining things.'

'I'm not imagining those.' Netta sat down on the edge of the bed. 'And Flori tried to tell me something a few weeks ago, but I didn't bother to listen...'

'Flori!'

'Oh, she sees almost everything that goes on. What was it she was saying? Something about ... a waggoner?'

Gaby suddenly felt incapable of going on with her denials. The urge to confide was irresistible. To tell someone, to ask advice! And especially to tell Cousin Netta, who had been so kind and good over Lucas Vourville...

'His name's Louis Peresqueau. You're right – it all began just after the vintage party.'

'And he did this to you?' Netta said, nodding at the bruised arms.

Gaby said nothing.

'Louis Peresqueau... Isn't he the man whose wife died in strange circumstances a couple of years ago?'

'She fell from the hay-loft in their stable.'

'Ah!' Netta remembered it all now. 'Of course. And there are some villagers who say he broke her neck himself.'

'Netta!'

Gaby had gone white. Netta leapt up to put her arms around her. 'My poor cousin! What have you got yourself into?'

Tears began to flow. Gaby's sobs came strongly, almost hysterically, as she tried to explain the hold that Louis had upon her. 'And he wants me ... to help him ... become a successful businessman... And he just won't listen when ... I try to tell him ... I have no influence with Papa and Uncle Gavin...'

'So he beats you?'

She nodded, her face hidden against Netta's shoulder.

'All you have to do, my love, is not see him any more.'

278

'If it were only that easy! The only way to steer clear of him is to stay inside the grounds. If I don't come to his house as promised, he puts himself in my way in the village or somehow manages to find me in Rheims or Épernay if I go shopping.'

Netta sat holding her cousin close. 'My dear Gaby, have you thought that you are laying yourself open to blackmail with this man?'

'No, no! You don't know him! He's straightforward in his own strange way. I'm his woman, you see – it's up to me to do all I can to help him. But he wouldn't stoop to blackmail, that would be a weakling's weapon. No, he wants my help, and won't believe I can't give it.'

Her tears had subsided now. She straightened, gathering her tangled mane of hair and twisting it up in a knot at the back of her head. She found a handkerchief and wiped her eyes. She looked at Netta, shaking her head.

'It's my own fault. I must find my own way out of this mess.'

'Not at all, little cousin. You could tell your father and let him deal with Monsieur Peresqueau–'

'Oh no! Oh, promise me you won't tell Papa! He'd be so ... disappointed in me!'

Netta got up and took a pace or two about the room, her long skirt dragging on the turkey carpet. 'To tell the truth, I'm a little disappointed in you myself, Gaby. How could you? A man like that?'

'But you don't understand! I ... I needed him. I can't live without love, Netta.'

Netta said nothing. She'd never been in this miserable situation. She'd never even thought about physical desire until Frederic aroused it in her, and ever since then she had found all the fulfilment she wanted in his arms. To go with first one man and then another in response to needs she couldn't control was an unhappiness she'd heard of but couldn't really imagine.

'But you've come to your senses about him now, I take it? You wouldn't care to end up with a broken neck like his wife?'

'Netta!'

'It's a possibility, isn't it? If he can do that to you-' she nodded to indicate the bruises she'd seen and perhaps others invisible under the silk robe – 'he can do worse. You must get rid of him.'

'But how? I've thought about going away, but where to?'

'No, *he* must go.'

'His home is here. His little house, his stable...'

'I imagine his house and stables are rented. If I remember aright, he's of half gipsy stock, settled here about six years ago...' Netta paced about, thinking. 'Gaby, will you let me tell Frederic about it?'

'Oh no!'

'Only a man can deal with this, dear. And Frederic's a man of the world – and used to dealing with bad cases like Peresqueau, he handled men worse than him in the Army, I'm sure... Let me tell Frederic.'

Gaby protested but in the end gave in. There was no one else to turn to, except her father – and the shock and disgust that would have caused were unendurable.

Frederic heard the tale from his wife with astonishment. 'How long's it been going on?'

'Something like six months now.'

'Good God!'

'Freddi darling, I'm afraid for her. He hits her! And you won't remember, but his wife died in a very strange way – the examining magistrate was very dubious about it although the certificate was issued in the end.'

'Oh, I'll see to him!' Frederic said, his dark eyes flashing with anger. 'Knocking a woman about? He must be a brute!'

'Well, not according to his lights. I suppose he thinks he's got a right. Anyhow, as far as I can gather, he's hanging on to poor little Gaby in hopes of doing well through her connection with the House of Tramont. He wants to be given a haulage contract, if you'll believe it.'

Frederic grimaced. A beautiful, young, passionate girl like Gaby – and all the man wanted was commercial advancement! It was an absurd waste.

'Well, I think we'll have to scare him off.'

'I don't think he scares easily.'

'Money?'

'It would have to be enough to persuade him to move away, to start somewhere else.'

'That sounds like quite a large sum. How could we find it, and not alert your Uncle Robert?'

They discussed it off and on for a day and a half. Then Netta came back to Gaby. 'Gaby, you know the pearls you inherited from your mother?'

'Yes?'

'Would you sell them?'

'Oh no! They were Mama's!'

'Dear, we need a good sum of money to buy out Peresqueau and persuade him to move right out of the district. Neither Freddi nor I can think how to raise the money without attracting attention.'

Gaby was unwilling but began to see the necessity when Netta explained Frederic's thinking. 'But how would I explain to Papa if I never wear them? He notices things like that – anything to do with Mama's memory...'

'We can have a replica made, my love. Frederic will take them to Paris next time he goes on business and have the duplicate made, then sell them. Believe me, he tells me many rich ladies do it – there are jewellers who specialise in it.'

Gaby never heard what happened at the two interviews between Frederic de la Sebiq and her lover. All she knew was that Frederic brought her a letter, ill-spelt and smudged, on a piece of cheap paper.

'You didn't want to hep me but things have settled sattisfactory. Shan't be seing you again. Thanks for evverything, Louis.'

She read it in the privacy of her room. She felt shivers down her spine as she sat staring at it. Could she really have been in love with a man who could write a farewell letter like that?

What could have got into her? She should never have let herself lose her head so wildly. She felt shame, disgust, regret.

After sitting a long time in the spring twilight with the paper in her hands, she rose stiffly. She picked up the matches from the china tray which held the emergency candle, always kept in each room in case the newly installed electricity should fail.

She lit a match with trembling fingers. She set fire to the letter, held it until the flame had consumed so far that it began to burn her fingers. She let the flinders drop into the tray, then with idiotic fierceness began to crush them into dust with her fist. When they were a little pile of black nothingness she drew a deep breath and blew them away into the air.

There... That was the end of it. From now on she would never surrender herself to anyone as she had to Louis Peresqueau or Lucas Vourville.

Love... It was a chimera, a mirage. It seemed she couldn't live without it but she would take care where she chose to find it in future. She would never let it become the master influence in her life.

And yet, what was there for her now? She shuddered away from the idea of an arranged marriage of the kind that Netta suggested. She knew her father would never force her into one if she refused. But what, in effect, could she do with her life?

She looked at herself in her dressing table mirror and saw a white-faced, tear-stained, whimpering fool. Anger raced up in her heart.

She sprang up and ran outside. It was a cool spring evening. The drizzle of late March touched her cheeks, cooling the shamed blood that had risen there. Calmer, she walked towards the vine rows at the far side of the estate.

There the workers were just beginning to wend their way home. Figures clad in dark blue trudged away into the grey-blue dusk, tools were stacked in little huts, a voice called a farewell.

She stood drinking in the scene, savouring the scent of the leaves in the wetness.

She was Gabrielle Fournier-Tramont. There was something here for her if she cared to take it up. After all, the old lady, Nicole de Tramont, had been the maker of this house, the head of a great wine firm.

She went to find her father in the big office behind the entrance to the cellars that ran into the hillside. He was working on invoices. He looked up in surprise when she came in unannounced, for the secretary had already gone home.

'Gaby! What are you doing here, dear? And without a coat in this dampness?'

'Papa, I wanted to ask you something.'

'Really? He could tell it was important, something that couldn't wait for the ordinary chit-chat of the family dinner table.

'Can you give me work to do on the estate?'

'Work? But, Gaby—'

'Like Old Madame, Papa. She held everything in her hands, didn't she – until the day she married Gri-gri.'

'Yes, of course. She was the moving spirit here. A wonderful woman.'

'I know that, Papa. I wish...'

'What?'

'Somehow I wish we were closer to her.

Not just adopted into the family, you know. I wish I were like Netta – a direct descendant.'

Her father took off the spectacles that had become necessary recently. He rubbed his eyes. 'Why do you say that, Gaby?'

'I suddenly feel I really want to *belong*,' she said with passion.

'But you do, dear. You do.'

'No, not just a member of the household. I want... Oh, I want it to be the most important thing in my life!'

'But Gaby dear, you'll get married, have children–'

She was shaking her head, with such vehemence and certainty that he sat back, alarmed. 'What is it, daughter? What's wrong?'

She sighed. 'It's love, Papa, what else? It all came to pieces. I've decided that I'm never going to get married. I just ... seem to choose the wrong men.'

'No, no – you mustn't talk like that! Good heavens, you're still only a girl!'

'Every other "girl" I know is married by now. No, Papa. I think I'm going to be a spinster.' She summoned an uncertain smile. 'But it doesn't matter, because I *know* I can be useful here, at the House of Tramont. It's only I don't want to seem to push myself in where I don't really belong.'

He rose, limped round the desk and took

her hands. 'You do belong, Gaby. In a way that you don't understand.'

'Oh, you mean I'm part of the tradition–'

'No.' He put her in a chair and leaned over her. 'I'm going to tell you something. I wanted to tell you but it somehow seemed a wrong thing, to burden you with a secret you didn't want. But now ... after what you've said...'

'What is it, Papa?' She was looking up at him with her wide, dark eyes, so like her mother's.

Robert took a deep breath. 'You are Nicole de Tramont's granddaughter.'

She frowned. 'No, Papa – or do you mean by adoption?'

'By blood. Nicole de Tramont was my mother.'

'No, no, Papa dear – she was your aunt–' She had thought at first that he was suffering from some delusion. But she saw his steady expression, his grave glance, and she knew all at once that it was true.

'Your mother?'

'And my father was Jean-Baptiste Labaud – you remember, the Californian who died last year? It's a long story. I only found out when I was a grown man.' He broke off, limped away, poured two glasses of the still wine made from the champagne grapes, and brought one to her. 'Drink, Gaby. And when you're recovered from the first shock, I'll

287

explain to you why you should feel that you have the greatest right in the world to play your part in the House of Tramont.'

Chapter Twelve

Mademoiselle Fournier-Tramont gave a hearty shove at the pile of correspondence on her desk. It cascaded over it to land on the floor.

'Gaby!' cried her brother in despair, leaping to save it.

'Leave it, leave it! Let it lie there until it rots. Or better still, set a light to it!'

'It's no use taking that attitude, Gaby. They've got to be dealt with.'

'A crowd of sour, cantankerous, stubborn, narrow-minded idiots! Why should we waste our time on them?'

'Because, sister dear, if we don't take them along with us in the Syndicat General des Vignerons, we may as well not bother to keep the association going.'

Gaby took hold of a little lock of hair either side of her head and gave them a tug. 'I've come to the conclusion that the Almighty has a spite against wine-growers.'

'Why d'you say that?'

'We find a way to counteract the

phylloxera. We finance the raising of grafts. We even arrange loans so the small growers can buy the grafts. We manage to make some decent champagne when the grapes are good. We economise when times are bad, and help the little vineyardists stay in business. And what happens? A bunch of fools plant vines all along the edge of the province and produce inferior wines, ship it off abroad where it disgusts our regular clients, the price of champagne takes a blow, and the small growers blame *us*. It seems we can't win their confidence no matter how hard we try.'

David Fournier-Tramont hunched his chin into his stiff high collar. 'If they weren't stubborn and cantankerous they'd never survive in a region like Champagne. It's a hard world there, Gaby – you know it from your own experience at Calmady.'

'Oh, you're too kind-hearted to them! I tell you, they're an impossible bunch. They keep turning and biting the hand that's trying to feed them.'

'It's because they don't trust us. You know yourself, my dear – the figures prove that twelve million more bottles of "champagne" are being sold every year than the Champagne vines can possibly provide.'

'But why must they be so certain that it's the big firms like Tramont and Moet and Pommery who are the guilty parties? You saw that shipment I sent back from Amsterdam – those labels referred to a totally non-existent firm in Épernay.'

Her brother inelegantly held his nose. 'That stuff really tasted vile, Gaby.'

'I know it did. I tried it myself. I hope to God no one in the household of King Edward of England is mad enough to buy it – the roar from His Majesty would be heard across the Channel.'

'Well,' said David, getting down on his knees and beginning to gather up scattered letters, 'what are we going to reply to these objectors?'

'We don't have to decide now.' Gaby stretched and yawned. 'We can talk to Papa about it at the weekend – you *are* going down to Calmady for Pierre's First Communion, I take it?'

'Wouldn't miss it for the world! I'm dying to see him in his new suit and holding a prayer book, trying to look saintly for the Bishop.'

He set the pile of disordered correspondence on the desk. They were in the offices of the Paris house of the wine firm. Here Gaby worked when she wasn't travelling on behalf of Champagne Tramont.

At twenty-six she had been accepted by her family and friends as 'odd'. She was clearly never going to get married. Some said it was a strange way for the Tramonts to treat their beautiful daughter, but that was the people who didn't know them very well. Those who were closer sensed that Robert Fournier-Tramont saw in Gaby a sort of reincarnation of the founder of the firm, La Veuve Tramont herself.

There was a difference, however. Nicole de Tramont had been an innovator, a power source. Gaby was content merely to help defend what her grandmother had built up. Times were so bad in the wine trade that it was all the winemakers could do to keep going.

Another different between Gaby and the great Madame Tramont, less well-known, was that Gaby lived outside the conventions when she was in Paris. She had friends her grandmother would have raised her eyebrows at – writers such as Colette, clothes designers such as Poiret. Paul Poiret actually had the shocking idea of raising skirt hems so that they showed the ankles – disgraceful!

Her family were vaguely aware that her life-style was unusual. But with the exception of her cousin Netta, they preferred not to inquire too deeply. Netta, on the other hand, was always avid for news of Gaby's activities.

'Well, who's the man of the moment?' she asked when she came into Gaby's room at the manorhouse to help her unpack.

'There's no one special at present, Netta.'

'Good gracious, what's the matter? Are the Parisians losing their attraction for you?'

Gaby gave a laughing glance. 'Contrary to what you seem to think, my dear cousin, I don't take lovers and discard them like Cleopatra.'

Netta was lifting a slender gown from the valise. 'My word!' She held it up. 'What do you wear *under* this? It's so flimsy your corset laces would show through!'

'Don't worry, I'm not going to appear in church like that. It's for a party in Épernay – the Rollins have invited me.'

'Oh, Gaby! I hoped you were going to give us all your time over this weekend!'

'Yes, yes – I'm dropping in on the Rollins en route back to Paris. Netta, what does Frederic say about this trouble with the *Vignerons?*'

'He's not playing too much part in that,' Netta replied, holding the silk gown against her body and examining herself in the cheval glass. 'He's concentrating more on this diversification that's become so important. Really, Gaby – what do you wear under this?'

'As little as possible. The whole point is that it isn't accentuating the waist so much – all the shaping is done by darts and tucks, not boning.' Gaby studied her cousin's appearance. 'I don't know whether it'll catch on. The "fine figure" outlook is still too strong. I told Paul I'd try it out for him – he calls it his "fish" silhouette but I think he's ten years too early with it. So what's Frederic suggesting we should diversify into?'

'Oh ... railways ... canal transport ... minerals... He and Papa and your father spend hours in the office poring over sheets of figures.'

Frederic wasn't really a big-businessman. He had been a shrewd gambler on the Bourse thanks to tips from well-placed friends, and now those same friends, and their friends, were part of an advisory service helping Champagne Tramont to survive.

The trouble was, some of the most earnest advice was to get out of the wine trade. 'There's far too much wine slopping around Europe,' they were told. 'Algeria produces a lot these days, and Spain's output is rising all the time now that the Bordeaux wine-growers have got the hang of the soil.'

'But it's not good wine!'

'People seem to like it. And it's a lot cheaper than vintage champagne, my friend.'

The Tramonts shook their heads. They couldn't give up the wine lands. Their lives were too intimately bound up with the grape.

Nevertheless they took some of the advice. They weren't likely to go bankrupt even if the bottom dropped out of the falling wine market. But in their view, the only reason to diversify was to survive until the wine market improved again.

'If it ever does,' said the bankers. 'And if it does, what about the phylloxera? There are still a lot of winefields where they aren't putting in American grafts – you're fighting a losing battle if you think you'll ever get back to growing Pinot grapes on Pinot stock.'

Yes, yes. They knew all that. It made no difference. Champagne had been made for generations along the River Marne and always would be, come hell or high water.

Pierre's First Communion was celebrated in the cathedral in Rheims, along with other children of the local families. Afterwards there was chat and congratulations before getting into the carriages and a few newfangled automobiles to go back to a luncheon party at the manor. Since the weather was fine and mild for this Easter season, the meal was held out of doors on the terrace. There were many guests from the neighbourhood.

The talk, of course, was all about the wine.

'What d'you think the outcome will be of this demarcation?' asked Marc Auduron, the family solicitor.

'One thing's for sure! Nobody'll be satisfied.'

'I hear the officials are insisting that the valley of the Cubry must be left out.'

'What?' It was a cry of indignation from a wine-grower from the Cubry.

Gaby sat under the shade of a garden umbrella, a glass of wine in her hand, listening to the argument. She'd heard it all before, not once but many times, in the course of the last year. The government of France was at last moving to delineate what regions could legally claim to make its most famous wine, champagne. Once the line was drawn, no one outside that area could claim to be making champagne. Sparkling wine, yes. Frothing wine, yes. They could choose any adjective they liked, but only the wines from inside the treasured area would legally be champagne made by the authentic method from the authentic grapes.

Naturally nerves were at full stretch all over the region. There were many growers who were going to be left out in the cold. Some, who had turned away from the Pinot grape to other, more juice-bearing varieties, would find themselves excluded even though their land lay within the boundary. Unless they returned to the select strains of the Pinot – the Pinot noir, the Pinot meunier, for instance – they wouldn't be able to call their wine champagne.

Some were saying they should never have edged the government into starting on the legislation. At the beginning, in the face of frauds carried out by other regions and even other countries, it seemed right to protect the precious champagne heritage. The trouble was, everyone who supported the idea at the outset couldn't possibly be included in the strict laws needed to protect the integrity of the wine.

Gaby did a lot of travelling on behalf of Champagne Tramont. She had found she had a natural talent for smoothing over difficulties that arose over faulty shipment and irate shippers. She had seen some very strange labels circulating in the capitals of Europe, and tasted some very weird 'champagne'. Some, it was said, was even made from rhubarb juice.

She supported the proposed legislation. So did the other members of the board of Champagne Tramont. But then, as others would say with a sneer, they could afford to. Their land lay easily within the demarcation zone, their grapes were expensively grafted Pinots, their cellar routines were a model of accuracy and purity, their name was unassailable. It was just like the Tramonts, implied the lesser growers, to act holier-than-thou about the wine. But what about the hundreds of little vineyards that were going to go to the wall?

She heard the exchanges becoming more heated around the long table under the young leaves of the vine arbour. She glanced about for a method to quieten them down before the effects of too much wine and too much enthusiasm caused the party to disintegrate. Even young Pierre, who always liked the grown-ups to get involved in conversation so he could get more than his share of the goodies, was looking apprehensive.

One of the villagers had brought his accordion. She drifted over to him. 'Play for us, Alain. Let's have some dancing.'

'Before we have some fighting, eh, mademoiselle?' He winked, unfastened the strap, and ran his fingers over the buttons. In a moment a bal-musette tune was fluttering among the vine tendrils.

'Louder, Alain.'

She turned, looking for a partner with whom to lead the way. A young man lounging with a group from Luzadon caught her eye. He sprang up as she tilted her head. 'May I, mademoiselle?'

'A pleasure, monsieur.' They put hands on each other's shoulders and danced off along the terrace.

The younger members of the party, bored by the arguments of their elders, followed suit. Pierre found himself a pretty little communicant in a dress of white lace. The grown-ups paused to watch them. The tension eased, the party spirit returned.

'I'm very flattered you chose me to help in your rescue operation, Mademoiselle Tramont.'

She didn't say, You were the first man my eye lighted upon. 'You're a stranger here, monsieur?'

'Oh yes, just passing through. I'm staying with the Jussarts in Épernay.'

'Oh, indeed?' That was impressive. The Jussarts were important people. 'You're in the wine business?'

'Not at all, mademoiselle. I'm an aviator.'

'A what?'

She stopped dancing, stood back, stared at him. 'Aeroplanes?'

'You've heard of them, surely? Lighter-than-air machines.'

'I've heard of them – I've even seen cinematographic film of them – but I never quite believe in them. You make a *career* of flying aeroplanes?'

'Yes, indeed. It's my business. I'm trying to interest people in using aeroplanes as a means of transport.'

'Of transporting what?'

'We-ell… People. Goods.'

'Goods?' Gaby laughed. It was all a nonsense. She swung into step with the music again. 'What's your name?' she asked.

'Charles Emeigart. You, of course, are

Mademoiselle Gabrielle Tramont. I've heard a lot about you.'

'None of it good, I dare say.'

'That depends on what you mean by good. I've heard that you're beautiful, which I find to be true. I've heard that you're clever, which I well believe. And I've also heard…'

'What?'

'That you like to live your own life.'

'Ah.' They polka'd to a halt as the music ended. Alain struck up a country tune. People gathered together to dance the *ronde,* a circular dance in which partners met and changed. She lost Charles Emeigart in the turns of the movements. Soon after she was called by her father to chat with old friends. When she thought of Monsieur Emeigart again, the Jussarts had taken their leave and carried their guest off with them.

To her surprise, she met him at the Rollins that evening. She was wearing the sensational dress by Poiret, which caused many indrawn breaths and surprised glances. 'Well, so this is why you thought I'd hear no good of you, mademoiselle,' he said teasingly when he came to speak to her. 'All my wicked men friends are saying your gown is a sheer enticement.'

'Not at all. It's a bid for freedom,' she said, taking her tone from him. 'I'll tell you something very shocking. This gown has no whalebone in it.'

'Really?' He came close, to slip his arm around her waist. 'Dear me. It's true.'

'Could you not have taken my word for it?' she asked, stepping back, smiling.

'But, mademoiselle, I'm a pioneer, an inventor. I have to test all suppositions myself.'

He was tall enough to top her by a head or more. He wasn't exactly handsome but he had an amusing face, the features a little askew, his nose broken. He told her afterwards that he had broken it in his first flying accident.

'Didn't that put you off flying?' she asked.

'Not in the least. It only made me more determined to master the art. Besides, it's the coming thing.'

'Nonsense.'

'I tell you, it's going to change the world. One day soon, an aviator is going to fly a machine across the Channel to England.'

'Don't be absurd! It would fall into the water!'

'Not a bit. You'll see.' He took her empty wine glass. 'Shall I fetch you more wine?'

'No, thank you, I must go soon. I have to be in Paris for an early morning appointment.'

'You're going to Paris tonight?'

She nodded. He glanced about the room. 'With your family? Your brother? I don't see anyone.'

'I travel alone, Monsieur Emeigart.'

It was his turn to be astounded. 'You haven't an escort?'

'None. I often travel alone.'

'But that's ... that's...'

'As strange to you as your flying machine is to me.' She tapped him on the shoulder with her fan. 'You see? The world is full of oddities.'

'Mademoiselle, may I offer myself as a travelling companion? I too have to be in Paris in the morning.'

'But, Monsieur Emeigart, I'm going by train, not by flying machine.' She was laughing.

'Well, so am I. It isn't always suitable to travel through the air. May I travel with you?'

'I see no reason why not.'

He looked at her from grey-blue eyes which had suddenly grown serious. 'I am very honoured, mademoiselle,' he said, and there was something in his tone that let her know he meant more than the mere fact of sharing a railway compartment.

Although they didn't sleep together that first night, her affair with Charles began from that moment. They had a lot in common – they were both adventurous, independent, yet glad to find a fellow spirit with whom to share something of their lives.

As spring gave way to summer, it began to

seem to Gaby that a marriage might emerge from their relationship. They had so much in common, yet each had separate interests that would prevent them from ever becoming too bound up in each other. True, there wasn't the same intensity about their love that she'd found with Lucas – but perhaps that was all to the good.

All the same, she waited to hear him suggest it first. Free-thinker though she was, she still thought it right for the man to make the offer. And as yet the word marriage had never crossed his lips when he spoke of the future.

That year the grape harvest was very poor. The little vineyardists everywhere were facing extinction and, in Champagne where they sold everything they grew to the big negociants, there was anger at the low prices. But it wasn't only in the wine industry that there was unrest. Everywhere there were strikes and troubles.

The final straw came when the railways went on strike. 'It's infuriating!' raged Gaby. 'I've got all these documents from David about the definition of the wine region, and I can't get down to Calmady to present them at the meeting.'

'You could go by road, darling.'

'Charles, you know the railmen have got barricades at the main outlets. I don't want to end up thrown out of the carriage and forced to walk.'

'Well then, I'll fly you there,' Charles offered.

'What?'

'I'll fly you. Why not?'

'You have an aeroplane available?'

'I've been demonstrating one in a field out towards the Bois de Vincennes. It's not exactly mine, but I can use it to fly you to Calmady.'

'But ... how would we get to Vincennes? We can't get a train, and carriages might be turned back.'

'By river, how else?' Charles said. He never admitted obstacles existed except to be surmounted.

The flight in the little bi-plane was the most exciting thing Gaby had ever experienced. The wind driving past the open cockpit was cold and hard as steel. Her hair, fastened down under the leather helmet on loan from Charles, nevertheless escaped in long tendrils which flew behind. Her stomach lurched and turned over as the fields and woods sped by below. When they landed at last, in a series of running bumps on a paddock at the far edge of the Tramont estate, she got down trembling with reaction – but eager to do it all again.

'Mademoiselle!' gasped the villagers who had run to see this wonder. They backed away, gaping, as she unbuckled the flying helmet and shook her hair free.

Her father's greeting was much the same. 'Gaby! How could you do such a thing!'

'But I had to get here with the papers from the parliamentary lawyers.'

'That didn't matter! You could have telephoned the main points–'

'Oh? And would our friendly vineyardists have believed what you reported? No, no, Papa, you know they need to see it in black and white from the government. And besides,' she added in a burst of enthusiasm, 'it was fun! I enjoyed every moment.'

Robert was re-introduced to Charles, whom he'd met once but quite forgotten. He took an instant dislike to him – this man who could risk his precious daughter's life in a flimsy flying machine. Although the journey had only taken about two hours, that was two hours too long for his child to be flying through the air in that dangerous fashion.

Charles had nothing to do while the meetings with the local vignerons and negociants went on. He went calling on his friends the Jussarts while Gaby and her father and uncle were shut up with the representatives of the big firms in Épernay.

But Robert had been alerted to the relationship between them. Something about their easy way with one another told him that they were more than just friends. He made inquiries. And then he called his daughter to the library for an interview.

'What is your relationship with Monsieur Emeigart, Gaby?'

She frowned. 'What makes you ask?'

'Are you expecting to marry him?'

She turned away from him to gaze out of the window at the dark green of the shrubbery. Yes, she was expecting to marry him. But she couldn't say so until Charles himself showed some willingness – she certainly didn't want her father making formal approaches.

'I haven't thought about that,' she lied.

'That's just as well, because he is already married.'

It was lucky she had moved away and was looking in the opposite direction. The pallor of her face would have told him that the cruel thrust had gone home. If he could have seen how he had hurt her, he would have been ashamed. But Robert was angry, angry that she should throw herself away so obviously on an adventurer.

'Did you know he was married?' he insisted.

She kept her voice absolutely cool as she replied, 'We've never talked about it. Ours is not that kind of friendship.'

'What kind is it, then? Is he hoping he'll persuade the Tramonts to invest in those ludicrous flying machines through his friendship with you?'

305

'Such a thought has never entered his head, Papa. I'm surprised it should enter yours. Why do you dislike him so much?'

'Anyone can see he's a ne-er-do-well.'

'He's nothing of the kind. Just because you can't see the possibilities of his machines, that doesn't–'

'They're toys for rich men! What can they possibly do that's useful?'

'Frederic says they can be useful. He says they would be invaluable in war.'

'In what way? To frighten simple natives by flying over their heads, I suppose!'

'No, by acting as scouts for the artillery. Charles is negotiating with the Bulgarian and Servian governments–'

'Bulgarians and Servians! My god! Anyone who expects to make money out of that crowd is a madman. Gabrielle! It would be better if you withdrew from any "friendship" you have with this fellow–'

'It would be better, Papa, if you refrained from meddling in my affairs!' She swept out, her head held high.

But of course she couldn't let what he had told her simply lie unspoken in her heart. Charles flew his machine back to Paris but she took the train, the railways having resumed a partial service by now. When they met again in his apartment by the university, he knew at once that something was troubling her.

'Your father didn't take to me, did he?' he suggested.

'Charles… He says you're married.'

'Why, yes.'

'You never told me.'

'I thought you knew.'

'How could I know?' she flashed.

'Well, the same way as your father presumably found out – by talking to the Jussarts.' Charles set down his Scotch and soda, stood up, and came to her. 'I'm sorry, darling. I truly thought you knew.'

She shook her head.

He put his arms about her and tried to draw her near. She resisted. 'Gaby,' he protested, 'don't be angry about it. What difference does it make?'

All the difference, she wanted to say. I thought we'd get married one day … I was hoping, planning…

She said stiffly, 'Where is your wife?'

'In Brussels. I haven't seen her in about two years.'

'What is she like?'

'Why on earth d'you want to know that?'

'What is she like?' she repeated.

For answer he went to a bureau, opened a drawer or two, and finally emerged with a leather portfolio containing photographs. He sorted through them, then turned to her holding one out. 'Our wedding photo,' he said.

It showed a much younger Charles in white tie and tails standing proudly beside a plumpish dark girl in a rather badly designed wedding dress. She was clutching a bouquet of orchids and fern.

'You want to know all about it?' he said, his voice bitter. 'It was a more or less arranged match. I saw nothing wrong with it at the time. That was fourteen years ago. I left university with my engineering degree and began getting interested in aeroplanes. Françoise thinks I'm literally mad. She says the Lord will punish me for daring to make men fly in the air like birds. She actually sabotaged one plane – that was how I got this broken nose.'

'Charles!'

'She's a religious lunatic. I left her for good in 1904, although I saw her from time to time while I was still living in Brussels. Since I came to France two years ago I haven't seen her and have only heard from her once, when her allowance was a bit late in arriving and she got her lawyer to send me a warning.'

'Oh, Charles! Darling!' She ran to him to throw her arms around him. 'I'm sorry! I had no idea!'

She clung to him for a time, until she'd got over the first distress. Then she murmured, 'And children? Do you have children?'

'We had a little boy, but he died of

meningitis. Françoise said it was God punishing me for my presumption.'

'Oh, my dear! She must be an awful woman.'

'Well, she's a great one for knowing what's in God's mind, though it's a mystery to kings and cardinals. As you can imagine, we ceased to have anything in common almost at once. Yet I'm tied to her, legally and religiously and of course she won't hear of a divorce.'

'No, I see that.' Gaby sighed and nodded. 'But, as you say, it doesn't make any difference. We weren't talking about marriage anyway.'

'No, that's out of the question.' He studied her with his alert blue eyes. 'Does that hurt you?'

'Not at all, Charles – what a silly thing to ask! Why, dozens of couples we know aren't married.'

'But in general they aren't so tied up with their ultra-respectable families as you are, my love. Tell me – would you have brought all this up if your father hadn't given you a lecture?'

She was honest enough to colour and shake her head. 'Let's forget about it, Charles. We'll go on as before. We were perfectly happy, weren't we?'

But things had changed, all the same. She'd had a secret hope before, that one day she'd be Mrs Charles Emeigart. She'd even thought about having his child. Now it was different. Although their relationship still seemed as permanent and strong as ever, something had shifted its foundations.

Because she felt guilty, she put herself out to help him in his career. He had the idea of starting a small air service for passengers and light cargo, and when in 1909 Bleriot actually crossed the Channel in his mono-plane, businessmen no longer sneered. Gaby gathered together the savings from her salary as a director of Champagne Tramont and a few investments, and gave it to Charles to help finance his project.

He found some clients. But it meant he spent less time with her in Paris, and more at the coast where the cross-Channel airfield was situated.

Netta greeted Gaby with a strange, secret smile on her lips on a springtime visit to Calmady. 'I've news for you, little cousin.'

'What sort of news?'

'I think it's good, but Pierre thinks it's rotten. I'm expecting another baby, Gaby.'

'What?' Certainly it was a surprise. Everyone had come to regard Netta and Frederic as the parents of an only child – a handsome, high-spirited, selfish yet loveable boy. 'My dear, of course it's good news! Frederic's delighted, I take it?'

'He hasn't got used to it yet. To tell the

truth, neither have I.'

'But it's lovely, Netta!' She hugged the older woman. Now that she looked at her carefully, she could see a golden glow under the fine skin, an added lustre to the bronze hair. 'It certainly agrees with you!'

'Yes, but Dr Cranne says I must be careful. After all, I'm going on thirty-seven – I'm not a girl any more.'

'Nonsense, you'll be fine, anyone can see that. Are you hoping for a boy or a girl?'

'Oh, a girl, I think. It would be nice to have another girl in the Tramont family, don't you agree? And Pierre would be less annoyed with a girl – he wouldn't feel he had a rival.'

'Good heavens, a fifteen-year-old boy shouldn't be too bothered about rivalry from a tiny baby!'

Netta sighed. 'Children are funny things, Gaby. You'll find that out if ever you settle down and start a family.'

Gaby shook her head. 'I'm destined to be the odd old spinster of the family.'

They had a long womanish chat over the five o'clock tea which the maid brought in. For once, they didn't talk about any of the problems besetting the wine industry. And when Alys came in, to find them comparing pictures of baby clothes in the *Ladies Compendium,* she smiled to herself. Even that strange niece of hers might one day

311

turn into a normal wife and mother, if only she could meet the right man.

The baby was born in the autumn, 'just at the most convenient time,' as Frederic observed, for the grapes were gathered and the pressing, though scant, had been successfully accomplished. The little girl was christened Elinore, after Frederic's dead mother. His father, an old and terrifying gentleman, actually made the journey to Rheims to see his granddaughter named in the great cathedral.

But that was the end of celebrations in the Tramont family for some time. Because in the following year yet another blight struck the vines. A new pest, a kind of mildew, spread among the young leaves as spring advanced into summer.

Almost every estate in France was affected. With two bad harvests recently behind them and the price of wine slipping yet lower, Robert and Gavin called a conference of the Tramonts.

'The question before this meeting,' Gavin said when they were all assembled in the library, 'is a simple one. We have to make a decision. Are we going to stay on here and struggle to keep the name of Tramont in being, or are we going to do the sensible thing and sell out?'

Chapter Thirteen

The discussion went on the whole day. In the end the family parted without making a decision. They needed time to think about it, to take further advice.

'It's all very well for your Uncle Gavin to be in favour of selling up,' Gaby's father sighed. 'He's a good fellow, but he's not a Champenois.'

'Neither are you, Papa,' Gaby said, shaking her head at him with a smile. 'You were born a long way from Calmady.'

'But blood and breeding tell, Gaby. I've got the blood of Champenois peasants in my veins. I *can't* give up the vines.'

Gaby couldn't help sympathising. Yet, as Gavin had pointed out, the young members of the family had their lives before them – were they to devote them to a failing industry?

She returned to Paris. There was business awaiting her at the office there. Moreover, she could meet there a member of the Rheims law firm who habitually advised the House of Tramont.

Marc Auduron was somewhat less than a friend and something more than an acquaintance. He had been at the dreadful coming-out party that ended in a fracas when the anti-Dreyfusards attacked the mansion and, if Gaby had but known it, he had played quite a part in the failed negotiations for her marriage to Lucas Vourville. He was now a senior partner in the law firm, spending a large part of his time in Paris working on behalf of the wine-firms over the legislation to define the champagne-making area.

Gaby invited him to dinner at the restaurant attached to the quiet hotel where she had a small residential suite. Charles was present too, because she wanted the benefit of his opinion. It was only fair. They were practically man and wife, and she was about to make a big decision on their financial status.

'We've been through all this before,' she remarked to Monsieur Auduron as they began on the soup course. 'And we ended up by holding on to most of what we own.'

'Yes, but you had to buy back what you'd sold in the end – that's a wasteful process. If you decide not to sell this time, you must make a long-term plan, and be prepared for hard times for perhaps three years.'

'If you ask me,' Charles interposed, 'there's nothing but hard times in the wine industry!'

'No, no.' Auduron frowned and smiled. 'In

314

the past, great fortunes have been founded on wine. It's unfortunate that we've had pests that we don't know how to deal with in the last twenty years or so.'

'I'd call twenty years of trouble "hard times",' Charles said. 'It comes of being in a dying industry. Now aviation–'

'Is just at its beginning – I quite see your point. But there has always been wine and there always will be. And modern science will show us how to conquer the new pests, just as it's shown you how to fly a heavier-than-air machine.'

'There's a difference, though,' Charles insisted. 'Wine isn't essential. Champagne especially is a luxury product.'

'But so is an Old Master, or a performance at the opera–'

'Oh, come on, Gaby,' said Charles with a laugh. 'Any ordinary man in the street can gain access to Old Masters or the Opera by a few centimes entrance fee. When was the first time you saw a poor man drinking champagne?'

'That may be true,' Auduron agreed. 'But special products must be made for special people.'

'Special people? You mean for fat old kings like Edward of England to give to his expensive tarts?'

Monsieur Auduron started. Gaby blushed, and luckily the waiter came to remove their soup plates and serve the fish. After that interruption the lawyer resumed tactfully on a different angle.

'You have to appreciate that the land along the Marne isn't much good for anything else except vines. The *Champagne pouilleuse* now … I've always thought that with modern farming methods it might be possible to grow grain there. But the hillsides are–'

'If you fly over the country,' Charles said, 'you can see acres and acres of vine-rows. It's a one-industry area. And that's dangerous.'

'Oh, certainly. That's why,' Auduron said, 'we've advised the House of Tramont to diversify. And I daresay Mademoiselle Tramont won't mind if I say we've been relatively successful.'

'But that's a totally different thing from selling out entirely,' Gaby said, looking anxiously at the lawyer. It was strange that at this moment she felt closer to him than to her lover. He was a Champenois, he understood the awfulness of the idea of giving up the land.

Auduron had a thoughtful, narrow face with long narrow eyes that made him look sleepy. Gaby had seen features like his here and there in the champagne region: it was said they came from conquerors just after the Romans left, barbarians led by Attila. But there was nothing barbarian about his shrewd lawyer's brain.

'Prices are low, of course. You'd lose a lot of money on a sale. Then there's the problem of what your father and uncle would *do* – they've been in wine all their lives, there's a human problem involved in taking their careers from them.'

'Well, they could retire,' suggested Charles. 'After all, your father must be – what, Gaby?'

'He's fifty-four – that's too young to retire.'

'It doesn't seem very young to me,' Charles insisted. He'd found that in trying to promote the idea of air transport, most of the opposition came from middle-aged men who'd become set in their ways.

Monsieur Auduron left with Gaby a set of figures he'd drawn up. They showed various alternatives and the financial results. 'I hope you find them helpful,' he said as he bowed over her hand at the end of the evening. 'Thank you for a most delightful meal, mademoiselle.'

'Thank you for giving me your time, monsieur.'

'A pleasure.'

When he had gone, Gaby went to her suite with Charles. The moment the door had closed behind them, she turned on him. 'How could you! How could you say things like that!'

'Like what?' Charles was taken aback.

'About champagne being what expensive tarts drink.'

'Oh...' He almost forgotten his own words. 'Oh, well, everybody's always said that champagne is a woman's drink.'

'That just shows how little you know about it! Vintage champagne is a great endeavour, appreciated by people of taste—'

'If you say so, darling. I don't really know much about it, you know I don't care for wine.'

'No, and that's just the point! You talk to me by the hour about your wretched flying machines, but if I want to talk about wine you get bored! Let me tell you, wine has made a lot more money for this country than aeroplanes!'

'Don't get in a tizz about it, Gaby.'

'Don't *humour* me! I'm trying to decide whether to vote in favour of annihilating something that's taken three generations to build up.'

'Look, I know you're anxious. I know it's a big decision. But if you're dispassionate you can see—'

'I can't be dispassionate about it. It's been our whole life at Calmady. And it doesn't just affect us, the Tramonts. It effects every grower in the region.'

'But you can't make your decisions on the basis of what's good for someone else. You have to decide what's best for the Tramonts. And I can tell you, Gaby, if your family were to realise their assets and invest the money in aeroplanes–'

'Oh yes,' she said bitterly. 'Papa said at the outset that you were looking for money to put into your silly schemes.'

'Silly? You know it's going to work, Gaby. You invested money yourself.'

'Only because … because… Well, that was my own money. Don't imagine for a minute I'd advise my family to invest in air transport!'

'You don't believe in it?'

She hesitated. They were having their first real quarrel. If she said what she felt, which was that she'd defend the vine rows to the death before she ever put a centime into flying machines, they might not be able to patch it up.

'Of course I believe in it,' she said after a hesitation. 'But don't let's pit one idea against the other, Charles. Help me! I've got to make up my mind how to vote.'

At the end of the week the family met once more and the vote was taken. Gavin and Alys voted to sell up. Their daughter and son-in-law voted to hold on. 'It's for Pierre and Elinore,' Frederic explained as he gave his decision. 'We feel we ought to inherit.'

Robert voted to stay with the business. He looked earnestly at Gaby as he did so, but the next to speak was his son David.

'I vote to give up,' he said. 'It's not that I want to, but the bankers agree that it will be hard going for at least the next five years – and I wonder if we can survive?'

That made three in favour of selling, and three in favour of holding on. Gaby's vote would settle the matter.

She'd come to Calmady half-decided to vote for selling. As if to reinforce her decision, Calmady was looking its worst in a grey day of heavy cloud and drizzle. The sick vines hung on the wires like men under torture. Among them moved the estate workers in their blue smocks and heavy clogs, sacking draped on their shoulders to protect them from the damp.

Who would want to hold on to a place like this? What did it have to offer except hardship and anxiety? It wasn't even as if the people cared about the Tramonts. They seemed to think the family were in some plot to do them down over grape-juice prices and the definition of the champagne area. Suspicious, stubborn, strait-laced…

Yet she loved them. They were her own kind. The land too – for all its tricks, for all the difficulties it caused, it was the home of the great wine that had given her family fame.

'I vote that we hold on,' Gaby said.

Later her father came to her and gave her

one of his rare embraces, with a fervour that touched her. 'I was afraid you'd say no,' he muttered. 'That man of yours... He thinks wine-making is an old-fashioned nonsense.'

'I'm afraid he does. But that couldn't alter the fact that our roots are as deep as those of the vines, papa.'

It almost seemed that the others were relieved to have been outvoted. The whole family sat down again to plan retrenchment. They discussed the plan David had concocted with his fellow-lawyers. The only way to keep going on a long-term basis was to mortgage the estate.

'It's nothing to be ashamed of,' Marc Auduron argued as they sat glum and unwilling. 'Land after all is only an asset—'

'What!'

'I mean, Monsieur Robert, viewed from a financial viewpoint. It makes more sense to mortgage the land and use the money when you need it, than to sell off little pieces or buildings or whatever.'

'We've never had a mortgage on any of our land.'

'But that doesn't mean it's a bad idea, Monsieur Gavin.'

Coaxing, arguing, the lawyers got what they wanted. A long-term plan was laid down. If the plant biologists could come up with a cure for the new mildew and everything else went well, by 1915 the

House of Tramont should be enjoying prosperity again.

The villagers of course got wind of the negotiations and mule-headedly decided that the Tramonts were about to sell them down the river somehow.

'They glower at me so,' Alys said in a voice quite unlike her usual firm tones. 'It's almost as if they know Gavin and I voted to sell up and leave. But they couldn't possibly know that.'

'I don't know so much, Aunt Alys,' said David, with all the insouciance of youth. 'The servants probably passed on the news – you know how they eavesdrop.'

'David! Don't say such things to Aunt Alys!' Gaby reproved.

'In any case, the locals feel like that towards all the negociants, not just us. They see their world going to pieces and they have to blame *someone*.' This was Robert, looking suddenly older than his fifty-four years. Grey had appeared in his dark hair. Although he'd always made a great effort to bear himself erect despite his lame leg, his shoulders had stoop now.

'Another thing you have to take account of is the fact that they feel we have no right to mortgage the estate.'

'No right?' cried David.

'No, not without consulting them,' Gavin explained. 'Old Madame bought their vine rows from them years ago and we have the deeds to prove it, but they still feel those rows really belong to them.'

'But that's not logical, Uncle Gavin,' David protested.

'What's logic got to do with it? It's a gut feeling they have. No one could argue them out of it.'

David looked as if he thought he could. With his new law degree in his pocket he was of the opinion he could win almost any argument he was put to.

'If they feel hard done by now,' muttered Robert, 'wait until our economy measures start to bite...'

Among those measures was a withdrawal from even rented living quarters in Paris. There had for years been a little pied-à-terre for the men, used mostly by David. There was also the little suite in the Hotel des Chataigniers where Gaby lived. A small apartment had been made of the attics at the office building in Rue Lelong where David could now take up residence, but it was thought unsuitable for Gaby to live above the business. She had to face the choice of removing back to Calmady or making some other arrangement.

When she told Charles of it, she expected him to say at once, 'You'd better move in with me.' She wanted him to say it. It was a good time to make their relationship more permanent, to make her family aware of it and accept it. When so much was changing, this final change would not shock them so much.

But Charles looked doubtful. 'I'd ask you to share my flat,' he said, 'but the fact is, I'm thinking of moving out of Paris quite soon.'

She stared at him. 'You never mentioned that?'

'No, it's a decision I'd been putting off. But it makes sense for me to move down to Calais where the airfield is likely to be.'

'I see.'

He came to sit next to her on the elegant little sofa in the drawing room of her suite. 'We can see each other often just the same.'

'Oh yes! It's so handy, isn't it – Calais to Rheims or Épernay!'

'It's only about a hundred and eighty miles. Distance doesn't mean so much now we have good train services. Besides, I'm thinking of investing in an automotive carriage.'

All at once she saw it from Charles's point of view. How much more romantic to come swooping east along the dark straight national routes in his wonderful machine, than to live prosaically together in a Paris apartment.

She began to laugh. 'All right, Charles. I can see it would be possible to keep in touch by means of modern inventions! I'll find something quiet and respectable in Épernay – in any case, it's a good spot to choose from the point of view of the wine industry. Most of the negociants have houses there.'

'I still think you should have persuaded them to sell up and get out.' But he turned away from the reproach in her great dark eyes.

It was all very well to talk about Épernay as quiet and respectable, but things had changed. During the following year the festering anger among the small growers began to erupt in sores that wounded the countryside. For some strange reason, they believed the big wine houses were importing cheap wine from North Africa to put into their champagne, instead of using the small crops, produced with such effort in the midst of the mildew attacks.

Riots broke out in the towns. Mobs began to march about at night in the countryside. The police were too few to deal with them, though they did their best.

'I was stopped on the way here,' Charles told Gaby as they sat down to dinner in the little restaurant attached to the Auberge du Marché in Épernay. 'They wanted to know who I was and where I was going.'

'I suppose they thought you might be one of the trouble-makers.'

'It's hardly likely any of the little vine-yardists would have a Benz tourer, my love!'

'You don't know! They've stolen motor-ised lorries and trucks before now. You must surely know that there are political activists from Paris stirring things up here – they know how to run a revolution.'

'Oh, revolution...' Charles sipped some beer. 'A few fights and a few windows broken.'

'It's easy for you to take it lightly,' she replied, annoyed. 'You're not living here in the midst of it.'

From the bar next door came the sound of raised voices. The owner could be heard shouting, 'Out! Out! I want no trouble-makers here!'

Charles half-rose. Gaby put a hand on his sleeve. 'No, stay out of it.'

But the door to the restaurant burst open. The owner and the waiter, struggling with a sturdy man, flailed in the doorway.

'Come *on*, Jules,' the waiter commanded. 'You know you're talking wildly. You've had too much to drink.'

'No, not *'nough!* If I'd had 'nough, I'd be with the boys... Still trying to get me courage up! Lemme go! I want another brandy–'

'You're going out of here, my lad,' said Monsieur Deneuf. 'I don't want your kind of talk in my bar.'

'Talk, talk – what's the use of that? Action, that's what we need, that's what the Reds tell us! You wait!' Jules kicked out at the waiter, who released his grasp to hop about holding his shin. 'I'm off, see – I'm going to help the boys make a lovely fire!'

'No, you're not!' Deneuf had held on grimly, and now Charles and one of the other male diners came to his aid.

The drunk stopped fighting. He stared owlishly at Charles. 'Ah, you're the fancy man that goes with the little dark Tramont! Ah, friend, what a sight you're missing! Great doings tonight at the Tramont house!'

Gaby heard it, and a frisson of fear went down her spine. 'What d'you mean?' she cried, running to grab his arm and shake him.

'Nah, nah, I'm not saying no more! But you'll see, you'll see – tomorrow when your boy friend's gone and you telephone Mama – no answer, heh? Nothing but the sound of sizzling, heh?'

'Charles!' she gasped. 'They've gone to burn down Tramont.'

He let go the drunk and half turned to her. 'I don't think so, Gaby – I just drove in, the police are all along the roads.'

'But if they go cross-country? They know the area like the back of their hand. Charles! We must get there, warn them!'

'Come on!' He ran out. His tourer was parked in the stabling behind the auberge. He cranked the handle while Gaby climbed

327

in. The big motor sparked, the car began to shudder with life. Charles leapt in beside her and took the high steering wheel in one hand while with the other he manipulated gear levers. They backed and turned, backed and turned.

'Hurry, hurry!' she urged, grabbing his arm.

'Let go, Gaby – I need both hands!'

Although it seemed an age to her, only a few minutes passed before they were speeding out of Épernay at thirty miles an hour. The night wind rushed into their faces, the headlamps picked up the metalled surface of the road and the boles of the cypress trees.

'Can't you go any faster?'

'We're topping thirty now – and I'm still running her in, she's not due to do anything like this,' he shouted back.

About an hour later Calmady came into sight against the starlit sky. A few cottage windows had lights: it was perhaps half past ten on a fine October night.

As they sped out and into the shallow vale between the village and the Villa Tramont, all seemed quiet.

But then, as they crested the rise, a glow in the sky.

Netta had woken from her first sleep to the smell of burning. She sat up.

'Freddi! Freddi!'

'Ah?' he grunted, rolling over on his back. 'Something's on fire.'

'Eh?' He pushed himself up on his elbows, sniffed the air. 'By God, you're right!'

He leapt out of bed. 'Get Elinore!'

She too was out of bed, scrambling into a dressing-gown while her husband pulled on trousers and slippers.

He was gone as she ran for the nursery. Flori was sound asleep, snoring. She kicked the nurse's bed as she ran past, snatching up her little girl. She pulled a cover from the bed to wrap round the child. 'Flori, Flori, wake up, wake up – there's a fire!'

The old nurse awoke in a daze. 'Eh, what? Is she crying? It's her teeth–'

'Something's burning, Flori! Monsieur's gone to telephone the fire brigade.'

Frederic was downstairs in the office, surrounded by smoke and fumes, jiggling the receiver uselessly. Either the line was down or had been cut. He could smell burning wood but the room in which he was standing was as yet untouched. He threw down the instrument, ran into the hall, shouting: 'Fire! Fire!'

Robert appeared at the top of the staircase. 'Where is it?' he called, dragging on a dressing-gown.

'Haven't found out yet – the smoke's blowing through from the back, from the terrace room.'

'I'll phone the–'

'Don't bother, the damn thing doesn't work.'

He found flames issuing from the big room they called the ballroom. Someone had got in through the terrace windows and set the place alight. The smell of kerosene was strong on the air, mingled with the smoke.

In the hall, flames were beginning to lick the oak panelling of the walls. Netta was there with the baby, Alys and Gavin came downstairs with an arm about each other. Flori was on the landing, foolishly gathering up things she thought she would save from the furnishings.

Frederic reviewed the inmates of the house. David was in Paris in the Rue Lelong, Pierre was at boarding school. The reduced staff of house servants was upstairs, furthest from the fire. Now they appeared, one by one the butler in an unexpectedly fine silk dressing-gown, the cook in shawl and curlers.

'Where are the maids? Where's Patti and – what's her name?'

'Suzanne? Yes, where's Suzanne?'

The groom appeared from outside. 'Sir, sir– Oh, you're all up–'

'How does it look from outside, Lenard?'

'The back of the ground floor is ablaze, sir, and someone's put a torch to the offices.'

'Get those damned women downstairs,' shouted Frederic to the butler in his officer's voice. 'Come on, the rest of you – this fire's going to burn right through the ground floor if we don't do something to stop it. Lenard, get the gardener and any other men you can find organise a bucket squad – try to get the fire extinguishers from the loading bays – quick, don't hang about.'

Flori, hearing the order from Monsieur in his 'impatient' voice, began to clamber upstairs to the attic floor to fetch the maids.

'Not you, Flori – stop!'

'It's all right, monsieur, I don't mind.' Up she went, Frederic shepherded everyone else outside. 'Gavin, Robert, see those men get to work. Where's Chausse?'

The gardener pushed forward. 'Here, sir.'

'Send your lad down to the village on the bay mare, she's reliable. Get some men to help here.'

'The fire brigade, sir?'

'I can't get through from here. Tell your boy to ask the mayor to telephone to Rheims for them.'

'Yessir.'

A sudden gust of wind rushed through the house. A sheet of flame seemed to spring up. It was greeted by a cheer from somewhere at the back.

'My God!' cried Robert. 'They're there – madmen!'

He went off at a limping run to see what was happening. He found a crowd of men, standing a few yards off among the shrubs, laughing drunkenly and clapping each other on the back.

'You fools,' he shouted. 'There are people in there!'

'Toadies to the rich! Let 'em burn!'

Some of the men from Calmady arrived, panting, having started to run as soon as they glimpsed the flames. Buckets were filled at the taps in the bottle-washing shed, but a milling crowd of intruders prevented them from getting to the fire.

'What about those women upstairs?' called Frederic.

To his dismay the butler replied from almost at his elbow. 'I couldn't get up, sir – the flames have taken the staircase.'

'*What?*'

Frederic ran back to the house. The back stairs were well alight, but the great front staircase was still passable. He raced up them. He could hear the women weeping and calling out for help.

They were in the passage outside their rooms, huddled together, two of them and Flori. They could hear the fire crackling and raging, they were engulfed in smoke that was drawn upwards as the old house burned.

'Come on – you can still get down the

front stairs.'

'No, sir – you can't see a thing in the smoke!'

'Come on, you idiots – you'll be burned alive!' He seized Patti by the shoulder and shoved her in front of him. Sobbing, coughing, she did as he urged. But as they moved along the passage, a tongue of flame came up to greet them.

The front stairs were alight.

'Damned idiots,' muttered Frederic. 'If they'd done as they were told they'd be safe by now.'

'I can't go down there, sir – I'll be burned.'

'Go on, go on – before the stairs fall in.'

'No, sir, no!'

But she went. The habit of obedience was strong. She ran down, fitfully lit up by the fire, holding her nightdress skirts close against her. But the moment she had passed, the stairs disappeared into the stair-well. Her weight had been just enough to break the burning planks.

'Oh, sir! What shall we do now!'

'We'll get out through the windows and on to the roof of the morning room.'

'Oh, no sir–'

'Yes, come on, the men will bring ladders.'

He ran into the room which had belonged to Gavin and Alys. It was full of smoke but as yet no burning had reached it. He threw up the big windows, but at once regretted it for the draught blew first in and then out, bringing a great rush of heat with it.

'Come on,' he urged the maids. 'Quick, out of this window before the fire gets here!'

'Oh, lord, I *can't,* sir!'

'Look, it's quite safe.' He got out on the sill to show how easy it was, then stepped along the coping to the ornamental stonework that ran down to the roof of the morning room.

'Hi! Look at him! Mr High-and-Mighty Himself has come out to wave to us!'

The crowd below him stared up, their attention drawn away from skirmishing with the fire-fighters.

'Getting toasted, are you, milord?' they mocked. 'Not so haughty now, are you?'

'Suzanne – Flori – quick, now – all you have to do is climb out, and walk along the balustrade and–'

'Get back in your fine house!' roared a bull-like voice from below. A stone came hurtling up towards him.

He heard it hit the roof, and automatically ducked. As he did so, his foot slipped, he went cascading down the sloping roof, and then off into the air.

He didn't feel the ground rush up to meet him.

Gaby and Charles arrived to find the men from Calmady engaged in a sort of hand-to-hand battle with a band of drunken rioters.

Only a few were able to do anything to fight the fire.

Netta was sitting on an ornamental garden seat in the courtyard, cradling Elinore and trying not to weep.

'Where's Papa?' Gaby asked. 'And – oh, there you are, Aunt Alys.'

'The men were trying to organise a water-chain. There's a fight going on – I don't know who they are, these people...'

Charles left Gaby to comfort her cousin and her aunt. He ran to the back of the house. One glance told him the fire-fighters were losing ground against the intruders, who outnumbered them.

He had taken to carrying a pistol in the car since the political troubles in the country-side became more frequent. He had it with him now. He took it from his pocket, and fired two shots into the air.

The effect was magical. The men stopped dead, drew back, gaped at him.

'If anybody moves without my permission, he gets a shot in the leg. I can see quite well in the firelight, thank you. Who are the fire-fighters?'

'We're here, Charles!'

'Oh, Monsieur Tramont – right – you and your helpers get on with it. The others, stand very still.'

From the distance came the clanging of the fire engine's bell. It was a horse-drawn vehicle, unlikely to make fast headway along the narrow lanes. But it distracted Charles enough so that he turned his head. The men he was trying to hold at gunpoint began to melt into the shadows.

It was then that he saw the body.

'Good God! Someone's been injured.'

Robert limped up. He threw himself down beside the fallen figure. 'Oh! Oh, no!'

'What? Who is it?'

'It's– Oh, God – it's Freddi!'

And now, easier to distinguish since the bellowing and shouting of the drunks had ceased, they could hear the screams for help.

Above, the window where the maids were calling out could be seen through the smoke. Then a great tongue of flame leapt out.

After that, there was silence.

Chapter Fourteen

The people of Épernay closed ranks to protect their menfolk. None of them, they insisted, would have been guilty of anything so wicked. The only name they were prepared to render up to the authorities was that of an interloper, a gipsy, a strange violent fellow liked by few and feared by most.

For twenty-four hours after his arrest Louis Peresqueau maintained a sullen silence. Then, unexpectedly, he laughed and admitted to being of the party that set alight the Villa Tramont.

The examining magistrate was surprised. The man was a small businessman, a haulier, not a vineyard worker.

'Why did you take part, Peresqueau?'

'Wanted to pay 'em out, didn't I!'

'You had a grudge against the family?'

He shrugged muscular shoulders. 'All of 'em. Wouldn't give me work, chased me out of Calmady just to show how powerful they were.'

'Chased you out? Who? When was this?'

'Couple of years back. That toy soldier Frederic de la Sebiq... Who did he think he was, throwing money at me and giving me my marching orders?'

That was all he was prepared to say about his reason. With a grin of hatred he confessed he had offered his wagon to convey the trouble-makers, had helped pour the kerosene.

'And what's more, when Mr High-and-Mighty came out on the roof, it was me who threw a stone at him and toppled him. Ha, toppled him, I did! Broke his stiff aristocratic neck, didn't he!'

He said he knew nothing about revolution or Reds plotting to overthrow the system. When the authorities offered a deal – his life would be spared in exchange for names of trouble-makers – he grimaced and shook his head. 'Kill me off if you like. Nothing's gone right for me since I took up with her.'

'With whom? There's a women involved?'

'Isn't there always?' But he wouldn't name her. 'She'll know,' he growled. 'She'll know, damn her.'

And Gaby knew. Every time his name was mentioned, she shuddered in horror. If only she could go back in time, steer clear of that physical temptation which had led her temporarily into his power...

At his execution there was a demonstration of protest outside the prison. But the police put it down with severity. And Gaby knew that Louis would have spat upon these political activists: he was a man out for himself all his life until the desire for revenge led him astray.

The following year there was war in Europe. 'Only in the Balkans,' they told each other with a laugh, because everyone knew that those little Balkan states were always squabbling with each other.

But it parted Gaby from Charles finally. He was to go to Servia to help them form an air corps. He and three other 'mercenaries' were to fly newly purchased machines to

Mitrovitsa and there train twenty young volunteers.

Their affair had been dying over the last twelve months, in any case. Charles didn't say: 'You should have sold up when you had the chance and invested the money with me.' Or 'You felt bound to those people, and look how they rewarded you!' But it was in his manner often, in his eyes.

She felt bound to defend herself against the unspoken criticism. She pointed out that the men of Calmady – 'our own people' – had rushed to help the minute they saw the fire. She told him that it was now known there had been political agitators at work, that the men had been drinking all day before they set the fire. She didn't say that one of the ringleaders had been a former lover.

The government sent in troops to quell the uproar. They stayed through the summer of 1911, but when it was time for the grapes to be harvested their quarters were needed for the transient pickers. With relief the Champenois saw them march out. And, oddly enough, it was a decent harvest: the mildew was being conquered.

Odder yet, the Tramonts benefited financially by the insurance compensation. They had an unexpected sum of money in hand. But they decided not to rebuild for the present. Netta, particularly, was against it.

'I never want to see the place again,' she said, holding the toddler close in the curve of one arm, grasping her tall teenage son with the other.

She and her parents removed to a rented house in Épernay. Robert chose to live in an apartment in the smoke-blackened manor houses. Gaby insisted in moving in with him. She was worried about him these days. He seemed so much older all of a sudden. He was fighting back against adversity, but stubbornly, dourly – not with the old enthusiasm and fire.

'I've decided,' her brother said to Gaby, 'I'm going to throw up the law and devote myself to the business entirely. You can see Uncle Gavin and Aunt Alys are giving most of their attention to Netta–'

'That's only natural, David.'

'I didn't say it wasn't. But the emotional shock has changed Uncle and Aunt. Papa can't do *everything*.'

'Please don't forget that I play a part, little brother!'

'No, no, of course not. But if you continue to travel abroad, it really needs at least one other member of the family here to be a support to Papa. I don't think he can expect much from Uncle Gavin for a while.'

It was true. And there was really nothing against David's plan. He had concentrated almost entirely on law concerning the wine industry, in any case. The laws regulating the champagne area had been passed and, as might be expected, had pleased almost no one – appeals and objections were being heard, and it needed a legal training to sort out which firms could go on selling wine to the Tramonts and which could not.

Gaby spent the night with Charles before he was due to fly his plane to Mitrovitsa. She wanted to find again the physical joy they had once known, to remember their affair as something grand and climatic. But in the end they were lying in each other's arms talking in soft tones, more like old friends than lovers. She kissed him farewell next day, listening to his promises to write often and knowing he would soon forget.

She plunged into the wine business. And strange to say, things began to go well. The mildew was conquered. They had two good grape harvests, two very passable vintages. Their new labels, with the government seal of approval incorporated, looked handsome. Prices went up, sales improved.

It really looked as if, by 1915, the bankers' plan would be fulfilled and the House of Tramont would be restored to its former glory.

But people began to read the newspapers with closer attention. 'It's not what's happening in the Balkans we should be worrying about,' they said. 'Look what

Germany's up to.'

The newspapers reported that the Reichstag had passed a bill to increase the already large German army. What could they want it for? European governments began to get worried – or perhaps had always been worried but now began to show it.

A few months later, France brought in a law that every young male must do three years' military service.

'No!' cried Netta. 'They can't take my son away from me!'

'Don't get in a state, Mama,' young Pierre said impatiently. 'It's not going to happen tomorrow!'

'Besides,' his grandfather put in, tugging at his grey beard, 'you'll get an exemption – an only son.'

Pierre nodded and said nothing. But Netta, watching the flash of his dark eyes, knew that he wanted to go. His father had been a soldier. It was a lot more impressive than going into the wine trade!

It seemed that war was expected. Yet why? What was there to fight about? Trade was good, science was providing new processes for the production of metals, manufacture was increasing, railways were spreading. And then came the information that young men attending university would not be called up until after they had gained their degree. Pierre, no scholar, was told he would be going to the Sorbonne.

'Utter nonsense!' he cried. 'They'll throw me out.'

'You'll do as you are told,' growled his grandfather. 'Your mother certainly doesn't want you called up.'

'But what difference does it make? If I go to university I'm parted from her anyway.'

'University is a lot safer than military service.'

'Oh, what rubbish, Grandfather! There isn't going to be a war.'

Why, then, was there all this frenzied diplomatic activity? Statesmen took trains hither and thither, French diplomats crossed the Channel to confer with their British counterparts.

It happened that Gaby was in London on business. Friends of her grandmother's late husband, Lord Grassington, were giving a small evening party for her when the startling news came.

The Archduke Ferdinand and his wife had been assassinated in Sarajevo...

Those present weren't the kind to say naively, 'Where's Sarajevo? What does it matter to us?'

'It's just the opportunity Russia's been waiting for,' said Newell Barr-Lavington of the Foreign Office. 'You can bet she'll start trouble if the Austrians take punitive action against the Serbs.'

All the talk was about what Russia would do. The party broke up in the early hours of the morning, the men shaking their heads and predicting weeks of diplomatic tension throughout Europe.

Gaby was worried too, but about trade. If by any chance hostilities should break out between Russia and Austria-Hungary over this matter, it meant chaos in the railroad system and so trade would be blocked. She knew there were shipments of sweet champagne waiting to go to Russia – she was pretty sure her brother put a 'delay' order on the loading.

All her anxieties were about upsets to business. She expected all the trouble to come from Russia. But none of her worries were strong enough to make her hurry home to France. David in Paris and her father at Calmady would handle everything. She still had business to do in London.

As expected, Russia ordered general mobilisation on July 30th. Her rail system, never of the best, became clogged with troops being shunted towards the Austrian frontiers.

The Austrian Empire was in turmoil. No one quite understood what was going on. Later it was said that the German High Command hadn't bargained for general mobilisation in Russia – whatever the reason, the German government, appealed to by Austria, sent an ultimatum to the Russian government demanding demobilisation. When the demand was rejected, the Germans declared war on Russia.

'Let them fight it out between them,' said London friends to Gaby as they sat in a box at the Haymarket Theatre. 'Serves 'em right!'

But two days later, for no reason that anyone could see, Germany declared war on France.

It was the 3rd of August. Many members of London society, and thus of the British government, were in the country getting ready for the shooting season. Everyone was stunned, amazed.

'I must get home,' Gaby said. 'I must get back to Paris at once.'

'My dear, don't be silly! Nothing's going to happen! The Prussians are just being noisy, as usual – they're not going to attack France, it's just a ruse to distract the Russians.'

'No, no–'

'Dear girl, travelling will be very uncomfortable in any case for a few days. Wait a little.'

Uncertain, anxious, she waited. Twenty-four hours. A fateful delay. In the morning came the news that the German Army had demanded passage through Belgium so as to attack France, had been refused, and nevertheless sent in her troops. The British, bound by a treaty to defend 'little Belgium', declared war on Germany.

And when Gaby tried to leave for her home, she found the travel system utterly clogged. The British Expeditionary Force was being moved to France. It was impossible to get on board a cross-Channel steamer without a pass.

She had friends, of course, who would provide her with one. But even for them it took time. Almost a week went by before she reached Calais on a crowded, dirty cargo boat. But at Calais things were even worse. No trains were running for the use of civilians. No taxis or hire cars were available – the vehicles had either been requisitioned or their drivers called up. When she tried to telephone she was told by the operator that only official calls were permitted.

The manager of the hotel suggested she ask for official help. She went to the Mayor's office, sending in her visiting card to introduce herself. A harassed secretary saw her. 'I'm sorry, mademoiselle, it is entirely impossible to do anything for you at the moment. Military traffic must take priority.'

'But surely I have a right to get home to–'

'Mademoiselle,' he said, fixing her with a grim, tired smile, 'this morning the Germans occupied Liège. Do you think your troubles are more important than that?'

There was nothing to say. With a little shake of the head she got up and went out.

The House of Tramont had shipping offices in Calais but all the horses for the heavy drays had been requisitioned. The shipping manager said he would do his best to find private transport for her. Next day she was called down to the vestibule of the hotel before breakfast. Piquet was there, the agent from the warehouse on the docks. 'Mademoiselle, an acquaintance of mine is going to Paris tomorrow on business, has permits from the Military Transport Officer. He says he'll take you as a passenger in his carriage if you don't mind being squashed in with him and two other people who have to get to the capital.'

'Oh, Monsieur Piquet, I don't mind anything so long as I can get there! Have you managed to get through to the Paris office yet?'

'They keep saying there will be at least two hours' delay, it's hopeless. Monsieur Ravelon asks that you'll limit your luggage to one valise, mademoiselle, as he doesn't want to overstrain his horses.'

The journey took four days, a trip that by train took less than that number of hours. The civilian traffic was kept off the national routes and continually held up at level crossings while troop trains went through.

Always the young men would hang out of the windows laughing and waving their caps. 'We're going to finish off the Boches!' they shouted.

'One hopes they soon will,' muttered Monsieur Ravelon. 'Friends of mine in high places–' he looked mysterious and important – 'say it will all be over by Christmas.'

They had problems getting feed for the horses, for often they had to pull in for long hours at the roadside with no village nearby. The inns where they put up at night had little to offer for either man or beast. They were continually stopped by military gendarmes to have their papers checked: spy scares were rife. Gaby heard of two men shot in Beauvais for asking questions.

Exhausted, cold and depressed, she thankfully said goodbye to her travelling companions in the early hours of 15th August near the Place Pereire and was lucky enough to get a hackney. She went at once to the office, hungry for news.

The office was of course open but the first thing she noticed as she entered the counting-house was that there were no young clerks at their usual posts. The counting-house manager hurried to greet her. 'Good God, Mademoiselle Tramont, I thought you were still in London!'

'No, no, I've been on my way for days – weeks, it seems. Is my brother here yet?'

He hesitated. 'No, mademoiselle, he got his enlistment papers four days ago.'

'Enlistment? At thirty-five?'

'Everyone not in an essential occupation is being called up according to age group and your brother–'

'Did he leave a message?'

'In his office, mademoiselle – a letter addressed to you in London with instructions to send it on as soon as the mail becomes organised again.'

She went ahead of him, up the short open staircase and along the passage to the big cold office where she and David had spent so many hours arguing over business problems. His desk was extremely tidy, but on the centre of the blotter was a large envelope with her name on it.

She tore it open. It contained a note from David with a letter, addressed to him in his father's handwriting.

'Dear Gaby, Clochinou will explain that I have gone to the Army. I'll write or telephone as soon as I have a settled address, I suppose a training camp. Please read Papa's letter for news of the family. I hope to be in touch soon, your affectionate brother David.'

She took her father's letter from its envelope. 'My dear son, It's said that there will be a postal collection from Rheims this afternoon so I am writing to give you the latest news here. You won't be surprised to hear your cousin Pierre volunteered the day after the war was declared and has gone, so far we don't know where. His mother felt she couldn't argue against it in the circumstances but she is very upset.

'Most of our men have gone or are going. I've asked your Uncle Gavin to come back to the manor to be more on the spot, for I think we're going to have big problems with the picking. The authorities have requisitioned almost all our horses and vehicles. All that's left are two teams of young horses, you remember the new ones we were going to train during the coming winter? Old Mellisot says we can get in some of the grapes using handcarts and there are of course some donkeys but you know the load-capacity of a donkey cart is low.

'I hope your sister has the sense to stay in London until this is over. I gather most people expect to have it finished by Christmas, thank heaven, as we want to concentrate on the new blend about then. I've written to Gaby by this same post but I really wonder how long it will take for the mail to get through under the present conditions. Your loving father.

'PS. Young Mellisot remarks to me that you too may be called up quite soon. He says two groups are being called, the twenty to twenty-one and the thirty-five to thirty-six – how he gets this information I've no idea, but he says your group are wanted for guarding installations and the like. As that seems a terrible waste, I'm asking to have your call-up indefinitely postponed on urgent business reasons.'

Monsieur Clochinou had stood by anxiously while she read this. He now said, in a troubled tone, 'Are there any instructions, mademoiselle? We don't know what to do here – the authorities have taken–'

'I know, I know, all your transport. It's the same everywhere.' She sank down in her brother's armchair behind the desk. 'See if you can get me some coffee and rolls, Monsieur Clochinou. I've been on the road so long… And, monsieur, ask the concierge to find someone to tidy the rooms upstairs. I'll be staying here a few days before I set out for Calmady.'

'Oh, mademoiselle…' He stood staring at her, the habitual frown between his brows deeper than usual.

'What's the matter?'

'I fear you won't be able to travel in that direction for a while.'

'I understand that. But in a day or two when transport gets back'

'No, mademoiselle. You haven't heard?'

'What?'

'Our Army launched a great offensive against the Germans in Alsace and Lorraine yesterday.'

She sat staring across the desk at him. After a moment she put up her hands and began to untie the veil that held her travelling hat in place. 'Very well,' she said in a voice that she kept very steady, 'please order my breakfast and then in about half an hour I should like to go up to the apartment to wash and change.'

'I'll tell Madame Debusse at once.'

'As you go, ask Monsieur David's secretary to come in.'

'I'm sorry, mademoiselle, he's gone too.'

'Then find someone – a dactylographist – I want to dictate some instructions. Is there any correspondence? When I've read it I'll want to do some letters.'

'Yes, mademoiselle.'

She could hear the note of thankfulness. Someone had come, someone had taken charge, he was no longer responsible for any mistakes caused by the chaos of the present times.

Later that day came news that the French flag was flying once more over Mulhouse in Alsace. Paris went wild with joy. As she worked at David's desk, Gaby could hear the shouts, loud flourishes by some amateur trumpeter, singing of patriotic songs. She went to the window to look out. Below, a little group were dancing and waving hats in the air. Good, she thought, the fighting will soon be over, everything will quieten down,

I'll be able to get home.

Home... How precious it had suddenly become. Often when she was abroad on business she'd think of Champagne with vague nostalgia, but life in St Petersburg or London had always seemed compensation enough for missing the pale grape blossom or the flurry of the harvest. But now she was filled with a fierce longing to see the vineyards again – the straight rows of vines, the chalky soil, the grey-roofed village with its quiet square and its weathered statue of an angel.

She'd go back the moment the Army had wiped up the German resistance. A week or two, at most.

That was her last day of real optimism for the next four years. For the following day the German army hit back at the French attack, two weeks later they were at the River Marne, and on 4th September they occupied the city of Rheims.

Chapter Fifteen

The Battle of the Marne banished any rejoicing from the streets of Paris. The capital, and beyond it the whole of France, watched in hypnotised anxiety and horror as the German Army came ever nearer and near.

Épernay fell, then Château Thierry, Compiègne, Villers Cotteret, and all the little towns and villages in between. Refugees streamed into Paris, haggard, exhausted, mud-spattered after heavy autumn showers.

The French government had gone to the safety of Bordeaux before the Battle of the Marne, for the capital was already threatened by the occupation of Brussels and the retreat from Mons on the coastal front. Two armies now came inexorably nearer. The sound of the great howitzers could be heard on the Champs Elysées.

Many decided to follow the example of the government and seek safety in the south. But Gaby Fournier-Tramont wouldn't even listen to the suggestion. 'We don't belong in Bordeaux,' she said curtly. 'We're champagne-makers.'

'But if the Germans come in, mademoiselle...?' faltered Clochinou.

'Then it's the end anyway. Besides...' She looked down at her desk, determined not to let the tears show. 'Bordeaux for me is too far from my people. I want to be here so as to get to them the moment the fighting stops.'

For nothing, absolutely nothing, had been heard from Calmady. She had only the letter her father had sent to David, dated

26th August. But now the Germans were in Rheims, had rolled over the village of Calmady with their gun-trains and their staff cars, had taken Épernay where Aunt Alys and Netta and little Elinore lived.

Where were they? Where were her family? What had happened to the workers of the Tramont winefield, to old Mellisot and Suchet and Madame Meniller?

The anxiety was almost unendurable. She couldn't eat, couldn't sleep. She carried out such business tasks as needed to be done in the Rue Lelong but Paris was almost paralysed not with fear, exactly, but with a kind of dreadful consternation.

On the 16th September the newsboys were running like greyhounds through the streets. 'Germans Retreat! Joffre Turns the Tide!' Gaby sent a clerk out to buy copies of the newspapers.

It seemed to be true. With the help of the British, who emerged from the Crècy forests, Maunoury was advancing from Meaux and d'Esperey was attacking the army of von Kluck. The Germans were being driven back to the River Grand Morin.

Now there was joy in Paris – not the foolish dancing in the streets, but the thankfulness of deliverance. People stood at street corners, tears streaming down their cheeks. Women hurried to church to give thanks. For twenty-four hours the tension was released.

But of course they had been over-optimistic. They watched as troops were rushed out of Paris to help the counter-attack, cheering but without the delighted patriotism of the early days. News varied: the British had driven the Germans across the Grand Morin and taken Coulommier, and Maunoury had smashed the centre of the orderly German retreat. No, on the contrary, d'Esperey was in trouble, the counter-attack had stopped.

Special editions of the papers contained little real news – nothing could be revealed, the situation was too desperate. Every morsel of information was seized on and turned into an epic. Rumours flew – the Germans were flying back to their frontier, they had turned and rent the French attack to pieces, von Hausen was advancing against Foch – confusion reigned.

But on the 11th September came a firm announcement. The Germans were in retreat. Paris was no longer in danger. How far they would retrace their steps remained to be seen. It depended on the energy of the French and British counter-attack, one could see – and that expended itself because of the difficulty in bringing up artillery and supplies.

The Germans took up a line running from

the Oise beyond Compiègne to the Aisne, along that river to Berry-au-Bac, and across Champagne in a wandering front to Verdun. There they stayed for the next four years, sometimes giving a few hundred yards or as much as a mile, sometimes gaining the same territory or a few yards either side.

They had been driven north from Épernay. They had settled just beyond Rheims. Their guns were trained on the city and the surrounding villages. Calmady was precisely in their range.

In a word, the House of Tramont was in No Man's Land.

Gaby pulled strings to get passes to go with the first civilian party to Rheims. The railway had been destroyed, partly by the battle and partly by demolition detachments to prevent it from being any use to the enemy. There were long delays, train travellers had to alight and take to such wagons and carriages as they could find. At Soissons Gaby was lucky enough to fall in with a party of staff officers in a closed automobile who gallantly offered her a lift.

She came in through the shattered suburbs of Rheims on the evening of 22nd September. She had been en route for three days. She was handed out of the staff car by a stout major who had decided to take a fatherly interest in her. She was tired, she had a headache from the jolting of the car over shell-holes, she longed more than anything else to get rid of her escort and run in search of a carriage or cart to get her to Calmady.

But there was something strange about the city. She stood on the pavement in front of the hotel where they had drawn up, and raised her head. There was a strange smell.

Burning!

Now she saw, now she understood. The strange glow she'd only been able to glimpse past her companions in the car, through the misty celluloid windows, was Rheims in flames. 'Oh, dear God!' she gasped.

'Mademoiselle, mademoiselle – pray come inside – this is an unsuitable sight for you!' The fat major hurried her indoors.

The manager of the hotel recognised her at once. 'Mademoiselle Tramont! We understood you were in England?'

'Lebel, where is my father? Have you any idea?'

He shook his head. 'Marie! Marie!' he was calling. 'Take Mademoiselle Tramont upstairs. There's a room on the second floor.'

The cage-like lift didn't work. She was led upstairs, protesting, asking questions. 'Sit down, mademoiselle. Wine and food will be here in a moment. I'll tell you what I know when you've eaten. There, there... Sit down, be calm.'

'I am calm, Monsieur Lebel. Please, please tell me!'

He stooped over her and took her hand. 'Your father, as far as we know, is still at the Villa Tramont'

'Still at the villa! But the invasion–'

'He said he would go down into the caves. You know how deep they go – he stayed with a few of the men, I hear he said no damned German was going to scare him away from his vines in September.'

'Oh...' She almost smiled. She could almost hear Papa saying it. 'You think he's safe?'

'We shall soon see. Once those swine stop firing their great guns – and God knows they must give up some day just for a rest! – your father will probably appear as cool as Marne water.'

'My aunt and uncle? In Épernay?'

Lebel clasped her hand tighter. 'We only hear rumours. The people of Épernay were ordered out by our army – an official proclamation, to clear the town so they could fight the German advance. Your people of course had to leave.'

'Where? Do you know where?'

'Well ... it's hard to say ... a lot of the Épernais have gone back, now the tide has flowed well north of them. But your aunt and uncle haven't shown up, nor your Cousin Madame de la Sebiq-Tramont, nor her little girl. At least, we haven't heard they've come back. We're all trying to keep track of what's happened, the Red Cross are trying to make lists – it's been such a muddle, people uprooted, shoved here and there either by the Germans or our own army.'

The door opened, the waitress appeared with a tray.

'Now, drink some brandy,' urged Lebel, pouring it with a trembling hand. 'Stay indoors. The city's on fire.'

'Yes, what in God's name is happening?'

'The Germans bombarded the cathedral three days ago.'

Gaby had been lifting the brandy glass to her lips with two hands. She paused now, stared at him. 'Bombarded the cathedral?'

'Yes.'

'On purpose, you mean?'

'Yes.'

'That's impossible!' She felt only incredulity. No one would deliberately... But Lebel was nodding his head with emphasis, his face distorted with grief and hate.

'They began getting the range on the 14th. Of course we knew they'd train their guns on Rheims, we have army HQ officers here, and thank God for it! You can't imagine, mademoiselle, what it was like while the Germans were passing through... Well, anyhow, they began to hit the cathedral three days ago. The first shell killed poor old Jacques.'

'Who? Oh, not the little beggar who always sat on the steps?'

'Yes, mademoiselle. In a way it seemed … what's the word … symbolic. An innocent, helpless little man. The cathedral was full of wounded and prisoners – French and German wounded, German prisoners. They, poor devils, hurried about trying to save the sacred statues and things... Useless, useless...' He faltered into silence. 'Drink your brandy, mademoiselle.'

She obeyed, fascinated into obedience.

'Abbé Thinot climbed up to the north tower and hung out a Red Cross flag. That was about two o'clock. The shelling didn't stop. About three o'clock some wood on the north tower caught fire and so did the Red Cross flag. I saw it myself, mademoiselle – it went brown and then burst into flames and fell away down the front of the tower in a little burst of sparks.'

'Monsieur Lebel, that's impossible. No one would fire on a Red Cross flag!'

'I would have agreed with you until three days ago, mademoiselle. Well, the cathedral roof caught fire, and the flames spread downwards among the beams and to the pews, and there were hundreds of straw paliasses for the wounded, you know, and they all caught fire, and then there was a terrible sort of explosion because you see, the lead on the roof had melted, and it all deluged down in the nave, and ... and...'

Tears were running down his face. He mopped them with his knuckles. 'Well, that was Sunday. The bombardment slackened off – I suppose the artillery commander could see the cathedral roof had collapsed, or maybe the light wasn't good enough because of course the smoke was causing great clouds... You know how the wind springs up here as evening comes on, mademoiselle – well, the flames ran before it, and the houses around the cathedral caught fire – well, Rheims is still burning.'

By the end of the week the fires were under control. The shells of the burned houses sagged in the bright autumn sun. On the cathedral, not a piece of standing masonry but was scarred with molten lead. The great Rose Window was gone.

Gaby decided to try to get to Calmady. She didn't tell anyone because officialdom would have announced, 'It's forbidden!' and friends would have cried, 'It's too dangerous!' The military were still trying to assess where exactly lay the front between the two opposing armies. As to danger – yes, it was dangerous, but a stubborn instinct was calling to Gaby that she must get home, must see her father, must, *must* find out what had happened to the precious vines.

She put on the leather coat she called her travelling coat, originally a gift from Charles to protect her from the cold of his Benz touring car. In her pocket she carried a pair of secateurs of the kind used for trimming the vines and an electric torch powered by a heavy, clumsy dry-battery.

She walked out of Rheims in the dawn light, past the burnt buildings, past the shell-holes in the square. She turned off into little lanes quite soon, partly to avoid being stopped but more so as to leave the main roads free for the trudging infantrymen.

Four miles out of the city, she passed the wreckage of Loucumire then turned east down a long narrow lane between vine rows scarred by shrapnel. The big guns were firing. From time to time she plunged into shelter in the roadside bank as a whistling missile went by overhead.

Presently she came to the spot to which she'd been heading. It looked like a passing point for two wagons in this narrow lane. Behind it was a bank of brambles and wild vines. She got out the secateurs, hacked a way through – it took a long time, she began to sweat but couldn't take off the coat because her arms would have been torn to pieces by the thorns.

At length the undergrowth began to give way. She was on an incline, partly cobbled. The bank of brambles thinned to little clumps, then she was entering a tunnel. It sloped gently downwards. She walked in without hesitation, and only when the wall on her left began to turn did she switch on the electric torch.

At length she came to a pair of heavy doors padlocked together across the tunnel. She felt for and found the big key in its niche in the wall. She unlocked the doors, put the key back in its niche, went through, closed them, found the duplicate key on the other side, re-locked the padlock and left it dangling on its chain this side of the lock – it could be pulled through if needed, through an aperture especially left for that purpose.

Now she was in a great underground hall. It used to be called the Still Wines Shed, when the drays used to come down into the tunnel to be loaded with still champagne when it was at the height of its popularity. It had become disused because Tramont no longer made still champagne for sale to the public.

She crossed the hall to a door in the far side. Once again she found the key and repeated the former process, though this time it was a single lock, not a padlock. She was now in a corridor carved through the chalk. She walked on, unperturbed by the faint scurrying sounds of little subterranean animals – shrews or voles or perhaps even rats.

When she reached the next door, she felt for a light switch once she had passed through it. But there was no electricity. She hadn't expected it – either the generator was wrecked or the petroleum to drive it had long since run out. It was no use attempting to light the gas brackets above her head in the wall – the gas for the Tramont caves came from Rheims, and Rheims had no town gas at the moment due to enemy action.

But there were always candles and small oil lamps in niches in the wall, together with matches in stainless steel boxes. She lit a lamp, leaving the heavy, unwieldy torch in its place.

She walked on. She was becoming weary now, for it was cold down here and she had worked hard hacking her way through the brambles. She'd been on this trek now for three hours.

There was a staircase to mount, about a mile of passageway to thread, a staircase to descend. Then she was among the carefully stacked champagne – she stooped now and again to see the date on the labels. 1874, 1876, 1880 (a blessed year), 1900 with its special label to celebrate both a great vintage and a great wine...

She passed through one cave after another. At last she was close to the outer cellars, so she must move with care. Who knew what was on the far side of the next opening?

In what was called the 'Farther Cellar' she found signs of recent occupation – a pair of shoes neatly left under a bench, a plate with a crust of cheese, a woman's pocket comb. Then she came to an entrance where something crunched under foot. She looked down – new cement, and at the side of the entrance clay bricks piled with a pickaxe alongside. She understood at once – the villagers had come down and bricked themselves in, leaving one member of the party to smooth old clay plaster over the new work to hide it from any investigating Germans. This last man would then make the long journey round to some other opening into the caves, to come down and join his friends much as she had just done. Now they had 'unbricked' the aperture.

She walked through. Once more her foot crunched on something, but she knew this sound – broken glass. She raised her lamp high to look round.

It was a charnel house for bottles. Not one remained whole unless it rolled empty away from her touch. The invaders had drunk all they could and then, forced to leave, had smashed all they could find. They didn't intend the winemakers to have anything to sell when they came back.

She smiled in grim triumph. Fools! Didn't

they know the cellar stretched for miles behind her, full of good wine?

She extinguished the lamp and put it in a niche before beginning the climb up the long zig-zagging staircase to the entrance tunnel. The lifts, of course, couldn't work without electricity.

The light of the afternoon was bright and golden, causing her to blink. She looked around in some anxiety. Figures moved here and there in the distance, but nothing like the number there should have been on a day of grape picking.

She hurried among the outbuildings to the porte-cochère of the house. Beyond, in the courtyard, two grey-haired men in peasant smocks were sweeping up broken glass with twig brooms. One of them limped aside to guide his fragments to a central pile.

She gave a great cry of joy and flew to him across the shell-pocked cobbles. Next moment she was in his arms, crying, hugging him, demanding to know what he was doing with a broom in his hands. He for his part was asking why she hadn't had the sense to stay in London.

'Oh, Papa, Papa! It seems like another century when I last saw you!'

'Let me look at you... My dear child, you look a wreck. Your coat is all torn–'

'Well, I had to fight my way through the thorns at the Still Wine Shed.'

'Oh, so that's how you got here! My love, you took a big risk. The Germans have an observation post–'

'Where are they? I knew they must have left when I saw you'd all dug yourselves out again.'

'That was only yesterday. There's been action over our heads for the last four days – that was the German retreat. We went below the first time about three weeks ago, when the Germans made their big advance.'

'Papa, why on earth are you wearing that ridiculous serge blouson?' she broke in, standing back to survey him.

'Well, you see, the Germans took all my clothes–'

She thought she'd misheard him. 'They did what? The Germans?'

'I was wearing a suit when we took cover a few days ago and it got all caked with damp clay, so Yssibiac lent me a smock.'

'Papa, you're not serious. Took your *clothes?*'

'Oh yes – everything portable – even the fresh-laundered caps and aprons of the maids.'

She started towards the house, to see for herself the truth of this mad allegation. He tried to catch her arm. 'No, daughter, don't!'

But she was running in through the open front door, suddenly avid to see her home again.

And paused, aghast, in the hall.

The place stank like a pig-sty, but it was men and not animals who had befouled it. The furnishings had been wrecked, someone had shot holes through the portrait of Old Madame which took pride of place over the staircase, the tapestry curtains had been dragged from their poles and where the pelmets had defied removal they'd been hacked with a bayonet. Every window was smashed in the drawing room. The turkey carpets had been carried off, and on the parquet floor empty or broken bottles lay about.

The little walnut table where the five o'clock tea was served had been taken. So had all the lamps, and the great chandelier, and the mahogany chairs. And in the dining room, because the table had defied efforts to get it through the door, someone had leapt his horse upon it – the weals and scratches of its shoes could be clearly seen.

Robert caught up with her as she was about to go into the music room. 'Don't go any further,' he said. 'It's too distressing.'

'They must really hate us,' she said in bewilderment, throwing out her hands to indicate the vandalism.

'Oh, my dear – it's just that they were crazy drunk.'

'Well, *I* hate *them!*'

Her father frowned. 'Well, don't waste too

much energy on that, because there's plenty needs doing here.'

'Oh – yes, you're right! I'll just go up and change out of–'

He drew her back, shaking her head. 'No, don't go up.'

'You mean – my room...'

'There's almost nothing there. All your clothes are gone. They've torn up some of your lace things and ... and... Well, it's better not to see.'

She went slowly to the piano and was about to sit down on the piano stool when she became aware it was covered with a sticky red substance. She recoiled. 'That's not–'

'Not blood,' he said with grim amusement. 'It's preserved plums from the kitchen pantry – they emptied about fifty bottles into the grand piano.'

She fell against him, hiding her face on his shoulder, 'Oh, Papa...!'

After a few minutes he drew back. 'I've got to get on, Gaby. The shelling may resume any minute, and then it's dangerous to work out of doors.'

'I suppose you'll get some of the villagers to help clean up?'

He shook his head. 'Their own homes have been treated the same. Besides, when they can spare time and energy for anything else – there's the grapes. I'm not going to let them rot on the vines if I can help it.'

She nodded in agreement. 'Is Uncle Gavin helping you? Where is he?'

He sighed, and she suddenly realised how drawn and worried he looked. 'I've no idea, Gaby. When we first went down to shelter, Gavin said he had to get to Épernay – he'd left Alys and Netta there, it was quite understandable. That was about three weeks ago. Of course, here at the villa we've been in the caves, so there's been little chance of getting in touch – but I can't hear any word of them.'

'You don't think… You don't think…?'

'Of course not,' he said with a false heartiness. 'In any case, we're likely to hear soon. There was a Red Cross official here earlier, asking what news we had of people, trying to collate information–'

'Had he heard of Uncle Gavin and the others?'

'No, but the whole situation is such a bedlam – he says that if we go to Rheims in about three days, they'll post lists of names and known whereabouts – but you see, people are still on the move, trying to get back to their homes now that the Germans have retreated…'

After a discussion Gaby decided to go back to Rheims to reclaim her valise from the hotel. Normally she wouldn't have bothered, but now she had nothing except what she stood up in, and who could tell whether it would be possible to buy new clothes if the Germans had looted the shops as they had the houses?

Her father asked her to stay in Rheims until the Red Cross information notice was posted. She was unwilling, but he pointed out that by the time she got back it would be the following morning, so that she would only have to wait two more days.

It made no difference, of course, whether it was night or day above ground as she travelled back through the tunnels. But she felt the weariness of night-time. She stopped to rest for an hour at the northern end of the caves before doing the walk to Rheims, and it was as she was trudging out into the wan morning light, still half asleep, that she was arrested.

'Now then, young woman, who are you and where have you come from?' It was a middle-aged soldier in a tin helmet and a rain-cape, pointing a rifle at her.

'Oh! Oh, good morning, corporal. My name's Gaby Tramont, and I came from down the road.'

'No you didn't, I had my glasses trained on that road not ten minutes since and there wasn't a soul in sight.'

'I came out of an underground passage.'

'A spy!'

'No, no, don't be silly – I'm Gaby

372

Tramont, of the wine firm.'

'You're a rotten German spy, that's what you are, my fine lady, and you're going straight into the guardroom!'

He marched her ahead of him, prodding her with the rifle. They soon came to a sentry post – it hadn't been there when she set out. She was taken to a ruined house on the outskirts of Loucumire, where a young officer listened to her explanation, examined her papers, looked willing to be convinced, but decided in the face of his sergeant's scepticism to have her taken to Rheims.

There the mistake was put right at once. 'I'm sorry, Mademoiselle Tramont, but you understand we have to be careful.'

'Of course, captain, I quite understand.'

'You say you'd been to your home – what is it name – Calmady?'

'Yes, I was naturally anxious to see–'

'But how could you get there?'

She explained about the tunnels. 'You're a stranger to these parts, captain, but us Champenois know how to get about the country even if the enemy are thick on the ground.' She told him the legend about Old Madame, sheltering in the caves and coming out to find the Uhlans in her courtyard.

'Well, then, it has its dangers, this troglodyte transport!'

'I suppose so, but it's also very useful. The Rhenois, for instance, will be able to live relatively safely in their city despite the German shelling – they'll just take to the caves.'

'Not very healthy, though?' He had a great distaste for the idea of underground life. He was a southerner, devoted to the sunny openness of Provence.

'Well, it isn't good for rheumatism, that's true. But on the other hand, I could take you by the hand and lead you to a spot that's quite possibly on the far side of the German lines.'

'No!' he said, raising his eyebrows.

'Yes,' she insisted, but she could see he didn't believe her.

The Red Cross lists were pinned up in the hall of the Mairie on the evening of the following day. With a crowd of others, Gaby went to find out what had been learned. In the flickering light of high-swung oil lamps, they read and exclaimed and groaned or laughed at the news they saw.

The names of Gavin Hopetown-Tramont and Alys Hopetown-Tramont were listed among the dead. 'Killed by shellfire at Chalons Crossroads.' Nicolette de la Sebiq-Tramont was among the wounded: 'Present whereabouts, Chalons Hospital.' But where was Elinore? Her heart beating hard in her breast, she hunted among the sheafs of paper and found her at last. 'Missing: Elinore de la Sebiq-Tramont, aged five, last seen at Chalons Crossroads.'

Gaby allowed herself to be edged out of the way as yet another anxious Rhemois searched for relatives. She went blindly out into the street. The sky was lit up by a green flare as the French gunners tried to illuminate the terrain to the north. Under its baleful light she made her way back to the hotel.

It was just possible to get to Chalons. She bribed her way aboard a travelling wagon. The journey was quicker than others she'd undertaken in the last month or two. In Chalons she was set down in what had once been the fine main street, hurried to the hospital, and asked for Netta.

'Are you a relative, mademoiselle?'

'Her cousin.'

'Papers, please?'

'Papers? To see a sick woman?'

'Mademoiselle, we've had enemy agents here picking up information from the refugees. We have to be careful.'

Her papers were in order. The Red Cross matron sighed, returning them to her. 'Mademoiselle, we have an official telegram for Madame Tramont. We haven't dared give it to her as yet.'

'A telegram? From whom?'

'The Department of War, mademoiselle. Her son Pierre was killed in the Battle of the Aisne.'

'But that's impossible!' Gaby cried. 'He couldn't have completed his training–'

'Oh, mademoiselle, every unit had to be thrown in to drive back the Germans! I hear there were fifty thousand casualties...' The matron's florid face crumpled into tears. 'Young boys... With their whole life before them...'

Gaby sat listening to the mourning voice. She tried not to hear it. Pierre dead?

After what seemed an eternity the matron was speaking in a firmer voice. She had dried her eyes. 'Will you take her the telegram, mademoiselle?'

'Give it to me.'

She was given the envelope, and a little girl in Red Cross uniform was to guide her. Netta was in a warehouse taken over by the medical authorities. It was heated by a stove at the far end. Someone had tried to clean the grimy windows but with scant success. There were no curtains. Truckle beds and mattresses took up most of the floor space.

Netta was sitting on a packing-case in a borrowed dressing-gown. One arm was in a sling, she had a dressing on her face held in place by a bandage. Her once-beautiful hair was badly brushed and piled up in a tangle. She looked up wildly as Gaby approached.

'I haven't seen her!' she cried. 'Have you? Those people who took her, they'll be looking after her – don't you think so?'

'Netta, it's me, Gaby!'

'It's not as if I wanted to let go of her – but they offered a lift, she was so tired, poor little thing – walking for nearly two days'

'Netta, don't you know me?' Gaby knelt by the packing-case, took her cousin's wildly gesturing hand. 'Netta, it's Gaby. I've come to take you home.'

'Home? Home – of course, that's where she is! Of course she'd go straight there as soon as she realised she was lost. She's always a good little girl – never strays far from home.' Netta dragged her hand away. 'Who are you? Are you from the Red Cross? They said... Someone said...'

Gaby turned to the little escort. 'Can she be taken home?'

'I think so, I don't think there's much we can do for her here. But of course she must be officially discharged. Matron will have her papers. Come along.'

Between them they got Netta to her feet. She came with complete docility, inquiring as they went whether they had seen her daughter and if she had had anything to eat today. 'She has to have milk every day. The doctor said milk is very necessary for good teeth. But milk's very scarce, isn't it? And so are potatoes – I've noticed it's difficult to get potatoes. Do you know where there are any?'

At the matron's office there was a short

wait. Then Gaby was called in to sign official discharge certificates. 'I hope your cousin will make a good recovery. She has had great misfortunes. How did she take the news of her son?'

'Oh, good God, the telegram – I forgot all about it.' Gaby automatically put her hand in her pocket for it, but couldn't find it. Then she realised she'd been holding it in her hand until she set her cousin down on a bench outside the matron's door. She turned quickly to retrieve it.

Too late. Netta was sitting on the bench with the opened telegram in her hands. She looked up as Gaby appeared in the doorway.

'Gaby!' she gasped. 'It says … my son… Oh, Gaby…'

With the paper still in her hands, she fell forward. The little auxiliary nurse leaped to catch her, but her thin arms were not strong enough to hold her.

Netta fell to the floor. Gaby threw herself down to help her, to lift her up.

But even as she put her arms around her, she knew it was too late. Her cousin had come to the end of her resources. Grief and despair had won.

Chapter Sixteen

The ruts in the lane had been frozen by the late spring frost. But the ice over the puddles broke under Gaby's heavy clogs. She could feel the cold water sometimes flow against her ankles in their thick wool stockings. In front of her face, her breath made a silver fog.

Overhead the stars of early morning were bright and clear, except when they were dimmed by an occasional gunnery flare. Somewhere to the west, a barrage was being put up – she could hear the yammering of the guns, see the flash of exploding shells.

She trudged on, shoulders hunched in her coarse peasant's coat. Over her arm there was a basket containing a man's suit, worn and much mended; a small sack of potatoes; and two vegetable pasties, made the previous morning by herself in the kitchen at Calmady.

If anyone stopped her, she was going to Rethel market to sell these items. She was Berthe Amouillet of Bazancourt, and she had the papers to prove it – good forgeries, provided by master engravers for French Intelligence.

Her briefing for this mission had been somewhat alarming. 'We have an agent on the run behind the German lines, mademoiselle. He has a rendezvous already arranged but we can't get to it because the enemy's on his trail and we've had to close down the network. It needs someone who knows the area to go there by an unexpected route and give him fresh clothes, new papers, and accompany him to a fresh safehouse.' Major Garouche had then paused, screwed his monocle in his eye, and added, 'Of course you are at liberty to refuse this assignment if you wish. You are a civilian – no one can force you to risk your life.'

Gaby had been recruited for French Intelligence when her remark to the provostcaptain filtered back to them; that she could take him by the hand and lead him to a spot behind the German lines. It had dawned on the HQ staff that this was literally true – that the Champenois knew an underground network of caves and passages in their chalk landscape. Mademoiselle Tramont knew more than some because she had access to the notebooks of an old friar who had made a hobby of excavating in the countryside.

For the last eighteen months she'd been leading small parties of men – with now and again a woman – to egress points north and north-east of Rheims. Some of them came out in No Man's Land, some of them came out about three-quarters of a mile behind the front line. She herself had gone on one or two forays, mainly to take messages to agents in place.

The one she was going to help now had been out of touch for over a week. 'Our problem is, mademoiselle, that the Germans may have captured him and put someone else in his place.'

'How am I to know? Is there a password?'

'Yes, but they might have got that out of him. In any case, we've had to junk them all – the Boches captured a lot of information when they raided one of our points in Laon.'

'What you're saying is, there's no way of knowing whether this man is ours or a plant put there by the enemy?'

'Exactly. But we do desperately want to get him out of the trap before it closes, if he's still at liberty and able to travel.'

'Am I to bring him back through the tunnels?'

'No, we've a place for him all fixed up. He can rest there...' Major Garouche hesitated. 'There's ... er ... a possibility ... er ... that you might do something else for us.'

'What's that?'

'You speak German, I believe?' She nodded. 'Could you speak German like an Alsacien?'

'We-ell ... I could speak it convincingly

enough to dupe a German, but not another Alsacien, if you see what I mean.'

He looked pleased. 'Well, we'll leave it for now. A lot depends...'

'On what?'

'On how you find our man. All we can tell you is he's going under the name of Emile Cellier and he's supposed to rendezvous at the ruins of the Church of Our Lady in Pettiloul every night as from the 10th May.'

'And what if the man who's there is a German?'

The major sighed, took out his monocle, polished it, and put it back in his eye. 'I can only say, mademoiselle, that you'll have to use your instinct. If he strikes you as ... not quite genuine, you'll have to pretend you stumbled on him by accident.'

'Oh, thank you very much,' Gaby said.

'You would like to withdraw?'

But of course she couldn't do that.

She had wanted with all her heart to do something to pay back the wounds the Germans had inflicted on her family. So many dead, so much suffering – and no one except herself and her brother left to take up arms against them. Her father was too old and unfit for military service and, besides, it had been decreed that he was of more use to the nation in helping to save the wine trade. 'After all,' said the Mayor of Rheims to him, 'when we finally gain the victory, we must have champagne to celebrate with, mustn't we?'

Gaby's brother David was on the Western Front now in Flanders. No question of an easy post behind the lines guarding some railway station or power works. Men up to forty-five were being called up for active service these days. The casualties had been horrifying since the war began. This new form of war – trench warfare, with huge guns firing from safe positions miles behind the lines took a dreadful toll.

Her little Cousin Elinore had at last been found, after a month of searching. The peasant family who offered her a lift had gone on with her to their relations in Niort. It had taken some time for them to realise that they ought to contact the Red Cross and say they had in their charge a little unknown child, answering to the name Elinore or Nora, whose parents had been last seen in Chalons.

Gaby had gone to collect her and take her to relations in Touraine. Frederic's father was dead now, but distant relatives gladly offered to give the little girl a home in that safe region until the war in Champagne should be over.

Nora had clung to Gaby as she said goodbye. 'You will come and get me, won't you?' she begged. 'You won't forget all about me again?'

'We didn't forget, Nora. We just couldn't find you.' Gaby held her tight. This little cousin was the only survivor of the branch of the Tramont family through Aunt Alys and Cousin Netta. The Germans had killed the rest. Oh yes, they had killed Netta too. Netta's heart had broken because of what they had done to her parents and her only son.

Gaby looked up now at the stars. They were beginning to fade just a little. It must be about four in the morning. Any moment she should sight the ruined steeple of the church of Our Lady. She had heard the sounds of men on sentry duty now and again, but each time she had quietly faded away among the trees. Now she skirted the woods to stare down the shallow slope.

Yes, there was the spire. She saw the glint of water or ice under the starlight – shell-holes full of cold winter rain, the rain that had reduced the whole countryside to one great mudbath. Whatever else she would remember about this war if she survived, the main thing would be the mud. Men marching through mud, guns being dragged by straining horses covered in mud, mud thrown up in a great lacey roundel when a shell landed, mud on her clogs, on her clothes, sometimes on the very bread that she put to her lips.

She took off her clogs. They were too noisy

for this dangerous moment. She went quietly down the slope, through the ruins of one or two village houses. In among the stonework of the church she thought she sensed movement.

'Monsieur?' she whispered.

No reply.

'If there's anybody there, please come out you're frightening me.' It was said in the patois of Champagne, with a whimper of fear in it.

A man's silhouette appeared against the starlight.

'Well, what is there to be afraid of?' he said in a gruff tone.

'So there *is* someone here! I thought so! Hiding like that, scaring a good respectable woman! Who are you, anyhow?'

He gave a grunt of laughter. 'If you must know, Madame-in-a-Fright, I'm Emile Cellier.'

'Oh, you are, are you! Let's have a look at you, Emile Cellier!' She got out a box of matches and in the shelter of the wreckage struck one. She held up the flame in cupped hands, and then dropped the match at once. 'Why!' she gasped. 'I know you! You did legal work for my family – Marc Auduron!'

'What – who's that – by God, it's little Gaby Tramont! What the devil are you doing here?'

'Looking for you, as it happens.'

'You?'

'And why not me?' she challenged, falling back into the curt patois of the region. 'You need a change of clothing – I suppose you don't care who brings it, my faith!'

'Gaby,' he said in wonder. 'Gaby Tramont!' He took her hand in both of his and shook it with vigour. She could feel that he was chilled through, but the grip was strong and with a warmth of its own. 'How did you get into this business?'

'It's a long story. How did *you?*'

'Oh, it seemed a thing I could do... There wasn't anybody to be hurt if I came a cropper, you see.'

'But your wife...?'

'I lost my family in an artillery attack at the beginning of 'fifteen.' There was a pause. She didn't know what to say. There had been so much loss... 'Well, little Gaby – did you bring me dry clothes? I've been wearing these soaking-wet things for two days now.'

'Yes, and in my basket, two tartines – are you hungry?'

'Famished!'

She put the food into his hands and, half-smiling in the darkness, heard him wolf it down. She produced from a pocket a tiny bottle of spirits, of the kind that the peasants took into the vineyards with them to wash down their midday snack. She gave that to him.

'Ah,' he sighed, 'now I begin to feel half-human again.'

'Get into these dry clothes. That'll complete the process.'

Without false modesty he peeled off the wet jacket and trousers. She turned away, although it was dark enough not to matter. After a moment he said, 'I'd better bury these old things.' When that was done he inquired, 'Now, who am I? Have I got papers?'

'You're my husband Gustave Amouillet. Just a moment, your papers are in a safe place.' She delved into the bodice of the thick serge dress. 'Here–'

'Oh, they're warm!' He laughed softly. 'I find that charming...'

'Come on now, Marc – this isn't the time for tomfoolery. You're a hard-working, heavy-handed peasant from Bazancourt and we're on our way to Rethel to try to buy a second-hand paraffin heater because your widowed father has the rheumatics and must be kept warm. Right?'

'Right.'

They set off. She saw at once that he was accustomed to letting himself slip into the landscape. He walked with the steady, somewhat heavy tread of the peasant. He let her carry the basket instead of, gentleman-like, taking it from her.

387

As they went they exchanged news. He'd been out of touch for a little over a week, with a German search party hard on his heels. She told him the group at Laon were 'blown', and he swore under his breath.

'Oh, God, Gaby – one of them was a boy of fourteen...'

He explained that he had been working behind the lines for about fifteen months. 'I learned German during my law studies, it made me useful.'

'What have you been doing?'

'Sabotage. Occasional information. I don't know what's in store now – presumably I'll have to be given a new identity and a new station if Emile Cellier is known to the *Burgerwehr.*'

'Well, it won't be Gustave Amouillet. He's a temporary figure because the papers, though good, are for an imaginary man.'

The best papers were those belonging to someone who had died. That was one of the things the underground agents did – they called it 'corpse-robbing', they took the papers from casualties of shelling or accident to be used again where possible.

The journey to Rethel was completed by rail. Their papers were checked once at the station and once on the train, but caused no comment. At Rethel they went, not to the market, but to the address that Gaby had memorised. It was a disused shop, its broken windows boarded up.

'Here?' she murmured dubiously. 'I think this must be wrong.'

'No, wait, the door's ajar.' He pushed it open and stepped inside.

At once an elderly woman came from the back. 'Oh, m'sieu, madame – you're rather late – I had given you up.'

'Madame?' Gaby countered. Then the password: 'The market's crowded today.'

'Ah, yes, too crowded for comfort.'

She offered her hand. 'Glad to see you. My name's Mili Ladour. You're Cellier, are you?'

'I was.'

'Yes, I heard there had been trouble. Come to the back room, I've coffee keeping hot. There's some bread, but no butter or meat, I'm afraid.'

'Oh,' sighed Marc, breathing in the aroma of the chicory-coffee, 'that's heaven ... I haven't had a hot drink in six days.'

Their hostess poured the drink into thick mugs. 'You're supposed to be looking over this shop to see whether you want to rent it. Take your time over the coffee. I have to go and collect someone – I'll be back in about half an hour.'

'Renting a shop?' Gaby laughed as the door closed behind her. 'I hope nobody comes and questions us – we don't look like people who could afford to rent a shop.'

But Marc wasn't paying any heed. He was gulping the hot coffee though it burned his throat.

The half-hour wait went quickly. They still had a lot of news to exchange. Marc had heard that she had lost members of her family but not that Elinore had been found.

'Safe and sound,' he said. 'Well, thank god for that at least!'

'I don't know if she's as "sound" as all that. She's with elderly cousins now, who don't really know how to look after a little girl. They write that she has nightmares all the time.'

'Who hasn't,' he said with a sigh.

Madame Ladour came back with one man, whom she introduced as Danny. 'Anne can't get away – she works for the German *Kommandantur* and they've given her a long proclamation to type out that'll take up her lunch hour. Well now… Did HQ put you in the picture?'

Marc looked at Gaby. Gaby shook her head. 'My orders were to collect Marc – I mean Cellier – and bring him to this address.'

'Hm… Which of you knows about Alsace?'

Marc looked mystified. Gaby said: 'Er … I was asked if I could speak German like a native of Alsace… But I wasn't given any more details.'

'Ah,' said Danny. 'Then let's explain. This

shop is to be let to a couple from Alsace who are supporters of the Germans. You know the way that goes – they get access to supplies of more or less luxury goods and their customers are German officers or favoured French citizens.'

'Have you papers for this pair?' Marc inquired.

'Papers, family photographs in an album, clothes – though I'm afraid the dresses won't fit you, madame,' said Mili, looking at Gaby with some envy. 'You're smaller than Madame Bleker, obviously.'

'You mean ... these are real things? Belonging to real people?' she asked, on an indrawn breath.

'Yes, it's quite a haul.'

'How did you get them?'

'That, madame, is the kind of question you don't ask,' said the leader with a frown at her. 'The point is, we got this windfall two days ago and we've *got* to use it within the next twenty-four hours, otherwise questions will be asked by the authorities about the non-appearance of the Blekers.' He hesitated. 'This has been sprung on you, that's clear. The point is, are you going to take it on?'

'What's the alternative if we don't?'

'Well, we'll pass you on to Mézières and keep you hidden until we can get new papers–'

'No, I didn't mean that,' Marc interrupted. 'I mean, if we don't take on this Bleker job, what happens to the set-up?'

'Oh ... we'll have to let it go. We can't keep it open any longer – the Blekers are supposed to be on their way from Strasbourg but though they could be delayed a day or two, we can't keep it going beyond tomorrow.' He looked first at Marc, then at Gaby. 'It would be a damned shame to lose it. We could get first-rate information. It's a near-perfect set-up.'

'Absolutely,' Marc said. He waited.

'I agree,' said Gaby.

'You'll do it? Thank God for that! Mili said she was sure the man would go along, but you, madame... You're an unknown quantity to us.'

'Do you want to know my real name?'

'For the love of heaven! Nothing I want less! Well, let's get this thing going. This is the shop you're to have. You have to report at the *Kommandantur* and claim it as soon as you can, and you'd better invent an excuse for being late – you were supposed to arrive yesterday. We've got the luggage and papers in a safe place...'

He gave them directions, then repeated them so that they would remember it. 'I'll go first, then you two. Mili will lock up and so forth, while you make your way ahead of her. She works for the Accommodation

Bureau which is how we knew this chance was coming up. You can change and make yourselves presentable. Mili will help. Then you'll go as soon as you can to the *Kommandantur* – clear?'

'Quite clear. How will we make contact with you?'

'Leave it a week or so. You'll be busy opening the shop and so on. I'll come in – I can't come as a customer, of course, but I'm a rail clerk, I could bring information about deliveries.'

'Deliveries of what?' Gaby put in as Danny headed for the door. 'What are we going to sell in this shop once we rent it?'

'Oh yes... That's important, you want to be able to make sense when you claim it. It's going to be a wine shop – I hope you know something about wine?'

Gaby looked at Marc. Marc looked at Gaby. Then they began to laugh with genuine amusement.

Adele and Thomas Bleker were, it ensued, a childless couple in their middle thirties. Thomas was the son of a family who wholeheartedly accepted the Germanisation of their region in 1870 and had grown up believing himself to be German. For this loyalty he was now being rewarded by a chance to better himself, to start up his own business instead of being a mere shop assistant. This was quite common in the occupied areas – empty shops and abandoned businesses were given to those whom the conquerors wished to reward.

The luggage and papers were in a cellar in the Rue de Givance. There were two suitcases and a trunk. As Mili had foretold, the dresses were too big for Gaby but with the use of pins and some hasty stitching while Marc shaved and changed she provided herself with an outfit which would pass muster. In due course she could alter the clothes, and with the help of a friendly photographer they could replace the photos in the family album with others showing themselves.

'What happens if anyone from Strasbourg drops in at the shop?' Marc murmured after he had hefted the luggage aboard the porter's handcart which Danny had sent.

'Let's hope it doesn't happen.' Mili surveyed him, in his good suit of brown broadcloth and high starched collar. 'You look quite convincing. Madame isn't so well-turned-out, but after a long and difficult journey perhaps she's not feeling too good. By the way, what's your excuse for being so late?'

Gaby fanned her face with Adele Bleker's gloves. 'Oh, mercy, I felt so bad,' she moaned. 'Long train journeys always upset my stomach...'

It had been uttered in the thickened

394

French of the Alsacienne. Mili stared at her. 'Good for you!' she cried. 'You know, I think this is really going to work!'

And it did. Their perfectly genuine travel documents and property claim were examined and accepted by the *Kommandantur*. They were given an escort to show them the premises they were to rent. A fat envelope was handed to them with details of how to apply for supplies of wine and cigars. Paint to refurbish the shop could be obtained from the Civilian Supplies Depot by special permit. New ration cards and clothing permits would come from the Mayor's office. Shop fittings and house furniture could be requisitioned from the *Stapelplatz*.

It was evening by the time they had been through all the formalities and signed all the papers. The last official wished them well and went out of the shop, closing the door with a friendly wave.

All at once Gaby began to shake. She felt blindly for a support, and felt Marc's arms come around her.

'What's the matter?'

'I'm frightened, Marc, I'm so frightened!'

'It's all right, it's just reaction–'

'What am I doing here? I told my father I'd be back in two days!'

'We'll get word to him, don't worry.'

'No, you don't understand! I don't want to

be here! I'm too scared to go through with it!'

'Now, now,' he soothed. 'I've always admired you, ever since that night at your coming-out ball...'

She jerked her head up to look at him, through her panicky tears.

'You were there? I don't remember that.'

For a moment there was a hurt look, but it was gone instantly. 'Why should you? That was the night you fell in love.'

'Oh... With Lucas Vourville... You know about that?'

'You forget, I was with your father's lawyers. I took part in the negotiations.'

She wiped her tears with the palms of her hands. 'I wasted half a year of my life on him... How strange it seems now.'

'Yes,' Marc said, setting her steady on her feet a few paces away. 'You see being scared out of your wits for a few minutes does you a lot of good. It cuts trivialities down to size.'

Despite herself she laughed – unsteadily, but it was a real laugh. 'And what's the next triviality we have to deal with?'

'Since we can't select our household furniture until tomorrow, we've got to go and get a room for the night.'

'Ah,' she said. 'I see. Come along then, Monsieur Bleker.'

'Very well, Madame Bleker.'

The innkeeper looked sour when they handed him their papers with the approval of the German authorities stamped all over them. He gave them the very worst accommodation on offer – an attic room full of draughts, bitterly cold in the May frost.

Since they were a married couple, there was a double bed. There was no pretence that Marc, a true gallant, would sleep on the floor while she took the bed. He was too exhausted after days and nights on the run, and for her part Gaby was too weary herself to worry about the decencies.

In the night she was woken by little starts of movement. She raised herself on her elbow. Marc was lying with his back to her, making little stabbing motions in the air in front of his face, as if he were fighting off an attack. He was muttering and protesting. But he was still asleep.

She turned, put her arms about him, laid her cheek against the nape of his neck. 'It's all right,' she whispered, 'it's just a dream, Marc, you're all right.'

And that was the closest to physical embrace they came on that first night.

The German officers at the barracks in Rethel soon grew fond of the couple who had opened the wine shop in the Rue de la Chappelle. The man was respectful yet friendly, always ready to lend a sympathetic ear if one had been passed over for promotion or been given orders for the front. The woman, though, was something special – mysterious dark eyes that betokened Latin blood, perhaps, and a golden smile like a madonna.

Not that it was much use trying to flirt with her. She and her husband were clearly head over heels in love with each other, for all that they appeared to have been married upwards of ten years.

Gaby and Marc turned to each other inevitably. Apart from the fact that they were physically attracted, they had no one else. They were isolated, vulnerable, with no friends apart from the few underground fighters who knew their secret. The neighbours disliked and distrusted them – dirty toadies of the Germans, taking some other man's home and livelihood, making a living off the goods the Germans 'requisitioned' for their own benefit.

In July came news of the French and British first offensive on the Somme. Marc sent back word that the German officers seemed unperturbed, expecting to hold their own against it at least and probably turn it back. There was certainly consternation among them in September, when a new weapon by the British was reported – the Germans called it *Ein Tank* but what it could be Marc couldn't fathom. In October Marc sent an urgent message – that the proposed French attack at Verdun was already expected, was spoken of as a matter of course almost, by the officers who came into the wine shop.

Christmas of that year was full of hope for the Blekers. It was said Germany had sent a peace note to the Allies, and there was a new French offensive on the Meuse which seemed to be doing some good.

'Do you remember, darling,' Gaby said as they came indoors from the midnight mass, 'that when the war first began, everyone said it would be over by Christmas?'

Marc sighed. 'What nobody mentioned was, *which* Christmas.'

'Perhaps it really is going to end soon. Perhaps this peace note...'

'Perhaps.'

But in the night they clung to each other in desperation. Time was going by, they were trapped here in enemy territory, there seemed almost nothing to hope for.

And yet, as 1917 began, such news as they could get from the Allied side sounded good. The Germans were withdrawing on the Western Front, the American President Woodrow Wilson was expressing indignation with German actions. The weight of events might yet force the Kaiser to negotiate a peace.

But then a jubilant *Kavallerie-Offizier* shattered all their hopes. 'Champagne!' he called, banging on the counter with a gloved fist. 'Champagne to drink the health of the Tsar!'

'Of the Tsar, captain?' queried Gaby, half-smiling, half-puzzled – for Russia was the enemy of Germany, the ally of the French.

'Yes, yes, to the health of the Tsar! He's abdicated, and the government of All the Russias is in a hell of a mess, and if they can go on fighting on the Eastern Front I'm the Sultan of Baghdad! My dear madame, it means the war in the east is over! Germany will be able to concentrate all her forces on those bastards the French and the British!'

'Oh, I see,' she said, turning away with her eyes suddenly flooding with tears. She spent a long time selecting two good bottles of champagne for the captain, ensuring that when she faced him again she was unperturbed and smiling.

'Damn them all!' cried Marc when she went into the cellar where he was stacking crates. 'Just when it looked as if it might be starting to turn our way...'

'I can't bear to think of it, Marc! Will the Russians really stop fighting?'

'I don't know ... I hope not... Oh, God, when will it ever be over?'

Their misery was lightened only a month later. Danny came late at night in great excitement. 'President Wilson has declared war on Germany,' he announced.

'A new rumour?' Marc said cynically.

'No, it's true – we got it on our network – the peace-lover declared war.'

'There's been nothing in the papers…'

'You don't think the Germans are going to let us know? They'll have to, eventually – but they'll play it down. But I can tell you, it happened a week ago and America has promised a huge amount of ammunition and weapons to the Allies.'

'Munitions and weapons… What we need is fighting men, Danny.'

Gaby had listened in silence. Now she said, 'Danny, can we go home soon?'

'What?' he blurted, taken aback.

'Can we pack up and go? I … I don't think I can bear much more of this.'

'Oh, look here, madame, that's not the kind of thing I like to hear.'

'I know, I'm sorry, but I have this feeling… It's time to go… We've been amazingly lucky so far, we've passed on a lot of useful gossip and a few bits of good information. But our luck is going to run out, Danny. I feel it in my bones.'

Marc took her hand. 'You must forgive her,' he said in apology to Danny. 'She's been a bit edgy recently.'

'I suppose it's no wonder. I understand, of course… But hang on a bit longer. We hear rumours of trouble with the civilian population in Germany. HQ would like to know if it effects the Army, they want to hear anything you can pick up.'

'But let them know at HQ – Danny, promise you'll pass back the word – I want us to leave *soon* – do you understand, Danny, *soon!*'

'Yes, yes,' he said. But she could see it had a low priority in his scheme of things.

In July a pretty French girl came into the shop one afternoon on the arm of a German officer. During the discussion about a good bottle of wine to go with the pigeons for the main meal, she managed to slip a tiny fold of paper to Gaby.

'Meet 2 am Ecu d'Or very urgent,' the message ran.

'It's a trap,' Gaby cried.

'No, I'm sure it's genuine.'

'She's hired by the Germans to–'

'I think she's Julie Delahaie – Danny's mentioned her. She's all right, Gaby, I'm sure she is.'

Despite her fears, he went out at ten minutes to two. There was a curfew, and Gaby sat for almost two hours imagining Marc arrested, dragged before the military authorities, tortured to make him talk, made ready to be shot as the dawn came up...

He came back about four. He gave his usual tap on the door before using his key. She flew to open it in the dark. He came in, but someone came just behind at his heels.

'Marc – who–?'

'Ssh… It's all right… Let us get inside and close the door.' He pushed her back up the stairs. She heard him follow up with the other man, and then the curtain was fitted against the door to keep in the light. He struck a match, lit the staircase lamp.

Behind him on the lower treads was a young man in an extremely ill-fitting grey suit.

'Gaby, this is Lieutenant John Stanner of the Royal Flying Corps. Madame Bleker, Monsieur Stanner.'

'How d'you do, madame,' he said in English.

'Marc! What is he doing here? Why have you brought him here?'

'He's got to be got out, Gaby. He's got information that needs to go back to British Intelligence at once. And you're going to take him.'

'Me?'

'Yes, my darling – you're right, it's time for you to go – and you must take this young man with you.'

'Go without you? Never!'

'Yes, you must,' Marc insisted. He turned to the newcomer. 'Please come upstairs, Lieutenant. We'll have a drink and explain things. Then you must get some sleep because you've a long trip ahead of you.'

'Marc,' Gaby said in an angry whisper, 'I am *not* leaving Rethel without you–!'

'Listen, Lieutenant Stanner's plane was hit two days ago above Tournai. He tried to make it back to the British lines but the wind forced him east and he came down near Le Cateau. Luckily some friends of ours collected him and brought him in a supply wagon to Rethel because he's got to be taken back, tomorrow morning – I mean, *this* morning – or this evening at the latest.'

'But why? I don't understand why?'

'Because he saw German reinforcements coming up in large numbers. Don't you understand, Gaby? The British are going to launch another offensive at Passchendaele and the Germans already know about it! When the British and French leave their trenches, they'll be walking straight into a trap.'

Chapter Seventeen

'Have I done something to offend you, madame?' asked Lieutenant Stanner.

Gaby paused in her rapid pace to stare at him for a moment. She shook her head and hurried on.

'I quite understand we couldn't speak on

the train because of my terrible French. But you haven't said a word to me even now we're on our own.'

'M'sieu, I'm taking you back behind the lines because I've been ordered to. But please don't ask me to be conversational.'

She saw him colour up, and was ashamed. But she couldn't summon the energy for apology or explanation. All her strength was needed for this journey.

It was the hardest thing she had ever done in her life. Every step was taking her further away from Marc. Every step, she died a little.

Their train journey from Rethel had been uneventful. No one had even asked to see their papers and permits. They had got off at a branch-line station near Pettiloul as dusk drew on. Curfew began now, and had they been stopped they would have had a hard time explaining their activities, but Gaby knew how to fade into the shadows of the trees.

The young aviator said nothing as he followed this beautiful but sombre French-woman. He gave an exclamation of astonishment when she skirted the side of a shallow incline and plunged in among the briars. But at her brief command: 'Help me,' he began to tear the bushes aside.

To do him justice, he was in good command of himself throughout their strange subterranean journey. Once he gave a start when some creature scurried away in the dark, and he was heard to say, 'My word!' when she found and lit the small lamp in the second of the underground chambers. Other than that, he was silent.

The journey took all night and part of next morning, so that the sun had been up for over an hour when she led him up a narrow unrailed staircase in the chalk and asked him to help heave aside a great stone closure.

She had no way of knowing if they were in No Man's Land or in French territory, because details of the exact lines were never made public. All they could do was move cautiously and surrender themselves if they saw French uniforms.

It was in fact French troops that they encountered. A platoon was being sent out on forage by a sergeant. Gaby walked up to the astonished soldier and said, 'I want to be put in touch at once with Major Garouche in Rheims.'

'Eh?' gasped the sergeant, bringing up his rifle. 'Where the hell did you spring from?'

'Never mind that. At once, please – take me to a command post and telephone to Major Garouche.'

Nothing is ever that easy. They were put under arrest, marched to a guardroom, the sergeant's officer was called, the subaltern thought it best to tell his captain in case the young man speaking atrocious French was a German spy, the captain called the provost marshal, and five hours went by before Gaby was invited to speak on the telephone to Garouche.

'Mademoiselle Tramont! It really is you! What on earth are you doing at Bledot?'

'It can't be explained on the telephone. Please send transport at once – I have someone with me whose report you must hear.'

'A foreigner, I hear.'

'It's a British airman. Please, Major – this is very urgent.'

An hour later a staff car arrived. They were driven at jolting speed back to Rheims.

How strange it all looked to Gaby now. She had been away eighteen months. The city had changed, there was more shell damage, the countryside to the north-east was a wasteland of trenches and redoubts. At HQ Lieutenant Stanner was asked to wait while Gaby was interviewed by Garouche.

He couldn't hide his surprise when she came into his office. 'Mademoiselle! Have you been ill?'

'No, I'm quite well. Only, please be quick. My companion has urgent information, and then I want to get back at once to Rethel.'

'Get back?'

'Yes, my partner – I must get back to him.'

Garouche had stood up to shake hands, and now he stepped back a little to study her. 'You aren't fit to go back.'

'Nonsense, I must!'

'A moment, mademoiselle – what was the cover story for your absence?'

'My mother is supposed to be ill in Strasbourg.'

'And you left the shop – when?'

'The night before last.'

'You certainly can't go back yet. It would take you a day at least to get to Strasbourg and one supposes you'd stay a few days with an ailing parent–'

'I'll say she was well when I got there...'

'Please, mademoiselle, I must insist that you remain in Rheims for a few days at least. We have many questions that you could answer, I think – questions of general background. And then the bona fides of this young man must be established before we can risk your going back–'

'Oh, he's genuine enough,' she said impatiently. 'One of his fellow officers will identify him at once – his squadron is based at–'

'Mademoiselle Tramont, you simply cannot be allowed to turn around and go back to Rethel. It wouldn't make sense – there are things we can arrange for you to take, if you give us a day or two to organise it. And besides, your father... Surely you want to see your father?'

She controlled a shiver of emotion. 'My father... How is he?'

'I believe, not well. I really think you should take a few days' leave to see him.' He was still holding her hand, and he pressed it now, warmly. 'It's time to stop being brave, Mademoiselle Gaby. It's time to be your father's daughter for a little while.'

She saw there was no help for it. She wouldn't be permitted to go back and it was useless to try to elude the authorities and go back on her own account. What the Major said was true – if she waited a few days, it would look more genuine when she got back to the shop. She could take new orders or information to the group in Rethel. And she ought to see her father.

She was given a room at HQ where she could telephone the villa in privacy. Her father's secretary, a new voice to her, said doubtfully, 'Mademoiselle Tramont? Not Mademoiselle Gaby?'

'Yes – please put me through to my father.'

There was a long delay. She began to think the call had broken down. Then Robert Tramont's voice, trembling and husky. 'Gaby? Is that you?'

'Yes, Papa.'

'Gaby... My dear child ... I ... I ... I never expected to be called to the telephone for a call from you … I'm sorry, dear, I can't…'

'Papa!' Now that she heard him, love and anxiety and remorse flooded through her. She couldn't really have been going to hurry back to an enemy city without even seeing her father? 'Papa, I'll be home in half an hour.'

'Home?'

'Yes, dearest Papa, yes – home – for a little while.'

He was standing in the archway of the porte-cochère when the official car drove up. She scrambled out, her thick country shoes catching on the running board so that she almost tumbled into his arms.

She was weeping helplessly. He held her close, supporting her, and yet unsteady himself. They leaned against the grey stone of the arch.

'My little girl,' he whispered. 'My only little girl…'

The servants were fluttering about in the background – the butler, expecting a suitcase to carry in, the housekeeper waiting to offer tea or coffee or whatever comforts the young mistress might want.

But they stood aside in silence as the two Tramonts walked indoors, arms about each other, lost to everything except their reunion.

When at last they were sitting side by side on a worn sofa in the former grand drawing room, they studied each other. He saw a woman in her mid-thirties, even more beautiful now than as a girl, though haggard and almost unkempt in the harsh afternoon light. She saw an old man – Papa was old! In his sixties but looking older, his dark hair streaked with grey, the stoop that was due to an old war injury much more pronounced.

They could only speak haltingly at first. He wanted to ask what she had been doing but knew that such questions were forbidden – she had been behind the enemy lines, on duty, like a soldier, and to speak of it might be to expose colleagues to risk. He took it for granted that she was home for good, and went white when she said she must go back as soon as possible.

'You don't understand, Papa. I've left my partner I must go back or he'll be unable to explain my absence.'

'But – but – surely you've done enough? Gaby, please ask for your release from this work. It's too dangerous – I can't bear to think of you–'

'It's not dangerous,' she lied with a false gaiety that convinced him not at all. 'It's not in the least dangerous. We run a shop – no one suspects us.'

'Please stay, Gaby.'

'I *must* go back. I can't leave him…'

Robert sank back into the corner of the sofa. 'Ah,' he sighed, 'I see. He's important?'

'Yes, Papa – important. If I could only tell you...'

'Never mind. How long can you be spared to me?'

'A few days.' To change the subject she said brightly, 'And how is David?'

As soon as she had said it, she knew the answer. Her father's face changed, he put a hand up to his brow as if to hide his eyes.

'Papa,' she said in a faltering voice. 'What happened to David?'

'He was killed in the spring, Gaby. In one of the "pushes" at Arras.'

'Oh God!' She folded her arms across her breast and huddled into herself, as if to protect herself from the blow. 'Oh, poor David, poor David... And I didn't even know!' Then she looked up. 'Why didn't you send word?'

'I gave the information to the authorities at Rheims and a Major Garouche came to see me. He said he thought it best not to send on the news – it would only unsettle you.'

'Unsettle me!' But the brief indignation died. 'Oh, poor Papa! All this time and you couldn't even let me know about my own brother...'

The housekeeper, unasked, had made hot chocolate and now brought it in. But though Gaby thanked her, she was unable to swallow even a sip. It wasn't that she was ill: it was simply that her body cried out for respite from the strains of the last few days, and the long months that had gone before.

'Is my room available? I'd like to rest, if I may.'

'Of course, Gaby – your room's waiting – I tried not to let it be used though we've had soldiers billeted – Madame Lousson, please run a bath for Mademoiselle – there is hot water, isn't there?'

The housekeeper didn't say she'd given orders to use precious coal to produce hot water the moment she heard Mademoiselle was coming home. She ushered Gaby upstairs like a mother hen caring for a frightened chick.

The bedroom, once so pretty, was scarred now by damp and war damage. But the linen on the bed was clean, there were roses in a chipped vase by the bed, and in the bathroom the mahogany trimmed bath was soon brimming with hot water.

Gaby's clothes had been carefully kept. She found a nightgown and a robe on the peg on the bathroom door. As she put them on she felt drained, dazed, lethargic. She could hardly make the few steps to the bed. She fell on it, clutched the pillow in her arms, and fell asleep.

When she woke she found that someone had lifted her into the bed and covered her. The light was quite different. She raised her head. Her father was sitting in an armchair by the open window.

'How do you feel?' he asked.

She blinked and rubbed her eyes. 'Better,' she admitted. 'What time is it?'

'You've almost slept the clock round, it's midday Wednesday. Are you hungry? Madame Lousson has some real coffee she's waiting to brew for you, and there are fresh rolls.'

She couldn't help smiling at him. He was treating her as if she were eight years old.

'I'd like some breakfast, Papa,' she said obediently.

Afterwards she found a dress laid out for her, a summer dress she'd managed to buy second-hand in Rheims market after all her clothes were stolen by the retreating Germans. It was strange to wear something she herself had chosen after being Madame Bleker for so long.

When she came downstairs there was a stranger waiting. Her father introduced him as Dr Didier. 'I'd just like him to take a look at you, Gaby.'

'Oh, Papa, don't be absurd. There's nothing wrong with me!'

'Now, daughter, please do as you're told,' Robert said.

She shrugged. What did it matter?

Dr Didier went up to her room. He took her pulse, her temperature, looked into her eyes, examined her hands, and pronounced her undernourished, overstrained, but otherwise fit.

'I could have told you all that.'

'Perhaps so. But I'm glad to have this chance to speak to you alone, mademoiselle. I've been looking after your father for almost a year now, and I must warn you, he's a very sick man.'

'Papa?'

'Didn't you think he looked unwell?'

'Yes, but... We're all under a great strain these days...'

'Quite so. But as I understand it, he was wounded in the last go-round with the Boches – quite a medical history, though all the records have been lost in the shellings. He shrugs and says every day he's lived since then has been a bonus. Well, mademoiselle, I must tell you that the bonus may be withdrawn at any moment.'

She gasped. He was alarmed and made her sit down. 'I'm sorry,' he said. 'I shouldn't have put it so bluntly.'

'No, no, it's better that you've told me. I had no idea! I thought ... I thought he was just older, that's all.'

'No, he has a heart condition now. He's been under strain all his life, making his body work under protest because he wouldn't submit to a wheelchair. Your homecoming has caused him to have a

415

slight attack–'

'What?'

'While you were asleep, Madame Lousson sent for me. He's recovered, and since I was here he asked me to take a look at you so I went along with it. But in fact, your father is the one who needs nursing. I hope you're going to look after him, Mademoiselle Gaby?'

There was nothing she could say. She simply sat staring at Didier, helpless in the grip of dismay and anxiety.

Two days later news came through of a big battle on the front in Flanders. There had been enormous casualties on the Allied side. Gaby read the flimsy newssheet with something like rage. All that urgency, all that desperation to get the news to Allied HQ that the Germans knew of the proposed attack and were prepared for it. And by the time the information had been sorted out and handed on, it had been too late.

She had left Marc – for nothing. She had saved no lives, done no good – except to return a lost flyer to his unit.

She went to see Garouche. 'When am I to go back to Rethel?' she asked, without even referring to the disaster at Passchendaele.

'Er... We have decided it's better if you stay this side of the lines, mademoiselle.'

'Decided? Who has decided?'

'Intelligence HQ, mademoiselle.'

416

'What utter nonsense! I must go back. Marc Auduron needs his "wife" there.'

'No, mademoiselle, that's all changed.'

She looked at him, suddenly tense. 'What does that mean? What's happened?'

'Nothing, my dear lady – there's no need to look like that'

'You fool, tell me what's happened!' she cried, jumping to her feet and leaning over Garouche's desk. 'What's gone wrong? Tell me!'

'Now, now...' He sat back, fixing his monocle in his eye and looking disapproving. 'We don't actually know what's happened.'

'Then I'll go back and–'

'No, no – your cover is blown, that's certain. The Bleker shop is finished.'

She could hear her heart thudding with heavy, forbidding beats. 'And Marc?'

'We don't know. He's gone.'

After a long pause she said, 'Tell me what you know.'

He was hesitant. 'The shop didn't open one morning. We hear that the gendarmerie eventually broke in and examined the premises. They found a body in the storage cellars.'

'A body? Not … not…?'

'Not Auduron. As far as we can piece it together – and you can understand that no one can just go and ask the German police what's been going on – it looks as if some

417

fellow from Strasbourg who knew the Blekers turned up in Rethel and decided to look up his old pal. And Auduron ... well, he...'

'He killed him.'

'Yes. As I see it, he had no choice. It looks as if he invited him down to the cellar, perhaps to find the real Bleker, and then bashed him on the skull and took off.'

'Where has he gone?'

'That we don't know,' Garouche said, shaking his head. 'But we haven't heard of any arrest or anything – at least so far. So he's hiding somewhere, and by and by he'll make contact with one of the underground groups so we'll hear something eventually.'

'Dear heaven,' Gaby said under her breath. 'Oh, why did I leave him?'

'It's better, mademoiselle. Don't you see? He's got a far better chance of surviving on his own.' He smiled at her. 'Oh, don't worry, Auduron's been on the run before. He'll be all right. We'll get word in the end.'

She tried to think of places he might go, friends he'd mentioned. But nothing seemed of any help. Garouche said: 'You see it would be of no use to send you back. You'd be arrested the minute anyone in Rethel saw you. And as for sending you elsewhere – well, to tell the truth, Mademoiselle Tramont, I think you're more use to us in your old role of organiser here in Rheims.'

'I see.'

'And in any case I hear your father…?'

'Yes, he needs me,' she agreed. 'Yes, it's true. I ought to stay here.' But oh, how she wished she had never left Marc…

From then events in the greater world moved with extraordinary speed. The Russian Revolution, of which they'd heard not a murmur under German censorship in Rethel, gathered pace. The new Soviet Congress asked for an armistice: Russia would be out of the war. The dismay engendered by the news was offset by the fact that the French forces had a great victory on the Oise-Aisne Canal, and then in November the Canadians and British captured the ridge at Passchendaele for which so many lives had been lost in August.

Just before Christmas, Robert Tramont died. It was mid-afternoon and the chief of cellar had come to discuss the blending of the new vintage which would start soon. He found the head of the firm in his chair behind his desk, one hand on the papers he had been reading, his glasses in the other. He had paused in the midst of studying a stock-taking list. It was the way he would have wanted to go – in harness.

That New Year was celebrated by the Germans outside Rheims with a particularly heavy and long bombardment. Nevertheless, people came from miles around to

419

attend the funeral. Even Lieutenant Stanner, in polished Sam Browne belt and leggings, hesitant and wary, appeared.

'I only learned who you really were a few days ago, mademoiselle, when I saw your photograph in the newspaper. I hope you don't mind my coming...?'

'Of course not. You're very kind.'

'I owe you such a lot.'

She shook her head. 'We achieved nothing, I'm afraid.'

'That wasn't our fault.'

'No.'

'I've thought about it since. That man we left in Rethel – you were worried about him. That was it, wasn't it?'

'Yes.'

'Is everything all right there?'

'Quite all right, thank you, lieutenant.' She excused herself to receive the condolences of other attenders. Lieutenant Stanner looked after her with regret. He hadn't understood enough. He'd thought her sullen and bad-mannered. And now here she was, with all these important people about her, and through the politeness and the dignity he sensed something verging on despair.

The months dragged on. The vintage was made – because the wine cannot wait even if men die. The vines were pruned in March, the stakes and supports were renewed by workpeople who crept among the rows at dawn and dusk and sometimes even with shaded lanterns at night.

And all for nothing because, on March 25th, 1918, all civilians were ordered by the military authorities to leave Rheims.

Gaby, along with many others, protested. 'Leave the vines? Are you mad?'

No, the authorities weren't mad. Less than a tenth of the population remained, the city would be better as a garrisoned fortress.

The citizens raged, but in the end they had to comply. By mid-April they trekked out, with the spring air full of the scent of the young vine leaves. Gaby, riding in one of the estate's carts, looking back to watch the towers of the cathedral disappear. We'll be back, she vowed, we'll be back.

It was as if, by losing her citizens, Rheims had lost her heart's blood. A month later, the German troops were in Rheims once more. Gaby read the news in Paris, where she had gone to take up residence at the Tramont offices. She crumpled up the newspaper and threw it on the floor. 'Is this what we fought so long for? To be forced by our own people to leave?'

'Never mind, mademoiselle,' said Monsieur Clochinou, though his own eyes were filled with tears. 'They won't be there long!'

Although at the time Gaby didn't believe him, it began to seem in July that he might be right. A great counter-attack was launched, taking the Allies back across the River Marne. Soon, very soon, Gaby Tramont might be able to return to her shattered home.

But first she ought to go and see her little Cousin Elinore. The child was nine years old, left for far too long in the care of an elderly relative although it had been meant for her own good. Gaby wrote to Cousin Cecile to say she was coming on a visit, and set about clearing paperwork from her desk so as to be able to give her time with a free mind.

It was a warm grey-blue evening at the beginning of August. She had worked hard all day and felt heartened, for great news had been announced – Soissons had been recaptured, any moment now the word would come that Rheims was free. She sat back, closed the last file, and rose from her desk. The long casement windows were open to the chestnut trees on the Rue Lelong. There was enough light to see a young soldier walk by with his arm about a girl in a light dress.

Passing them there came a tall man in a wide-brimmed hat. Something about him held her attention. Her heart gave a heavy beat.

Could it be?

She knew. She *knew*. She flew from the

room and down the stone staircase, almost colliding with the concierge in her mad race. A man was coming up the shallow steps of the outer entry. She flung herself upon him.

'Marc!'

He tottered on the steps, they swayed to and fro for a moment, then he regained his balance and swung her round, off her feet, the world wheeling.

'Darling! How on earth did you know?'

'From the window – I saw you – I knew you–'

'But Gaby, it's almost dark!'

'I knew it was you! I just knew!'

They kissed with a passion of greeting and welcome that made the whole world erupt in a blaze of glory. When at last they stepped apart, all she could do was laugh and cry.

'That hat! That absurd hat! Where did you get it?'

'In Switzerland, from an artist who befriended me. Don't you like it? I think it's rather dashing!'

'Marc, how did you get here? Where have you been? All these months – I've been nearly out of my mind!'

'I'm sorry. I couldn't get any word to you. I wanted to – can we go inside? Can we talk?'

'Oh, yes, come along, come in, my apartment is upstairs, the one David used to have. Oh, Marc, my darling, if you only knew...'

'I do know, Gaby. I do.' With his arm firmly round her waist, he went indoors with her. She called in at her office door that she had finished work for the day and was going up to her flat. The office staff were looking at each other in bewilderment to see the usually self-controlled Mademoiselle Tramont laughing and chattering like a girl. But they smiled. Happiness was so rare these days. How lovely to see someone incandescent with happiness.

In her apartment Gaby drew the blinds and switched on the light. 'Let me look at you,' she said. She took the wide-brimmed hat and threw it on a table. They were devouring each other with their eyes. 'Tell me what happened,' she demanded.

But the need for words had left him. He picked her up in his arms and carried her into the little bedroom. They undressed each other urgently, and made love with all the pent-up longing of a year of parting. Then they lay murmuring to each other, not really talking, merely comforting and soothing with gentle sounds, until they were ready to turn to each other once more.

Midnight had come when at last they sat up together, drinking weak coffee and making long explanations.

Marc had had to stay under cover for

weeks. The German counter-espionage machine had been out looking for him in earnest. Finally, luck – if it could be called that brought him to the scene of an accident – runaway horses had dragged a cart over a cliff onto the road below, smashing the cart, killing the driver.

'I changed clothes with him and took his papers. I became Lucien Despaz. I reported the accident in the next town, Dieuze, giving the impression that the load on the cart was urgently needed in Strasbourg – so I got official help to commandeer another cart and horses, which got me to Strasbourg. I just kept working my way towards the Swiss frontier. Getting across was more difficult – that took me two weeks, but I fetched up in Delemont.'

'Why didn't you write to me then, Marc?' she protested. 'You could have written–'

'No, because I was caught up in the organisation to get prisoners of war across the frontiers – I spent some months helping them – well, to cut a long story short, it wasn't until ten days ago that I was given leave to go home.'

'But of course it's all under German occupation–'

'So I headed straight for Paris, in hopes of finding you here.'

'Thank God you came today and not tomorrow! I'm off to Tours tomorrow, to see

Elinore. Oh, God, Marc – just think if we'd missed each other by a few hours!'

He put down his coffee cup and held her close. 'I'd have followed,' he said. 'Nothing would have stopped me from finding you, once I knew you were alive and well.'

They hardly slept, there was so much to tell and so many kisses to exchange. In the early hours they dressed, then breakfasted at the station while they waited for the train for Tours.

The house in the village outside Tours was owned by Cecile de la Sebiq, a second cousin of Gaby's Uncle Frederic, the father of Elinore. Cousin Cecile was a small, delicate woman with a face like a withered pink rose. Her maidservant was just such another – two elderly ladies from a posy of dried flowers.

'Cousin Cecile, I want to thank you with all the warmth at my command for taking in little Elinore.'

'My dear girl, what could one do? There was no one else, you know, and all the money was gone – I don't speak ill of the dead, of course, but old Monsieur de la Sebiq mortgaged everything up to the hilt and it all went when he died. And then poor Frederic had gone before him – poor dear boy, how like him to die trying to save somebody else...' She sighed and wiped away a tear. 'Well, now, as to the child ...

I've done my best... She's a funny little thing, lives a life of her own, you know...'

The maid had gone to summon Elinore. She came into the room a few minutes later, dressed in the obligatory school pinafore which she wore until it was time for the evening meal.

'How do you do,' she said, shaking hands and curtseying first to her cousin and then to the tall, tanned stranger.

She was an odd little thing – she had none of Netta's fair-skinned good looks nor Frederic's dramatic darkness. Instead she was mousey, thin, with bony wrists and ankles. Her only claim to beauty was her grey eyes, large, clear and strangely deep.

Her appearance hadn't been helped either by wartime stringency nor her elderly cousin's notion of suitable garb. She had hand-knitted stockings, thick sensible shoes, a dark brown and white gingham dress still too big for her and clearly inherited from some other child. Her straight hair was worn in two wispy plaits coming down behind her ears.

'Have you come to take me home?' she asked Gaby.

Gaby was about to say no. After all, what home was there to take the child to? Rheims was still a battlefield, the apartment in Paris was unsuitable for a little girl.

But something about the desperate appeal

in Elinore's eyes made her change her mind.

'Yes, of course,' she said.

'Cousin Gabrielle!' cried Mademoiselle de la Sebiq in reproach. 'Where could the child go? The war'

'The war will soon be over,' Marc said, speaking for the first time since the little girl came into the room. 'I know from what I heard in Switzerland – the German government is tottering, there's a secret peace offer and if it isn't agreed to, there will be rebellion in Germany before the autumn. So of course Elinore must come home.' He glanced at her. 'It's time, isn't it, Elinore?'

She nodded gravely. 'I've quite liked being here,' she said, with a little embarrassed smile towards Mademoiselle de la Sebiq, 'but … you see … I'd like to have somewhere really of my *own*.'

Gaby knelt to put an arm about her. 'Tramont is yours,' she said in a low voice. 'You're a champagne girl, and you belong in the champagne country.'

'But the place is all in ruins!' protested Mademoiselle de la Sebiq.

Marc laughed. 'That's just the point, mademoiselle. We have to rebuild it. You can't leave the world in ruins.'

Elinore studied him over Gaby's shoulder. 'Are you Cousin Gaby's husband?'

'Not yet. Ask me again in a week or two.'

'Will that make you my cousin?'

428

'Of course.'

The little girl turned to the old lady. 'I think it's time I went to proper cousins,' she said in a quaintly polite tone. 'Thank you for having me all this time, but I really must go home.'

Mademoiselle de la Sebiq gave a helpless little laugh. 'I see it's settled.'

Gaby straightened. 'Yes, I believe it is. With your agreement, Cousin Cecile, we'll take Elinore with us when we leave – let's say in two days time?'

There was no question of permission. And truth to tell, the old lady was glad to think she would be relieved of the responsibility, glad to get back to her own world of tisanes and quiet games of euchre with friends as quiet and timid as herself.

A strange excitement took over her little house as, for the next two days, they packed Elinore's belongings. They all went into one medium-sized trunk: it contrasted strangely with the pile of toys and clothes Gaby used to take with her when she went to the seaside at the same age.

On the train, the child sat between the two grown-ups. She watched the countryside as if fled by. After a long silence she said: 'Is it pretty, the Champagne region?'

Gaby was seized with doubt. What was she doing, proposing to take this little girl to Paris, and there to wait for nothing better than a wrecked house and a ruined land?

But Marc reached across Elinore to take Gaby's hand. 'It's all right,' he reassured her. 'It may not be as pretty as Touraine, but it's where she belongs.'

One day the war would end. One day they would begin again, thought Gaby.

And so the train sped on, taking them towards their future.

The publishers hope that this book has given you enjoyable reading. Large Print Books are especially designed to be as easy to see and hold as possible. If you wish a complete list of our books please ask at your local library or write directly to:

Magna Large Print Books
Magna House, Long Preston,
Skipton, North Yorkshire.
BD23 4ND

This Large Print Book, for people
who cannot read normal print,
is published under the auspices of

THE ULVERSCROFT FOUNDATION

... we hope you have enjoyed this book.
Please think for a moment about those
who have worse eyesight than you ...
and are unable to even read or enjoy
Large Print without great difficulty.

You can help them by sending a
donation, large or small, to:

**The Ulverscroft Foundation,
1, The Green, Bradgate Road,
Anstey, Leicestershire, LE7 7FU,
England.**
or request a copy of our brochure for
more details.

The Foundation will use all donations
to assist those people who are visually
impaired and need special attention
with medical research, diagnosis
and treatment.

Thank you very much for your help.